A FATAL CROSSING

A FATAL CROSSING
TOM HINDLE

CENTURY

1 3 5 7 9 10 8 6 4 2

Century
20 Vauxhall Bridge Road
London SW1V 2SA

Century is part of the Penguin Random House group of companies whose
addresses can be found at global.penguinrandomhouse.com.

Penguin
Random House
UK

Published in the UK by Century in 2022

www.penguin.co.uk

A CIP catalogue record for this book is available from
the British Library.

ISBN 9781529135695 (hardback)
ISBN 9781529135701 (trade paperback)

Typeset in 13.5/17 pt Fournier MT Std
by Integra Software Services Pvt. Ltd, Pondicherry

Printed and bound in Great Britain by Clays Ltd, Elcograf S.p.A.

The authorised representative in the EEA is Penguin Random House Ireland,
Morrison Chambers, 32 Nassau Street, Dublin D02 YH68.

Penguin Random House is committed to a sustainable future for
our business, our readers and our planet. This book is made from
Forest Stewardship Council® certified paper.

For Hayley, without whose endless support
this book would not exist

A list of notable passengers and crew travelling on board the Endeavour. *Compiled by ship's officer, Timothy Birch.*

First-class
Miss Hall
Mr and Mrs Green

Second-class
Mr Temple
Monsieur Dupont
Mr Blake
Mr and Mrs Webber
Mr and Mrs Morris
Mr and Mrs Hewitt

Third-class
The woman
The brawler

The officers' quarters
Captain McCrory
Mr Birch
Mr Wilson

Below deck
Mr Seymour
Mr O'Shea

The rain fell all night. It poured relentlessly, hammering upon the *Endeavour*'s deck and rattling against her steel funnels. Still, she carved her way through the Atlantic. She might be slowed, but even in conditions as hostile as these, she could never be stopped. Stretching the best part of nine hundred feet from bow to stern, the lights from countless portholes glinted in the darkness. As long as her engines burned, she would continue defiantly on her path to New York.

Once the clouds were empty and had begun to part, a tired grey sun shimmered high in the sky. Rainwater clung to the foremast and dripped from the rigging, glistening in puddles upon the deck.

On a summer's day, passengers would start emerging the moment the sun rose, those in first- and second-class keen to explore the ship, while their companions in third-class clambered simply to escape the confines of their own cramped cabins. They would stroll on the promenades that ran along the *Endeavour*'s flanks, lean upon the railings and look out to sea, or rush to claim the wooden benches on the main deck. But in the middle of November, there was less enthusiasm.

Even in third-class, the prospect of staying in a warm cabin was a great deal more inviting than stepping outside into the winter chill.

The first passenger to appear on deck that morning was a small boy in a brown woollen jacket and shorts, followed by his mother.

The child had complained all night. He had been hungry. He had felt seasick. Watching him now, skipping happily up the starboard promenade, his mother knew that he had simply wanted to leave the cabin. The ships belonging to the Aurora Cruise Line were built for luxury rather than speed, and it was true that the *Endeavour*'s third-class quarters were more comfortable than the dingy conditions in which they had initially travelled from Russia to England. Even so, a cramped room shared with five other people, all of whom spoke different languages, was no place for a restless child.

Pulling her coat tightly around herself, she hurried after her son, calling for him to be careful as his shoes slipped and squeaked on the damp wood. Oblivious to her pleas, the boy ran the length of the deck, a neat row of portholes on his left and the *Endeavour*'s lifeboats lined up like sentries on his right. Heavy beads of rainwater dripped steadily through cracks in the deck above.

Without warning, the boy came skidding to a halt. Usually, when he reached the corner of a street he would turn around, hopping from one foot to another and beckoning her to catch up. This time, at the bottom of the companionway leading up to the second-class deck, he stood and stared. His mother was so taken aback that she, too, stopped as she tried to guess what could have transfixed him.

She had chance only to consider for a few seconds before her son began to scream.

She ran the last few metres, all fears of falling on the slippery deck gone. When she reached him, she seized him by the jacket and clutched him to her. Then, as she laid eyes on his discovery, she gasped in horror.

At the foot of the steps was the body of an elderly gentleman. Dressed in a sodden black suit, he looked as though he might just have been plucked from the ocean and dropped upon the deck. His skin was deathly pale, his thin white hair plastered to his scalp and his eyes staring vacantly towards the sky. Still grasping her trembling son, the woman dragged him away and began to cry for help.

Within moments, other passengers emerged from their cabins. None of them understood Russian, and so at first they looked irritable and confused. Still dressed in their nightclothes, a small number rubbed sleep from their eyes – but when they saw the body, a uniform expression of shock set in.

Some turned away, anxious not to be involved. Others came closer, eager for a better look. Those who wore them removed their flat caps, one man whistling and remarking to himself what a mess had been made. Another joked loudly that it seemed the toffs in first- and second-class didn't even have the decency to die in their own sections of the ship. He was greeted with a small chorus of gruff laughter from the rowdiest of his companions, but it was perhaps a more astute observation than he realised. The gentleman lying on the deck was the only one wearing anything resembling a suit.

Within minutes, two of the ship's officers came running, leather boots squeaking on the deck and black woollen coats billowing behind them. Upon seeing the body, the younger of the two took off his peaked cap and ran a hand through his hair. His colleague grasped him roughly by the arm and sent him to fetch help, before stepping towards the growing crowd of passengers, hands outstretched, calling out that there was nothing to see and asking them to move along.

His efforts were futile. By the time his companion returned with help, it seemed as though half of the passengers in third-class had turned out to investigate. Having either heard the screams or caught sight of the commotion outside their cabins, they jostled and strained their necks to see, gasping at the sight of the body and whispering to each other in hushed tones.

The officers tried in vain to move the thronging crowd along, while two porters placed the body on a stretcher that had been fetched from the ship's infirmary and covered it with a sheet. But as the stretcher was lifted away, revealing the puddle of blood and rainwater upon which the man had lain, there came the cry that they had dreaded.

'He's been killed!'

Panic ensued immediately, the officers struggling hopelessly to calm the heaving, shrieking mob of passengers. Those who spoke English barged their way to the front, demanding an explanation as to exactly who had been killed and what was being done about it.

Despite the icy wind that was buffeting the deck, it would be a long while after the body was removed before the crowd finally dispersed and sought shelter. And even then, the officers knew better than to hope that they had heard the last of the morning's proceedings.

They had no doubt of how quickly talk of this morbid discovery would spread among the *Endeavour*'s two thousand passengers and crew. Just as they knew how rapidly the first-hand reports would turn to gossip, each detail becoming embellished with every retelling.

They had four long days ahead of them before they docked in New York. Within hours, the ship would be rife with talk of death, blood and murder.

Wednesday 12 November 1924

1

I had already been awake for an hour when the knock came at my door. I was lying in my bunk, starting intently at a yellow ribbon that I held gently between my fingers.

In all honesty, it had been the best part of two years since I last enjoyed a full night's sleep. Two years since I had managed to close my eyes and slumber peacefully. Of course, the memories were always there. The lingering sense of guilt never quite went away. But it was only at night – alone, in the darkness – that it truly revealed itself. No longer trailing like a shadow, but instead, looming overhead, as though taking on some physical form of its own.

Even when sleep did finally take me, there was no escape. I would wake – often several times each night – clammy and gasping in my bunk. This particular morning was no different. Jolting from sleep in the early hours, I scrambled for the ribbon and clutched it close.

Taking deep, soothing breaths, I felt the material between my fingers. It was a scrap of yellow velvet, worn so regularly that it had begun to fray slightly at one end. I pictured the way it used to flutter in Amelia's hair. The way that Kate had always tied it so lovingly in a perfect little bow.

Slowly the panic faded and, as it always did, a numbness took its place. A sense of hopelessness that, if I let it, felt as though it could very well swallow me whole. Because it was my fault that I couldn't sleep. My fault that all I had left of Amelia was a scrap of yellow ribbon. My fault that everything had gone wrong.

It was around quarter to eight when the knock came at my door, sharp and urgent. 'Birch! Captain's briefing. Fifteen minutes!'

Setting the ribbon down, I frowned. Captain McCrory was a man insistent upon punctuality. In my time on board the *Endeavour*, just shy of five years, his daily officers' briefing had never once taken place other than at nine o'clock. Even during my year away, I'd often looked at the clock and known that somewhere in the Atlantic, the men were gathering for their morning ritual. Before I could call out a response, though, the speaker moved along, apparently interested neither in receiving a reply nor in giving an explanation.

Casting back the covers, I sat up on my bunk, and was greeted by a searing flash of pain. I had managed during the night to roll onto my right-hand side, and as I hauled myself from the mattress, the old wound in my shoulder throbbed.

Gritting my teeth, I reached for the scar and brushed it with my fingertips. Somewhere in my memory, I heard the crack of rifles and the frantic cries of men scrambling for cover. I felt a sudden agony, burning white-hot in my shoulder as a German bullet found its mark. Blood staining my uniform, I remembered tumbling to the ground, before an American soldier seized me under the arms and dragged me roughly to safety.

Despite my best efforts, I didn't suppose I would ever forget that day. Just like the scar, it seemed I would for ever carry it with me.

Screwing my eyes shut, I waited for the pain to subside. Then I flicked a switch on the wall, casting the room in a dull electric light, and dressed hurriedly in my officers' uniform.

The *Endeavour*'s first- and second-class accommodation might very well be considered the peak of luxury, but the officers' quarters were significantly less comfortable, and in the depths of winter, you felt it. We were situated halfway down the ship, barely above sea level, but with just enough decks between us and the engines that we failed to benefit from any of their residual warmth. What little heat there was, the cabin itself did nothing to retain. The carpet was rough and threadbare, the walls exposed metal.

Shivering, I donned a crisp white shirt with a black tie, long woollen coat and peaked cap. Last of all, I folded the yellow ribbon carefully and tucked it into the pocket of my coat.

I had thought on more than one occasion that it would be safer to leave it in my cabin, hidden away in a drawer perhaps. But I hadn't yet found the strength to leave it behind. It was a piece of Amelia that I could still carry with me, a token of everything I intended to reclaim. Truthfully, I couldn't bear to be apart from it.

By the time I arrived in the officers' mess hall, the other men were already congregating, eating slices of toast and sipping from steaming mugs of tea and coffee. They barely looked up as I slipped into the room. It had become a habit, in the six months since my return to the *Endeavour*, to wait until they had all gathered before making my own arrival, unnoticed and unannounced. At the best of times, this was a simple task. A record would be playing on the gramophone, and there would be chatter and laughter as we prepared for our daily duties. That morning, however, was different, an air of hushed anticipation having settled over the room. Even though I would rarely join in, it was still an unsettling departure from the usual cheerful atmosphere.

'Wilson,' I said, seating myself beside a stocky fellow with cropped black hair.

'Birch,' he replied.

'What's this all about?'

Wilson shrugged. 'Damned if I know.'

'You've never known the captain to call one of these early?'

'Never.'

When Captain McCrory joined us, we stood as one to attention. He was a large man with a stout build, and a neat grey beard, perhaps to mask the creases that were just beginning to line his face and pinch the corners of his eyes. Not a thread was out of place on his uniform, the silver buttons on his black captain's jacket gleaming.

I was all too aware that I owed McCrory a great deal of gratitude. As gruff as he might sometimes be, there couldn't be many commanders who would allow me to return to the *Endeavour* after a year's absence. On my first day back I had gone to his office, with the intention of shaking his hand and thanking him in person for the understanding he had shown, but he had promptly sent me away.

'That won't be necessary, Mr Birch,' he had said, clapping me roughly on the back. I remembered flinching as his palm caught the old bullet wound, but had forced a smile.

Looking back on that meeting, I suspected I would never know whether he had been sparing me from explaining myself or had simply wanted to avoid witnessing an emotional display from one of his officers. I supposed it didn't matter. All that was important was that he had let me return. He had welcomed me back when I needed it most.

In the mess hall, the men who had been on duty that morning explained why we had been gathered so early. The younger of the two – a relatively new officer by the name of Travis – was white-faced as his companion shared the news. A passenger appeared to have fallen down a companionway during the night, between the exterior second- and third-class decks, and had been found dead just an hour ago.

Captain McCrory listened silently, iron-like intensity fixed upon his face as we heard that the body had been taken below and a coroner would be telegrammed ahead of our arrival in New York. The reporting officer then paused a moment, waiting, apparently, for some acknowledgement of this tragedy from the captain, or perhaps even further instruction. None came. Instead, McCrory gave a single nod, prompting the officer to hurriedly describe how minor repairs were also required to the rigging in the wake of the previous night's storm, and how the lifeboats would need checking for damage.

With the report concluded and various duties distributed, the captain dismissed us and returned to his office. The hush that had preceded the briefing hung over the room for several minutes, as if our congregation was wary of breaking the unnatural stillness. Soon enough though, the men returned vigorously to their breakfasts, a record began to play and the noise and clamour that was synonymous with the mess hall started up again.

'Poor old boy,' Wilson observed cheerfully, smearing a dollop of marmalade onto a thick slice of toast.

'The passengers are bound to be worried,' I said.

'A few of them.'

'Only a few?'

He shrugged. 'You know how bored they become on these crossings. For most of them, a body turning up is likely the first interesting thing that's happened since we set out. Some will be upset, but most will be intrigued to know all about it. You wait and see. We'll have more of an issue with them gossiping than panicking.'

I struggled to share his casual optimism. In many ways, the *Endeavour* was a melting pot. A community of strangers brought together for six nights, with no option to leave. Nowhere for anybody to escape to. It wouldn't take much to disturb such a delicate balance.

'Have you ever had a passenger die before?' I asked.

'Once. Not long before you first arrived, actually. An old bird snuffed it in her sleep. Gave her husband a shock by all accounts, when he woke up next to her the following morning.'

'What did they do with her?'

Wilson shrugged again. 'The same thing I suppose they'll do with this fellow. Kept the body out of the way until we docked and she became someone else's problem.' He caught sight of my frown. 'Accidents happen, Tim. People die. There's no sense in getting worried about it.'

He realised his mistake the moment the words had left his mouth.

'It's all right,' I said quickly.

'Christ, Tim, I didn't mean to—'

'It's all right, Wilson.' I forced a smile. 'Honestly. No harm done.'

An uncomfortable silence descended, and I turned my attention to the mug of tea that sat on the table in front of me. For all of his good-natured concern, Wilson had never possessed any kind of discretion. It wasn't the first time he had blundered into a difficult spot and I doubted it would be the last.

Still, it seemed he was right. According to the reporting officers, the body was out of sight and a team of porters had already cleaned away the bloody puddle that had been left behind. The new fellow, Travis, had spoken about a crowd of inquisitive third-class passengers turning out to join in the commotion, but for the time being at least, it sounded as though there was little left to see.

Having finished his toast, Wilson stood abruptly and brushed the crumbs off his coat.

'You're on duty?' I asked.

'McCrory has me doing rounds. You?'

'Not for another hour.'

'Are you joining the other chaps?'

I glanced towards a table at the other side of the mess, where three of our colleagues were sharing breakfast. One appeared to tell a joke and the man beside him burst into a fit of roaring laughter. Travis was the third member of the group, some of the colour having returned to his face as he nursed a mug of coffee.

'You can't cut yourself off for ever, Tim,' said Wilson. 'Perhaps you should go ashore with them after we've docked. They're bound to want some decent food by the time we arrive. Lord knows they won't find any here.'

I said nothing, glancing instead down at my tea.

'Look, I know it's not your sort of thing,' he continued, a sudden eagerness in his voice. 'But some time together away from the ship might be just what's needed. You could do with—'

'I can't,' I said, a good deal more abruptly than I intended. 'I'm ...' I shuffled awkwardly in my seat, acutely aware of how closely Wilson was peering at me. 'I'm meeting someone when we dock.'

'*Meeting* someone?' Wilson frowned to himself, apparently wondering who on earth I might possibly have to meet. I might have been offended if I weren't so painfully aware of what an unusual prospect it must seem. After several seconds, the frown disappeared, his eyes lighting up. 'Your American friend?' he asked. 'The soldier.'

'That's right.'

'Raymond, wasn't it?'

I nodded. 'He wrote to me a short while ago and insisted that I visit. Seems to think that a friendly face might do me some good.'

'Well, I, for one, agree.' He forced some cheer into his voice again. 'But you need more than one friend on the other side of the world, Tim. The trick with the others is to—'

'Wilson,' I urged. 'Please ... Even if I could, you know that they wouldn't want me joining them.' I forced a smile. 'I'm not exactly cheerful company these days.'

He looked at me, an unreadable expression on his face. Then he sighed. 'Fine,' he said. 'Suit yourself.'

I waited until he had left and then glanced over at the other table again.

It wasn't that I didn't want to join them. Wilson knew that much. But over the past two years, it had become a struggle to take joy in virtually anything at all. Even something as simple as sharing breakfast with fellow officers. I'd become a creature of solitude, much preferring to keep my own company than attempting to make forced conversation. And yet I knew all too well that Wilson was right. As deeply as my affection for Raymond ran, I needed more than just one friend in New York.

To their credit, the other officers had tried at first. On my return to the *Endeavour*, they had been warm and inviting, encouraging me to smoke with them and play cards. But it hadn't taken them long to recognise that I wasn't the same man who had left. As the weeks went by, they'd gradually allowed me to cut myself off; to sink deeper into my regret. After six months, just Wilson remained, and I would often wonder if even he, deep down, only continued to bother with me out of pity.

Absent-mindedly, I slipped the ribbon from my pocket. It was comforting just to feel the material between my fingers. To have something of Amelia that I could see and touch. It didn't quite heal the pain, but it did, at least, numb it a little.

At the other table, Travis turned and, before I could glance away, we locked eyes. For several seconds, neither of us moved. Then he smiled and nodded in my direction.

I couldn't say exactly how long we looked at each other, the smile on Travis's face taking me so completely by surprise that it seemed to pin me in place. When I failed to return it, though, the smile started to fade. He tilted his head slightly, his brow creasing into the makings of a quizzical frown as his eyes strayed to the ribbon in my hand.

The sound of a door being knocked upon brought me abruptly back to my senses. It had come from outside, four sharp raps echoing down the adjoining corridor.

Declaring that I would answer it, I rose clumsily to my feet, stuffed the ribbon back into my pocket and hurried from the mess, where a door at the far end of the corridor connected the officers' quarters to the rest of the ship. I cursed myself silently as I went. I needed to be more careful. It would hardly do for the other officers to think not only that I was a recluse, but also that in my solitude I'd taken to fondling anonymous pieces of ribbon.

As I strode towards the door, the knocking came again, more intently than before. Whoever was there was clearly anxious to be seen. It was a member of the crew, I supposed. An officer would be required to oversee the repairs to the rigging or the lifeboat drill mentioned during the briefing, and I imagined the porters would be keen to get on with it while the weather remained fair.

Or perhaps it was a passenger. Wilson might be right about news of the old man's death spreading quickly. It could very well be a concerned bystander, hoping to ask what was being done.

18

Passenger or otherwise, I supposed I ought to be grateful for the escape that they had just afforded me. Perhaps, I thought darkly, I should even thank whoever was calling.

But when I grasped the handle and opened the door, I couldn't believe my eyes.

2

After a brief discussion with the other men, I hurried to Captain McCrory's office to inform him of our visitor. He listened silently as I made my report: that a passenger had come to the officers' quarters demanding a meeting to discuss the body that had been found on the promenade. Then, with a grim expression on his face, he sat back in his chair and stirred his tea, the spoon clinking softly against the porcelain.

While he seemed to consider this development, I glanced towards the window, to hide my face as much as to admire the view. The bullet wound in my shoulder was still aching from having been lain on during the night, and I was eager for the captain not to see me grimace. All the same, there was certainly a view to be admired.

Situated on the *Endeavour*'s uppermost level, the little office offered an aerial perspective as she carved a path through the waves. On a clear day, I thought that there must only be a few vistas in the world to match it. This was not one of those days. Though the rain had stopped falling early that morning, dark clouds still peppered the sky, the water was rough and grey, and the wind could be heard buffeting the ship from all sides.

With some unease, I brought myself to break the silence. 'He's eager to speak with you, sir,' I said. 'He's quite insistent, in fact.'

Captain McCrory snorted quietly. After nearly thirty years at sea, he wasn't the sort of man to appreciate having personal meetings forced upon him by passengers. But all things considered, nor was he the sort to enjoy being woken with the news that one of them had died during the night.

'He's a police officer, you say?'

'That's right, sir,' I replied. 'A detective, apparently. His name is James Temple.'

'And what do you make of him, Mr Birch?'

'I can't say I've had the opportunity to make much of him, sir. We've tried to ask a few questions, but we couldn't get anything out of him. As I say, he is adamant that he wants to speak with you personally.'

McCrory stopped stirring and carefully placed his teaspoon on the saucer. 'The nerve of it,' he muttered.

'Would you like me to send him away, sir?'

He didn't answer. Instead, he glanced down at his desk. His papers and stationery equipment were neatly arranged beside three framed photographs: one of his wife, another of the *Endeavour* docked in Southampton, and a third carefully clipped from a newspaper, in which he was shaking hands with a member of the Royal Family on the day of her maiden crossing. There was a typewriter too, though I knew it had barely been touched. Captain McCrory was a man who clung steadfastly to more traditional ways of doing things.

On any other crossing, I might have thought that he was inspecting one of the photographs. But in that moment, I knew his attention was elsewhere entirely. He was looking at an ornate wooden box which the officers were all aware contained a selection of fine cigars. It was a new addition, purchased especially for this voyage to mark a long-awaited and much-anticipated retirement. Though he was a proud Scotsman, his wife was American, and we all knew that the box would be opened the moment we docked in New York.

For several seconds, Captain McCrory gazed at it, a faraway look in his eyes as though he could actually see the moment he would step from the *Endeavour* for the last time and light that first cigar. He sighed.

'That won't be necessary, Mr Birch. Show him in, please. Let's get this over with.'

As instructed, I opened the door and Temple stepped through.

To say that I had been surprised to find him knocking on the door to the officers' quarters – declaring that he was a police officer and demanding to speak with the captain – would be quite the understatement.

He was lean and wiry, with a head of thick brown hair and a square jaw. He looked younger than any of the ranking police officers I had ever spoken to – I guessed that he could be no older than thirty – but there were shadows beneath his eyes and his forehead seemed creased in a perpetual frown. A three-piece charcoal suit hung from him, with a thin tie and a shirt that looked as though it had already seen at least a day's wear. A grey woollen coat was folded over one arm and he carried a matching fedora in his hand. There was a small cut on his neck, as though he had shaved in a hurry, and I noticed a few specks of dried blood on his collar.

When I first showed him into the mess and explained to the other officers who he was, there'd been some discussion about sending him away. The captain would often say he had no patience for troublemakers or attention-seekers, and the verdict among the men was that Temple would quickly be labelled as both.

But I'd been keen to get the measure of the young police officer. Despite the frustration that he might cause the captain, I was curious to hear what it was that he had to say. When I volunteered to be the one who introduced him, the other men had only been too happy to let me proceed.

I wondered now if my curiosity might get the better of me. Temple slipped into the office even before I had fully opened the door, as though he had been waiting with his ear to the wood. Ignoring me entirely, he crossed the room in a couple of steps, seated himself opposite the captain and placed his fedora on the desk. It was probably for the best that he didn't extend a hand. I doubted the captain would have shaken it that morning. Instead, the two men watched each other cautiously, as though each was weighing the other up before making the first move.

It was McCrory who broke the silence. 'Would you like me to send for some tea, Mr Temple?'

'No, thank you.'

A fresh silence descended.

'I understand that you're a detective.'

'That's right.'

There was yet another pause, as the captain waited for Temple to elaborate. Knowing him to be an impatient, straightforward sort of man, I was painfully aware that such a tedious exchange couldn't go on for long.

'And you would like to take a look at the gentleman who was found this morning.'

'I think it would be best.'

'May I ask why?' As if on cue, the first hint of irritation began to manifest itself in the captain's voice. 'I don't know what you might have heard from the other passengers, Mr Temple, but this is quite clearly an elderly man who slipped and fell down a flight of steps. It is, of course, a serious accident and we are treating it with all due sensitivity, but I see no need for the involvement of a police officer.'

'You might be right,' Temple replied. 'But in my experience, there's no way of being sure until a proper investigation has taken place.'

'In your *experience*?'

If Captain McCrory was trying to point out the detective's apparent youth, it seemed to have no effect. Temple might have looked young, but there was something in the way he sat stoically in the face of the older man's frustration, one leg crossed lazily over the other and with an expression of complete neutrality, that spoke of a self-assurance beyond his years.

'Where exactly have you come from, Mr Temple?' the captain demanded. 'A big city, I expect. London? Birmingham?'

'London.'

'Well, let me make something clear to you, sir.' The captain clasped his hands on the desk and leaned forward, steel flashing in his eyes. 'This is not London. There isn't danger lurking around every corner. I have sailed on civilian vessels such as this for near-enough my entire career, and in *my* experience, people don't make a habit of killing each other. I won't have you spreading such talk among my passengers just so that you can take a good story back to your station.

'May I also point out that while you have command of the law in England, you have no authority aboard this vessel. I know how these things work. We are in international waters and in four days, we will dock in New York where, of course, the Americans will have jurisdiction. What I'm saying, Mr Temple, is that any investigation you would like to conduct aboard this ship must be sanctioned by me, and I am of no mind to have you spreading panic over a simple accident.'

Captain McCrory leaned back in his seat, and now it was Temple's turn to consider his options. He had listened attentively to every word, breathing deeply, like a chess player deliberating over his next move.

'I understand your position, captain,' he said carefully. 'And it's not my intention to cause alarm. But consider this. You say that your passengers don't make a habit of killing one another. Today, one of them might have done just that. You have a dead man on your hands and nothing but speculation as to what could have happened to him. What you also have is a representative of Scotland Yard offering to help resolve the situation.'

The captain's nostrils flared, but Temple continued, undeterred.

'I'm asking for the opportunity to inspect the body and make a few inquiries. And you're right –' his voice rose a semitone as he saw the captain preparing to interrupt him – 'I don't have jurisdiction aboard your ship, but I know how these things work too. Until you can demonstrate that I have committed some kind of crime, you have no authority either to prevent me from speaking to anyone who is willing to talk. I'm asking for your assistance. Not your permission.'

Silence hung heavily in the air as Captain McCrory weighed Temple's retort. He wasn't accustomed to being spoken to so abruptly. I'd heard of men under his command being dismissed for discrepancies half as severe. The honest truth, however, was that Temple made a convincing argument.

'Is it true that he was found without a coat?' asked Temple.

The captain frowned at him. 'I haven't the faintest idea. Why should something like that be important?'

The detective gave a little shrug. 'I'm sure you noticed that the weather last night was less than accommodating. Does it not strike you as unusual that an elderly gentleman would be out in such conditions for as simple a reason as an after-dinner stroll, but not wearing a coat?'

'I fail to see what you're suggesting, Mr Temple.'

'I'm suggesting that we have a duty to question what he was doing when he fell, before we declare it a simple accident. Where was he going? What was he doing? Surely you'll agree that these are questions which need to be answered.'

Captain McCrory picked up his teaspoon again and began tapping gently on the rim of his teacup. 'What's your business aboard my ship, Mr Temple?' he demanded.

'I can't discuss that with you.'

'That won't do.' He jabbed the teaspoon at Temple like a dagger. 'I have a dead man at my feet and no sooner than the body has gone cold do I also have a detective from London at my door, talking about murder and insisting that he be allowed to inspect it. You explain to me why I shouldn't be suspicious.'

Temple took a long, measured look at Captain McCrory, his eyes seeming to narrow a fraction. I heard a soft, rhythmic tapping sound and, glancing down, realised that he was bouncing his heel upon the floor.

'I'm sorry, captain,' he said, 'but I can't tell you why I'm travelling to New York.'

'Then I see no reason why I should trust you to inspect the body. Even if I did give my consent, we dock on Sunday. What kind of investigation do you plan to conduct in the space of just four days?'

'If you're correct and this fellow's death was truly an accident, a short one.'

'And if I'm wrong?' There was suddenly a hint of menace in the captain's tone. 'If there is a crime to be pursued, what sort of investigation do you suppose you'll conduct then?'

Temple leaned forward, looking McCrory straight in the eye. 'An efficient one.'

For what felt like an eternity, the two men watched each other across the desk like boxers in a ring. I was beginning to wonder if I ought to interject when, finally, the detective spoke.

'I can tell you that I'm travelling on business,' he relented. 'Police business. But I can't elaborate any further.'

For several seconds, the only sound was the soft tapping of Temple's heel upon the floor. Captain McCrory glanced at the cigar box, his eyes once again glazed over with the same wistful look that I had seen before Temple stepped into the cabin. Still, however, it seemed he was remaining defiant.

'Captain,' said Temple flatly. 'If a crime has taken place, does it not occur to you that when this ship docks and its passengers disembark you will be allowing the culprit to walk free into the streets of New York? Free, not only from justice for their actions aboard the *Endeavour*, but perhaps even to strike again? Why not give me the chance to conduct a small investigation? To put your conscience at ease, if for no other reason.'

The captain ran a hand across his beard. Again, Temple made an alarming compelling argument, something that I suspected even McCrory would be unable to deny. Finally, like a mighty oak giving in to a woodman's axe, he relented.

'Very well,' he said. 'If you wish to inspect the body, you may. But I have one condition.'

Temple's eyes narrowed.

'Mr Birch, here, will accompany you.'

'*No*,' Temple snapped.

The captain raised an eyebrow. 'No?'

'It's quite unnecessary.'

'These are my terms, Mr Temple,' said McCrory, raising his voice to silence the detective's protests. 'If you wish to conduct an investigation aboard my ship, Mr Birch will escort you and see that none of my passengers are troubled.'

His composure now completely gone, Temple shifted his features into a vicious scowl. I could see him preparing his next assault; almost *hear* the gears grinding in his mind.

'Does that suit you, Mr Birch?' Captain McCrory addressed me for the first time since Temple had sat down. 'You will stay by Mr Temple's side until he is satisfied that a suitable investigation has been carried out.'

'Perfectly, sir,' I said. 'But my duties ... The rigging, the lifeboats—'

The captain waved a hand. 'Your fellow officers are perfectly capable of tending to your duties until Mr Temple is satisfied.'

Temple twisted round to inspect me and our eyes locked. They were like shards of ice, with not even the slightest attempt to hide his utter contempt for the captain's decision.

'Does that suit you, Mr Birch?' the captain repeated.

'Of course, sir.'

'I won't be escorted,' Temple growled, turning to face McCrory again. 'It's absurd.'

'Then you won't see the body.'

For several seconds, the two men glared at each other once more. Then, without another word, Temple stood, snatched his fedora from the table and swept from the cabin.

3

While the view from Captain McCrory's office was certainly impressive, it was on the *Endeavour*'s bridge that I felt most at home. The room from which the ship was commanded, it sat high above her prow, boasting a polished wooden deck and broad windows that looked out towards the ocean. The helm stood in its centre, with the engine order telegraph beside it, while a telephone and a lavish compass hung upon the wall.

As often as I could, I tried to be on the bridge whenever we left port. Kate always said that I must imagine it, but I would swear that you can *feel* the engines beginning to roar and burn beneath your feet as the *Endeavour* makes way. Smoke starts to guzzle from her three iron funnels, her four propellers – each twenty feet across – begin to churn through the water and the best part of fifty thousand tons is propelled through the waves. In my mind, there was little that could match that particular thrill.

Three days into our journey, however, there was no such excitement to be found. The *Endeavour* had reached a steady pace, and while formality required that an officer always be on hand, the man who I relieved had already taken the necessary bearings after the previous night's rough weather, and it seemed we had no reason to change speed or course. I could quite easily go for a walk around the main deck if I wanted to, return an hour later and find that nothing had changed. The helmsman might not even notice I had gone.

And it was also true that there were matters elsewhere which could use my attention. There was Mrs Fitch, the sour old widow from Cambridge who, upon boarding the *Endeavour* on Monday morning, had complained that her first-class cabin didn't offer enough room to exercise her dog. Her Yorkshire terrier was a nasty little creature that had nipped at my heels as I promised to investigate the availability of a larger cabin. Likewise, there were reports that Mr Seymour, one of the ship's porters, had been drinking on duty and required a stern dressing-down.

And, of course, there was James Temple.

Needless to say, my association with the detective had not begun well. After he had barged from the office, I'd closed the door behind him and Captain McCrory remarked upon what a cocky young sod he was.

'How old would you say that fellow was, Birch?' he had asked, the leather squeaking as he settled back into his chair. 'About your age?'

'Thereabouts, sir. Perhaps a few years younger.'

'And do you imagine that you would ever presume to sweep into a police station and begin making demands of a senior officer?'

'No, sir.'

'No, sir, indeed.' The captain shook his head, a distant look in his eyes.

31

'Sir?' I had asked cautiously. 'You don't suppose this gentleman's death does warrant further investigation? I agree that it was most likely an accident, but I can't help thinking about what Mr Temple said. About if there *were* someone responsible. When we arrive in New York, they would—'

'Birch,' the captain had sighed. 'Enough. If Mr Temple won't agree even to be escorted in his inquiries, then he clearly doesn't feel that there is enough of a threat for us to pursue.'

'But if he changes his mind, sir, should I still accompany him?'

Captain McCrory had given a low chuckle and sipped from his teacup. 'I wouldn't worry, Mr Birch. I don't think our detective friend will be bothering us again.'

For the time being, at least, this final observation seemed to have rung true. When I left the office, I had half-expected to find Temple waiting for me outside, ready to apologise for his lack of composure and ask if I might still consider escorting him to the body. But there had been no sign of him, and so I was happy, for the time being, to be left to enjoy the simple tranquillity of the bridge.

I was sure the other officers must have noticed me volunteering to spend more and more time up there. Just as I was sure they must have noticed I was always the last to arrive for the daily briefing. If I was correct in either suspicion though, nobody had questioned it.

The truth was that the bridge was an escape. It wasn't just the endless sky and rolling ocean that had such a soothing effect. It was the polished instruments, the stillness and the open space. I felt at home amid the functionality of it all, the simplicity. It was a place where I didn't have to pretend not to notice the way the other men looked at me, with sympathy in their eyes, or struggle through forced, uncomfortable conversation.

Of course, I wasn't so self-centred that I believed I was the only one grappling with the weight of the past. Many other officers had suffered harrowing experiences during the war, and it was true that I, myself, would revisit those years often enough in my mind. The wound in my shoulder acted as a constant reminder of the mud, the wire and the lingering stench of death.

I touched my lapel and my mind drifted to rural France. To the small group of German soldiers who had ambushed us, trying hopelessly to defend the farm buildings that they had chosen as their refuge. And to Raymond, who had dragged me behind cover and stood guard over me after I had been hit.

I was all too aware that I owed him my life. Perhaps in more ways than one. We had kept in touch after the war, each sending a handful of letters to the other every year. We shared memories of the weeks spent trudging through forests and fields. Fears of whether we would ever return to a normal life.

But over the past two years, those letters had taken on an altogether different purpose. Perhaps it was simply easier to put my thoughts to paper than to voice them aloud. Whatever the reason, as I gradually cut myself off from the rest of the world, Raymond had become my closest confidant.

Gazing out to sea, I took Amelia's yellow ribbon from my pocket and felt the material between my fingers. Raymond had invited me on several occasions to visit him in New York, but

I had always declined. Just as he had politely declined to visit me in England, or to see the daughter who, if it weren't for him, I might never have had.

That is to say, I had declined until now.

I tried to picture the moment we would meet in the harbour on Sunday morning. Would he look different? Surely, he must. The last time I saw Raymond, I was being stretchered into the back of a truck, ready to begin the long journey to the nearest field hospital. He had been caked in mud and sweat, a rifle slung over his back. After six years at home in New York, would I even recognise him?

Slipping the ribbon back into my pocket, I sent for a pot of Earl Grey and tried to busy myself by studying some charts. But my mind wandered restlessly to Temple's meeting with the captain. The truth was that the detective had unnerved me. He made a compelling argument, of course, that if some-one were truly responsible for the old gentleman's death, they mustn't be allowed to simply leave the *Endeavour*. But his own silence – his stout refusal to disclose his business in New York – was just as troubling.

I thought of the way he had glared at me when he heard the captain's terms. Perhaps I should be glad that our paths had crossed for only a moment.

I was nursing a second cup of Earl Grey when the telephone began to ring on the wall behind me, the brass receiver rattling in its cradle with every chime. Settling my teacup back in its saucer, I crossed the room in three strides and picked it up.

'Bridge,' I said.

'Is Birch up there?' a voice crackled in my ear.

'Speaking.'

'Thank God, you're the third line we've tried. It's the mess. There's someone here asking for you. A passenger.'

'Oh yes?'

'He's bloody rude, but we've given him a coffee and that seems to have calmed him down a little. If you wouldn't mind popping down and taking him off our hands, I'm sure we'd all be much obliged.'

'Who is he?' I asked warily, though I suspected I already knew the answer.

'Not a clue,' came the gruff reply. 'He won't give us his name. He just keeps saying that he's a police officer.'

Before I could speak another word, the line went dead.

4

It was with growing unease that I returned to the officers' mess hall, where I found James Temple sitting alone, draining a mug of coffee.

The stillness of the room was unsettling. There would usually be at least a couple of men playing cards, listening to the gramophone or flicking through a novel while they waited to be called up for duty. I wondered what the detective had said to send them on their way.

'Mr Temple.' Cautiously, I seated myself opposite him. 'What can I do for you, sir?'

He looked me up and down, and I shuffled uncomfortably under the intensity of his gaze, struggling to forget the disdain with which he had glared at me when the captain first made his ultimatum.

'It was Birch, wasn't it?'

'That's right, sir. Timothy Birch.'

His leg bounced restlessly beneath the table, the heel of his shoe tapping out the same faint rhythm that I had heard in the captain's office.

'I'd like to inspect the body,' he said, his voice level and measured.

'We've been over this already, Mr Temple,' I replied. 'We offered to escort you and you turned us down.'

'I didn't turn you down.'

'You stormed from the cabin, sir. I'd say that it was implied.'

The detective scowled.

'If I were to take you to the body,' I said, 'can I ask what it is that you'd expect to find? Captain McCrory has made it quite clear that this death is being treated as an accident.'

'Doesn't that feel a little naive?'

I thought for a moment, trying to predict what trap he might be about to lead me into. I was eager not to underestimate him, as I had when he first sat down in McCrory's office.

'You asked the captain if the gentleman had been found without a coat.'

'I did.'

'Do you truly think a detail like that would be relevant?' I asked. 'I'll admit that it might be strange for him to have gone out without a coat. But would it really be enough, in your mind, to throw into question how he fell down that companionway?'

Temple settled back in his seat, pausing as though for some deliberate effect. 'Answer something else for me,' he said. 'We don't know exactly what time this fellow fell, but we do know that it was raining for most of the night. So, it stands to reason that your captain is right about at least one thing. He almost certainly *was* out in the rain when he fell.'

'Go on.'

'The steps that he fell down were conjoining the outer sec-
ond- and third-class decks. Correct?'

'Yes ...'

'Is there not a staircase inside that would have taken him
the same way?'

I didn't answer straight away. I could see where he was
going and knew that unless I was prepared to lie, I had lost.

'Yes,' I admitted.

'So, why did he feel the need to go out in the rain?' There
was a hint of triumph in Temple's voice.

'He might already have been out,' I replied, aware of how
unconvincing I sounded. 'For all we know, he was outside
when the rain started and he was on his way in when he fell.'

'He might well have been,' Temple agreed. 'But we're
still talking about an elderly man taking an evening walk in
the middle of November. In the middle of the Atlantic, no
less. You can't tell me that, if such an outing had been
planned, he wouldn't at least have *thought* about putting
on a coat.'

His leg was still bouncing beneath the table, his heel tapping
out that same infuriating rhythm.

'You seem very keen to pursue this, Mr Temple,' I said.
'Did you know this man?'

'I don't even know who he is.'

'Then why take such an interest?'

Now, it was Temple's turn to remain silent.

'Why couldn't you tell the captain your business in New
York?' I asked, seeing that I had caught him off guard. 'Will
you at least tell *me* what it is?'

'Police business,' he replied, without a moment's hesitation.

We sat in silence, neither one of us prepared to budge. I looked at Temple intently, as though, if I tried hard enough, I might actually be able to *see* what he wasn't telling me.

'I don't understand how you can expect me to trust you when you seem so adamant not to do the same,' I said.

Temple grimaced, and then, with a loud clatter that echoed around the mess like a gunshot, he brought his mug down upon the table.

'Fine,' he muttered, standing to leave. 'I told your captain that I'll do this myself if I have to. It seems I will.'

I watched as he picked his fedora up from the table, swept his grey woollen coat around his shoulders and strode towards the door. Just as he was about to disappear from view, I found myself calling after him.

'Mr Temple.'

He turned and, for the first time since I had sat down, met my eye.

'Do you really believe there are passengers who will talk to you about this?'

Temple snorted. 'They're already talking. How did you think I knew about it in the first place?'

I cursed inwardly. Wilson had been right; gossip was already starting to spread.

'And say you're right,' I said. 'Say a crime has truly taken place, is it not for the police in New York to investigate? Surely, they're far better equipped than we are here. They'll have resources, men—'

'I understand there are two thousand people on board this ship.'

'That's right.'

'Do you happen to have all of their names and addresses?'

I fought back a scowl. 'No.'

He nodded and tucked his hands into the pockets of his coat. 'There'll be no way of investigating this when we arrive in New York. Not once the passengers have all disembarked. If a crime has taken place, either we reach a conclusion, here and now, or we accept that we're letting the culprit walk.'

I looked down at the tabletop. 'How long would you need with the body?'

'Only a few minutes.'

With a heavy sigh, I slipped my hand into my pocket and felt the material of Amelia's ribbon brush my fingertips.

I was all too aware that I had no choice. Temple had me beaten. For the briefest of moments, I wished I had taken my chances with Mrs Fitch and her Yorkshire terrier.

'Five minutes,' I said. 'But that's all.'

5

On a clear morning, you would hear accents and languages from all around the world on the *Endeavour*'s various outer decks as passengers strolled, sunbathed and sat down for breakfast with steaming cups of tea and coffee, and plates laden with toast, bacon and eggs. You might even see some running. While there was a fully equipped gymnasium for first- and second-class passengers to make use of, covering the length of the promenade a few times would provide a decent run for those keen to stretch their legs.

But on that particular morning, the deck was still wet and slippery from the rain that had fallen during the night, and the winds that came buffeting in from the sea were freezing. Only a brave few would be outside by choice.

I turned up the thick collar of my officer's coat, though to little effect. Temple, meanwhile, didn't even flinch. There was a determined expression on his face as his own coat billowed behind him, a hand keeping his fedora firmly in place upon his head.

Despite this apparent show of bravery, Temple had made something of a protest just moments before at having to step out into the elements. I had explained that the *Endeavour* was like a warren. Corridors and staircases twisted and wrapped around each other in ways that, to anybody unfamiliar with them, made little sense. To reach the room in which the body was being kept, it would be quicker to go around a section of the outer deck and re-enter the ship further down.

A flash of gratitude danced across his face as we finally stepped inside. Closing the door behind us, I led him down three flights of stairs, deep into the belly of the ship.

The aesthetic of the *Endeavour*'s lower levels was so markedly different to those occupied by many of her passengers that I often felt as though you could descend a single deck and believe yourself on a completely different vessel. The soft carpets and polished wood that furnished the first- and second-class accommodation gave way to hard floors and cold metal walls. In place of floral wallpaper and framed artworks, the corridors were adorned with bare pipes and harsh electric lights.

Stopping at a metal door, I drew a key from my pocket and led Temple into the makeshift morgue. The room that had been chosen to house the body was, in actuality, little more than a cupboard. Just a few hours earlier, the shelves that lined the walls had been stocked with bedding, cleaning supplies and tinned food, all of which, in the interest of hygiene, were now stuffed into other cupboards or piled up in the corridor outside.

A table that had been brought in to lay the dead man on filled most of the cramped room, and a sheet had been found to cover him. But the first thing that struck me as I opened the door wasn't the lack of space. It was the smell. With no porthole and therefore no chance of fresh air, the place was filled with the musty stench of sodden clothes. I dearly hoped that this would be our only visit. Given another day, the odour that greeted us would be that of the body itself.

It felt a disrespectful resting place, but the simple truth was that we had nowhere else to keep him. There had apparently been some discussion of putting the body in one of the cold rooms used by the *Endeavour*'s kitchens, but it would have meant sacrificing too much food and our return schedule didn't allow for the time it would take to have the room suitably cleaned when we reached New York. It wasn't an ideal situation, but as Wilson had put it – albeit somewhat indelicately – we had only four days left until we docked, at which point the body would become someone else's problem.

Without a moment's hesitation, Temple pressed his fedora into my hands and whipped the sheet away. It was the first time I had seen the dead man and, with the damp smell already filling my nostrils, my instinct was to look away. After taking a moment to steady myself, I turned, slowly, to survey him.

He had been placed on his back, staring at the ceiling with vacant eyes. In life, I was sure that he had been a very presentable gentleman. He must have been around seventy, with thin white hair, a black suit and tie and a well-kept moustache. Somewhat ironically, it occurred to me that he could easily have passed for an undertaker. But now his suit was sodden and his skin damp and puffy from hours of lying in the rain. His hair was plastered to his head and a shallow puddle was gathering beneath the table, drops of rainwater falling occasionally into the slowly expanding pool.

I had seen more than my fair share of corpses during the war, broken and mutilated in countless unspeakable ways, but this felt different. To see a life ended in a civilian setting was something else entirely. Our examination felt like an intrusion, as if a curtain had been drawn back and some gruesome secret revealed.

And, of course, there was one detail in particular about this man that set me on edge. It seemed the reports that Temple had heard were correct. He wasn't wearing a coat.

'He was found just after seven o'clock this morning,' I said as Temple leaned over the body. The detective had taken a handkerchief from his pocket and was using it to cover his hand as he lifted the dead man's head. He peered intently at the base of the skull, his nose just inches away from an angry, open wound. Looking more closely, I saw for myself that the hair around it was matted with blood. The poor fellow must have lain where he fell for some time before he was found.

'A child in third-class was the first one out on deck after the rain had stopped,' I continued. 'His mother took him outside and they found the body on the starboard promenade, at the bottom of the companionway leading up to second-class. It came as quite a shock to them both, I'm told.'

Temple snorted. 'I'll imagine it did.'

I hesitated for a beat, caught off guard by his apparent amusement.

'A man has died,' I said sternly.

He ignored me, continuing his examination of the body. I was becoming increasingly aware of how cramped the room was, of the damp air and of the bare bulb casting a harsh, unnatural light. I took a deep breath.

'Our medical officer has already inspected him,' I continued, clearing my throat. 'The verdict is that he slipped and fell backwards down the companionway, hitting his head on a step on the way down. They say he was dead before he reached the bottom.'

'Or was pushed,' Temple murmured.

'I'm sorry?'

He said nothing, his focus still firmly on the body.

'Mr Temple,' I pressed. 'I'm sorry, I think you may have—'

'Your medical officer can't know for sure that he slipped.' Gently, Temple set the head back down. 'We can agree on one thing, though. Our friend, here, certainly fell backwards. This blow to the back of the head is the only injury. If he fell forwards, you would expect there to be other marks to the face.'

'Do you think that's relevant?' I asked.

Temple cast me a glare. 'If he fell backwards, he must have had his back to the stairs.'

'I suppose that's true.'

'But why?'

I shook my head. 'I'm sorry, I don't follow.'

'Consider the possibility that he really did slip. That it was truly as innocent as your medical officer describes. Why was he facing away from the stairs? Did something on the deck cause him to turn around? Or is your theory that he was simply walking backwards in the direction of a flight of stairs?'

I looked down at the body, a sense of dread beginning to form in the pit of my stomach. 'You're suggesting that he might have been speaking to someone,' I said. 'Someone who pushed him.'

Temple didn't answer. He had come alive in the brief time that he had been inspecting the dead man. The cautious,

45

calculative figure who had visited Captain McCrory's office just a few short hours ago was now moving nimbly, an intense look of concentration on his face. He reminded me of a hound, rummaging around the mouth of a rabbit hole with a scent in its nostrils.

'Do we know who he is?' he asked.

'He wasn't carrying much in the way of personal effects,' I replied, clearing a lump from my throat. 'But, yes. An officer searched his pockets and found a wallet with a few English notes inside and a key to cabin 203. It's a second-class cabin, occupied by a Mr Fisher.'

'Was he travelling alone?'

'We believe so. Or, at least, it looks that way on paper.'

'On paper?'

'We have a ledger,' I explained. 'Containing the names of the passengers with cabin reservations in first- and second-class. We've checked it this morning and Mr Fisher is the only passenger whose name is against cabin 203.'

Temple nodded. 'So, we have nobody to ask about his business? Where he was going or what he might have been doing at the time that he died?'

'It does seem that way.'

Temple thought for a moment, staring intently at the body. As he did, a drop of water fell from the hem of Fisher's trousers.

'Can we speak to the woman?' he asked.

'I'm sorry?'

'The woman who found him,' he said irritably. 'Has anybody spoken to her? Or the child?'

I shook my head. 'I don't think you'll learn much from her. She's Russian. The officer on duty tried asking a few questions

46

shortly after they found the body, but it seems she doesn't speak much English.'

Temple grimaced, evidently displeased.

'All right,' he said. 'I think we're done.'

'That's all?'

'Unless you've made some other observation that I have missed?'

'No,' I stammered. 'No, of course not. I just ... I supposed you would want longer with him.'

Temple shrugged. 'Besides the injury to the back of the head, there isn't much else to see.'

'So that's it? You can see it was an accident.'

The detective shook his head. 'No.'

'I'm sorry?'

'I don't believe this was an accident. Or at least, I don't believe it's a simple case of Mr Fisher here slipping on his evening walk. Tell me, Mr Birch, is this the first time you've clapped eyes on the man yourself?'

'It is.'

He motioned towards the body with his handkerchief. 'And now that you've seen him, are you really compelled to believe that a man his age would take a simple evening walk in last night's conditions, but not think to put on a coat?'

With an effort, I forced myself to look over Fisher again. I surveyed the polished leather shoes, the wet skin and the dull, glazed eyes.

'Where was he going?' Temple continued. 'What was so important that it couldn't wait? Or, indeed, what was he walking away *from*?'

'Really,' I began to protest. 'Mr Temple, I—'

'The fact that he has fallen backwards also warrants further investigation. I wonder, when was the last time you stopped at the top of a flight of steps and turned your back to it?'

I had no answer for him. My lips remained firmly sealed.

'I'd like to look around Mr Fisher's cabin.' Temple covered the body again and wiped his handkerchief on the sheet before returning it to his jacket pocket.

'I really don't think that would be approp—'

'But before I do,' he interrupted me again. 'I'd like to speak with the maître d'.'

'The maître d'?'

'Precisely.'

'Mr Temple,' I said, forcing as much authority into my voice as I could muster, 'my instructions from Captain McCrory were—'

'Your instructions were to keep me from bothering any passengers. The maître d' is not a passenger and it would seem, therefore, that you can't stop me from speaking with him. So, while I would much prefer to be unaccompanied, I suggest that if you insist on following your captain's orders, you lead the way.'

I was silent.

'Now,' he said briskly. 'Will the maître d' still be in the restaurant?'

'He ought to be,' I muttered. 'The breakfast service will just be finishing. But will you at least tell me why you want to speak with him?'

Temple cast me a quick, frustrated glance. Much like Captain McCrory, I had the impression that this wasn't the sort of man who appreciated being questioned on his profession. Certainly not by civilians.

'Mr Temple,' I pressed, 'what does this have to do with the maître d'?'

With his hand already on the door handle, the detective turned and looked me in the eye. 'I think he and I will have something in common.'

'And what is that?'

He nodded towards Fisher's corpse. 'I suspect we'll both have seen this man before.'

6

Temple and I occupied a little table for two in the far corner of the restaurant. Like a scolded child, he sat with his arms folded, elbows propped upon the pressed white tablecloth.

In all the time that I had served aboard her, Captain McCrory had been immensely proud of the *Endeavour*'s capacity to provide the pinnacle of luxury for those passengers with deep enough pockets to afford it. But it was the restaurant that was truly the jewel in her crown.

Open only to first- and second-class passengers, the entire length of one wall was sheet glass, framed with thick velvet curtains, to offer diners a panoramic ocean view. The other three were occupied by gold-framed paintings, each so broad that they, themselves, might easily have been windows into various beautifully captured landscapes. An oak bar was well stocked with wine, whisky and gin, a bartender polishing its top with a silk cloth, while a string quartet played on a raised podium. The carpet was a deep red and the room was softly lit by a dozen ornately sculpted glass chandeliers.

Even though it had been five years since my first crossing on board the *Endeavour*, I still burst with pride at the sight of it. Elsewhere on the ship, we offered a saltwater swimming pool, a café and various reading and smoking rooms. The first-class cabins had even been famously modelled upon London's Ritz Hotel. But to my mind at least, nothing could match the grandeur of the restaurant.

Temple, however, was scowling. Upon arrival, we had been met by the maître d', a short fellow dressed in a black suit and tie named Robert Evans. He had made no pretences about resenting being brought away from his duties, but having explained our investigation and that Temple needed to ask him a few questions, he had agreed to speak with us. His only conditions were that we waited for a gap in the breakfast service and that we took ourselves out of the way while we did so. Temple had been about to protest, but I quickly said that we would be happy to oblige.

On the surface of our table, the cutlery glinted in the light from the chandeliers, the distance between each utensil so perfectly judged that it might have been hand-measured with a ruler. Robert Evans ran an impeccably tight operation, despite the restaurant's capacity to seat the best part of five hundred diners at any one time. If we had visited an hour earlier, we wouldn't have been able to find a table. But in that moment, it must have been less than half-full, the remaining passengers finishing their breakfast and making cheerful conversation.

I had suggested to Temple that we send for some food, hoping I could spark some friendly conversation that might clear the air between us. The menu had been written by the famed Italian chef, Luca Rossi, and I was sure that a decent breakfast would help to ease the detective's irritable demeanour. Perhaps he might even be a little more forthcoming about his work in London and business in New York. But he had abruptly declined, asking instead only for some coffee.

'Isla says he was an old gentleman.'

I glanced over at a nearby table, where a group of finely dressed passengers were tucking into heaped plates of bacon and eggs.

'He lost his balance and slipped,' a woman continued eagerly. 'That's what she heard.'

'How dreadful,' one of her companions exclaimed.

'Nonsense,' a young man chipped in. 'It must have been a younger fellow. Probably just had a little too much of the old ...' He drank from an imaginary bottle, to the apparent amusement of a couple of his companions.

'No,' the woman insisted. 'Isla was *sure* that he was an older gentleman. A crowd turned out to see the body. She says that she saw him.'

'How could she have seen him? He was down in third-class. Isla wouldn't dare stray even to second!'

Returning to my tea, I thought uneasily that Wilson had been right. It seemed there really would be no chance of containing this news while Temple conducted his investigation.

I nodded towards the window. 'It's quite a view,' I said, hoping to break the silence. It was a poor attempt at conversation. On a bright day, it was, indeed, quite a sight. Now, the clouds remained grey and the waves were rough and hostile.

Temple's eyes snapped in my direction.

'The view.' I nodded awkwardly towards the windows again. 'It's impressive.'

He turned to survey the angry landscape. 'I've seen better.'

'In London?'

He fixed me with the same piercing gaze that he had the captain, and I braced myself for what I was sure would be a clinical response. But the rebuttal didn't come. Instead, he gave a small shrug and returned to his coffee.

I took the opportunity to steer the conversation in a different direction. 'Can I ask why we're here? When did you and the maître d' see Mr Fisher?'

'If you'd let me speak with him, you would have known fifteen minutes ago.'

'You heard my instructions as clearly as I did, Mr Temple. If the maître d' asks us to wait until he's available, then that's what we'll do.'

The detective said nothing.

'Look,' I said, aware that a hint of irritation was beginning to creep into my voice. 'I'm sorry if this isn't how you're used to doing things in London, but I have my instructions and I intend to follow them.'

He scowled into his cup. Before I could press the issue further, though, his eyes flicked over my shoulder, and I turned to see the maître d' bustling over to our table. He pulled out a chair and sat down next to me, dabbing at his receding hairline with a handkerchief.

'Mr Birch,' he said.

'Mr Evans.' I put out a hand for him to shake.

Having been recruited as the *Endeavour*'s maître d' during my year away, I hadn't had the opportunity to know Robert Evans in any more than a professional capacity. It seemed, however, as he looked with a nervous expression at the hand I was offering, that in the six months since I returned he had

certainly heard about me. I had hoped that the rumours surrounding my reclusiveness had made it no further than the
officers' mess. But as Evans took my hand, grasping it for the
most fleeting of moments before whipping it away, I was
reminded of just how widely my reputation seemed to have
spread among the crew: the curious officer who seemed so
insistent to keep to himself.

'This is Mr Temple,' I said. 'He's a detective, investigating
the body that was found this morning. I'm sure you've probably heard about it.'

'Of course,' Evans replied, a harassed expression on his
round face. 'News spreads quickly in here. The passengers
have been discussing little else all morning. They're all telling
slightly different stories, mind you. It seems nobody actually
knows the truth of the matter, but it's a terrible business however you look at it.' He hesitated for a moment, suddenly
becoming defensive. 'I'm not quite sure why you'd come to
me about this, though.'

'He was in here,' said Temple. 'The night before last.'

Evans frowned.

'I was at the bar,' Temple continued. 'At about nine o'clock. I
heard shouting behind me and when I turned around, I saw the
deceased arguing with a gentleman from that table.' He pointed
to the far end of the restaurant, near the musicians' podium.

I was taken aback. It seemed foolish in hindsight, but under
the circumstances of our partnership, I'd barely considered
that Temple was, himself, a passenger. I briefly wondered who
he had been at the bar with. Was he waiting for someone?
Having a quiet drink with his wife before sitting down to dinner perhaps?

'Yes, I remember that.' Evans rubbed his chin. 'He was a short fellow, wasn't he? Older chap. Had a moustache.'

Temple nodded. 'How did it look to you?'

'The argument? It looked as though he had wound the young gentleman up in quite a big way. I ended up having to step in and ask him to leave.'

'Just a moment,' I interrupted, prompting a glare from Temple. 'He was arguing with someone at a table?'

Evans shook his head. 'Not at the table. They'd gone to the other side of the restaurant.' He pointed. 'The younger fellow was sitting there, having dinner with two ladies and another gentleman.' He then gestured vaguely to the opposite end of the room. 'But when your man came to the table, the younger gentleman took him over there.'

'Why would he do that?' I asked.

Evans shook his head again. 'I suppose he didn't want his companions to hear whatever it was they had to talk about.'

'Could *you* tell what they were arguing about?' Temple cut in.

'I wasn't listening, truth be told,' Evans replied. 'They were making quite a scene, disturbing the other passengers. The particulars didn't interest me. I just wanted to get them out.'

'And you haven't seen either of them since?'

The maître d' began to shuffle nervously in his seat. 'Look, I'm sure it can't be related—'

'Answer the question, Mr Evans.'

Evans sighed. 'The older gentleman came back,' he said. 'Yesterday morning. He came early, before the first passengers started arriving for breakfast.'

'What did he want?'

Evans grimaced. 'He wanted the cabin numbers of the people at that table.'

'And you *gave* them to him?' I gasped.

'I didn't just hand them over.' The maître d' flashed me a vicious look. 'I'd imagine it's all right for you gentlemen in the officers' quarters, Mr Birch. Running the restaurant isn't exactly a well-paid job, you know.'

'So, he gave you money?' said Temple. He didn't seem half as offended by the idea as I was.

'Look,' said Evans sternly, 'he was offering five pounds for their names and room numbers. Five pounds!'

'And that didn't seem suspicious to you?'

'Of course it did. But I thought, what harm's he going to do? He looked like he was pushing seventy, for God's sake. For all I knew, he wanted to find the younger gentleman and apologise. Tell me, sir, how I was supposed to turn that down.'

I shook my head, appalled.

'I'll need those names and cabin numbers,' said Temple. 'Is there anything else you can tell us about him? Anything he said, perhaps?'

Evans thought for a moment, his cheeks flushed. 'He was French.'

'French?'

'He spoke good English – perfect, I'd say – but he was definitely French. Beyond that, gentlemen, I simply didn't want to know.'

Temple nodded. 'Thank you, Mr Evans. You may go.'

Evans frowned, apparently unaware that he had required the detective's permission to leave. He stood up without a word and scurried away.

'Scandalous,' I muttered. 'Utterly scandalous.'

'Don't do that again,' said Temple sharply.

'Do what?'

'Don't interrupt when I'm conducting an interview. You want to know why I objected to you following me around? This is why. If I'm to investigate this, the last thing I need is you disrupting my train of thought.'

'Following you around?' I began to protest. 'Let's just make something clear—'

Before I could go any further, the maître d' returned with his book. I swiftly made a mental note to have stern words with Temple later on about just who was in charge of this arrangement.

'There were three reservations for that table.' Evans ran a finger down the list of names. 'A Miss Vivian Hall in cabin 112, a Mr Arthur Blake in cabin 237 and a Mr and Mrs Webber in 226. I believe it was Mr Blake that your man had this argument with.'

'Three bookings,' Temple mused. 'Is that unusual?'

Evans shook his head. 'We ask for a cabin number when we take a reservation, but the first- and second-class cabins only tend to fit a couple of people. If there's a larger group having dinner together, you'll often have a few different cabin numbers reserving one table.'

He watched in horror as Temple produced a pen from his jacket and scribbled down the names and cabin numbers on a thick white napkin. Having apparently decided against commenting, though, he hurried back to his booth, taking care, I noticed, not to look me in the eye.

I was beginning to feel uneasy. Despite Temple's observation of how curious it was for Fisher to be outside without a coat, or indeed to have fallen backwards down the companionway, I had still clung to my hope that he might simply have slipped. That his death would prove to be no more than a tragic accident. Now, having heard that in the twenty-four hours before he died, he had not only had a heated argument but had gone out of his way to find the offended party, I was struggling to suppress the feeling that there might be more to this than Captain McCrory wanted to believe.

Meanwhile, the enthusiasm that Temple had gained from our conversation with Evans was making me even more nervous. The boyish eagerness I had seen in his eyes when he examined Fisher's body was back. With a small smile, he folded the napkin bearing Mr Blake, Miss Hall, and Mr and Mrs Webber's cabin numbers and tucked it into his jacket pocket.

7

After leaving Robert Evans in the restaurant, Temple was insistent that our next port of call should be Fisher's cabin.

'I thought you would want to meet Arthur Blake,' I said, Evans's account of the argument in the restaurant still fresh in my mind.

The detective shook his head. 'We gather facts before we speak to witnesses. First, I want to know everything I can about Fisher.'

The idea of letting Temple inspect the cabin made me uneasy, but I knew that I had to allow it. If his earlier observations about the circumstances surrounding Fisher's death hadn't been enough, I couldn't deny how suspicious it was for the man to have been involved in a heated public argument just twenty-four hours before his death. In Temple's mind, he seemed to be chasing down a murderer, and the thought of such an individual roaming the *Endeavour* – free, if they saw fit, to act again – was deeply unsettling.

And so I led the way from the restaurant to the Great Staircase. For most passengers, the first few visits to this particular spot were a thrill. Carved from solid oak, it was often thought to be the heart of the *Endeavour*, situated in the centre of the ship and spanning six decks. On each level, the polished banisters spread like a pair of outstretched arms, bearing carvings of roses and lilies that were so lifelike, you would need to feel the wood on your fingers to be sure they weren't actually blooming. It was rare to walk past it without catching at least a couple of visitors marvelling at either its size or craftsmanship. Temple, however, barely seemed to notice it. Instead, his feet clicked smartly on the polished floor as he marched in the direction of second-class.

On arrival, we found that Fisher had occupied a snug cabin with a neatly made single bunk, a narrow wardrobe and a desk and chair. A washbasin and a mirror were mounted on the far wall, beneath a small porthole which allowed a little natural light.

I'd heard the second-class cabins described by some passengers as cosy, which seemed a fair assessment to me. Fisher's room was perhaps ten feet across and just large enough for Temple and me to both move comfortably around. It was a fraction of the size of the suites offered in first-class, although a good deal more luxurious than a cabin in third-, the majority of which saw four passengers crammed into a similar space.

I held the door open for Temple before quickly following him inside. I had half-expected him to insist that he inspect the cabin alone, and I wasn't about to wait in the corridor while he carried on without me. I had restrained myself in the restaurant, but I was determined to remind him that our investigation was being conducted entirely at my discretion.

I thought of Kate, a frown on her face, shaking her head at my stubbornness. 'Let it go, Tim,' she would say. 'Just leave it be.'

Closing the door behind me, I watched as Temple took up a position in the middle of the cabin. Fisher had apparently been travelling light, with not much in the way of possessions for him to inspect. Still, he swept a glance around the little room, his eyes coming to rest upon an ornate walking stick that leaned beside the door. It was a pretty object, with a curved handle like a shepherd's crook and varnished to an impressive shine.

'Might that be ornamental?' I asked.

Temple grimaced, as though my question was a fly buzzing around his ear. He picked up the stick and turned it upside down. 'It's well worn,' he said, peering closely at the bottom. 'This was used regularly.'

Apparently finished with the stick, he pressed it into my hands and fished a leather suitcase from beneath the bed. Finding it empty, he closed it again, deposited it on the bed and turned his attention to the wardrobe. Over his shoulder, I spotted a few white shirts and a sharp brown suit. After a brief inspection, Temple turned and held out a black item for me to take. At first, I thought it was a jacket or a blazer. On closer inspection, I realised it was an overcoat.

'He really did leave this behind,' I murmured. 'And the walking stick.' I shook my head, my sense of unease building. '*Where* was he going?'

Temple ignored me. Still at the wardrobe, he pushed the shirts to one side and began to rummage inside the suit, albeit with a great deal less reverence than I would have hoped for. I thought better than to question him, though. Instead, as we stood among his possessions, I couldn't help but wonder who, exactly, this man Fisher had been. Was there a woman somewhere who would need to be told that her husband wasn't coming home? Children who no longer had a father? There might even be grandchildren. He had, after all, appeared to be an older gentleman.

The more I thought on it, the less, I realised, we knew. Surely, there must be someone who would be bereaved by the news of Fisher's death. Perhaps this Arthur Blake might prove to be one such person. If the story of their argument in the restaurant and Fisher's eagerness to then seek him out proved anything, it was that they certainly knew one another. When Temple was finished with the cabin, perhaps these were questions that he could answer.

Moments later, Temple emerged from the wardrobe with a small wad of paper in his hand. On the top was Fisher's ticket; a return from Southampton to New York, stamped by the inspector as he'd boarded the *Endeavour* on Monday and printed with the blue stripe of the Aurora Cruise Line. He put the ticket down on the desk, revealing a paper booklet inscribed with '*République Française Passeport*'.

Flipping it open, Temple frowned, and then the corners of his mouth twitched into a smile.

'What is it?' I asked warily.

He said nothing.

'Mr Temple?'

He held the passport out to me. 'Do you still think we're dealing with a simple case of an old man falling down the stairs?'

I placed the coat and walking stick gently on the bed and took the passport. Inside was a black-and-white photograph of Fisher. Printed underneath was his date of birth: 2 April 1854. Then, I saw the name, *Denis Dupont*.

Temple grinned triumphantly.

'Denis Dupont,' I murmured. 'Is it a forgery?'

'Unlikely.' Temple took the passport from my hand, and held it up to the light to inspect it more closely. 'It looks genuine. A forgery as well made as this would be difficult to come by.'

'You think he's boarded the ship under a false name?'

'How many seventy-year-old Frenchmen do you know with the name Fisher?'

I nodded slowly. 'So, the question is *why* Monsieur Dupont would take a false name.'

'That's not the only question.' Temple handed me a slip of paper. 'You said that he was travelling alone. So who gave him this?'

Scrawled on the paper was: *Saturday. Nine o'clock.*

'What makes you think someone on the ship gave it to him?' I asked, peering at the note. 'This might just as easily have already been in his pocket before we left Southampton.'

'Look at the paper,' Temple said irritably, like a schoolmaster scolding a young boy. 'It's in pristine condition. If that had been in his pocket more than a day or two, it would be creased or smudged. Someone gave that to him very recently.'

I stifled a heavy sigh, my stomach sinking as I held the note in one hand and the passport in the other. What little hope I had still harboured that Fisher's — or should I now say Dupont's? — argument in the restaurant might somehow be unconnected to his death was rapidly fading. And judging by the small, satisfied smile on his face, Temple knew it as well.

8

As luck would have it, Arthur Blake's cabin was not only in second-class, but also happened to be just a short walk from Denis Dupont's. Leading the way, I stepped up to knock on the cabin door, when I felt Temple clasp me on the shoulder.

'Don't you think you should let me do it?'

I paused, not quite sure that I understood. Then the penny dropped.

'You don't even want me to knock on a door?'

Before Temple could reply, the door opened a crack and a lean, boyish face peered out at us.

'Mr Blake?' I said, speaking hurriedly before Temple had a chance. 'My name's Timothy Birch, I'm one of the ship's officers. This is Mr Temple. Could we speak with you for a moment, sir?'

The door opened a little further and the nervous expression on Arthur Blake's face turned to one of confusion. He wore chequered trousers and a matching waistcoat, with a pale green shirt underneath. It was a fine suit, but the cuffs of his shirt were rolled back and the collar was wide open. Likewise, his sandy hair, which I imagined would ordinarily be neatly brushed, was wildly dishevelled, a few strands hanging idly over his face.

'How did you know to come?' he said, his voice barely more than a whisper.

Temple and I exchanged a glance.

'Are you expecting us, sir?' I asked.

'Mr Blake,' Temple cut in. 'I'd like to speak with you about the man who approached you in the restaurant on Monday evening.'

Blake's face dropped. 'What about him?'

'Have you not yet been out this morning?'

Blake shook his head.

'He was found dead. Just a few hours ago.'

Blake's eyes went wide. 'I suppose you'd better come in,' he said quietly.

We followed him into the cabin to find it was identical to Dupont's in size and decoration, but with one unmistakable difference. Specifically, it had the distinct appearance of having been rocked by an earthquake. A leather suitcase lay in the middle of the cabin, the wardrobe was wide open and clothes were strewn across the little room: pink, blue and white shirts dumped unceremoniously on the floor. The sheets had been ripped from the bed and the drawers wrenched from the desk.

'Dear God,' I murmured. 'When did this happen?'

'Last night.' Blake stared down at the floor, massaging his forehead with one hand, as though nursing a splitting headache. As he spoke, I detected a polished, refined accent. 'I came back and found it like this.'

'Back from where?' asked Temple.

'The restaurant,' Blake replied. 'I went for dinner, stayed for a drink at the bar and when I returned ...'

He looked up and waved a hand around the cabin. I turned to inspect the door and immediately saw the splintered lock. There was no questioning that it must have been forced.

'What time was this?' said Temple.

'Around midnight, I suppose.'

'That's a late supper, Mr Blake.'

'Well, as I said, I sat for a while at the bar.'

Temple was still assessing the room, taking in every detail with needle-like precision. Again, I was reminded of how this ferocious intensity seemed so poorly matched with the creased charcoal suit, the thick, unkempt hair and the specks of blood on his collar.

'Have you not slept?'

'How am I supposed to sleep? I've hardly known what to do. Been in some sort of shock, I suppose.'

'But you didn't think to report this?' Temple lifted the suitcase to reveal a small pile of colourful socks nestled underneath. 'You seemed surprised to find us at your door.'

Blake shuffled uncomfortably. 'No,' he said. 'I haven't.'

'Why not?' I heard my voice rise, furious that such vandalism could be allowed to take place on my watch without even being reported.

'Look, I'd really rather not say,' Blake began to protest.

'This isn't a social call, Mr Blake.' Temple straightened up and glared at him. 'A man has been found dead, not two days after you were seen having a public and, by all accounts, very heated argument with him. You're now addressing a member of Scotland Yard and a ship's officer. It's not in your interest to withhold anything from us, sir.'

Blake seemed to think for a moment. As he did, his eyes flickered nervously to the desk, where a pointed object had been covered with a knitted jumper. I'd been so taken aback by the rest of the room that I'd barely noticed it until now. Blake's lips quivered as he looked at it, but before I could ask what it concealed, he swallowed back a large gulp, reached into the pocket of a blazer that hung over the back of his chair and fished out a cigarette case, shortly followed by a box of matches.

'Do you mind?'

'Not at all,' Temple replied.

Blake sat down on the bed and, with a trembling hand, lit a cigarette. He drew on it deeply, before slowly exhaling. I took a short step back. The cabin might very well have been the same size as Dupont's, but in its dishevelled state and with a thin cloud of smoke forming above our heads, it was beginning to feel a good deal smaller.

'How did he die?' asked Blake.

'He fell down a flight of steps,' said Temple. 'He lay there all night and a boy found him this morning on the deck.'

Blake ran a hand through his hair, brushing the stray strands from his face, and let out a long sigh. 'Christ, that's a nasty way to go.'

'Who was he?' asked Temple.

'You're looking into his death, but you don't even know who he is?'

'Answer the question, Mr Blake.'

Blake frowned and took another drag on the cigarette. 'His name is Denis Dupont. He's an art dealer – or *was*, I should say. He has a little gallery in Bath. Opened it after the war when his place in London was bombed.'

'Did he ever go by the name Fisher?'

Blake's frown intensified. 'Not that I know of.'

'And how did you know him?'

'I did a little work for him.'

'In the gallery?'

'No.' Just for a moment, an unpleasant flicker of amusement danced across Blake's face. 'No, I paint. My interest has always been more in the history of art, mind you. But times are … let's say a little tough at the moment. So, for the past year or so, I've been doing some work for Dupont.'

'He sold your paintings?' said Temple.

'That's right. I produce portraits, mostly. Every so often, Dupont will have a businessman or a landowner visit the gallery, wanting to commission a painting of their family or their dog. Something like that. Dupont doesn't paint, so he employs me on a freelance basis to do the work.'

'And this arrangement works well for you both?'

'I suppose so.' Blake shrugged. 'We both make a little money from it if that's what you mean.'

'So, what prompted Monday evening's argument?'

Having already smoked his cigarette to the end, Blake motioned for me to pass him a glass ashtray from the desk. Pressing the butt into it, he reached for his cigarette case and immediately lit another. I noticed his hand was steadier than it had been a few moments earlier.

'Look, gentlemen,' he said curtly. 'As you're here, I'll happily assist with an investigation into who's broken into my cabin. But I'd like you to understand that there are two reasons I have chosen not to report this. The first of which is that I am travelling to New York on both a sensitive and deeply private matter—'

'Mr Blake,' Temple interrupted, his patience apparently wearing thin. 'Whether we hear it from you or from one of the many other diners who witnessed your argument with Monsieur Dupont, I intend to find out exactly what the subject of that disagreement was. If it gives me reason to suspect you of any involvement in his death, I can assure you that it will not be in your favour to have withheld it from me.'

Blake sat silently, weighing up his options. Recognising an impasse, he gave an exasperated sigh. 'Does the name Ecclestone mean anything to either of you?'

'No,' Temple answered for us both.

Blake sat up straight on the bed and took a long drag on the fresh cigarette. 'Joseph Ecclestone was a painter,' he said. 'Most of his work was done in Devon, during the late eighteenth century. He would paint the ocean, the coastline, the hills ... He never achieved quite the same popularity as some of the European artists working at the time, but there's no questioning that he was one of the most talented English painters in recent history.

'Now, the funny thing about Ecclestone is that he never painted portraits. He would often write about how his interest lay solely in the power of nature, so he only ever produced landscapes.'

Blake paused a moment. Having overcome the initial shock of our arrival, it seemed to me that he might actually be enjoying the attention of his audience. The more he spoke, the clearer and bolder his voice seemed to become.

'Except,' he continued, 'there are some historians who believe that he worked on a single portrait shortly before he died. They say that he painted a woman – mind you, nobody knows who she was. Ecclestone was never married, so some speculate that the subject was his mother. Others think he fell in love in the later years of his life and died before they could be married.

'He kept journals, which, of course, I've studied. But he seems to have been a private sort of fellow. There's nothing in any of his writing to suggest who she might have been, or, for that matter, even confirming that the portrait actually existed.'

I was starting to become impatient with Blake's story, having hoped instead for some new detail about his argument with Dupont or the ruined cabin. Temple, however, seemed to be transfixed, hanging on every word.

'But *I* know the portrait is real.' Blake's eyes were gleaming.

'How's that?' asked Temple.

'Because I've found it.' Blake took another long drag on his cigarette, as though for dramatic effect. 'A chap from the West Country came to Dupont's gallery, looking to sell some artwork that had been left to him when his mother died. The house must have been stuffed with it because he brought in three full crates and – low and behold – the portrait was in the collection.

'Here's the thing, though. Dupont had *no clue* what it was. I suppose he thought it was just another pretty piece, because he put it up for sale at a price ten, maybe even twenty times less than it must be worth.'

'So you bought it?' asked Temple.

'That's right,' said Blake proudly. 'I'm taking it to the New York City Art Fair.'

'I suppose that's an auction of some kind.'

Blake rolled his eyes. 'It's the largest art auction in the world. Every year, the most prolific collectors come together for one grand event. Although it's a particularly special occasion this year – Winston Parker, of all people, is opening it. Surely, you must at least know of *him*?'

I glanced quickly at Temple, hoping to gauge his response to this name. It was certainly one that I was familiar with. Raymond mentioned Winston Parker regularly enough in the letters that we exchanged, but even in England, he was well known. The youngest of four sons born to an immigrant family in New York, he had supposedly become one of the most successful men in America. He owned hotels, land, racehorses; I'd even heard that he had a small stake in the Aurora Cruise Line. I could understand why Arthur Blake would be excited to show him his painting. According to Raymond, Parker was thought by many to be the American Dream personified.

And yet, as I looked at Temple, I was met with a curious sight. At the mention of Parker's name, his jaw seemed to clench and his eyes widened. I watched him closely, but Blake was now so caught up in his own narrative that he continued without even noticing the effect that Parker's name seemed to have had.

'God only knows how much the lost Ecclestone would sell for in front of an audience like that,' he said. 'I'm quite sure

71

that even Mr Parker himself would place a bid. Now *there's* a man whose acquaintance would most certainly be worth making, don't you think?'

'I think I'd like you to move on, Mr Blake.'

'But surely you'd agree that—'

'*Now.*'

Whether Temple had meant to be quite so aggressive, I couldn't say, but he snapped at Blake with such ferocity that the artist and I both physically recoiled.

An uncomfortable silence followed, during which I peered at Temple. He'd already made it quite clear that he wasn't looking for a friend in Arthur Blake, but the sudden hostility with which he had just chided the young man was something else entirely.

'Of course,' said Blake, the wistful expression that had overcome him fading away as quickly as it appeared. 'Yes, quite right. Not relevant, I suppose.'

Knocked off balance, he took a drag on his cigarette, struggling, it seemed, to meet the intense glare with which Temple was now fixing him. To tell the truth, I could hardly blame the poor fellow. There was no denying the detective's sudden change in temperament. It may have been a trick of the light, but he seemed even to have paled slightly.

Surely, he couldn't suspect Winston Parker of some role in the theft of Blake's painting? How would he steal it – or, for that matter, even know of it – ahead of the Art Fair? I would need to put it to him, I realised. To determine, if it was indeed Parker's name that troubled Temple, why it had prompted such a sharp response.

'As I say,' Blake continued, a slight tremor to his voice, 'my plan was to sell the portrait at the Art Fair to the highest bidder. Only—'

'The painting's gone.' Temple cast an eye around the ruined cabin, straining, apparently, to return to the problem at hand.

Blake looked down at his feet, a few rebel strands of hair dropping in front of his eyes again. 'I spent everything I had left,' he murmured, more to himself than to us. 'Buying the portrait and the ticket for this damned ship. It was supposed to fix everything.'

'How did you know the painting was by Ecclestone?' I asked, ignoring a venomous look from Temple. 'How can you be sure if nobody's ever seen it before?'

'It had to be.' Blake shook his head, a wistful look in his eyes. 'The Devon coast in the background. His use of colour and light. The brushwork ... To someone truly familiar with his work, it could only be Ecclestone's.'

'Then how did it go so long without being recognised?'

'I've thought about that. As I say, Ecclestone's work is valuable, but he never achieved the same prestige as some other artists working at the same time. I can only imagine that the old bird who owned it was a distant relative or friend of the family who was bequeathed it over the years and didn't know its true worth any more than Dupont.'

Blake stubbed out his second cigarette in the glass ashtray. He seemed barely to have smoked this one, he had been speaking so much about his painting, and I could have sworn that I noticed his hand beginning to tremble again. I was surprised to see that he didn't immediately light a third.

'I presume, Mr Blake,' said Temple, 'that this painting is the reason Dupont approached you on Monday evening?'

In an instant, Blake's face shifted from an expression of wistful self-pity to one of anger. 'He'd found out about it,' he spat. 'God knows how, but he'd worked it out. I couldn't believe it when he came up to me in that restaurant and tapped me on the shoulder.

'And that's when the argument took place?'

'Yes.' Blake glanced down at his feet. 'I'd had a little too much to drink and ... well, I'm ashamed to say that I lost my temper.'

'Why did you take him away from the table?'

Blake frowned.

'You took Dupont to the other side of the restaurant to discuss the painting,' explained Temple. 'Why couldn't you speak with him at the table?'

'I was dining with a group of friends. They're a good sort, but I haven't told them about the portrait. I haven't told anyone about it because I wanted to avoid exactly *this* sort of scenario.' He waved a hand around the cabin. 'Of course, I knew the moment I saw Dupont what he wanted. I took him away so that I could keep them in the dark. That's when he told me he wanted to negotiate its return. Said I'd cheated him out of it but he'd pay a fair price to have it back.'

'Were they not suspicious?' asked Temple. 'By all accounts, the argument was quite public.'

Blake shrugged. 'Harry and Cassie asked what the fuss was all about. I told them that he was a client and we'd had a disagreement over a job. Neither of them knows very much about the art world, so they didn't ask any more than that. As for Vivian ...'

Blake's eyes went wide, as though he had been struck with a sudden jolt of electricity. I briefly thought Temple might press him to complete his train of thought, still wary of how he had snapped at the mention of Winston Parker. If he meant to, though, the artist gave him no opportunity.

'Vivian needs to be warned,' he said frantically, getting to his feet. 'Dear God, how could I not have thought—'

'You're speaking about Miss Hall, I presume?'

'Of course. I should have gone last night. Should have thought straight away—'

'Mr Blake,' said Temple sternly. 'Sit back down, sir, and explain to us exactly what it is that you believe Miss Hall needs to be warned about.'

Blake glanced at the door as though thinking about making a dash for it, but seemed to think better of the idea and sat down again. His gaze flickered to the desk, settling on the pointed object that remained obscured by a jumper.

It felt too foolish to voice in front of Temple, but there was something about it that set me on edge. The placement of the jumper seemed so deliberate, when the rest of the cabin was in such disarray. I'd almost have said that it had been arranged in order to hide the object on the desk. But before I could give it any further thought, Blake continued with his account of Monday's events in the restaurant.

'The fourth member of our party,' he said. 'Vivian Hall. She was away from the table when Dupont arrived, ordering herself a cocktail at the bar. I was rather pleased about that.'

'Why was that, sir?'

'Because she knew Dupont.' Blake paused to let this new detail sink in. 'Vivian is an artist herself, and a gifted one at

75

that. She's produced four extraordinary portraits these past two years, all of which have been sold by him. I'm quite sure she must have seen us arguing. But for her to have been away from the table meant, at least, that I could keep his identity – and by extension the existence of my portrait – a secret from Harry and Cassie.'

'So Miss Hall isn't aware of the painting?' asked Temple.

'Certainly not. I managed to steer the conversation along before she returned to the table.'

'Even so, she didn't ask about the subject of the argument? Or reveal to Mr and Mrs Webber that she knew Dupont?'

'She did not. She returned with her cocktail and sat back down. Nothing more was said.' Blake gave a little shrug. 'Harry and Cassie looked a little uncomfortable, but Vivian seemed happy just to move on.'

Temple paused a moment. When he spoke again, he did so cautiously, asking his question as though it might somehow crack if he delivered it too aggressively.

'Did Miss Hall have any grievances of her own with Monsieur Dupont?'

'Nothing that would justify pushing him down a flight of steps, if that's what you're suggesting.'

The detective raised an eyebrow, prompting Blake to sigh.

'Vivian is something of a rising star,' he explained. 'Dupont has done a good job with her work so far, but with each new piece that she produces, it's becoming clear she is meant for greater things than his little gallery in Bath. That's why she's decided to take her latest painting to New York and sell it at the Art Fair.'

'I imagine Monsieur Dupont would have been less than pleased with such a decision,' said Temple.

'As would I,' agreed Blake. 'But do you not see, gentlemen? This is exactly what Vivian must be warned of! If some lunatic is roaming the ship, breaking into cabins and stealing art-works – not to mention attacking art dealers – she needs to be told.'

'She will be,' I said firmly.

'Perhaps I should find her,' said Blake, glancing nervously again towards the door. 'Make sure she hears it from a friendly face. She's travelling alone, you understand. The thought of whoever's done this targeting her as well is just too much to—'

'*We* will warn Miss Hall,' said Temple sternly. 'I fully intend to speak with her today as part of our inquiries. If she is, indeed, in danger, we will ensure that she is aware.'

'What in heaven's name are you talking about?' Blake's voice began to rise. 'It seems to me that anybody who is bound for the Art Fair must be in danger. For God's sake, look around you! Look at what this madman has done to my cabin!'

'I *am* looking,' said Temple. 'And it is the question of your cabin to which I am going to insist that you now return. Calm yourself, Mr Blake, and tell me what, exactly, happened in the hours prior to finding it in this condition. You told us that you had been drinking in the bar. I take it you were alone?'

Blake looked as though he might try to resist, just as he had our first few questions. But whether he remembered Temple's warning about the consequences of holding back or had decided that we might actually be of some help, he seemed to think better of it.

'I haven't seen Dupont since our argument,' he muttered. 'I had the day to myself yesterday, went for a late dinner in the evening, and that was when I met ...' He tailed off, a grimace dancing over his face. 'That was when I met *her*.'

Temple was silent, waiting patiently for Blake to elaborate.

'I ate by myself in the restaurant,' he continued. 'When I'd finished, I wasn't quite ready to come back to the cabin and it wasn't the sort of night on which you'd want to go for a walk, what with the rain pouring down, so I sat at the bar for a while. I was having a quiet drink when a woman came and sat next to me. She looked straight at me and said, "It's Beatrice. Beatrice Walker." Naturally, I shook her hand, said how much of a pleasure it was to meet her and bought her a drink.'

'How long did Miss Walker spend with you?' asked Temple.

'A couple of hours, I'd say. She asked me all about what I did for a living, so I told her that I was an artist and we spoke about what we were each going to do in New York.'

'And that didn't strike you as suspicious?'

'Not at the time. To tell you the truth, I couldn't believe my luck.'

'You didn't tell her about the painting?'

'Of course not.'

'So what happened?'

Blake paused, a fresh grimace forming on his face. 'I asked if she'd like to come back with me for a nightcap. *That's* when she chose to tell me she was married and that she ought to be getting back to her husband. I was more than a little peeved, I can tell you, but she left before I could say another word. Stormed off as though I'd offended her somehow. It was about midnight at that point and the bartender had called time an hour ago, so I came back.' He waved a hand around the cabin. 'To find this.'

'And the painting was gone,' Temple concluded.

Blake didn't reply.

'Could Mrs Walker have known about it by some other means?' asked Temple. 'It seems fairly evident that she was keeping you occupied while the theft took place.'

Blake shook his head. 'I've been wondering the same thing. Of course, I wouldn't be telling you a word of this if I didn't think she was involved. But I've told no one about the portrait. If Dupont worked out what it is on his own, he would have been the only other one who knew it even existed. Which means that if she knows, she must be with him.'

'And yet, you still haven't reported any of this?' I said.

Something dark blazed in Blake's eyes. 'This could be the most valuable artistic find of the century,' he said quietly, as if suddenly worried about being overheard. 'And believe me when I tell you that I won't be the only one aboard this ship who's bound for the Art Fair. The last thing I need is for word to get out that the fabled lost Ecclestone is somewhere on board.' He shook his head vigorously. 'I had planned to find Dupont today and confront him.'

Temple snorted. 'You'll struggle.'

Blake glared at him.

'Can you describe her?' I asked, keen to steer the conversation to safer territory. 'Mrs Walker, I mean.'

'She was a pretty thing. Tall, pale, short black hair.' He flashed me an unpleasant grin. 'Marvellous figure.'

'And she didn't mention anything else about who she was travelling with?' said Temple. 'Or where she was going?'

'Aside from her husband, you mean? Just that she was visiting New York. Beyond that, she only wanted to know about me. It all seemed perfectly innocent.'

'And I assume that you have no way of contacting her again?'

'None at all.'

Temple nodded. 'Your other companions,' he said. 'The couple who dined with you and Miss Hall on Monday evening. Who are they?'

Blake frowned. 'I've told you – I took measures to ensure that they aren't involved in any of this.'

'All the same, I'd like to know.'

'Suit yourself.' He gave a little shrug. 'My friend, Harry Webber, and his wife, Cassandra. He's an estate agent.'

'And what about Mrs Webber?'

'She studies law,' Blake replied. 'She's American but she came to England to spend a year in Bristol. That's where she met Harry.'

Temple nodded and cast one last cursory glance around the dishevelled cabin. Bitterly, I wondered how much effort it would take to convince him to share whatever conclusions he had arrived at.

'What's the second reason?' I asked.

Blake frowned at me.

'You told us there were two reasons you haven't reported any of this,' I pressed. 'The first was to keep the painting a secret. As much as I disapprove, I suppose I can understand that logic, given your suspicions about other collectors being on board. But what was the second?'

Blake took a deep breath, as if to steady himself. Once again, he glanced at the pointed object on the desk.

'The second,' he said, 'is that I believe whoever has taken the painting has made a threat against my life. Foolish as it might seem to you gentlemen, I thought that I would be safer if I searched for it alone.'

Temple's eyes narrowed. 'What do you mean, you *believe* there is a threat?'

'The thief and I didn't exactly have a conversation.'

'Then how has this threat been made?'

Without a word, Blake stood and moved to the desk, where he grasped the jumper and whipped it away, revealing the object it had concealed.

Buried in the wood, its hilt pointing proudly towards the ceiling, was a knife.

9

Temple was pacing back and forth on the outer deck in a state of the most fevered agitation.

I was in something of a dour mood myself, my head bowed as I sat on a nearby bench. The clouds had begun to clear and a pale sun was attempting to shine, a crisp breeze sweeping the deck. Passengers strolled arm in arm in the direction of the restaurant for lunch and a group of children played with a skipping rope.

I watched them for a short while, allowing my mind to drift briefly to Amelia. They looked a few years older than she was, and yet, I knew that she would have wasted no time in walking up to them and insisting that she be included in their game. She would want to know their names; where they were from; their favourite subjects at school. She had always been such an inquisitive child.

As I watched them, I slipped her yellow ribbon from my pocket and ran it through my fingers. When I first joined the *Endeavour*'s crew, I'd fantasised on more than one occasion about taking Kate and Amelia to sea. It would be a great adventure for Amelia. She would run the length of the promenade, the yellow ribbon fluttering in her hair. In reality, though, I'd never supposed that it would happen. Our finances would barely stretch to a holiday at an English seaside, let alone a voyage on the *Endeavour*. Even so, it had always been a comforting image.

With an effort, I withdrew from the fantasy, burying it deep inside. Slipping the ribbon back into my pocket, I turned my attention to Temple, as he continued to march upon the deck. He had convinced me that Dupont's death required the attention of a detective. The various questions surrounding the old man himself, the raid on Arthur Blake's cabin and the missing painting had already left no room in my mind for any further doubt. But the discovery of the knife in Blake's desk had taken our investigation to a different level entirely.

The moment he revealed it to us, my heart had sunk. I had still been clinging quietly to the hope that our inquiries would end with Dupont tumbling tragically down that companionway of his own accord. But the gleaming blade buried in the wood of Blake's desk spoke plainly enough.

On closer inspection, I'd quickly identified it as a steak knife; one of a few hundred which could easily have been taken from the *Endeavour*'s restaurant. Its blade was only a few inches in length, but the message it sent was clear: wielded correctly, it could kill. If Temple was right, and the thief had known that Blake was at the bar with Beatrice Walker, it seemed they had meant to use it only as a threat. A warning not to pursue them. But if Temple was wrong; if the culprit had *not* been in league with Beatrice Walker ...

Perhaps the answer still lay with Dupont. He was, after all, the only one other than Blake who seemed to know that the painting was on board. Perhaps he had planted the knife before hiding the painting and falling to his death. It was a theory that I caught myself desperately hoping we would prove to be true. If we didn't, the only conclusion left to us was that the culprit was still at large, somewhere on board.

I thought of Vivian Hall and the many other passengers who must also be travelling to the New York City Art Fair, carrying priceless paintings of their own. Were they all fair game to whoever had raided Blake's cabin? Was the culprit already planning their next move?

After leaving Blake, Temple had declared that our most urgent priority should be to find and question Beatrice Walker. To determine if she really had been in league with the thief. Finding no reason to disagree, I had taken him to read the ship's ledger. The detective had received some unsavoury looks as I led him through the officers' quarters to the record room, though he seemed barely to notice. For Beatrice Walker to have been allowed in the restaurant suggested that she must be travelling in first- or second-class. In either case, finding her name and cabin number ought to be a simple task.

But it was here that our trail had quickly run cold and Temple's mood been catastrophically dampened. When we had taken the heavy book from the shelf and scoured it from front to back, we found nothing. According to the ledger, there was no Beatrice Walker on board.

'For God's sake, Mr Temple,' I said. 'Speak to me. Let me help you.'

The detective was still pacing relentlessly, muttering to himself and drawing nervous glances from a nearby group of passengers. At the sound of my voice, he stopped and fixed me with a quizzical expression, as if he'd just remembered I was there.

'How do you propose to help?' he demanded. 'Have you seen something that I have missed?'

'Of course not.'

'Have you perhaps spoken to someone that I have not?'

'You know I haven't.'

'Then tell me, Birch, how do you plan to help?'

'Mr Temple,' I said as sternly as I could manage. 'Regardless of your objections to my accompanying you, I am part of this investigation. Surely we stand a better chance of finding our culprit if we do so together?'

He glared at me, a ferocious intensity in his cold eyes. Then he stopped pacing, propped himself against the railing and stuffed his hands into the pockets of his grey woollen coat.

'We know that Monsieur Dupont sought out and paid the maître d' for Mr Blake's cabin number yesterday morning,' I said. 'He must then have stolen the painting last night, while Beatrice Walker kept Mr Blake occupied at the bar.'

Temple shook his head. 'You saw as clearly as I did that the door to Blake's cabin had been forced. There's little chance of Dupont managing that.'

'But he must be the thief,' I urged. 'What other option did he have when Blake refused to sell the painting back to him? He must either have hidden it before falling to his death or someone found it with the body and has taken it for themselves.'

Again, Temple shook his head. 'If Dupont decided to steal the painting, why would he do it on the second night of the voyage, with four more to go before arriving in New York?

Blake seems to have gone to some lengths to make sure that nobody else on this ship knows it even exists. Surely, Dupont would have known that if anything happened to it after he'd approached Blake on Monday evening, his involvement would be assumed. Why steal it now and leave so much time for Blake to find and confront him?'

'What if his plan was always to steal it?' I suggested. 'What if he boarded under a false name to conceal himself from Mr Blake after he'd taken it, just as Mrs Walker seems to have done?'

'Then why reveal himself to Blake on Monday evening?' Temple protested. 'There'd be no sense in hiding behind a false name when Blake had already seen his face. And what about the note we found in his cabin? *Saturday. Nine o'clock.* What do you make of that?'

I opened my mouth, but no answer came. It seemed we were well and truly at a dead end.

'We need more evidence,' said Temple bluntly. 'There's no time to be wasted on what would almost certainly be a fruitless hunt for Beatrice Walker. She is clearly a woman who doesn't want to be found and we have no further leads. The only line of inquiry available to us right now is to speak with Blake's companions from the restaurant on Monday night: Miss Hall, and Mr and Mrs Webber.'

'What do you expect to learn from them? If Mr Blake went so far out of his way to make sure that they didn't know about the painting—'

'What else do you suggest?' Temple spat, his temper finally overcoming him. 'We both saw the walking stick in Dupont's cabin. Do you honestly believe a man who apparently relied on such a thing is capable of forcing a locked door? Somebody else planted that knife in Blake's desk – the same somebody who now has his painting and who most likely threw Dupont down those steps. Blake's companions might very well not know about the painting, but it's surely better that we speak to them than do nothing.' Something dark flashed in his eyes. 'Or is your intention that we leave our man free to act again, should he require it?'

I pressed my face into my hands. 'The knife is alarming,' I agreed. 'And whoever planted it certainly needs to be held to account. But we can't simply assume that Dupont was pushed.'

'Are you so sure?' Temple rounded on me, his voice rising. 'What if he boarded under a false name to conceal himself from someone other than Blake? What if, when he approached Blake in the restaurant, he was being forced to retrieve this painting for another party? Someone on board the ship wants that painting, Birch. They may have it already or they may not. Either way, if it's truly as valuable as Blake claims, can you afford not to accept that they have shown they would be willing to kill for it?'

My lips remained firmly sealed. I had no answer.

'We have less than four days to reach some kind of conclusion before arriving in New York,' Temple continued. 'The police will not be in a position to investigate this once the passengers disembark, so if our conclusion is that there is indeed a murderer to be caught, we must do so before they have the opportunity to escape into the city and strike again.'

'The captain—' I began to say.

'Never mind the captain,' Temple interrupted. 'Do you really believe he'll vouch for us if we can find no solid proof?'

I thought of Captain McCrory and knew that, as we spoke, he was likely counting down the minutes until we docked in

New York and he could step into the arms of retirement. He was thinking about the box of cigars on his desk, a house in the countryside and a life free of bureaucracy. Dealing with a murder and the theft of a mythical painting was not on his agenda.

Likewise, it seemed just as clear that Temple wasn't going to be argued with. He had snapped at me in exactly the same way as he had in Blake's cabin, at the mention of Winston Parker. Even now, while I sat and considered his argument, he glared at me, his jaw clenched.

This couldn't go on. Murder or not, I couldn't have him roaming the *Endeavour*, losing his temper with every passenger with whom he came into contact. Remembering my resolution in Blake's cabin – to determine exactly why Parker's name in particular seemed to have prompted such a hostile response – I took a deep breath.

'Who's Winston Parker?' I asked.

The effect was immediate, a glimmer of what seemed almost to be panic passing across Temple's face.

'Winston Parker?' he repeated.

I nodded. Then, keeping my voice as level as I could, said: 'Who is he?'

'He's a businessman.' Temple's usual defiant tone quickly returned. 'An American businessman.'

'But who is he to you?'

He didn't reply, a fresh breeze across the deck causing his coat to flutter.

'The way you snapped at Mr Blake when he mentioned Parker's name,' I pressed. 'And the look on your face – it was more than just recognition. If I didn't know better, I'd have said that you looked worried. Winston Parker means something to you.'

Temple said nothing, his nostrils flaring.

'Is he involved in this business of yours in New York?' I insisted. 'Is that what you—'

'That's enough,' Temple snarled. 'If we have neither culprit nor evidence of any kind when we dock on Sunday, whoever has killed Dupont and stolen Blake's painting will walk free into the streets of Manhattan. It may indeed be the case that Miss Hall and the Webbers have nothing to offer, but we are running out of options and the clock is ticking, Mr Birch. So please, if you have any other suggestions, do share them. If not, may I ask that you stop wasting what little time we have?'

Well and truly silenced, I looked out over the ocean and breathed in the salty air. I was certain, now, that I hadn't simply imagined Temple's curious reaction to the name Winston Parker. There was a secret there, and if it was truly liable to affect him in the way that it had in Blake's cabin, it suddenly seemed my duty – both to the captain and to our passengers – to uncover it.

For the time being, however, he was giving nothing away. Perhaps I would coax more out of him as we proceeded, but in that moment, he had returned to the matter at hand. Somebody on board the *Endeavour* had Arthur Blake's painting. Somebody was likely responsible for Denis Dupont's death, and we were trapped with them, with nothing but ocean for days in each direction.

I thought again of the ribbon in my pocket. I yearned to be home. To feel Kate wrap her arms around me and see Amelia playing among the trees in our garden.

'You need to understand, Birch,' said Temple gruffly, 'if you are to accompany me on this investigation. We don't have time to allow our culprit the benefit of the doubt. There's too much overlap. Too much about Blake and his painting that they simply shouldn't have known. This has to be approached in the most serious way possible.' He looked at me intently. 'Do you understand what I'm telling you? Until we have proven, without a shadow of doubt, that whoever broke into Blake's cabin, stole his painting and planted that knife didn't also throw Dupont down those steps, we have no choice but to treat this as murder.'

10

The woman who greeted us in cabin 226 was clearly surprised to find two strange men knocking upon her door. She composed herself quickly though, smiling warmly and asking in an American accent, 'Can I help you, gentlemen?'

After Temple had introduced us and explained that we were investigating a break-in to Arthur Blake's cabin – omitting, to my relief, any details of the knife – she held open the door and invited us in.

'Cassandra Webber,' she said, offering a hand to Temple and then to me. The detective made a quizzical face at the prospect of shaking hands with a woman but did so without passing comment. 'Harry's not here right now,' she said. 'But if you'd like to come in, I'll certainly help you if I can.'

Mrs Webber was a striking woman. Blonde curls bounced around a pale, slender face, while a chequered tan dress hugged her waist. A pair of rings nestled on her finger; a wedding band and an elegant engagement ring bearing a single glistening stone. They were beautiful, but I couldn't help feeling that their simplicity was at odds with the extravagant string of pearls that hung around her neck.

'I'd invite you to sit,' she said cheerfully, 'but I'm afraid I don't have much in the way of places to offer.' She sat herself down at the desk, crossed one leg over the other and draped an arm lazily over the back of the chair.

Occupying a twin room, the Webbers had been provided with a bunk bed in which to sleep. Without any further invitation, Temple seated himself on the lower bunk, perching on the edge of the mattress. I couldn't bring myself to join him, my officer's instincts restraining me, and settled instead for standing nervously by the door.

'What's this about then?' she asked. 'Is Arthur in some kind of trouble?'

'You might say that,' Temple replied. 'I'm sure you'll remember, Mrs Webber, that a gentleman approached your table in the restaurant on Monday evening.'

'Of course. He and Arthur made quite the scene.'

'So I understand. And that's precisely why Mr Blake may be in trouble. The gentleman who approached you was found dead early this morning.'

'My God.' Mrs Webber brought a hand to her mouth, the little diamond on her engagement ring glinting. 'I heard talk when we went out for breakfast that a man had died but I hadn't realised ...' Her eyes snapped up and locked with Temple's. 'You can't think Arthur's involved?'

'We're not leaping to any conclusions, ma'am,' I said, fretting over Temple's blunt delivery. 'We're simply gathering as many facts as we can.'

'Of course.' She nodded, her eyes filled with concern. 'Well, ask me whatever you need to and I'll tell you what I can.'

'Do you think we might also be able to speak with Mr Webber?' asked Temple. 'As you both witnessed Mr Blake's argument with the deceased, it would be helpful to hear both of your points of view.'

I caught myself flinching at the word 'deceased'. I thought of the man that we had seen lying on a table just a few short hours ago and it somehow felt too clinical a term. If Cassandra Webber was similarly fazed, however, she didn't show it.

'You've actually just missed him,' she said. 'He wasn't coping so well with the sea this morning, so he's taken himself for a walk. He thought some air might help.'

'Has he not struggled with seasickness before?' asked Temple.

She shook her head. 'Not until this morning. If I'm completely honest with you, I wondered if it might actually be cabin fever setting in. These rooms are comfortable, but Harry's never been the sort to sit still for very long.'

'Are you more accustomed to the ocean, ma'am?' I asked, hoping to lighten the tone.

'I ought to be. I swam for Bristol, so I've had my fair share of time in the water.'

'Bristol is where you studied?'

She flashed me a quizzical look. 'You know that I studied?'

'Mr Blake mentioned that you came to England to study law.'

'Oh. Well, yes, he's right. I spent three years studying in New York and then I came to England for my final year.'

'Is that not quite unusual?'

'I'm the only woman in my class, if that's what you mean.' A hint of ice crept into her voice.

It was not what I had meant, and I was grateful, as I began to stumble over a clumsy reply about not meaning to be presumptuous, when Temple stepped in.

'Is that where you're travelling now? Back to New York?'

'Boston. We're visiting my parents there for Thanksgiving. It's Harry's first time meeting them and he seems pretty nervous.'

'He proposed without meeting your parents?' I asked.

'Well, it all happened rather quickly.' She looked down at the ring for a moment, before glancing back up at Temple. 'Listen, I don't mean to be rude, but I can't imagine that these are the questions you gentlemen came here to ask. I'm sorry to be so direct but I'd like to know how you think Arthur might be involved with this poor man who's died.'

'Not at all,' Temple replied. 'Perhaps you could tell us what you saw on Monday evening. We've heard Mr Blake's side of events, but I'd like the story in your own words.'

'Sure.' She settled back in her chair. 'Well, Arthur had suggested that we all go for dinner together. Harry, myself and Miss Hall. He was in such a good mood – the happiest Harry and I have seen him in months – and he said he wanted to celebrate.'

'Did he say what it was that he was celebrating?'

'Not exactly. He just mentioned something about being commissioned to do a painting in New York. It sounded like a big deal, but he said he wasn't allowed to tell us the details. We knew it must have been important though, because he kept insisting that we order champagne. Not that the rest of us ended up having much of it.'

'And why was that?'

Mrs Webber gave a short laugh. 'Well, I suppose Harry wouldn't have had much anyway. He's never been fond of wine and certainly isn't one for champagne. But Arthur ended up drinking more than a bottle by himself. He was in such a good mood; he just kept pouring more and more ...'

An involuntary noise escaped from the back of my throat. Despite the vast sums that Blake believed his painting to be worth, I still hadn't fully understood why he would be so angered by Dupont approaching him in the restaurant. The influence of an entire bottle of champagne might go some way towards explaining it.

'Anyway,' she continued, 'Harry and I were chatting away, and Miss Hall had gone to order a drink from the bar, when the old gentleman came to our table and tapped Arthur on the shoulder. He turned around and this gentleman asked if he might speak with him. Honestly, Arthur went so pale, he looked like he might collapse. Before the gentleman could say another word, he stood up, grabbed him by the arm and marched him over to the other side of the restaurant. We couldn't hear anything they said after that – the musicians were playing, you understand – but we could see this gentleman speaking for a minute or so and then ... well, Arthur just went mad. I don't know what the gentleman had said to him, but I'd never seen him so angry. The maître d' ended up having to go over and break them up.'

'And Mr Blake didn't explain himself to you?' asked Temple.

'He did tell us a little. Naturally, I turned to Harry and asked him what on earth was going on, but he had no clue either. When he finally came back to the table, Arthur said that this gentleman was a dissatisfied client. Apparently, there's a big event happening in New York and lots of people from the art world are travelling to it. I suppose it was just bad luck that he happened to be on the same ship as us. Even so, I couldn't believe he would come over and approach Arthur so brazenly. It's disgraceful, no matter what kind of disagreement they might have had.'

'And that was the last you saw of him?'

'That's right.'

'What about Mr Blake?'

I may have imagined it, but I could have sworn that Cassandra Webber seemed to hesitate.

'We're having dinner with him on Saturday night,' she said. 'Before we dock. If this commission in New York is as big as he claims, he seems to think it's unlikely we'll see him again for a little while. Harry's insisting on one last evening with him before we go our separate ways.'

Temple nodded, apparently satisfied. 'I understand that the fourth member of your party, Miss Hall, was away from the table when this gentleman first approached.'

At the mention of Vivian Hall's name, her affable demeanour seemed to falter slightly. 'That's right. She was ordering a drink at the bar.'

'But I suppose she must have seen the argument.'

'I suppose so.'

'Did she not seem interested in who the gentleman was?'

Mrs Webber gave a little shrug. 'She came back to the table just as Arthur was explaining to Harry and me that he was a dissatisfied customer. She didn't ask any questions, so I suppose that must have been enough detail.'

I looked at Temple quizzically, wondering if he might press the matter. I was sure it wouldn't have escaped him that Blake believed he had successfully moved the conversation along before Vivian Hall's return. If Mrs Webber was correct, it seemed that, in reality, she had heard – and presumably recognised – that he was lying about Dupont's identity.

'Did this gentleman try to speak with Miss Hall?' asked Temple.

'Not that I saw. Why? Did they know one another?'

Temple shook his head. 'It sounds as though they're both members of the art community. I wondered if perhaps they might be acquainted.'

'Well, if they were, she didn't say as much.' Her expression darkened. 'But then, with that woman, who knows?'

Temple's eyes narrowed. 'Is there any sort of bad blood between you and Miss Hall?'

'No. I'm sorry, that was uncalled for. To tell you the truth, I barely know her. She's a friend of Arthur's.'

'And how exactly do you know Mr Blake?'

'Through Harry. He used to work with Frederick Scott, Arthur's father-in-law.'

I glanced at Temple. It was evident from his momentary look of confusion that this new piece of information had taken him by surprise just as much as it had me.

'Mr Blake didn't tell us that he was married,' I said.

'Well, he's not any more.' She frowned. 'Evelyn divorced him last year. It's why we were so surprised when he told us he was coming on this trip in the first place, let alone when he started ordering champagne. It made more sense, of course, once he explained about this commission, but since Evelyn cut him off, he's been completely broke.'

'I'm sorry,' said Temple. 'What do you mean, she cut him off?'

Mrs Webber's frown grew more intense. 'How much do you know about the Scotts?'

'I've heard of Frederick Scott,' I said. 'He owns a great deal of land around Bristol and Bath.'

'Right.' She nodded. 'Frederick is Evelyn's father. Arthur wears his suits well and he might speak as though he went to Oxford, but before he married Evelyn, he hadn't a penny to his name. At least, that's what Harry tells me. He's known Arthur a lot longer than I have.'

'You think he married Miss Scott for her money?' said Temple.

She drummed her fingers on the desk. 'Honestly, I couldn't say. I first met Arthur just before he and Evelyn divorced, so I never really saw them together.'

'But you did meet her?'

'Briefly. Harry and I had just started seeing each other and he took me to one of Frederick's garden parties – it was Evelyn's birthday, if I remember rightly. Incidentally, that was the only other time I've ever met Miss Hall. Oh, but you should have seen these parties ... Everyone who was anyone would be there. Arthur loved them, of course. He loved everything about the lifestyle that came with marrying Evelyn. But you'd like to believe he loved her, too.'

It didn't take much to imagine why Blake might crave the lifestyle that came with marrying into a family like the Scotts. I pictured a long gravel drive leading to an imposing stately home, countless windows glinting and sand-coloured brick glowing in the summer heat. The perfectly mown lawns would no doubt be full of Frederick Scott's friends and business acquaintances, dressed in light linen suits and striped blazers, their wives in extravagant hats and bright summer dresses. Waiters in dinner jackets would patrol the gardens, each with one white-gloved hand fixed stoically behind their back while the other proffered a silver tray of champagne, and the air would be rich with the velvet tones of a string quartet.

'Why did they divorce?' asked Temple.

'For various reasons, I believe. Frederick was never in favour of the marriage, for one thing. When Evelyn met Arthur, she'd been all set to marry the son of a local MP. But I'd imagine that was one of the things that appealed about Arthur. When your father's planning to marry you off to the son of his wealthiest friend, being with a handsome young artist must be quite a romantic prospect. Of course, Frederick hated Arthur, but the marriage happened too quickly for him to do anything to stop them.'

'They can't have been together long,' I said.

Mrs Webber shook her head. 'About a year, I think. As I understand it, after a little while Evelyn realised that, deep down, Arthur was no different to any of the men that Frederick would have picked out for her. He was just spending *her* money because he didn't have any of his own. They ended up divorcing last year. But Miss Hall would be the person to ask, if you're interested in the particulars.'

'Why is that?'

'Because she's a friend of Evelyn's. The only one who'd give Arthur the time of day, by all accounts. Harry says they connected over their love of art.'

'But they've stayed in contact since he and Miss Scott divorced?'

She shook her head. 'They bumped into one another on Monday, while boarding the ship in Southampton. They hadn't seen each other since Evelyn sent Arthur away, so he insisted that she joined us for dinner. A chance to catch up. At least, that's what Harry told me.'

As she spoke, I couldn't help but wonder if I heard a hint of resentment in her voice. Before I could pursue it, Temple cut in.

'I do find it somewhat curious that your husband has stayed in touch with Mr Blake,' he said. 'Considering he's employed by Blake's former father-in-law.'

'Oh, Harry and Frederick don't exactly see eye to eye these days. Harry was taken on as an apprentice when he was younger and Frederick taught him to run the Scott estate. He was learning to oversee land, property – you name it. It's actually how we met. I stayed in one of Frederick's apartments while I studied at Bristol and it was Harry who met me at the railway station and moved me in. But that feels such a long time ago now. Harry left Frederick to start his own estate agency last year, around the same time Arthur and Evelyn divorced.'

'I can't imagine Mr Scott took that well.'

'That's putting it lightly.' Mrs Webber laughed bitterly. 'Frederick trained Harry for years to take over his estate. I don't think it ever occurred to him that he might have aspirations of his own.'

'And how is Mr Webber's company faring?'

'It's been a little up and down,' she admitted, drumming her fingers again on the desk. 'He had some good business with a few of the local landowners when he first opened, but Frederick was very unhappy and he's an influential man. Once he started shooting his mouth off, Harry's business began to dry up. It's picking up again now, though. He prefers not to talk about the finer details any more, but he tells me that he's had plenty of new clients over the last few months. I can't tell you how proud I am of him.'

Temple nodded, taking it all in. I was both amazed and concerned that in our conversations with Robert Evans, Arthur Blake and now Cassandra Webber, he hadn't written down a single detail. I almost wondered if I ought to make a few notes myself, but I couldn't imagine anything that might frustrate him more than the suggestion that he wasn't conducting his investigation with the necessary care.

'Can you please recount your movements yesterday, Mrs Webber?' he asked.

'Why would you need to know that?'

'Just as a formality. I'll be asking everyone who came into contact with Mr Blake or the deceased prior to the break-in.'

She thought for a moment. 'Well, let's see. I woke up early and went swimming in the pool, then Harry and I caught the end of the breakfast service in the restaurant. After that, I spent the rest of the morning and most of the afternoon reading.'

She motioned towards a stack of handwritten notes and a heavy, leather-bound book on the desk. *Legislative Process Regarding the Acquisition of Land Volume IV* was emblazoned in gold on the spine.

'In the evening, we went for dinner and then I came back to the cabin while Harry went to check on his car.'

Temple cocked an eyebrow. 'His car?'

'It's his pride and joy.' Mrs Webber rolled her eyes, though the traces of a smile seemed to suggest that she found her husband's passion more endearing than genuinely frustrating. 'He bought it straight after opening the firm and winning his first few clients. Says he likes the idea of driving it on Broadway. If you ask me, though, the real reason he's brought it along is that he's hoping it will impress my parents.'

'Was it unusual for him to check on the car?'

'Not especially. He went on Monday night, too. But he was away for longer last night. When he came back, he said he'd found a big scratch down the side of it and had to file a report with someone.'

'A scratch?' Temple repeated.

She nodded. 'I haven't seen it myself, but it must be bad. He was in a terrible state when he got back.'

'Do you know the name of the man he reported it to?' I asked.

'I didn't ask.' She frowned. 'Should I have?'

I opened my mouth to reply, but Temple leapt in.

'How long was Mr Webber away for?'

She thought for a few seconds. 'I'd say a little over an hour. It took him a while to find someone to report the damage to.'

'Do you remember what time he was out?'

'It must have been between ten and eleven o'clock. It was pouring with rain. He was soaked when he came back.'

'And you were here, in the cabin, while Mr Webber was checking on his car?'

'That's right.' She began drumming her fingers on the table again.

Temple nodded. 'We'll leave you in peace in just a moment, Mrs Webber. But before we do, there are just two more things that I need.'

'Oh?'

'First, I'd like to see an example of your handwriting.'

'My handwriting? That's certainly an odd request.'

'I'm afraid it's rather important.'

'Well, I suppose you can see some of the notes that I've been making from my reading, if you'd like?'

She reached into a drawer of the desk and drew out a thick stack of paper, from which she handed the top sheet to Temple.

Of course, I realised why he was making such a request. He must be trying to identify the handwriting on the note that we had found in Dupont's cabin. Although why he thought Cassandra Webber's might present a match, I couldn't possibly say.

From my vantage point by the door, I had no hope of inspecting it myself. In any case, Temple scanned the page and then returned it to her waiting hand.

'And finally, Mrs Webber, one last question before we leave.' He paused for a moment. 'I don't suppose the name Beatrice Walker means anything to you?'

Without a second's hesitation, she shook her head. 'No, I'm sure I don't know anyone by that name.'

11

'I don't understand,' I said as we descended a rickety iron stairwell into the depths of the *Endeavour*. 'Why not wait in the cabin for Mr Webber to return?'

'Damn you, Birch,' snapped Temple. 'I've told you already – facts before witnesses. If Webber roamed the ship unaccompanied for an entire hour, I can't believe a word he says about using that time to report the damage to his car until I've seen it for myself.'

I didn't reply. Temple had been in a foul mood since we left Cassandra Webber, berating me once again for interrupting his interview process.

'And, of course,' he continued, 'we need to find a way of proving the truth in Mrs Webber's own story.'

'Be serious,' I scoffed. 'Surely you can't suspect her of having a role in any of this?'

Temple sighed. 'Does it not occur to you that while her husband was checking his car, she was, by her own admission, alone for an hour? She claims she spent the time reading in their cabin, but what evidence do we have to support that?'

'You believe she might be involved?'

'I'm simply saying that we can't overlook her being alone while Blake was in the bar with this Beatrice Walker. And we both heard her say that she swam for Bristol. She's clearly an athletic young woman, maybe even capable of forcing the lock on a cabin door if suitably motivated.'

'Next you'll be telling me that she threw Monsieur Dupont down that companionway,' I muttered.

Temple didn't reply.

We reached the bottom of the stairwell and I led the way through a warren of narrow corridors. We were now just a few decks above the engine room and the metal walls hummed faintly around us. Thick pipes criss-crossed the length of the ceiling while harsh lights buzzed and flickered. It was a stark contrast to the grandeur of the upper levels, with their polished wooden staircases, soft carpets and majestic views of the ocean.

Porters and chefs bustled around us, appearing and then vanishing again into cupboards and rooms that opened on either side of the corridor. Some carried sacks of vegetables or joints of meat that were bound for the kitchens. Others grasped brooms and mops as they hurried on their way to clean the passenger areas. A few cast curious glances in Temple's direction. All, however, nodded towards me or touched their caps with brisk calls of 'sir' as we passed.

I brought Temple to a halt at a broad iron door, which, to my shoulder's complaint, I heaved open to reveal the cargo hold.

After his first visit, I'd recently heard Travis, the new officer, describe the hold as large. He wasn't wrong, but that didn't come close to doing justice to the cavernous space. I was fairly sure that, during the war, I'd seen smaller aircraft hangars.

Along the entire length of one wall, wooden crates were arranged in towering piles that stretched towards the ceiling, lashed together with thick netting. There were trunks and chests stacked in mountainous heaps, and parked tightly in three rows down the middle were the cars. The humming of the ship's engines was tremendous, echoing around us as if we had descended to the belly of some enormous beast.

Temple led the way, weaving between the cars until he came to a halt at a navy-blue Ford Model T, described to us by Cassandra Webber. It was a neat little vehicle, with a canvas roof and bright round headlights that resembled a pair of wide, unblinking eyes. It had been freshly polished, the bodywork and spokes on the wheels glinting.

My officer's salary didn't provide anything like the means to own a car in England, but I had occasionally driven military vehicles during the war. As we inspected Harry Webber's Ford, I couldn't help but imagine myself behind the wheel, with Kate in the passenger seat and Amelia in the back.

I watched as Temple circled it, taking in every detail, before his gaze came to settle on the scratch that ran the length of its passenger side. His brow was furrowed in intense concentration, his eyes piercing. Then, like a medic inspecting a wound, he crouched and traced the scratch delicately with a finger.

I was about to ask if there was some way that I could help, when there came a rustling, scurrying sound behind us. I turned and peered into the gloom. While the lighting in the corridor might have been harsh, there was a good deal less to see in the cargo hold. A regiment of sparsely placed lanterns provided a gentle glow, although depending on how the contents of the hold had been organised, casting long shadows in some places and completely obscuring the light in others, it was often a struggle to see more than twelve feet in front of you. I stood and watched, straining my eyes as I searched for the source of the noise. A pile of trunks and suitcases had been heaped just a few yards ahead, a wall of wooden cargo crates stretching eight feet tall behind it, but there was no sign of any life.

I turned back to Temple. 'Did you ...'

He didn't respond, apparently too engrossed in his inspection. If he had heard the sound too, he seemed to have ignored it.

I ushered the thought away. Though you wouldn't know it to look at some of the passenger accommodation, the *Endeavour*'s lower decks were home to a great number of rats. I shouldn't be so alarmed to hear them scuttling around down here, where it was warm and dark and they would be left largely undisturbed. All the same, I found myself shuffling nervously on the spot.

'What do you make of it then?' I asked, returning my attention to the car. Temple seemed deep in thought, so much so that I wouldn't have been surprised to learn that he had forgotten I was there.

'The scratch isn't deep,' he murmured. 'It shouldn't be too much of a job for a garage to repair.'

'Mr Webber will be pleased.'

'No doubt.'

'Does it look as though it could have been done maliciously?'

He stood and observed the gap between Webber's car and its neighbour in the adjacent row. 'Difficult to say. This is

107

certainly a tight space. I suppose it's possible that if something large was being carried past it might have scraped the side.'

'So you believe Mr Webber's alibi?'

'I believe that his car has been damaged.'

He looked around intensely, his brow furrowed. 'How was Webber even allowed to come down here? Is it not off-limits to passengers?'

'It's something of a grey area,' I admitted. 'It's unusual for a passenger to ever want to come here, so the only ones who do tend to have a genuine reason. We would, of course, always discourage it, but we've never had much of a need for any strict rules prohibiting it.'

Temple grimaced, as though this explanation was utterly ridiculous. 'Mrs Webber says that her husband had to search for a crew member to report this to. Would there not be a man on duty?'

'There's no need. As I say, it's unusual for anyone unauthorised to come down here.'

Temple rolled his eyes, and I struggled to restrain a sudden swell of resentment. 'It seems Webber must have found someone though,' he said. 'If he managed to file a report.'

I opened my mouth to reply, but before I could, there came a crash from behind us.

Snapping around in unison, we squinted into the darkness. Something heavy had been knocked over, the sound of metal tumbling to the ground echoing around the hold. We stayed silent, watching for any further clue that might betray its source.

'You said there wouldn't be anyone down here,' Temple whispered.

I couldn't answer. I must have jumped a foot at the sound of the crash and my mind was racing, every nerve tingling with a sudden burst of adrenaline.

'Birch!'

I shook my head, my mouth hanging open. 'There shouldn't be.'

Without another word, Temple sprang in the direction of the sound. I scrambled to follow, but he had taken me by surprise and already disappeared behind the wall of crates that I had been peering at just moments before.

'Wait!' I called, but it was no use. He had broken into a run, fedora in one hand and grey coat fluttering behind him as he plunged deeper into the cargo hold. Crates, leather trunks and thick rope netting all flew past as I hurried to keep up with him.

He ran several yards and then skidded to a stop, a furious expression on his face as he scanned the room.

'What are you—'

'Shh!' he hissed. 'Get down!'

He grabbed my wrist and wrenched me into a crouching position behind a mound of luggage. I withheld a gasp, the ferocity with which he pulled me to the ground causing my shoulder to sear.

Slowly, we peered over the top of our makeshift cover. There was nothing to be seen. Nothing even to be heard except the sound of our panting and the rumbling of the engines.

'Come on ...' he growled, his eyes flitting from one pile of cargo to the next. 'Where have you gone?'

There was no reply. Looking out into the darkness, there was only stillness and silence.

'There's nobody here,' I whispered.

The detective ignored me.

'Temple. There's nobody—'

I was cut off by the frantic patter of feet. Spinning around, we saw a figure bolting towards the door. Silhouetted against the light from the corridor, I could see clearly that it was a woman, but there was no making out her face. Her back was turned to us and she was moving as though pursued by a pack of snarling hounds.

Temple sprang to his feet, vaulting over the trunks and breaking into a run. 'Stop!' he bellowed. 'Stop right there!'

As he leapt our makeshift barrier, something tumbled from his coat pocket and clattered to the ground. Catching a glimpse of black metal, I tried to call out, but he paid me no attention. He was charging towards the door, desperate to catch up with the woman.

Scooping up the fallen object, I hurried to follow, but could see already that it was no use. Temple had miscalculated when he first gave chase, taking us in entirely the wrong direction, and she had a good lead. We burst from the cargo hold into the harsh light of the corridor, but there was no sign of her. Temple cursed, sweeping his head to left and right.

'This way!' he cried, choosing a direction and breaking once again into a run.

We rounded the corner and saw immediately that it was futile. The corridor stretched out before us, a dozen doors on either side. Temple's eyes darted from one to the next, but he must have known as well as I that it was no good. Even if the woman had come this way, there were too many options. Far too many ways for her to have escaped.

'Dammit,' he hissed. 'Dammit!'

He was panting slightly, his thick hair tousled as the realisation that she had eluded us seemed to fully take hold. For me though, the identity of the woman had almost become a secondary concern. As Temple turned and saw the concern on my face, his brow creased.

Without a word, I held out the item that he had dropped during the chase. In my hand was a revolver.

12

Over the course of the past two years, I'd done all I could to avoid the feeling of being watched. I would take care to be the last into a room, hover in corners and speak only when addressed. Even in England, when I was on leave from the *Endeavour*, I would barely leave the house.

At first, the only way that anyone would look at me was with eyes full of pity. I grew to hate it. I wanted to tell our neighbours that if they were going to look at me with anything at all, it should be scorn. Resentment. Anything but pity.

Kate was the only one who obliged. Because she knew just as well as I did that it wasn't pity I deserved. That if it weren't for me, things would never have gone wrong.

In time, I got my wish. As the months rolled by and things seemed to become more and more hopeless, the pity faded, though it didn't come as the release that I had imagined. I realised that I was still being watched, but with something else entirely. I was becoming an oddity. A strange, sad fellow who people would quickly nod to in the street, before dropping their gaze and hurrying past.

Even when I returned to the *Endeavour*, the other officers would stare uneasily at me. I'd hoped the ship would be a place of sanctuary. Instead, it was as if I had some kind of terrible wound that they were doing their best not to stare at. I'd see them looking at me across the mess hall, and then quickly glancing away when I caught their eye.

As time passed I retreated further into solitude. To adopt the mentality that, when you're regarded as a curiosity, it's better not to be seen at all. But even with my general aversion to being watched, the woman from the cargo hold made me feel an altogether different sense of unease.

I had expected that I would be relieved to be out in the open air again. But as I stood upon the deck, my hands tucked into the pockets of my coat and my collar turned up against the breeze, it soon became clear how deeply the encounter had troubled me. Even now, the best part of an hour later, I couldn't help but look around, as though I might spot her peeping from behind some form of cover or dashing around a corner. I supposed that the thought of not only being watched, but also being pursued, was an especially uncomfortable one.

And then, of course, there was the question of Temple's revolver. After the woman had vanished, he snatched it from my hand and stuffed it back into his coat pocket, a furious expression on his face.

'Why do you have that?' I had demanded.

He didn't answer.

'Is it loaded?'

'Of course,' he snapped. 'It's not unusual for a police officer to carry a firearm.'

'On the streets of London, perhaps. Why are you carrying it now?'

'Why shouldn't I?'

I had no answer. I supposed that, ultimately, he was right. There was no reason a police officer shouldn't carry a gun if they felt the need. And yet, that logic in itself made me even more uneasy – the fact that Temple clearly did feel a need was what I found so troubling.

I wondered if he anticipated needing it during our search for Arthur Blake's painting. After all, we had no way of knowing what the woman in the cargo hold might have intended for us if she hadn't given herself away. Likewise, the knife that we had found in Blake's cabin might suggest a need to defend ourselves if we succeeded in identifying whoever had planted it. But Temple had been by my side since I'd agreed to show him Dupont's body, and at no point had he had a chance to fetch a revolver. Clearly, it had been with him all day.

Again, I couldn't help but wonder about the mysterious police business that awaited him in New York, and his sharp response to the name Winston Parker. The more I did, the more fiercely determined I became to understand what he was keeping from me.

With our chase declared thoroughly unsuccessful and no clue as to the woman's identity, Temple had insisted our only option was to pick up the investigation where we had left off. It was this course of action that brought us to the promenade, investigating the place in which Dupont's body had been found that morning.

'Should we not be looking for her?' I had asked as we climbed to the surface.

'Where do you suggest we start?'

'What about Beatrice Walker? The woman who kept Mr Blake occupied while his cabin was being raided?'

Temple frowned. 'What about her?'

'What if that was her? What if she's learned somehow that we're investigating? It would make sense for her to follow us, wouldn't it?'

'It might indeed, but if this ship is as difficult to navigate as you claim, there's no chance of rooting her out below deck. Assuming she is connected to either Blake's painting or Dupont's death, the only way we'll find her is by returning to the task in hand.'

Begrudgingly, I had agreed with the detective's argument. Of course, it hadn't stopped him from asking virtually every porter and engineer who we passed on our way if they had seen her. But it was no use. Nobody seemed to know anything about a woman fleeing from the cargo hold.

To make matters worse, up on the promenade there was just as little to be learned. A small team of porters had worked hard with rags and buckets of soapy water, and we found Dupont's final resting place spotless. There was no sign of last night's storm, nor that his body had ever lain at the foot of the companionway.

I could sense the change in Temple's mood as he surveyed the scene. Having failed to catch the woman in the hold and now finding virtually nothing in the way of clues to inspect on the deck, his frustration was building – a development that

115

did nothing to ease the nerves caused by my discovery of a revolver in his pocket.

But the site made me uncomfortable for another reason. It wasn't just the knowledge that this was where Dupont had died or even the lack of clues for us to inspect. It was the total absence of any passengers in this area. On other parts of the deck, we had seen couples strolling and children playing. I thought of Wilson's theory that we would have to contend with passengers gossiping more than panicking. It seemed they were avoiding the place altogether.

'You mentioned that your medical officer inspected the body,' said Temple.

'That's right. As soon as he was placed below deck.'

'Did he have any idea of what time Dupont might have died?'

'As I understand it, it's difficult to say. The rain started to fall at eight o'clock and didn't let up until around four in the morning. Any passengers who were moving around the ship will most likely have used the indoor staircase to stay dry, which, it seems to me, is why Monsieur Dupont lay here all night without being found.'

'So he could have fallen at any point within that time.'

'I suppose so. But with the condition of the body ...' I thought of Dupont's face, the damp skin puffy and swollen. 'I gather that it would be impossible to appoint a specific time of death without an autopsy.'

Temple knelt to examine the spot at the foot of the companionway and I tried not to think about which step might have delivered the killing blow. Tried not to wonder whether Dupont had been killed the moment his skull had connected with it or if he had lain for a while in the rain, waiting to die.

'Cassandra Webber told us that her husband had been soaking wet when he returned from checking his car,' said Temple. 'Why wouldn't *he* have kept out of the rain? Surely there's an inside route that he could have used to reach the cargo hold?'

I shook my head. 'There's no internal access from the passengers' accommodation. It's another reason we don't tend to worry about needing a man on duty down there. If Mr Webber wanted to check on his car, he would have had to go outside.'

Temple thought for a moment. 'And say that he went after Dupont had fallen,' he mused. 'Would it be possible for him to reach the cargo hold without passing the body?'

'I'm afraid so. There are outdoor companionways on either side of the ship; it allows for an easier escape should the passengers ever need to evacuate. Monsieur Dupont was found at the bottom of this one, but if Mr Webber had used the other, he wouldn't have seen the body.'

'But if he used this one and *didn't* see the body, that would at least help to narrow down the time of death.'

A hint of his earlier enthusiasm was returning to Temple's voice. Before I could answer, he leapt up the companionway, taking the steps two at a time, and surveyed the next deck, scanning the neat row of portholes.

'Are these passenger cabins?' he called.

'Yes,' I answered, scrambling to follow him. 'Second-class.'

My shoulder was still aching from being dragged behind cover in the cargo hold, and it complained all the worse as I jogged up the steps to join him. When I reached the top though, and the reason for his question became clear, all thought of it vanished from my head.

'Do you think someone might have seen something?' I asked.

'Or heard it.' He pointed to the porthole nearest the top of the companionway. 'Can you tell which cabin this is?'

'Certainly,' I answered, counting the portholes. 'Each cabin has one porthole and this one's the twelfth from the end.'

Without a moment's hesitation, Temple took off in the direction of the nearest door. Once inside, I followed him down the corridor, our footsteps muffled by the rich red carpet as he counted down the cabins. Arriving at his mark, he knocked sharply.

At first, it seemed as though the occupants might not be in. Then I heard the sliding of a chain. I swept a glance down the corridor, wondering how many other doors were locked – and how many had only been so since the discovery of Dupont's body.

The door was opened by a weathered-looking gentleman, dressed in a worn charcoal suit. He peered at us through a pair of thick-rimmed spectacles, while a woman who I supposed must be his wife looked over his shoulder. Flecks of grey were beginning to streak her hair.

'Pardon the intrusion, sir,' said Temple. 'I'm investigating an accident that took place last night and I hoped—'

'An accident?' the man repeated in a broad American accent. 'What sort of accident?'

'A gentleman fell down the stairs. Just outside your cabin. I'm trying to determine at what time he might have fallen.'

The man's eyes went wide. 'We wouldn't want to be involved with anything like that,' he said hurriedly.

'Nobody is accusing you of any involvement,' Temple replied. 'I only wondered if perhaps you or your wife might have heard something.'

'No.' He shook his head aggressively. 'We didn't hear anything.'

'Are you quite sure?'

'I'm telling you, we didn't hear anyone fall.' He licked his lips nervously, his voice rising. 'We went straight to bed after dinner, and even if there *had* been any accident while we were here, the porthole was closed. The rain was really coming down, you know? I'm sorry, but we can't help you.'

Over his shoulder, I saw the woman open her mouth as if to speak. She seemed to think better of it though, her eyes falling to the ground.

Temple grimaced. 'You had dinner in the restaurant?'

'Yes, sir.'

'And at what time did you return to the cabin?'

'Around nine o'clock, I should think.'

'You went straight to bed at nine o'clock?'

'That's right.' The American nodded eagerly.

'You didn't stay up at all?'

'We did not.'

'Mr Temple ...' I said, wary of the man's growing distress.

'So, you might have been asleep by, say, half-past nine?' he pressed, oblivious to my concern.

'I suppose so.'

Temple nodded. While I was wary of him snapping as he had done at Arthur Blake, I shared his frustration. The American gentleman seemed far from cooperative. I suspected

that Temple might have had more luck trying to coax information out of a tree.

'Thank you,' he said. 'Mr …?'

'Hewitt,' the American replied, with the air of a man who
had just surrendered the keys to his house, rather than simply
his name.

'Thank you, Mr Hewitt.'

The door closed and I heard the chain slide back into place.
As disappointing as the conversation had been, I breathed a
quiet sigh of relief. I didn't believe there was any serious danger of it being drawn, but as Temple seemed to have grown
increasingly frustrated, I couldn't help but think of the revolver
in his pocket.

'Do you believe him?' I asked.

'Difficult to say. He certainly didn't seem keen to talk.'

'Dupont's story appears to be spreading quickly. I'm sure
Mr Hewitt won't be the only one who wants to stay as far
away from all of this as he can. But let's say that he's telling
the truth. What does it tell us?'

Temple sighed. 'If he really is telling the truth, I suppose it
tells us that Dupont must have fallen at some point after half-
past nine, when the Hewitts went to sleep.'

'Could he not have fallen before nine o'clock?' I asked.
'Before they returned to their cabin, I mean? It had already
been raining for the best part of an hour at that point, so there
wouldn't have been anyone outside.'

Temple scowled and shook his head. 'I can't see it. The rain
might have started falling at eight, but it must have been at
least an hour before it started to come down hard. If Dupont
fell much earlier than half-past nine, I suspect there would still

have been people using the outdoor companionways who would have found him. It makes more sense for him to have gone down them later in the evening.'

I thought about this for a moment, remembering the coat and walking stick that Dupont had left behind in his cabin. To think that he must have fallen later in the evening, when the rain was coming down even harder, certainly made it more curious for him to have not brought them with him. My first assumption was still that he must have been hurrying some-where. Perhaps even to meet someone. But could Temple's earlier theory in the captain's office be correct? Could he, in reality, have been running *from* something?

I pressed a hand to my forehead, my thoughts swirling. 'So the question we need to answer is: why was he out so late in the pouring rain?'

13

The second-class accommodation was pleasant enough –
certainly more luxurious than the quarters which the other
officers and I occupied – but as we set off in search of Vivian
Hall, I was reminded that first-class was something else
entirely.

Having risen to the top of the Great Staircase, we found
ourselves standing beneath an enormous glass dome, light
pouring through like rain. Even Temple stopped to admire it,
his eyes widening for the briefest of moments. Taking the lead,
I guided him towards the mouth of a nearby corridor. Just like
the restaurant, the first-class quarters had been modelled on
the finest London hotels, with polished oak underfoot and
great vases of flowers and exotic ferns adorning the corridors.
On our right, magnificent paintings hung upon the wood-
panelled walls. On our left, there were windows so broad that
they made the portholes in second-class look laughable.

Glancing through one as we passed, I saw the sun brush the
horizon. Within the hour it would be completely dark, the
ocean a canvas of black beneath a starry sky. With a worrying
realisation, it occurred to me that the first day of our

investigation was almost over. Just three more remained before we docked in New York on Sunday morning and our killer walked free.

A gentleman wearing a spotted bow tie and sporting what might well have been the most impressive moustache that I had ever seen strode towards us. A much younger man in a dark suit followed closely behind, carrying what I took to be the moustached gentleman's briefcase in one hand and clutching a fat pile of papers in the other.

'Mr Shaw is expecting you presently in the reading room, Your Lordship,' I heard him calling out as they brushed past. 'If we make our way now, we should be just in time.'

I turned and watched them hurry towards the Great Staircase. It was sometimes difficult to imagine that such grandeur could even exist when, on the same ship, four strangers would bunk together in a single third-class room.

Arriving at the cabin number which he had noted down in the restaurant, Temple stepped up and knocked briskly on the door. When no answer came, he knocked again more sharply.

Irrational as it might seem, I couldn't help but feel unnerved by the lack of response. I remembered the knife protruding from Arthur Blake's desk, and for a split second I caught myself questioning whether the thief might already have paid Vivian Hall a visit.

If Temple was similarly concerned, he didn't show it. A grimace passed across his face, as though her absence was some personal affront.

'Already gone for dinner perhaps,' I suggested. 'I suppose we'll wait until she returns?'

Temple shook his head. 'We'd be better off finding Harry Webber. Miss Hall may come back by the time we're finished with him.'

'And if she doesn't?'

'We'll have to call on her in the morning.'

'But she needs to be warned of what's happened to Mr Blake,' I protested. '*We* need to warn her.'

'And how do you propose we accomplish that if she is nowhere to be found? We have no sense of where she might be, nor when she will be back. We don't even know what she even looks like, for pity's sake. Short of setting up camp outside her room, I don't see how you expect to find her.'

'Perhaps that's exactly what we ought to do. You've said yourself that we need to treat this as a murder investigation. How can you know that Miss Hall's painting won't be stolen next? That it won't be her desk with a knife planted in it?'

Temple glared at me. 'We will warn Miss Hall. It will ideally be done this evening, but if it has to wait until tomorrow morning, I am content with that.'

'How *can* you be?'

'Because Blake's painting was evidently the focus of a highly targeted attack.' Temple snapped at me, his voice rising. 'Dammit, Birch, you heard as clearly as I did – he has gone to considerable lengths to keep his painting a secret from virtually everyone that he can. It was taken by someone who knew exactly where it was and, quite possibly, even that it was unguarded while he sat with Beatrice Walker. Someone who wanted that painting specifically.'

'But what if Miss Hall's painting is also in their sights?'

'Blake's portrait, if we are to take him at his word, is a mythical item of untold value. Miss Hall's is an original work by an up-and-coming talent. The only thing they have in common is their owners' relationships with Dupont—'

'Who is now dead,' I interrupted. 'A death which you, yourself, are insisting we treat as murder.'

Before Temple could protest further, a skinny young man hurried over to us, running frantically from the direction of the Great Staircase. A faded brown jacket flapped about him as he scurried our way, drawing disparaging glances from a nearby group of finely attired ladies.

'Sir!' he gasped, his eyes coming to rest upon my cap. 'They said on the stairs that an officer had come this way. Please, sir, you must come and help.' He paused a moment, panting as he tried to recover his breath. 'There's a fight,' he said. 'Broken out between two men. Down in third-class.'

I glanced at Temple.

'I hardly you think you need me to join you for this,' he muttered.

'And I can hardly trust you not to break off on your own by the time I return.'

Temple scowled and looked at Vivian Hall's door. Then, apparently recognising an impasse, he gave a single curt nod.

I faced the young man. 'Lead the way.'

He turned on the spot and hurried back towards the Great Staircase. Scrambling to follow, we descended through second-class, until the oak came to an end and we dropped onto a narrower, iron stairwell. As we emerged into the third-class common area, the tranquillity instantly gave way to a frantic clamour of noise and activity. Dozens of passengers chattered in different languages, seated on rough wooden benches that ran, like a spine, through the length of the vast space. Children chased each other in rings, oblivious to the scoldings being cast at them from all sides, while a gentleman wearing a flat cap and braces played a cheerful tune on a tired old piano.

In the middle of the hall, I saw from our vantage point on the companionway that a crowd of perhaps forty onlookers had gathered in a circle, cheering and taunting as two brawlers danced in the centre of the makeshift ring.

'Let me pass,' I cried, wrestling my way into the circle. 'Let me through!'

I broke through to the middle just in time to see one of the fighters land a savage blow on the other's jaw. He was lean and wiry, barely more than half the size of his opponent, with a shaven head, broken nose and the cuffs of a grubby shirt rolled up to his bony elbows. If he was intimidated by the other man's stature, he didn't show it. His eyes lit up as his knuckles connected with his opponent's mouth, yellow teeth bared as his lips drew back into a grin. To see him apparently getting the better of so much larger a combatant was such a sight that, for a split second, I simply stood and stared. It was like watching a Jack Russell sizing up to a bear.

As his opponent staggered backwards from the force of the blow, the shaven-headed man's gaze settled upon me. I was recovering my wits, bracing myself to jump between them and break up the fight, when something in his expression stopped me. His eyes went wide, the grin slipping from his lips. If I didn't know better, I'd have said that it was a look of recognition.

We stayed there for a moment, his expression rooting me to the spot, until I realised it wasn't actually me he was focusing on. He was looking just past me. Turning to follow his line of sight, I saw Temple hovering at my shoulder. He seemed to have gone deathly pale, his lips parted as he locked eyes with the shaven-headed brawler.

With a start, I realised exactly what I was seeing on his face. It was sheer terror.

Our intrusion must only have distracted the man for a matter of seconds, but it was all the time his opponent needed to regain his footing and land a blow of his own. With the force of a sledgehammer, his fist connected with the smaller man's brow, the crowd cheering with delight as he went tumbling to the ground.

'Enough!' I roared, leaping to stand between them. 'Stop this at once!'

Immediately, the cheering faded. Recognising either my officer's uniform or that the entertainment was over – perhaps both – the spectators quickly began to scurry away.

The larger man was the first to respond. 'This thieving rat was going through my cabin,' he snarled.

'Liar!' The shaven-headed fellow scrambled to his feet, a drop of blood trickling from the corner of his mouth. His opponent's final blow had left a mark, it seemed. Although, to look at the cut on the larger man's cheek and the black eye that was already starting to glisten, it seemed the fight hadn't been going his way. If it hadn't been for our intervention, I struggled to believe he would have pulled it back.

'What proof do you have?' I asked him.

'Proof?'

'What has he taken?'

'Nothing. I caught him before he could make off with anything.'

'On your way then,' I said as sternly as I could manage. 'Both of you.'

'You aren't going to punish him?'

'I can't pass punishment for a crime that there's no proof has been committed,' I said. 'If you have any evidence, sir, please share it. If not, I suggest you move along and be grateful that you caught him when you did. I'll remember both of your faces. If either of you cause any further trouble, I'll see that you're dealt with by the police on our arrival.'

The larger man gawped at me, his fists clenched as though he might strike me with one of the hammer-like punches that had floored his adversary. He thought better of it though, turning instead and barging a small group of remaining spectators out of his path.

I went next to address the shaven-headed man, who was watching his opponent walk away as he wiped blood from his mouth with the back of his hand. Then he looked me in the eye. Without thinking, I took a step back, causing him to grin at the sight of my discomfort. I steeled myself, clenching my fists, but he was already turning his attention elsewhere.

Just as he had during the fight, he looked over my shoulder and locked eyes with Temple. The grin became a sneer, his thin lips curling. From the corner of my eye, I saw movement at his sides; he was flexing his fingers, clenching his fists over and over. The detective's expression, meanwhile, remained unchanged, lingering somewhere between panic and amazement. In an instant, the bravado with which he had been conducting our investigation had all but vanished. To look at him now, I wouldn't be surprised if he turned and fled.

For several seconds, I watched as they weighed each other up. Then, just as I was becoming sure that I would need, in some way, to intervene, the shaven-headed man spat upon the floor, nodded at Temple and slunk away.

'Birch,' said Temple quietly. 'You must lock that man up.'

'How can I?' I protested. 'If there's no proof of his crime, I can't confine him based simply on another man's accusation.'

'For God's sake, you just saw the look on his face as plainly as I did. You can't seriously believe that he isn't guilty.'

Temple was right. I had seen his expression. But however threatening he might have appeared, it wasn't the sneer that bothered me. Nor was it the delight when he landed such a savage blow on his opponent. What genuinely troubled me was the recognition that I was so sure had passed between him and the detective.

'Do you know him?' I asked.

Temple recoiled, a grimace taking form on his face. 'I hardly need to. It's clear as day that he's an unsavoury sort.'

'I don't believe you. I saw the way that you looked at each other and I'll be damned if you don't know that man.'

'That's absurd.'

'Is it?' I pressed. 'Because I'll tell you what I saw – I saw the exact same expression on your face as when Arthur Blake asked you about Winston Parker.'

The instant I'd spoken, I wondered if I had pushed him too far. If, perhaps, a more subtle approach would have served me better. When he spoke again, his voice had dropped to little more than a growl.

'I'm warning you, Birch. That man needs to be locked up.'

'Not until you tell me who he is.'

Temple glared at me, his jaw clenched, but I stood my ground. I knew what I'd seen.

After several seconds, when he realised that I wasn't going to budge, Temple's expression softened. His eyes widened, and the same fear that seemed to have overcome him when he first saw the shaven-headed man began to show once again.

'If you want to let a man who is evidently a criminal roam your ship, that's your prerogative. But you have my opinion.'

I opened my mouth to protest, but he continued before I had a chance.

'We're done for today. I need some space. Some time alone to think.'

'But Mr Webber,' I said. 'And Miss Hall—'

'We're done!' he snapped. 'If you still insist on following me in this absurd fashion, we will meet again tomorrow at ten o'clock on the promenade. That's ten o'clock sharp,' he added. 'I don't care what your captain says. If you're late, I swear to God I'll carry on without you.'

Without another word he was gone.

14

In the day that we had spent together, Temple had shown himself to be nothing if not tenacious. Infuriating perhaps, but tenacious, nonetheless. The boldness with which he had demanded to inspect Denis Dupont's body, interrogated Robert Evans and Arthur Blake, and pursued the woman in the cargo hold might even have been admirable, had I not found myself so often on the receiving end of a significant amount of scorn.

But it was this very tenacity that troubled me. As I returned to the officers' quarters, I was growing increasingly concerned by how panicked he seemed to have been by the sight of the shaven-headed brawler.

They knew each other. Temple might deny it, but I was certain. The way that our arrival had thrown the man off balance during the fight, the sneer with which he had fixed Temple and the nod that he had given him before slinking away ... There was surely no other reason for someone as seemingly unshakeable as Temple to have been so unnerved by the mere sight of an unsavoury character. Nor to be so insistent that he should be locked up.

Could he be a criminal who Temple had encountered in London? Might that even be why he carried a revolver? To protect himself in the event that he ran into an old foe? But if that was the case, why not simply say as much? Why deny so passionately that the two of them knew each other?

I was so caught up in my thoughts that, as I arrived at the officers' quarters, I barely noticed Wilson hailing me from down the corridor.

'Tim,' he said, striding over to meet me. 'There's someone here to see you. A woman.'

'A woman?'

He nodded. 'A Miss Hall. Asked for you personally.'

In an instant, all thoughts of the brawler were gone from my head.

'*Vivian* Hall?' I asked.

'I couldn't tell you. She isn't the sort to be on first name terms with the likes of us. She's waiting for you in the mess.' Wilson dropped his voice to a murmur. 'I'd be quick about it, if I were you. She's been here a little while already and seems not to have enjoyed being kept waiting.'

For a split second, I was so surprised that I simply stood there, looking at Wilson with what I was sure was an expression of pure bemusement. It must be Vivian Hall, I decided. But how could she possibly have known to find me?

'She's waiting,' Wilson prodded.

I nodded, straightened and allowed him to usher me into the mess hall.

As I entered, I caught myself wishing, absurdly, that he had somehow found a more comfortable place for Miss Hall to wait. Or, at the very least, somewhere more private. The new fellow, Travis, and an older officer called Davies were seated at a nearby table, warming their hands on steaming mugs of coffee. If Vivian Hall seemed troubled by their presence, though, she didn't show it. While they cast curious glances at her from across the room, she, to all intents and purposes, might not even have known they were there.

Wearing a bright cloche hat and long, fur-trimmed coat, she was inspecting an old painting that hung upon the wall, portraying a galleon docked in an eighteenth-century harbour. In the five years since I had first boarded the *Endeavour*, I can't say that I'd ever paid it a great deal of notice. Miss Hall, however, was peering at it, her face so close to the canvas that I thought she might risk leaving a smudge of crimson lipstick.

At the sound of my arrival, she turned to face me. Unlike Cassandra Webber, she didn't extend a hand for me to shake.

'Mr Birch?'

'Miss Hall. I hadn't expected to find you here, ma'am.'

'Nor would I like especially to be here. But Arthur has told me what's happened and I thought it prudent to meet you.'

'You've spoken with Mr Blake?'

'I have. He came to my cabin this afternoon in a dreadful state.'

I withheld a sigh. While I understood Arthur Blake's eagerness, I was sure Temple would be less than pleased that the young artist had so quickly failed to follow his instructions.

'Would you mind accompanying me to second-class, Miss Hall?' I asked. 'The gentleman who is leading this investigation would very much like to—'

She pursed her lips. 'I don't have long,' she said curtly. 'I was rather hoping that we could do this quickly.'

The thought of telling Temple that I had spoken to one of his witnesses without him was a daunting one. But it was clear that Vivian Hall wasn't going to take no for an answer. Though her tone was courteous enough, she looked at me with the expression of someone used to giving instructions, rather than following them.

Consoling myself with the knowledge that Temple would have another three days in which to seek her out and conduct his own interview, I adopted a smile and motioned towards one of the tables.

'What I'd like to know, Mr Birch,' she declared as I pulled out a chair for her, 'given the terrible misfortune that has befallen Arthur, is whether you believe I have reason to fear a similar attack. I understand he has told you that I, too, am carrying a valuable painting to the Art Fair.'

She spoke directly, fixing me with a pair of dark eyes. Curiously, however, there was no sign that the prospect of falling victim to the thief who had targeted Arthur Blake frightened her. At least, none that I could see. It was as though she was addressing a simple point of business. A minor nuisance that she was keen to resolve so that she could return to her evening.

'Mr Blake has told you about his painting?' I asked.

'To a certain extent.'

'How do you mean, ma'am?'

'He wouldn't tell me what it was. Nor, for that matter, who the artist is. Only that he is travelling with a valuable piece which he had hoped to keep secret.'

'Does Mr Blake's secrecy seem at all curious to you?'

'To be quite honest, Mr Birch, it explained a great deal.'

134

'How so, ma'am?'

She exhaled sharply, as though this were an especially tedious question. 'On Monday evening, when Denis approached Arthur in the restaurant, I was ordering another drink at the bar. By the time I'd returned to the table, the maître d' had asked Denis to leave and Arthur was telling Mr and Mrs Webber some bizarre story about him being a dissatisfied patron.'

'Mr Blake was under the impression that you failed to hear that,' I said.

Miss Hall gave a little nod. 'So I understand. In fairness, I only caught the tail end of it. I gather that he was trying very quickly to move the conversation along when I returned.'

'But you knew in that moment that Mr Blake was lying?'

'Immediately. I've worked with Denis a few times over the last couple of years, so you might say that I knew him rather well.'

'May I ask why you didn't call Mr Blake out on his lie?'

'I had half a mind to,' she admitted. 'It seemed quite clear that he was up to something, and when I returned that evening to my cabin, I wondered if I might track him down and ask what it was. But in the end, I decided against it. Arthur can be a fool, but he isn't an idiot. I supposed he must have had a decent reason for being so secretive. Of course, that reason became perfectly clear when he visited me this afternoon. Which returns me to my question.' She leaned forward in her seat. 'Do you believe that I should be concerned?'

It occurred to me that there was still no sign of any fear in her voice. In truth, there was something a little unsettling about the entirely practical way that she approached this conversation. It did nothing to ease the nerves that I could feel building as I wondered just how forgiving Temple might actually be when he learned about it. As I considered Miss Hall's question, I thought about the conversation we'd had before our encounter with the shaven-headed man. Tried to imagine exactly what guidance Temple, himself, might give.

'It seems to us that Mr Blake's painting was a targeted theft,' I said cautiously. 'As you've heard yourself, he went to some lengths in order to keep its existence secret, suggesting that this wasn't a random attack. The thief knew exactly where to find it and wanted to take that painting specifically.'

She nodded approvingly and clasped her hands on the table, fluffy white lace protruding from the sleeves of her coat.

'That being said,' I continued, 'I do think it would be prudent for you to be on your guard. However targeted the theft of Mr Blake's painting might have been, it doesn't excuse the fact that somewhere on board the *Endeavour* is a thief with an eye for valuable art.'

'That doesn't fill me with a great deal of confidence, Mr Birch.'

'I quite understand. Perhaps I could hold the painting here, and return it to you when we dock. There's no safer place than the officers' quarters.'

'You really believe that such a precaution would be necessary?'

'I would like to hope not, ma'am. But I would be very happy to take it if it would put you at ease.'

Vivian Hall paused a moment, apparently considering the proposition. For the first time, she looked genuinely troubled.

'I understand that the painting you're carrying is one of your own,' I volunteered, hoping to lighten the mood.

'It is,' she said proudly. 'I've produced five these last couple of years. It's how I know Denis. He sold the first four in his gallery.'

'But not your latest?'

'No.' She gave a little smile. 'Denis has been good to me. He's shown me that there's appetite for my work. But if I'm going to truly make a name for myself, I'll need to set my sights somewhat higher than his quaint little gallery in Bath. The New York City Art Fair seems the perfect venue.'

'You must have been sorry to hear about his death.'

Miss Hall had sat up a little straighter as she spoke about her work, as if the discussion of her art itself was a great deal more interesting than the prospect of it being stolen. At the mention of Dupont's death, however, she frowned.

'Of course. As I say, I think our business together was complete. But it's a terrible thing to happen. He was a decent sort. A respectable kind of man.'

I paused a moment, choosing my next words with care. 'I'm sorry to ask you this, Miss Hall. I'm sure it must seem very indelicate, but—'

'You'd like to know where I was last night.'

'I would, ma'am.'

'I was alone in my cabin.'

'Is there anyone who can confirm that?'

She shook her head. 'I'm travelling alone. It's another reason I wanted to find you myself, Mr Birch. When Arthur told me that you were investigating Denis's death, he said you might not believe it to have been an accident. I appreciate that it could look somewhat suspicious for me to have both known that Arthur was lying about Denis's identity and been alone with no alibi at the time his painting was stolen. I rather hoped that if I were forthcoming it would help to quell any suspicions you might have about my whereabouts.'

Again, I had the sense that this conversation was merely a point of order for Vivian Hall. I nodded, though I silently wondered whether Temple would be so easily swayed.

'I understand that Mr Blake plans to have dinner with Mr and Mrs Webber again on Saturday evening,' I said, 'before we dock in New York. May I ask if you intend to join them?'

'I shouldn't expect so. To be frank, I'm surprised that I was invited to join them on Monday.'

'May I ask why?'

She hesitated a moment. 'You must understand, I'm Evelyn's friend, not Arthur's. I do have a soft spot for him – he knows a great deal more about art than anyone else in Evelyn's circle and I used to enjoy speaking with him when they married. But while it was pleasant enough to see him again on Monday, it doesn't change the fact that the two of them fell out. Nor that Evelyn is an important contact. It wouldn't do for her to somehow find out that I had been spending a great deal of time with Arthur.'

'But if Mr Blake is no longer in contact with his former wife,' I said, 'surely you could have dinner together on board the *Endeavour* and she would be none the wiser?'

For the first time, a glimmer of discomfort showed on Miss Hall's face. 'This is somewhat personal, Mr Birch,' she said. 'But I suspect I wouldn't have joined Arthur for dinner at all had I known that Mr and Mrs Webber would also be there.'

'Why is that, ma'am?'

'Because Mr Webber and I were briefly ...' She hesitated again. 'We were briefly *involved*. It was a few years ago now, while he still worked for Frederick Scott. It didn't last long, you understand. A few months perhaps. I had already been growing a little tired of him, but I brought it to an end when Evelyn quite rightly pointed out that it wouldn't do for one of her friends to have such a relationship with a member of her father's staff.'

There was something distinctly unpleasant in the way she said 'staff'. It reminded me of the look on Arthur Blake's face when Temple had asked if he worked in Dupont's gallery. He might not actually be cut from the same cloth as Vivian Hall and Evelyn Scott but, faced now with a true member of the world that he seemed so desperate to be a part of, it appeared to me that Blake put on a good show.

'Miss Hall,' I said. 'Are you saying that you didn't know Mr and Mrs Webber would be joining you on Monday evening?'

'Quite so. I bumped into Arthur while I was boarding in Southampton and he insisted that I join him for dinner.'

'Why would he not tell you that Mr Webber was also attending?' I heard my voice rise slightly, surprising myself by how much this revelation shocked me. 'Surely, he must have realised what an uncomfortable position he was putting you both in. Mrs Webber too.'

'Harry and I always kept things very quiet. Unless Evelyn told Arthur about us, I think it's quite possible that he might never have known.'

'But he and Miss Scott were married,' I protested. 'You don't think she would have confided in her own husband?'

139

Miss Hall gave a little smile. 'Arthur can be fun when he's on form. But he's not the sort of person one turns to when in need of subtlety. Evelyn learned that quickly enough. Although I'd imagine she wishes she'd learned it a good deal sooner.'

I thought about the troubling condition of Arthur Blake and Evelyn Scott's marriage. The more I learned about it, the more tumultuous it seemed to have been. Then I thought about Kate; how blissful our own first years together had seemed and how desperately I yearned to return to them. To hear how this couple had used their marriage as a tool – one seeking wealth and the other to spite her father – made me sting with resentment.

'I ought to be getting back.' Miss Hall rose to her feet, then said in a tone that suggested to all intents and purposes that she was doing me a favour, 'But I'll consider your offer. To leave my painting here, that is. I'm sure you can appreciate that it's very precious to me. It would be difficult to be apart from it, but if there really is a thief on board, perhaps it would be best.'

'Of course, ma'am,' I replied. 'I'll escort you back to your cabin, if you'd like. Perhaps I could—'

'No,' she said quickly. 'That's decent of you, but I'm sure there's no need. I'll return here if I change my mind.'

I was slightly taken aback by the sharpness with which she repelled my offer. But her mind seemed made up, so I nodded agreeably. I walked her to the end of the corridor, asking as I did that she made sure to lock her cabin door and open it only for people she knew. Then, as I held the door to the officers' quarters open for her, a fresh thought came to me.

'Miss Hall,' I said. 'If I may ask – your painting ... Is it a portrait?'

She nodded. 'Of my sister. Is that important?'

I remembered Arthur Blake's description of his own painting. A portrait of a woman, he had said. The only one that the artist had ever produced. Briefly, I considered revealing this to Miss Hall but instead I forced a smile. She had been warned of the danger. It wouldn't do to worry her unnecessarily.

'Merely a point of interest.'

She seemed to consider this for a moment, before giving a single curt nod and turning to leave. I waited until she had gone, then hurried immediately in the direction of my cabin. There was a scrap of paper on my bedside cabinet, on which I knew that I needed to write down everything I had just learned. If I could at least report the details of our conversation word for word, perhaps Temple would be less furious that I had spoken to Vivian Hall at such length without him.

Of course, the revelation of her history with Harry Webber was a curious detail, and one that I would need to ensure I relayed. But I knew which discovery Temple would be most interested in: that Vivian Hall had realised Blake was lying to the Webbers about Dupont's identity on Monday evening. Not to mention that she had no alibi for the time that the painting was stolen and Dupont met his death.

As I jogged down the corridor, I caught myself wondering – could her visit to the officers' quarters have been a front? An effort to dissuade us from the possibility of her being the culprit? She clearly had an eye for fine art. Perhaps she intended to add Blake's painting to a collection of her own.

141

I was in such a hurry to write down my muddled thoughts that, as I returned to my little room, I almost missed the note that lay on the floor. It was a single sheet of paper, folded twice over and apparently pushed underneath the door.

I stooped and gingerly lifted it up. It was tattered, with one rough edge as though it had been torn from a book or journal. Unfolding it carefully, I found it contained a short message written in a scrawling hand. Six words, to be precise.

As I read it, all thoughts of my conversation with Vivian Hall tumbled from my mind. I stared at the page, unable to tear my eyes away, reading it over and over until my hands began to tremble.

Finally, when I could bear it no longer, I flung open the door, ran back to the mess and held the scrap of paper aloft. 'Who delivered this?' I demanded.

Travis and Davies, who had acquired fresh mugs of coffee since I had shown Vivian Hall out, both glanced up.

'It came from a passenger,' said Travis.

'You're sure?' I asked frantically.

'Quite sure, it was a woman. She handed it to me personally, no more than an hour ago.'

'But who was she?'

'She didn't leave a name. Just asked me to make sure that you got it.'

'Can you at least describe her?' I urged.

Travis shrugged. 'She was young. Scruffy-looking thing.'

'And she asked for me by name?'

'Not by name. She just asked for it to be given to the officer escorting the detective.'

Davies, apparently intrigued by my agitation and the increasingly nervous expression on Travis's face, set his mug down on the table and cast me a quizzical glance. I felt the weight of their eyes upon me. Could almost hear the pair of them wondering what on earth I was raving about now. Realising that I would likely be made to share the contents of the note if I stayed any longer, I retreated to my cabin.

Slamming the door closed, I unfolded the paper and stared at it, poring over the words until they barely made sense. Until I could hear them echoing in my mind. Feel them on my tongue.

It was a threat. A warning of the most terrible kind.

Keep away or you'll be next.

15

Once my wits had returned to me, my first course of action was running straight to find Temple. He might well have insisted on solitude after our encounter with the shaven-headed man, but he needed to see the note. *I* needed him to see it. Clutching it in my hand, I ran to second-class and hammered on his cabin door, desperate to hear what conclusions he would draw.

But it was no use. Either he was ignoring me or he wasn't there. I cursed under my breath. Thinking back to the moment he'd left me in third-class, I supposed he hadn't specified that he would be returning to his cabin. Only that he'd wanted to be alone.

I tried briefly to deduce where else he might be, but again, to no avail. Then, I began to wonder if it might simply have been a lie. A ruse to get rid of me, so that he could resume the investigation on his own.

There was no way of knowing. Wherever Temple might be, it seemed, for the time being, that I was alone. Resigning myself to the fact that I would need to find some other way of taking my mind off the troubling contents of the note,

I returned to the officers' quarters, where I was accosted by Wilson.

Of course, despite my best attempts to hide it, my friend had seen straight away that I was troubled. That is, more so than usual. He pressed me for details and I settled for telling him that the investigation had taken a toll, recounting some of the most puzzling questions that Temple and I had encountered. Without a word, he took me by the shoulder and ushered me into his cabin.

'Dammit, man,' I said, allowing myself a nervous chuckle as he fished a bottle of Laphroaig from under his bunk. 'The captain will have you thrown over the side if he catches you with that.'

Wilson waved my concern away, swatting it from the air like a fly buzzing around his ear. He reached underneath the bunk again and fetched out a pair of glass tumblers. Uncorking the bottle and giving the whisky a sniff, he poured a generous measure into each. I took one gratefully.

'This detective sounds like an absolute sod,' he said, seating himself upon the bed. 'Suppose I ought to be grateful. The way you tell it, I'd much rather he gets lumped with you than with me.'

He flashed me a grin and I forced one in return. But before I could reply, he frowned suddenly.

'Do you think there's anything in it?' he asked. 'This old fellow's death, I mean? Some of the other chaps were speaking over dinner about restless passengers; gossiping about foul play and demanding to know what's being done about it all.'

'I suppose they didn't want to ask me themselves,' I muttered, prompting a grimace to pass over Wilson's face.

'I'm sorry,' I said, my eyes dropping to the floor. 'I didn't mean ...' I blew a heavy sigh. 'There must be something more going on. The missing painting, Monsieur Dupont boarding under a false name and now this Beatrice Walker apparently vanishing into thin air ... There has to be some kind of connection.'

'You agree with the detective, then? You think he might not have fallen of his own accord?'

I didn't answer straight away, sipping my whisky and savouring the warmth of the alcohol.

'I would like to think that he did,' I said cautiously. 'Whatever else might be going on, it would certainly please me to learn that Monsieur Dupont's death, at least, was an accident. But for him to have fallen just a day after his argument with Mr Blake and at the same time that the painting was stolen ...'

Wilson cocked an eyebrow, and for the briefest of moments, the image of the knife standing to attention on Arthur Blake's desk flashed in my memory.

'Yes,' I said finally. 'I think it's possible that he might not have done.'

My friend let out a long sigh. 'McCrory won't have it,' he said. 'He's thinking about nothing but the moment we arrive in New York and he lights that first cigar.'

'Quite so. Mr Temple's insufferable, but if I want to know what's truly happened to Monsieur Dupont – or indeed to find that painting – I'm going to have to let him do his work.'

'Do you think he has a chance of pinning the culprit down?'

'Who can say? Two thousand people on board and just four nights until we dock.' I shook my head. 'Temple might very

146

well be insightful, but you've got to wonder how he could make any real progress on his own.'

'He isn't alone.' Wilson stood and raised his glass, a fresh grin on his face. 'He has you. Timothy Birch, the great detective!'

I gave a weak smile and raised my own glass in response.

I was becoming quite certain that I had made a mistake letting Wilson sweep me into his cabin. Of course I appreciated his good-natured concern, but a conversation about Dupont was hardly the distraction that I had been seeking. As he sat down again on the bed, I thought again of the message:

Keep away or you'll be next.

The most pressing question, of course, was who had sent it. I briefly considered whether it might have been delivered by Vivian Hall; if slipping it beneath my door had been her true reason for visiting the officers' quarters.

But then Travis had mentioned receiving it by hand, before pushing it under my door himself. The woman who had given it to him to was 'young' and 'a scruffy-looking thing'. She might well have youth on her side, but with her lace cuffs and fur-trimmed coat, scruffy was the last word I would use to describe Vivian Hall.

Instead, I had settled on the troubling conclusion that the woman Travis had met must be the same one who Temple and I had pursued in the cargo hold. Whoever she might be, the meaning of her message was clear. She wanted to put an end to our investigation. The question at hand, though, was how serious was her threat?

147

I thought again of the knife in Arthur Blake's desk. Could this woman have been the one who planted it there? Could she have played a role in sending Dupont tumbling down that companionway? And if so – if we failed to heed this warning – would she genuinely see that Temple and I shared a similar fate?

'Any improvement with Kate?' asked Wilson abruptly. He held up his free hand defensively. 'I know that you prefer me not to ask. Believe me, Tim, I'm well aware. And I know that this detective's given you a rough time today, but you seem ...' He adopted an uncharacteristic frown. 'Quiet. Even more so than usual.'

For a moment, I simply looked at him. This was now far from the distraction that I'd hoped for. For a split second, I considered even returning our discussion to Dupont.

'No better than before,' I said. 'I tried to call on her again before we left Southampton, but she wouldn't see me.'

'She sent you away?'

'Not quite. Her mother told me that she wasn't there, but I can't believe it. Her sister says she barely leaves the house.'

'I'm sorry, Tim.'

We sat in silence until I noticed him fidgeting uncomfortably with his whisky glass.

'What is it?'

'It's nothing,' he said, shaking his head. I peered at him, my eyes narrowed, until he relented. 'Only ... I can't help wondering why you're stopping in New York.'

I frowned at him. 'I've told you. I'm visiting Raymond.'

'I know. But you're usually itching to get back to England. With good reason, of course,' he added hurriedly. 'But I can't help wondering what's different this time.'

I took a deep breath. I had resolved to keep my purpose in New York a secret, a visit to an old friend being all the detail I would allow myself to share. Of course, I should have known that it wouldn't be enough for Wilson. He knew all too well that I wasn't the sort to simply visit old friends.

'Raymond ...' I said quietly, looking down at the ground. 'He thinks that he can find her. He thinks he can find Amelia.'

Wilson's face dropped. 'And how does he plan to do that?'

'You know who his father is. He has connections, influence—'

'Connections and influence that Raymond's waited two years to offer?'

I closed my eyes. 'Wilson, this man saved my life. When I was shot, he was the one who dragged me to—'

'Hardly out of the goodness of his heart. We were at war. If you hadn't been wearing an Allied uniform, he'd just as likely have left you in a ditch.'

'Wilson,' I snapped, my voice rising. 'For God's sake, that's enough. I trust Raymond. If he says he can help, then I must let him try.'

Wilson shook his head. 'I'm not sure about this. I know that you're—' He stopped, apparently rethinking his approach. 'I know how badly you want to find Amelia. And I know that you share a history with Raymond. But for him to offer something like this ... How can you be sure that he'll come through?'

'Because he's already started.'

Wilson had no answer for me this time. He watched, wide-eyed, as I reached into my pocket and fished out the yellow ribbon, holding it high so that he could see.

149

'Raymond sent this to me a week ago,' I said. 'He has a man in England already. He's been searching for a few months and has so far found this.'

Wilson stared at the ribbon for the best part of an entire minute before shaking his head. 'Tim ...' he said, a slight tremor to his voice, 'you know that I don't want to ask you this ... but how can you be sure it's Amelia's? I don't doubt Raymond's intentions, nor his father's connections. But even I've seen that before. She wore it in the picture that you put in the newspaper.'

'She wore it everywhere,' I replied.

'Precisely my point. How can you know that this is hers?'

'Because Raymond wouldn't lie to me.' I folded the ribbon and returned it carefully to my pocket. 'I have to trust him, Wilson. Searching by myself is getting me nowhere. Kate still won't speak to me and it's been so long that the police have all but given up. Frankly, I don't see what other choice I have.' I heard my voice begin to tremble. 'I have to do something. Anything I can. I have to make things right.'

This time, seeing that my mind was made up, Wilson didn't even open his mouth to protest. Even so, his disapproval was painted plainly on his face. An uncomfortable silence settled over the cabin as we returned to our whisky. When we had both drained our glasses, he waved the bottle in my direction.

'Top-up?'

'That's all right. I need some air.'

'I'll come with you.' He stood, but I waved him back down onto the bunk.

'I'll be fine. There's no sense in both of us being even colder.' I took my coat from a hook on the door and threw it around

150

my shoulders. As my hand settled on the door handle, though, Wilson called me back.

'Tim,' he said sternly. 'You know that it wasn't your fault, don't you? What happened to Amelia – it was ...' He frowned, apparently struggling for words. 'You couldn't have known what would happen. Kate must realise that, underneath it all. She'll come round.'

For a brief moment, I was blindsided. Wilson regularly offered to lend a sympathetic ear, but he had never been quite so forthcoming with his own stance. I forced one last smile as I opened the cabin door.

'I won't be long,' I told him. 'I promise.'

I stepped out and made my way quickly down the corridor. A burst of laughter erupted from the mess, but I hurried past, silence and solitude beckoning me on. Climbing all the way to the main deck, I made a couple of laps of the port-side promenade. Eventually, the night air seeming to numb some of my nervous energy, I found a quiet spot beneath an electric lantern and leaned against the railing.

Most nights, you could see stars in the sky, so clearly that a skilled navigator could plot a course by their position. I caught a glimpse of a distant crescent moon, but any stars on that particular evening were hidden away by thick black clouds. Still, the water was so calm it would have been easy to forget the storm that had raged the previous evening. Looking out at the ocean now, it might have been the surface of a mirror, the lights from a hundred portholes glittering like fireflies.

With a cursory glance about the deck, I propped my elbows upon the railing and pressed my hands to my face, the breeze whispering in my ears.

'You know that it wasn't your fault, don't you? What happened to Amelia ... Kate must realise that, underneath it all. She'll come round.'

That parting comment had caught me like a blow to the gut. Wilson had never before been so brazen and, truthfully, I couldn't say what was worse: that he seemed so earnestly to believe what happened wasn't my fault, or that I might never bring myself to do the same.

When I had first taken up a post on board the *Endeavour*, five years earlier, Kate made her disapproval all too clear. *What if something happened? What if she or Amelia needed help while I was away? What would she do?*

Despite her concerns, I'd accepted the position. Nothing would happen, I had insisted. I would have so much leave that she'd be glad to see the back of me when I returned to sea.

But of course, I'd been wrong. Devastatingly so. Looking back, I wished that I had listened to Kate's pleas. That I had never set eyes on the *Endeavour*.

I slipped the ribbon from my pocket and ran it through my fingers, thinking back two years to the night I had arrived at home and found that Amelia had gone. I remembered my surprise, as I returned from Southampton, not to have seen a light flickering in the kitchen or bedroom window. Amelia would certainly have gone to bed, but Kate always waited up for me when she knew I was coming home.

Panic had taken me as I scrambled from empty room to empty room, searching for a message; a clue of some kind that would reveal where they had gone. Blood had thumped in my ears and I jumped so violently at the sound of a sharp rap on the front door that I knocked over a vase. It had tumbled to the ground and shattered, water spreading across the carpet.

Barely noticing, I'd run to answer the door, only to find our neighbour waiting for me on the doorstep. Her face wrought with sympathy, she had seen me return and come to break the news that Amelia was gone. Vanished without a trace. And that Kate, apparently inconsolable, was at her sister's house.

Immediately, I resigned my post on board the *Endeavour* in order to join the search. Kate came home and we spent each waking moment exploring every avenue that we could. But after eighteen months without a single lead, our finances had been in tatters. We had already lost our daughter. If I didn't return to work, we would lose what little else we had left. And so, when I announced my decision to return to the *Endeavour* – however reluctantly – Kate's bitterness towards me reached a new peak. Since Amelia vanished, she had never looked at me in the same way. But upon hearing the news that I would be going back to sea, she had been so repulsed that she packed a bag and went again to stay with her sister. This time, she hadn't come back.

I looked down at the yellow ribbon and thought again of Wilson's comment, *'It wasn't your fault.'*

Of course it was my fault. I knew it just as well as Kate. I understood the resentment with which she glared at me. I had left and Amelia had vanished. There was nothing else to be discussed. It would always be my fault.

And what of Raymond? Could his offer really be too good to be true? In two long, agonising years, he had given me my first – and only – glimmer of hope. He had resources at his disposal. Powerful people whose support he could offer. Surely, I had no choice but to trust him.

'*It wasn't your fault.*'

The words rattled around my mind, slipping just out of reach each time I tried to grasp them. Wilson seemed to believe it. Perhaps, one day, I might too.

16

I couldn't say exactly how long I'd stood on the promenade, gazing at the ocean as I sank under the weight of my own thoughts. But at the sound of my name, I whipped around with a start. It was a female voice, and for a split second I expected to find myself face to face with the woman from the cargo hold. Instead, I saw Cassandra Webber approaching, wrapped in a long coat and carrying an umbrella.

'I'm sorry, Mr Birch. I didn't mean to frighten you.'

'Quite all right, ma'am,' I said, returning Amelia's ribbon hurriedly to my pocket. 'No harm done.'

'Are you sure? I hope I'm not intruding.'

'Not at all.'

I felt a drop of rain on my skin. Then another. Within seconds, it was falling all around us, pattering lightly upon the deck.

She opened the umbrella. 'Would you care for some shelter?'

'That would be very kind.'

She came to stand next to me, huddling so closely that I found myself breathing the floral scent of her perfume.

'You're out late, ma'am,' I observed. 'Is anything the matter?'

'Perfectly fine,' she replied, her breath steaming in the cold air. 'I've actually just been to see Arthur.'

'How is he?'

'Oh, he's a nervous wreck. He can't tell whether your detective friend wants to arrest him for murder or thinks he's going to be next.'

'I'm sure Mr Temple didn't mean to frighten him,' I said.

'As am I. Regardless, it was kind of you to put him in a first-class cabin.'

My instinct was to tell her that it was the least we could do. But this would only have been half-true. After seeing both the knife and the broken lock on Blake's door, we could hardly have expected him to spend the remainder of the crossing in his own room. The only available cabins, however, were in first-class. Having now heard the story of his marriage to Evelyn Scott, I had no doubt that it would suit his tastes significantly better than the second-class cabin in which he had left Southampton.

Catching sight of Cassandra Webber's rings, I seized the opportunity to move the conversation along. 'Are you and Mr Webber quite recently married?'

'Very recently. Three months, to be precise.'

'It sounds as though you hadn't known each other long when he proposed?'

'I suppose not.' She glanced down at the little diamond, before pulling back her hand and tucking it into her coat pocket.

'Are you quite sure that you're all right, ma'am?' I asked. 'I don't mean to speak out of turn. Only you seem somewhat subdued.'

'Am I really putting on such a poor performance?'

'I couldn't possible say. Although if you were, I hardly think I would be in a position to criticise.'

She gave a little laugh, though it seemed to vanish as quickly as it had appeared.

'To tell you the truth, Mr Birch, it's this trip. Of course, there's the death of the gentleman from Monday evening. Even though I didn't know him, to think that he died just a single day after he approached us has certainly cast something of a cloud over this crossing. But if I'm honest, it's Harry who's troubling me. He's so nervous about this visit to Boston – about meeting my parents. The very idea has him completely on edge. And I'm ... '

She broke off. 'Well, I've learned something about him these past two days that I hadn't known before. A silly thing really. But something that's caught me truly off guard.' A yearning expression took form on her face. 'I keep wishing that it could all just be simple again. When Harry proposed, I thought that it would make me so happy. And it does. *He* does. But things seem to have become so complicated. Sometimes I just can't help wondering how we might go back to the way things were. In the beginning.'

She breathed a small sigh.

'I told you that we met when Harry showed me around my place in Bristol?'

'It was one of Mr Scott's properties.'

'That's right. Frederick owns quite a few around Bristol, as I understand it. I was in a gorgeous little apartment, right in the middle of town. Harry had picked me up from the station and moved me in, but he kept on finding reasons to come back. A lock needed changing or a light bulb replacing. Of course, I knew he was just looking for excuses to come by and see me, and after a month or so, he finally asked if he could take me to dinner.'

She looked wistfully out to sea, her eyes locked upon the horizon.

'He proposed just five months ago. I'd come to the end of my year in Bristol and was making arrangements to move back to Boston, when he came to the apartment and asked if I'd consider staying in England with him. He said that business was picking up again at the firm, so he wanted to provide for us both while I looked for a legal position.

'Of course, he wanted to wait a little while, to make sure that my parents approved, but I told him no. I said that if we were going to do it, we ought to do it right away. He took a little convincing, but he agreed in the end and we married in August.'

She turned and looked me in the eye. 'That's why he's so nervous about this trip to meet my parents. And why he's brought his car along to impress them. They don't yet know about him. Nor that I'm planning to stay in England. We're breaking the news to them when we arrive in Boston.'

'I can certainly see how that would be intimidating.'

Mrs Webber gave a little smile. 'It was the only way. They'll like Harry well enough, I've no doubt about that. But they would never have agreed to their only daughter spending the rest of her life on the other side of the Atlantic. It wouldn't have mattered how much they approved of him as a match. If we'd asked for their blessing, they would never have given it.'

She gave a hollow laugh. 'I'm sorry, Mr Birch. I'm sure you haven't the faintest interest in any of this. But what about you? Are you married?'

It took me a few seconds to decide how best to answer, the rain pattering above our heads on the canvas of the umbrella.

'Do you know,' I said quietly, 'the honest truth is that I'm not entirely sure.'

'That certainly sounds confusing.'

'You might say that. My wife and I aren't speaking.'

Cassandra Webber's neatly plucked eyebrows furrowed in concern. 'I'm sorry. I didn't mean to pry.'

'No, that's quite all right. It's my fault really. We've been going through something of a difficult period and I ...' I forced a smile. 'We're working it out. I'm going to set things right.'

We stood there in silence for a moment, gazing out into the darkness. I thought of what she'd spoken about a moment ago; that she had learned something of her husband since boarding the *Endeavour*.

'Mrs Webber,' I said cautiously. 'I feel I ought to mention – I spoke a short while ago with Vivian Hall.'

At the sound of Miss Hall's name, her eyes narrowed.

'I owe you an apology,' I continued. 'I hadn't realised when we called on you this afternoon that there was a history between her and Mr Webber. I do hope that Mr Temple's questioning wasn't ...' I paused a moment, struggling to meet her eye. 'That it wasn't indelicate.'

She shook her head. 'It's me who owes you an apology, Mr Birch. I ought to have told you when you called this afternoon. I'm sure it sounds odd, considering it was a number of years ago now that they were together – and only for a short while at that – but it's rather raw. If I'm honest, it's quite a recent discovery for me.'

'I take it then, ma'am, that this is what you have learned about Mr Webber these past two days.'

'It is. When Harry told me on Monday that Arthur had invited Miss Hall to dinner with us, he was ... different. Acting in a way that I'd never seen before. I pressed him on why the idea of dining with her seemed to make him so uncomfortable and he eventually told me about their ...' She scowled. 'Their history.'

'I quite understand. For what it's worth, I apologise if our questioning was out of turn.'

'You were only doing what you had to.' Mrs Webber's expression changed slightly, her voice hardening. 'Out of interest, Mr Birch, what did you make of Vivian?'

'She's ...' I hesitated, searching carefully for the most appropriate words. 'She seems very sure of herself.'

'I think you're being very kind. I ought not to say what I thought of her. To sit with us at dinner like that, when she must have known how it would make me feel ...'

'Perhaps she didn't realise that you knew.'

'Perhaps. But it doesn't change the fact that *she* knew. And then there's this painting of hers. She was telling us all on Monday, she hasn't a shred of interest in marrying or starting a family. All that matters is her art.' Mrs Webber shook her head. 'I suppose she and Harry would never have lasted. Not if that's her attitude. Still, I can't imagine them together. I can't imagine him wanting to be with *any* of those people. He always told me that he hated working for Frederick. That Evelyn was such a brat. To think that he and Vivian were together at all, however briefly, is ...'

She gave another little laugh, her face lighting up as though she was snapping back into focus. 'I'm sorry, Mr Birch. I'm sure I must have said quite enough.'

'Not at all. It must have come as a shock.'

She forced a smile and glanced up at the umbrella. 'This rain seems to be letting up,' she said. 'I ought to get back. Harry will be wondering what's keeping me.'

'Of course. Although if I may say, Mr Temple is still very keen to speak with your husband. Just to ask him the same questions that he asked you this afternoon, you understand. I'd hate to cause any inconvenience, but is there any chance we might meet him tomorrow?'

Cassandra Webber seemed to think for a moment, before giving a nod. 'Why don't I send him to meet you both for lunch? I'll have him come to the restaurant at one o'clock.'

I nodded my gratitude and she turned to leave.

For a long while, I stayed where I was. Another glass of Wilson's Laphroaig would have warmed me through nicely, though I couldn't face any more talk of Kate and Amelia. Still, I couldn't stay on the promenade much longer. It was growing colder and the wound in my shoulder was aching again. Not to mention that I couldn't help but glance around every so often, looking for the woman from the cargo hold. Cassandra Webber had given me quite a start, and it was becoming increasingly difficult to deny just how much the note in my cabin had troubled me.

Where in God's name was Temple? Could he really be pursuing the investigation without me? Or was it the shaven-headed brawler who had caused him to vanish? I remained convinced that they knew each other, but could this man really have unnerved him so much?

I suddenly longed for the sedate routine of my officer's duties. To find a larger room for Mrs Fitch and her damned Yorkshire terrier or to investigate the claims that the porter, Seymour, had been drinking on duty. For a split second, I even wondered about showing Wilson the note. He'd make some smart comment or other which might, at least, make me smile.

Finally, unable to stand in the winter air any longer, I relented. Turning the collar of my coat up against the cold, I stuffed my hands into my pockets and marched across the deck.

Thursday 13 November 1924

17

When I woke on Thursday morning, I was in no hurry to see Temple again.

As I'd returned to my cabin the previous night, the one thing I was sure of was that there was a great deal I wasn't being told. I lay in my bunk, holding Amelia's ribbon, and realised just how desperate I was to know why he was so reluctant to share his business in New York. To uncover why the name Winston Parker elicited such a bizarre reaction and understand the nature of his apparent connection to the shaven-headed brawler.

The truth, it seemed to me, was that there was something very wrong with this detective. There must, surely, be a reason he carried a revolver. And if I were to stay true to Captain McCrory's orders, I was determined to discover what it was.

As usual, in my efforts to avoid idle chatter with other officers, I ensured I came last into the mess for the captain's daily briefing. They barely looked up as I slipped in, sipping from mugs of coffee while a Gene Austin record crackled from the gramophone. Travis, however, cast me a wary glance. I felt a twinge of guilt at the way that I had interrogated the young man over the note he'd delivered to my cabin. No doubt the others had since advised him to give me a wide berth.

When the captain joined us, Wilson took the needle off the record and the reporting officers declared that we were still due to arrive in New York on schedule. The lifeboats had all been inspected, with no damage found as a result of Tuesday night's rough weather, while minor repairs to the rigging were well under way. Satisfied, the captain nodded his approval, but before he could dismiss us, one of the men spoke up.

'It's worth considering, sir, that a great many of the passengers seem to be concerned about yesterday's ...' He swallowed, paling a little under McCrory's piercing gaze. 'Yesterday's incident. They've been asking what's being done about it.'

'What's being done?' the captain repeated.

'Yes, sir. Several have asked if an investigation is taking place.'

Murmurs of approval sounded around the room, heads nodding in agreement.

'Now listen here,' said Captain McCrory, silencing the group in an instant. 'We all know how gossip travels on these crossings. The gentleman's death was an accident, d'you hear? And until we have any reason to believe the contrary, that is what we will tell the passengers. None of you are to say anything that might cause further alarm.' He swept a fearsome glance around the congregation. 'Is that understood?'

There was a sharp response of 'Yes, sir,' and with a clattering of chairs, plates and mugs, we were dismissed.

Glancing at the wall clock, I saw that the briefing had been short, leaving the best part of an hour to fill before I was due to meet Temple. With Wilson on the bridge that morning, I had no desire to sit with the remaining men in the mess hall. But I didn't fancy waiting in my cabin either, alone with the threatening note.

Instead, I thought of the duties that I was failing to fulfil by accompanying Temple on his investigation. Specifically, I thought of Seymour, the porter who had supposedly been drinking on duty. As the crowd in the mess thinned, and those officers who were left began to glance in my direction, I wagered that I must, surely, have time at least to see about him.

You would often hear grumbling in the mess about the quality – or lack thereof – of our quarters. It was certainly true that, compared to some of the passengers' accommodation, our own cabins were far from luxurious. But visiting the quarters occupied by the porters and men from the engines always reminded me that we could have it a great deal worse.

Situated just two decks above the engine room, there was a dull, constant rumble that caused the floor to vibrate beneath your feet. More often than not, I couldn't help but be reminded when I visited the lower decks of my time in the trenches. While it was often difficult to think in such terms, I knew that I was one of the lucky ones; fortunate enough to have only heard stories about the living nightmares that were Passchendaele and the Somme. Even so, the wound in my shoulder was a constant reminder of the combat I'd seen. The sense of claustrophobia and the filthy, lingering stench of death could never be truly forgotten.

And yet on this particular morning not even the memory of the trenches could stop me glancing around every so often, looking out for the woman who had been watching us in the cargo hold.

Keep away or you'll be next.

Was she still following? Lurking around a corner to make sure that Temple and I were heeding her warning? Whoever she was – Beatrice Walker or otherwise – I suspected she would be sorely disappointed if she thought it would deter the detective.

With a sigh of relief, I reached the door that I'd been searching for and, after giving a precautionary knock, let myself in. The cabin was barely larger than my own, with a pair of narrow bunks crammed tightly together. Two men lounged upon them, one shuffling a deck of cards while the other wrote in a leather-bound journal. At the sight of my officer's uniform, they sprang to their feet and stood to attention with cries of 'sir'.

Both men looked to have been on duty during the night. They still wore their white shirts, black trousers and braces, but the red jackets that distinguished them as porters were discarded onto their respective bunks and both had rolled their cuffs up to their elbows.

'Mr Taylor,' I said. 'I'd like a moment alone with Mr Seymour, if you wouldn't mind.'

The man holding the cards nodded, and with another 'sir' he stepped from the cabin, closing the door as he went. The other, Seymour, began to shuffle uncomfortably on the spot. I was sure he knew exactly why I was visiting.

He was a young lad, slim and pale, with the makings of what he presumably hoped would one day be an impressive moustache furnishing his upper lip. He couldn't have been much older than twenty.

'Now listen here, Seymour,' I said. 'I won't keep you in suspense. There have been allegations that you've been drinking on duty. This will turn out better for you if you play along, so I'm giving you an opportunity to come clean.'

Seymour swallowed nervously, his eyes darting around the room.

'Last chance,' I said sternly. 'Last chance before I search the cabin.'

The young porter's eyes flickered momentarily to his bunk.

'Fetch it out,' I instructed.

'Sir?'

'Fetch it out, man. Or would you rather watch me do it?'

With a sigh, Seymour crouched beside the bunk and produced from underneath a small bundle wrapped in a thick woollen jumper. He unwrapped it, revealing a half-empty bottle of Famous Grouse. With a twinge of guilt, I couldn't help but be reminded of the Laphroaig that Wilson kept under his own bunk.

'That's the lot, is it?'

'That's it, sir.' He pressed the bottle into my hand. 'The rest is—' He stopped himself, realising his mistake just a second too late.

'There's more?' I demanded.

'There was, sir. But I've barely touched it.'

'You've hardly been giving it away for free, have you?'

A grimace passed over Seymour's face. 'No, sir. Not for free.'

I felt my eyes go wide. 'You've been *selling* it?'

169

'Just the odd bottle, sir,' he said hurriedly. 'I didn't mean any harm. I've never drunk on duty, I can promise you.'

'That's enough.'

The young man fell silent, looking to the floor.

'I'll need the names of the men you've sold it to.'

Seymour's eyes went wide with panic. 'Please, sir. if they get wind that I've told you, I'll be in for it.'

'You're in for it already, Seymour. Their names.'

He sighed again. 'I only ever sold a couple, sir. The last one went just yesterday to a fellow from the engines called O'Shea. Said he's come into some money and wanted a bottle of something to keep in his cabin.'

I frowned. 'What do you mean, come into some money?'

'I didn't ask, sir. I suppose he might have done an odd job for someone.'

'You mean one of the passengers?'

'Perhaps, sir. Like I say, I didn't ask.'

I nodded, committing O'Shea's name to memory. 'Who else?'

He gave another sigh. 'Well, sir. There was ...'

But he didn't finish. A quizzical expression took form on his face as he realised that something else had caught my attention. Following my gaze, he saw that I was looking down at the journal he had tossed onto his bunk. Except it wasn't a journal at all. It dawned on me that I was looking at a sketchbook.

'Are you something of an artist, Seymour?'

'I don't know if I'd go so far as to say that, sir.' He spoke slowly, as though waiting for some kind of trap to be sprung.

'I can do a decent sketch, but I haven't studied or anything. You can take a look if you'd like.'

He picked up the book and pressed it into my hand. Turning the pages carefully, I saw sketches of a dry-stone wall next to an oak tree; a cocker spaniel with its tongue lolling out; a young woman sitting on the bank of a river.

'These are impressive,' I said. 'Do you draw just for your own amusement?'

'Thank you, sir.' He was becoming more enthused, apparently pleased by the praise. 'Yes, sir. For the most part. Though some of the other men do make requests from time to time.'

He took the book from my hands and turned to one of the final pages, where there was a sketch of a woman still in progress. Her face appeared to be finished, as did her neck and shoulders, but he seemed to have only just started working on her hair.

'That's Taylor's wife,' he said proudly. He picked up a black-and-white photograph that lay face down on the bed. 'See? I only started working on it yesterday.'

I nodded. It was certainly an impressive likeness. No doubt Taylor would be pleased when it was finished. Skilled as Seymour appeared to be, however, it wasn't his sketches that I found myself interested in. It seemed to me that an opportunity had presented itself in the form of this young porter. One which I was suddenly eager to seize.

'Do you know much about famous artists?' I asked.

'Not much, sir.' He closed the sketchbook, suddenly deflated. 'That's to say, I do take an interest, so I might know a little more than the next man. But as I say, sir, I haven't studied.'

'What about an artist called Ecclestone?'

'Oh yes, sir.' He nodded enthusiastically, the eagerness quickly returning to his voice. 'There can't be an Englishman alive who takes an interest in art but doesn't know Ecclestone. There was an exhibition at the town hall in Portsmouth. I took my mother to see it.'

'And what do you make of his work?'

'It's beautiful, sir. Some of the finest landscapes I've ever seen.'

'Would I be right in saying that he only painted landscapes?' I asked. 'Only, I've heard stories about a portrait.'

Seymour lowered his voice and leaned in a little closer, as though telling a ghost story around a campfire. 'Nobody knows about that, sir. At least, not really.'

'How so?'

'Well, because nobody knows if it's real, sir.'

'Do *you* think it's real?'

He scratched his chin. 'I couldn't say with any certainty, sir. But I'd like to think so.'

'And why's that?'

'Just imagine it, sir! If it turned out that one of the greatest artists England's ever known had done a whole other painting which nobody's ever seen. And even if he hadn't, well, every-one likes a bit of mystery, don't they, sir? If nothing else, it makes for a good story.'

I didn't reply. It occurred to me that I already had a great deal more mystery on my mind than I cared for.

'I didn't know you were interested in this sort of thing, sir?' he said eagerly.

'My ... wife has taken an interest.' I was painfully aware of how unconvincing I sounded, but Seymour didn't seem to have noticed. He was like a Labrador puppy, a cheerful grin plastered across his childlike face.

Growing wary of the time, I thought of Temple's warning; that he would begin today's inquiries without me if I was late for our appointment. But I couldn't leave yet. A thought had vaguely occurred to me as I descended to Seymour's cabin and realised its proximity to the cargo hold; an idea that I was now considering putting into motion. Of course, I knew that Temple wouldn't appreciate me orchestrating any kind of plan without first consulting him. If it paid off, though, it would be worth whatever scolding I might receive.

'Now listen, Seymour,' I said, brandishing the whisky. 'We have a problem here. But there's something you can do for me. Something that might help to make it disappear.'

The young man nodded eagerly. 'What would you like, sir?'

'On Tuesday night, a car was damaged in the cargo hold. You're going to ask around and see what you can find out about it.'

'You want me to find out who did it?'

'If you can. I know there won't have been a man on duty in the hold itself, but the damage was apparently reported to a member of the crew. Perhaps you could start by finding out who that was. Whatever you learn, I want to know about it. See what you can dig up.' I held the whisky up again. 'And perhaps I won't need to pay O'Shea a visit.'

'Yes, sir,' he nodded enthusiastically. 'Thank you, sir.'

Certain now that I would be late to meet Temple, I made to leave. But as I grasped the door handle, Seymour said, 'I can tell you one thing for sure, sir.' There was a sudden intensity in his voice. 'About Ecclestone, that is.'

I turned to face him. The wild look that had been in his eyes when he spoke about the portrait had once again returned.

'If that painting ever turned out to be real,' he said, 'it'd be worth an absolute killing.'

18

After scrambling up to meet Temple on the promenade, I was surprised to find that he wasn't alone. Wrapped in a long overcoat, wearing a black bowler hat and swinging an umbrella in one hand, was Arthur Blake.

'Mr Birch!' he exclaimed.

'Mr Blake.' I was panting slightly from having jogged most of the way. 'I hadn't expected to see you this morning.'

The artist was bristling with enthusiasm, striding towards me and extending a leather-gloved hand. I might have believed him to be an entirely different man from the one who presented us with a steak knife plunged into the surface of his desk.

'Mr Blake came to my cabin a short while ago,' said Temple. 'He has some new information that I thought you ought to hear from him personally.'

The last time I had seen Temple, he'd appeared so panicked by the sudden appearance of the shaven-headed brawler that he had fled the third-class common area. Wherever he'd been when I tried to call on him with the note I'd received, he certainly looked to have regained his composure. His eyes were as sharp as ever, his fedora in place upon his head and his hands tucked into the pockets of his grey woollen coat.

Blake, meanwhile, nodded eagerly at the prospect of assisting in our investigation. 'Yes, indeed,' he said. 'I was returning to my cabin last night when I ran into an old contact, one Nathaniel Morris.'

'I'm sorry, sir, Nathaniel …'

'Nathaniel Morris. He's an acquaintance from Bath. To tell you the truth, Mr Birch, he's a terrible bore. But he runs an art gallery in the city – has done for the last forty years or so. What I thought might interest you gentlemen is that he and Dupont don't see *at all* eye to eye.'

'Is that so?'

'Quite so. I mentioned to you yesterday that Dupont set up his gallery in Bath after the war? In doing so, he became Morris's sole competitor. I gather that Morris had hoped to retire some years ago, but Dupont completely derailed his business.'

'Mr Blake,' I said. 'Are you trying to suggest that this Mr Morris may have meant to harm Monsieur Dupont?'

'I couldn't possibly say,' he replied, with the slick authority of a salesman. 'And I certainly wouldn't want to lead you gentlemen to any kind of false conclusion. But I understand that you're treating Dupont's death as suspicious. Perhaps even as murder. Surely, if that's the case, Morris's presence warrants some kind of investigation? A conversation, if nothing else?'

'I have his cabin number,' Temple chipped in. 'It seems he's travelling in second-class with his wife.'

I frowned and turned again to address Blake. 'Where did you say that you saw this gentleman?'

'In first-class, soon after eleven o'clock. But he must have been visiting another passenger. As Mr Temple here says, he's travelling in a second-class cabin.'

I may have imagined it, but I was sure that I caught something unpleasant in the way Blake said *second-class*.

'You didn't stop to greet him?'

'I'm afraid I only saw him from a distance. But I'm quite sure it was him.' Blake gave a short laugh. 'If you do decide to meet him, I think you'll see what I mean.'

I glanced at Temple. He was tapping his foot against the deck, apparently eager to be off.

'Morris knows Vivian, too,' said Blake. 'After her first two paintings did so well, he tried to convince her to sell her last couple in his gallery. But she's remained with Dupont.'

'Are you saying that there's bad blood between them?'

'Not between Vivian and Morris. At least, not that I'm aware of. But I can't imagine it did anything to improve his opinion of Dupont.'

I thought back to my conversation with Vivian Hall in the officers' mess, trying to remember if she had said anything that might suggest a meeting with Morris. Nothing came to mind. Instead, I could think only of how abruptly she had brought our conversation to an end. How she had refused so adamantly to let me accompany her to her cabin. It had certainly seemed that she'd had somewhere to be.

'Are you suggesting that's where Mr Morris might have been going when you saw him last night? To see Miss Hall?'

'Again, I simply couldn't say,' Blake replied. 'Although Vivian is travelling with a new piece. I suppose it's possible that Morris hopes he can convince her to sell it with him before she makes it to the Art Fair.' He was so eager now that he seemed to be trembling. 'Shall I come with you? Morris can be something of a prickly character, but I've dealt with him before on several occasions. I'd be happy to introduce you.'

'I'm sure there's no need,' said Temple.

'But—'

'If Morris has any further information about your painting, Mr Blake, you'll be the first to know.'

Blake hesitated, clearly deflated. His mouth hung open for a short moment, as though he was preparing to press his argument, but a stern look from Temple seemed to change his mind.

'Of course,' he said, quickly adopting a cheerful smile. 'I understand. No room for bystanders in an investigation like this! In that case, I shan't hold you gentlemen up any longer. You know where to find me if I can be of further service.'

He tipped his bowler to us and left, swinging his umbrella as he went. I wondered if he had some romantic vision of joining Temple in his investigation. Perhaps he thought a story about a daring attempt to steal the painting and the intervention of a Scotland Yard detective would boost its value even further in New York. All suitably embellished, of course. In Blake's chain of events, I suspected the knife in his cabin would instead have been held to his throat. I smiled to myself at the thought of how much time it might take with Temple to put him off such an idea.

'He seems to have perked up,' I observed.

Temple snorted. 'He was beside himself when he knocked on my door this morning. I suspect Mr Blake believes he's solved this case for us.' He turned to face me. 'You're late.'

'I know. I was seeing a man about Mr Webber's car.'

'The car? What about it?'

'I've tasked one of our porters with seeing if he can turn up any new leads. He's well acquainted with the goings-on below deck. If the crew knows of anything suspicious that happened on Tuesday night, with a bit of luck he'll hear about it.'

Temple shook his head, a grim expression on his face. 'You should have asked me about this. He might frighten the culprit off.'

'He'll be discreet,' I said, thinking of the leverage I'd acquired with Seymour's whisky. 'I'm sure of it.'

'Fine,' he muttered. 'The car's unlikely to be of any real consequence, I suppose. But it's on your head if it goes wrong.'

I bit my tongue, forcing myself not to retort.

'We'll call first on Mr Morris. See if we can't rule him out. That is,' he said drily, 'unless you need a few more minutes.'

Again, I thought of a few choice words with which I'd like to reply, but I held my tongue. 'There is something,' I said. 'Something you ought to see.'

I reached into my pocket and fetched out the scrap of paper. Temple took it with a frown.

'That was pushed under my door last night,' I said in the most confident voice I could manage. 'It was given to one of the other officers by a passenger. A young woman.'

Temple said nothing. His eyes were fixed on the note, the frown still firmly in place. If he was intimidated by the message it bore, he didn't show it.

'I take it you got one too?' I asked.

'No.'

For a brief moment, I wondered if he had misunderstood my question.

'Why would it come to me but not to you?' I asked. 'You're quite sure you didn't receive one?'

He scowled. 'I imagine I would remember receiving a death threat.'

'Of course you would. I only wondered ...' I stopped to reconsider my approach, wary of pushing him too far. 'Well, what do you make of it?'

'It seems fairly evident to me.'

'The message perhaps. This woman from the cargo hold wants to put a stop to our investigation. But is there nothing you can tell from it? You said yesterday that we wouldn't be able to find her again without further evidence. Surely this must count for something?'

Temple looked up. 'What do you expect to learn about her from this?'

'I was thinking about the note we found in Dupont's cabin. *Saturday. Nine o'clock.* Perhaps the handwriting—'

'It's not the same,' said Temple bluntly.

'I wasn't so sure either. But perhaps we ought to just—'

'It's *not* the same.'

I recoiled, taken aback by the sudden severity of his tone. 'So we ignore it?'

'No,' he spat. 'We don't ignore it. We gather more evidence. A witness account. A handwriting sample that matches this one. Something that could actually help us. On the subject of which –' he tucked the folded note into his pocket before I could protest – 'Mr Blake is of the opinion that Vivian Hall came to speak with us yesterday evening. He must be mistaken, of course. I certainly haven't spoken with her.'

I shuffled uncomfortably, struggling suddenly to meet his gaze. 'She came to the officers' quarters last night,' I said. 'Not long after we'd parted ways in third-class.'

'And you spoke to her?'

I nodded.

Temple looked out to sea, his jaw clenched. 'I told you explicitly—'

'*She* found me,' I protested. 'I told her that it was you she would need to speak to, but she wouldn't have it. What was I supposed to do?'

'You should have insisted that she seek me out,' he snapped. 'You should have told her that if she refuses to speak to me, she speaks to nobody at all. I am the one investigating this case, Birch. Not you.'

'Are you really so against my helping that you won't allow me to speak to a witness who seeks me out?'

'Wholeheartedly.'

I felt my cheeks flush, embarrassed by how much this stung.

'I barely spoke with her at all, if you must know,' I said. 'She was keen to be off.'

'Where to?'

'She didn't say.'

'Did she have someone to meet? Somewhere to be?'

'I'm telling you, she didn't say.'

'What *did* you learn, then? Did you ask her for a handwriting sample, perhaps?'

'No.'

'Or if she knew of any reason why Dupont would go by the name Fisher?'

'No,' I repeated.

Temple rolled his eyes. 'So you have not only ignored my instructions,' he said darkly, 'but you have done so with nothing to show for it.'

'Not quite,' I said sharply. 'We might not have spoken for long, but I did learn something. Miss Hall most definitely heard Mr Blake trying to convince Mr and Mrs Webber that Monsieur Dupont was a dissatisfied customer. She knew that he was lying to them.'

'But she didn't know why?'

I shook my head. 'The first she learned of Mr Blake's painting was when he warned her of the danger to her own piece yesterday afternoon. She did admit, though, that she has no alibi for Tuesday evening.'

'None at all?'

'None. She says that she was alone in her cabin. Her hope was that by being so forthcoming, it might absolve her of any suspicion.'

'I'd say it does precisely the opposite.'

'I thought you might. In any case, there was more. It seems Miss Hall and Mr Webber were together for a short while. While Mr Blake was married to Evelyn Scott.'

Temple glanced in the direction in which Blake had just walked. 'He failed to mention that this morning.'

'I don't believe he's aware of it.' I struggled to keep a smug note out of my voice. 'Mr Webber was still working for Frederick Scott at the time, so it sounds as though they kept it rather quiet. Miss Hall brought the relationship to an end when Miss Scott decided it was no longer appropriate.'

Temple turned and looked out to sea.

'Cassandra Webber was unaware of their history, too,' I continued. 'Mr Webber only revealed it to her on Monday, after Mr Blake had invited Miss Hall to join them for dinner.'

Temple frowned suddenly. 'How do you know this? About Mrs Webber? It can't have come from Miss Hall.'

'I ran into her last night.'

'You've spoken with *her*, too?' A look of pure fury took form on Temple's face.

'Only briefly,' I said hurriedly. 'And I've made us an appointment with Mr Webber. She's sending him to meet us in the restaurant at one o'clock.'

'I don't care,' Temple snapped. 'What must I say to make you understand? You don't speak alone with *my* witnesses.'

'They're *my* passengers! I can hardly help it if they seek me out or if we both happen to be walking upon the promenade. What do you expect me to do? Turn and run in the other direction?'

'I expect you not to take it upon yourself to further my investigation. I expect you to bring them to *me*.'

'And how should I do that when you're nowhere to be found?'

Temple's eyes narrowed a fraction.

'I came to your cabin last night to show you this note,' I said. 'You weren't there.'

'I needed some solitude. Some space to gather my thoughts.'

'And where were you doing that?'

Temple was quiet, suddenly unsure of himself.

'Who was the man in third-class?' I tried instead.

'I have no idea.'

'I don't believe you. You snap at Arthur Blake, you insist on carrying a revolver and then you're so startled by the sight of this man that you completely disappear. For God's sake, just what is your purpose on board this ship? This "police business" of yours in New York. What are you—'

'That's enough,' Temple barked. 'My business in New York is just that – business. I don't know what you think you saw take place in third-class, but you have no right to ask my purpose aboard this ship.'

I had known he would be unhappy, but I still wasn't prepared for such a reaction. His shoulders were heaving, and I was alarmed to realise that his hand had gone to rest in his coat pocket. The same pocket into which he had tucked his revolver the previous day.

Temple stood glaring at me as I wondered if I had angered him so much that he might actually draw the gun. Then, with a vicious scowl on his face, he turned and swept in the direction of second-class. Timidly, I made to follow. We walked to Nathaniel Morris's cabin in complete silence, and when we arrived, I let him knock on the door without protest.

19

The gentleman who opened the cabin door squinted at us through a small pair of round spectacles and an enormous set of ginger whiskers. His hair was receding and he wore a black suit and tie, his neck spilling over the top of a crisp white collar and waistcoat straining against his bulk. He loomed over us, filling the entire doorway.

'Mr Morris?' asked Temple.

'Yes?' Nathaniel Morris raised a white silk handkerchief to his mouth and coughed violently, his bushy eyebrows knotting in suspicion as Temple introduced himself. 'I can't imagine why I would want to speak with a police officer,' he muttered. 'It's not convenient, gentlemen. Not convenient at all. My wife and I are about to—'

'It's regarding Denis Dupont.' Temple raised his voice to be heard above Morris's protests. 'I understand he's an acquaintance of yours.'

At the sound of Dupont's name, Morris widened his eyes. His hands clenched into meaty fists and his jowls trembled, little stammering noises tumbling from his quivering lips.

'That ... damned French swine!' he finally managed to blurt out, his shoulders heaving with rage. 'What fresh misery has he sent you to my door to deliver? That man has nothing to offer but lies and deceit. From the accursed day that he was born, I would wager—'

'He's dead,' said Temple, so bluntly that it made me wince.

Morris fell silent for a moment. 'Dead, you say?'

'Yes, sir. I suspect you'll already have heard about it. His body was found yesterday morning, aboard this very ship.'

Morris's eyes flew wide again behind his spectacles and his whole body began to tremble. 'Now, hold on just a moment,' he roared, his cheeks turning crimson. 'You think that because he and I had misgivings, you can come to my door the second he turns up dead and pin it on me? The nerve of it! How was I even to know he was aboard this damned ship?'

A woman appeared at the door and laid a hand on Morris's shoulder. She looked tired, with heavy bags beneath her eyes.

'Nathaniel,' she said. 'What on earth is all this noise?'

'Go back inside, Eleanor. That Frenchman's been topped and these work-a-days think I have something to do with it. Well, let me tell you, sir, I won't have it. I'll be making a serious complaint to your superior officer the moment we return to England.'

'Calm yourself, Mr Morris,' said Temple. 'Nobody is accusing you of any crime. My investigation is simply to determine what Dupont might have been doing at the time of his death.'

'Let them in, Nathaniel,' said Eleanor Morris, gently squeezing her husband's shoulder. 'Answer their questions and I'm sure they'll be on their way, won't you, gentlemen?'

'Certainly, ma'am,' I replied, earning a fresh scowl from Temple.

Morris disappeared into the cabin, coughing and muttering, while his wife beckoned for us to follow. He seated himself at the desk, the chair giving an alarming creak under his weight.

Just like the Webbers, Nathaniel and Eleanor Morris had been provided with bunk beds in which to sleep. Temple nodded at the neatly made lower bunk.

'May I sit?'

'If you must,' Morris grunted.

He sat and looked intently at the art dealer. Huddling awkwardly together by the door, Eleanor Morris and I shared a fleeting, nervous glance. Temple hadn't spoken a word to me since our argument on the promenade, and I wondered if she was as concerned about her companion's composure as I was about mine.

'You say that this is the first you've heard of Dupont's death,' said Temple.

'Obviously.'

'We'd heard—' Eleanor Morris began.

'We'd heard that a man had died,' her husband cut in. 'The way people are talking about it, I doubt there's anyone left on this ship who hasn't. But as I said, I didn't even know that ...' He took a deep breath, as though physically struggling to even say Dupont's name. 'I didn't know *that man* was even on board.'

'Would I be right in assuming that you're travelling to the New York City Art Fair?'

'You've heard of it, have you? I'm taking a Navarrete. It's a beautiful piece. Ought to fetch a good price. I take it you must have an interest in art?'

'I'm afraid not,' replied Temple. 'I believe Dupont may have been travelling there as well.'

Morris's nostrils flared and he coughed loudly into his handkerchief. It was a booming sound, echoing around the small cabin, though I barely registered it. All I could think of was whether he might become another target for our culprit. An acquaintance of Dupont, travelling to the New York City Art Fair with a valuable painting in tow. In my eyes, at least, he seemed a suitable candidate.

'No doubt planning to swindle some poor fool out of their life's savings,' he wheezed, when the fit had finally subsided.

'What do you mean by that, sir?'

The art dealer shook his head. 'Nothing. It's not important.'

Temple made no reply, fixing him with a piercing stare. After a while, Morris gave a sigh, his bushy eyebrows knotting together in the middle.

'How much do you know about this man?' he asked.

'Enough. I know that he had a gallery in London, but it was bombed during the war, so he set up shop in Bath. And I know that he was travelling on this ship, presumably to the New York City Art Fair, when, on Tuesday night, he took a tumble down a flight of steps.'

'Nasty way to go,' Morris observed, though I couldn't help but wonder if I heard a hint of satisfaction in his voice. 'You're right. Dupont did set up in Bath after the war. That's when I first met him.'

'I understand you have a gallery of your own?'

'Morris and Son,' he said proudly. 'My father's gallery. We've traded for nearly sixty years. It's the oldest in the city.'

'I can't imagine you were too pleased to see Dupont setting up shop.'

'Quite the contrary. I suppose you haven't visited Bath before, Mr Temple. Well, we aren't speaking about a country village. The city is more than large enough for a little friendly competition.'

'Then why were you so offended by Dupont moving into town?'

Morris took a deep breath, his nostrils flaring. I exchanged another nervous glance with his wife, my fingers straying to the ribbon in my pocket.

'You don't *know* this man,' he muttered. 'You haven't the faintest idea what you're talking about.'

'So enlighten me.'

'Why?' Morris brandished his handkerchief. 'Why, exactly, should I explain the details of my business to you?'

'Because a man who it seems you had a serious disagreement with has been found dead. And I am still looking for a reason to dismiss you from my investigation.'

Morris glared at the detective, his shoulders heaving. Then he gave another long sigh, a great rasping sound like the final breath of some dying animal. From the corner of my eye, I saw Eleanor Morris's shoulders sink.

'I had arranged the biggest sale of my career. Just last year. A beautiful piece by a German artist called Liebermann.'

Temple waited patiently while the art dealer broke off again to cough loudly.

'I had agreed to buy the painting from its original owner. A fellow in Wiltshire. And had arranged to sell it to a serious collector in America. I'm not exaggerating when I say that with the profit from this single sale, I would have been planning my retirement.'

'So what went wrong?'

'That damned Frenchman got involved.' Morris began to tremble with rage again. 'I don't know how, but he got wind of the sale, contacted the owner of the painting and offered him nearly double what I had agreed to pay.'

'That must have been a substantial amount of money.'

'An extraordinary amount. How he had the funds to make that kind of offer, I shall never know.'

'Who was his buyer?' Temple leaned forward on the bed. 'I assume that he must have been acting on behalf of a client.'

'As did I,' said Morris. 'But that might very well be the most frustrating part of the entire affair. This happened a year ago, and yet, I haven't been able to determine who the buyer was.' He shook his head, a wistful look in his eyes. 'We're a close-knit bunch in the art community. Dupont must have had a serious collector lined up to have made such a large offer, but for nobody to know who that person was is beyond belief. I've asked all my contacts, and not one of them has any idea what he did with the piece.'

Morris's cheeks had turned a violent shade of red as he told his story. I almost suggested that Temple let him rest for a moment before continuing.

'What can you tell me about an artist called Ecclestone?' he asked.

'A Devonshire artist.' Morris mopped his brow. 'A wonderful talent.'

'Have you sold any of his work in your gallery?'

'A few pieces.'

'Landscapes?'

'Ecclestone *only* painted landscapes.'

Temple paused for a moment. Then he said very innocently, 'So I'd been led to believe. Only, I've heard recently about a portrait.'

'It's a fairy tale. You'll never find anyone worth their salt who genuinely believes it exists.'

'What if I were to tell you that Dupont thought he'd found it?'

The art dealer laughed. 'I'd say it sounds exactly the sort of trick that he would try to play. Have you listened to nothing I've told you, Mr Temple? Dupont was a con man – a liar and a thief. I'm sure he would quite happily have tried to convince you that he'd come across Ecclestone's mythical portrait, but you'd be a fool to believe him.'

'It's not actually Dupont who we've been asked to believe,' said Temple. 'I've heard this news from Arthur Blake.'

'Then you'd be even more of a fool. Blake's a decent enough fellow, harmless, but he's got a head full of sawdust.'

'You don't believe the painting exists, then?'

'No, sir, I do not.' Morris raised his handkerchief to his mouth to stifle another cough. 'And I would advise you to do the same.'

I thought back to my conversation with Seymour earlier that morning. Could he and Morris both be right? Could it be possible that Ecclestone's portrait didn't exist? Arthur Blake certainly seemed to think that it was real. But if he was wrong, what, exactly, had he bought from Dupont? Had he been conned, just as Morris had apparently been?

'What of your movements over the last few days, Mr Morris?' Temple asked. 'I'd like to know where you were on Tuesday evening.'

'I knew it!' the art dealer cried. 'I knew you were trying to put this thing on me!'

He began to cough violently, his sudden outburst bringing on a new fit that seemed to rattle the very walls of the cabin.

'Gentlemen,' said Eleanor Morris, moving the short distance to stand behind her husband. 'You can see that Nathaniel is not well. Since boarding the *Endeavour*, we have left this cabin only for meals. The remainder of our time has been spent resting and sleeping.'

She laid a hand on Morris's shoulder. He reached up, his own hand dwarfing hers, and gave it a gentle squeeze.

'So you didn't witness an argument between Dupont and Arthur Blake on Monday evening?' asked Temple. 'At around nine o'clock in the restaurant?'

'We couldn't have done,' Eleanor Morris answered. 'We've been taking our meals earlier in the evening so that Nathaniel can return to bed. We haven't once been in the restaurant any later than eight o'clock.'

'You haven't been for any walks? Or taken tea in the reading room?'

'Dammit, man,' Morris grumbled. 'Has my wife not made it clear enough already? I am not well. I'm not drinking, I'm not smoking and I'm certainly not taking tea in the damned reading room.'

'How about first-class?' The question was innocent enough, and yet there was suddenly an edge to Temple's tone. 'I don't suppose you've been to call on any other passengers?'

Morris glared at him. 'I've told you, I have left this cabin only for meals.'

'Then perhaps you could explain why Mr Blake saw you roaming the first-class corridors last night?'

'He must be mistaken,' said Eleanor Morris.

'No, he's quite sure of himself,' Temple replied. 'He says that just after eleven o'clock, on his way back to his cabin, he saw your husband. Of course, he may have mistaken you for someone else. But considering that this sighting is the only reason we knew to call on you this morning, that would be quite a coincidence, wouldn't you say?'

Eleanor Morris fell silent, and Temple turned his attention once again to her husband.

'Perhaps you were paying a visit to Vivian Hall? I understand that the two of you are acquainted.'

'Barely. I tried to convince her to sell her last two paintings with me, but she always worked with *him*. In any case, it's irrelevant. I didn't even know that she was on board.'

'Then I'll ask again.' There was a menacing tone now in Temple's voice. 'If you weren't visiting Miss Hall, what were you doing last night in first-class?'

For several seconds, he and Morris glared at each other. The detective's expression was one of defiance, his foot tapping against the floor. Even Eleanor Morris appeared less sure of herself, glancing down nervously at her husband. I was bracing myself to intervene when finally Morris spoke.

'I have left this cabin,' he rasped, 'only for meals.'

Temple seemed to consider. 'All right,' he relented. 'You can hold that line if you'd like. But you'll appreciate, I suppose, that it makes it difficult to believe you couldn't have witnessed Dupont's argument with Mr Blake on Monday. Or indeed that you couldn't have been roaming the ship on Tuesday evening, when he was killed.'

Morris's nostrils flared, a guttural sound rumbling in the back of his throat.

'What about the name Beatrice Walker?' asked Temple.

'What about it?'

'Does it mean anything to you?'

'Not a thing.'

'Or Fisher? Can you think of any reason why Dupont would board this ship under that name?'

'I've told you already, he was a con man. No doubt it was part of some hellish new scheme that he was operating. Who knows? Perhaps he was trying to hide from someone.'

'Would he have reason to need to?'

'I couldn't possibly say.'

'You wouldn't say that he had any enemies, then?'

'Get out.' Morris jabbed a stubby finger in Temple's direction. 'I won't sit here and indulge this any further. Get out of here, now.'

Eleanor Morris fixed me with a pleading look and I knew that our time was up.

'I think we have what we need,' I said. 'Don't you, Mr Temple?'

At first he didn't move. Then without a word, he stood and swept from the cabin, leaving me to murmur hurried apologies as I scrambled to follow.

20

'What in God's name was that?' I demanded. 'Were you trying to pick a fight or am I supposed to believe that's just how
things are done by the police in London?'

Temple turned and fixed me with a glare of such intensity
that it became an effort to maintain eye contact. I clenched my
fists, determined to stand my ground.

'I agreed to remain silent in these interviews,' I said, 'on
the condition that none of my passengers were inconvenienced.
You can throw convenience out of the window. The way you
conducted yourself in there was borderline harassment. Do
you not realise that if Nathaniel Morris were to make a complaint about your behaviour to the captain – and I'd say that
he has every right to – this investigation would be over?'

Temple was a coiled spring, his jaw clenched and cold eyes
blazing. He breathed deeply, as if to calm himself, and for a
split second I wondered if I had pushed him too far.

'Listen,' I said. 'I know that you want to keep whatever
you're doing in New York secret. But if your lack of composure in there was because I asked—'

'When you're dealing with someone like that,' he said sharply, 'who holds you in the same regard as the dirt on their shoe, you need to make it quite clear that they are not in charge.'

His voice was measured and level, as though he was explaining the simplest of concepts to a child, but he bristled with a fury that I could see he was wrestling to control.

'You need to elevate yourself in their mind to a position of authority,' he continued. 'Sometimes that means trying to frighten them, others it means becoming their best friend. In the case of Mr Morris, it meant ensuring that his wasn't the loudest voice in the room. Either way, you won't get anything useful out of them until you've convinced them that they are not on your level.'

'You must see your interview as a resounding success, then,' I said bitterly.

'I do. We have a new suspect who is not only hiding something from us but who also harbours a long-standing grudge against Dupont.'

'Be serious,' I scoffed. 'You saw the state of that man's health. Are you honestly going to accuse him of throwing someone down a companionway? Or forcing a cabin door?'

'It would only take a moment's exertion to push a seventy-year-old man down those steps. You saw as clearly as I did the contempt that Morris has for Dupont. I'm sure that, given the opportunity, he could muster up the strength to do the deed. And if nothing else,' he continued, raising his voice before I could object, 'we've learned that Dupont's finances don't add up. Where did he get the money last year to swoop in and steal Morris's sale? Where did he even find the money to set up in Bath? If his gallery in London was destroyed, he won't have been able to make anything from selling the property. It must have been done with existing capital.'

'He might have had insurance.'

'He might. Which would go some way towards explaining the gallery. But insurance wouldn't give him the funds to steal Morris's sale. It seems our dead Frenchman had several questionable dealings that we aren't yet fully aware of. The kind that could likely get someone into serious trouble.'

'You mean that could cause someone to find a knife planted in their desk.'

'Quite possibly. And there's still the question of why Morris is lying about his visit to first-class.'

'Could Mr Blake not have confused him for somebody else?'

'Does that really seem likely?'

Truthfully, it did not. I remembered Blake's comment that, even at a distance, he would struggle to mistake Morris. At the time, it had seemed a curious thing to say. Now, though, as I thought of the art dealer's enormous frame, great ginger whiskers and terrible rasping cough, I understood how unlikely it was for there to be anyone else aboard the *Endeavour* with a genuine resemblance.

'Surely Mr Morris would make a more likely victim than a culprit,' I said. 'He's carrying a painting to the Art Fair, just like Mr Blake. And in any case, he didn't even seem to know that Monsieur Dupont was on board. He might well be lying about his visit to first-class, but could it not be unrelated?'

'It could. But until we expose whatever it is that he's hiding, we can't discount him as a suspect. However you choose to look at it, there's no denying that he has a serious motive for doing away with Dupont.'

I had to concede, Temple made a convincing point.

'I suggest we part ways,' he said sharply. 'And meet again in the restaurant.'

'You want to split up?'

'We have a good couple of hours before our appointment with Harry Webber. I don't see any need for me to take up time that I'm sure you could put to better use.'

His concern almost sounded sincere, I thought.

'But what will you do?' I asked.

'I hardly see how that's your business.'

'Until you tell me where you were last night, I'd say it's entirely my business. How can I trust that you aren't simply shaking me off in order to investigate on your own? For God's sake, man, you might not want to tell me what you're doing in New York, but can you not see how suspicious it looks for you to keep vanishing?'

Temple scowled and glanced down at the ground. I let the silence hang between us, until he finally looked up again and met my eye. 'If you must know, I'm returning to third-class.'

'So you did know that brawler.'

The detective nodded. 'He's a criminal. A dangerous sort who you should have damn well locked up when I told you to.'

'If you'd told me this at the time, perhaps I might have.' I shook my head. 'Is he a suspect?'

'Not where Dupont's concerned.'

'Then what business does he have on board the *Endeavour*?'

'That's precisely what I mean to find out.'

I nodded. 'I'll come with you.'

'You'll do no such thing.'

'But if this man is a danger to the passengers, surely I have a duty to—'

'If you follow me, we are through.' Suddenly, there was iron in Temple's voice. A hint of menace that was so palpable, I took a step back. 'Dupont be damned. You might need to accompany me in order to investigate his death, but this is police business and I will not have you involve yourself. '

He glared at me with such ferocity that I thought I might be about to see his revolver. 'The restaurant,' he growled. 'You will meet me there and I will interview Webber. Until then, do not think to follow me.'

Without another word he turned and strode away. His departure was so abrupt that, for several seconds, I found myself standing alone in the corridor, cursing under my breath as he rounded the corner and disappeared from view.

I had thought that to learn I was right – that Temple did, indeed, know the shaven-headed man – would come with a sense of vindication. Perhaps even satisfaction. Instead, the discovery that he was some kind of criminal had me wanting even more desperately to understand the nature of Temple's business in New York. To explain his aversion to Winston Parker's name and the need that he apparently felt to carry a revolver.

Despite his warning, I was filled with a sudden determination to follow him. Didn't I have a duty, after all? Ensure that the investigation was appropriate; that had been the captain's instruction. If whatever awaited Temple when we docked was driving him to speak in such a hostile fashion to Blake and

Morris, and spend valuable time searching third-class for the shaven-headed man, then it seemed to me that I was all but obliged to uncover his secret. If I kept my distance, I was sure that I could pursue him without being seen.

I cursed again. The risk was too great. If he caught me and was so enraged that he followed through on his threat to abandon me, I might never find Dupont's killer. Nor return the stolen painting to Arthur Blake.

Still, I wasn't going to stand idle. There were other ways that I could investigate.

I had wondered already about visiting the *Endeavour*'s telegram office and sending a message to London, enquiring about Temple's records. But I had quickly abandoned the idea. For one thing, I didn't know who I would contact. Scotland Yard? Even if I could pluck up the nerve, they would surely have no reason to indulge my request for information on the business of one of their officers.

Then there was my second idea, which had come to me as I'd lain in my bunk the previous evening. I could search Temple's cabin, looking for anything that might explain exactly what he was keeping from me. The door would be locked, no doubt, but the skeleton key, kept in the officers' quarters, would allow me in.

It was risky, of course. If I went through with it and was caught, and my actions reported, Captain McCrory would dismiss me immediately. That is, if Temple didn't get his hands on me first.

And yet, despite the danger, I knew that I had to try. I needed to know Temple's story, and if he wasn't prepared to share it with me, I would discover it for myself.

I set off at pace, the carpet muffling the rhythmic thumping of my boots. Hurrying down the Great Staircase, I reached the entrance to the officers' quarters and, stepping inside, heard a Duke Ellington record crackling down the corridor. Two off-duty men were playing cards in the mess, but I brushed past, hoping that I would slip by unnoticed.

Rounding a corner, I came to a stop at a broad metal cabinet. I eased it open, grateful to Duke for masking the squeaking of the hinges. Inside was a collection of gleaming rifles, lined up neatly beneath a single brass key on a metal hook. I swept a glance around the corridor; the rumours that would spread if I were caught in this particular cabinet didn't bear thinking about. With the coast clear, I took the skeleton key, tucked it into my coat pocket and then quickly shut the metal door.

Retracing my steps, I climbed the Great Staircase to the second-class deck. I was struggling to maintain a regular pace now, wrestling with a desire to get the job done and my natural instinct to turn and abandon my mission.

My heart was thumping in my ears when I reached cabin 212. I knew even before opening the door that it was an inside-facing room. It was the cheapest cabin that you could have without bunking with strangers in third-class. Scotland Yard must have shallow pockets, I thought. Or perhaps it was simply reluctant to put its hands in too deep at the expense of its officers.

I knocked sharply on the door, on the off-chance that Temple had come this way before visiting third-class and should happen to be inside. Receiving only silence in reply, I drew the skeleton key from my pocket and, with a nervous glance up and down the corridor, slipped inside.

Leave. Kate's voice echoed in the back of my mind as I closed the door behind myself. I pictured her face, creased with concern at the idea of me executing such a foolish plan. *You've already taken this too far, Tim*, she seemed to whisper. *Just leave, before it gets any more out of hand.*

With a deep breath to steady my nerves, I ushered her voice away. I was here now. If I were caught, there was no way that I could make my punishment any more severe by staying a while longer to look around.

Temple was travelling alone, that much was plain to see. The cabin contained only a single bunk, and there were no possessions that looked as though they might belong to a companion. A leather suitcase had been deposited in one corner and the charcoal suit that he had worn the day before was strewn carelessly over the back of a chair.

A book sat on the desk, a history of the Napoleonic wars. I flicked through and saw that many of the pages were worn and shabby. It had been well-thumbed. Next to it was a hip flask, which I lifted to my nose and caught a whiff of whisky.

I was beginning to feel foolish, realising how much I had risked for so little reward. But I couldn't leave yet. Not until I had searched the cabin thoroughly.

I eased open the bottom drawer of the desk to find it empty. As was the middle one. The top drawer, however, was not. It contained a leather-bound journal and a small paper carton about the size of a cigarette packet.

I recognised the carton immediately. I had seen similar packages countless times during the war. My heart now pounding, I picked it up and heard a metallic clinking as its contents rattled around inside. Tipping them into my hand, I found myself holding a pile of bullets. If I had been in any doubt before, it certainly appeared now as though Temple's revolver must be loaded. The bullets were small, the kind that wouldn't do much damage at any kind of range, but up close they would kill.

I tipped them back into the carton and returned it carefully to the drawer. Then I turned my attention to the journal. Laying it on the surface of the desk, I flicked through the opening pages and saw several neatly written lists of names and addresses. At first, I wondered if these might be Temple's notes from the case, but I quickly dismissed that theory. There were far too many names and none that I recognised – certainly no sign of Arthur Blake or Cassandra Webber.

It occurred to me instead that I must be looking at an account of Temple's work with Scotland Yard. I'd only ever visited London a handful of times and the vast majority of the addresses meant nothing to me. But I glimpsed a few familiar names: Kensington and Hackney, for instance, were undeniable.

I continued to flick through the pages, breezing past more lists of names and addresses, until I found a handful of newspaper clippings, tucked carefully into the centre of the journal. There must have been at least a dozen, reporting on various burglaries, assaults and even murders. I skimmed through, setting each delicately aside until one short piece caught my eye. One which bore a name that I most certainly recognised.

Scotland Yard has confirmed the arrest of Violet Parker, an American citizen associated with a string of violent crimes throughout London. Miss Parker, who is understood to be a cousin of the prominent American businessman, Winston Parker, has been returned to America, where she remains in custody. The charges being brought against her date back almost six years, and include bribery, assault and conspiracy to commit murder.

Among the gravest of the crimes of which Miss Parker is accused is the kidnap, torture and subsequent murder of Edward Pearce, a Scotland Yard officer who is reported to have played a crucial role in her arrest.

A date for further proceedings has not been publicly confirmed.

My heart pounding, I read the clipping several times before carefully placing the entire bundle back inside the journal.

What exactly was I looking at? A record of some kind, but of what? My mind began to race. Was this why the very mention of Winston Parker's name seemed to fill Temple with dread? Was he somehow involved in whatever Violet Parker had been doing in London? And what of the shaven-headed brawler? Temple had said that he was a criminal – was one of the names in this journal his?

A knock on the cabin door came like the strike of a hammer. Three sharp cracks against the wood, shattering the silence.

Instantly, panic took hold and I snapped around, my immediate thought that it must be Temple. That he had followed me here. But that made no sense. Why would he knock on his own door?

The knock came again. Three more raps.

I looked frantically around the cabin, but of course there was nowhere to hide. Nowhere to go and the door wasn't locked. If the visitor tried the handle, I would be completely exposed.

But who in God's name could it be? Temple was clearly travelling alone and he hadn't mentioned having any companions aboard. Who would be knocking on his door?

Treading lightly, I crept towards it, and with my hand pressed flat against the wood, looked through the peephole.

Instantly, I recoiled, clapping a hand to my mouth.

It was a woman. She was young, with a slender, freckled face and wild eyes that darted around the corridor. A grey cardigan hung loosely from her skinny frame and strands of ragged, sandy-coloured hair clung to her cheeks.

The warning in the note from my cabin echoed in my mind, along with Travis's description of its courier.

'*She was young. Scruffy-looking thing.*'

It must be her. It didn't matter that there were hundreds of young women aboard the *Endeavour*. In that moment, I was sure that the woman who had been watching us in the cargo hold – the one who had threatened me with the same gruesome fate as Dupont – was now knocking on Temple's door.

As quickly as it had taken hold, my fear gave way to a surge of resentment, a barrage of new and troubling questions racing through my mind. Was she an ally of Temple's? Was that why she was here? Had he recruited her to frighten me away? To shake me loose so that he could pursue the investigation unhindered?

My hand quivered above the door handle. What if I was wrong? Surely, Temple wouldn't have pursued this woman so earnestly in the cargo hold if she was an accomplice. But if that were the case – if she did mean us both real harm – then she wouldn't simply step up to knock on his door.

There was only one way that I would find answers. I had to confront her.

I took a deep breath, grasped the handle and threw open the door. But where the young woman had stood only seconds before, there was now just an empty corridor.

Once again, I began to panic. I had to find her. I had to know why she had come. I sprang from the corridor, sweeping my gaze right and left. There she was, about to round the corner. At the sound of the door opening, she stopped and turned around. Our eyes locked.

For a split second, I was taken aback by her expression. She was a good distance away, but there was no mistaking it. Where I had expected malice and resentment, I saw only surprise.

We stood, each of us apparently as bemused as the other. Then, as if in slow motion, the confusion in her eyes gave way to fear. Already, I knew what was about to happen. But it was too late and she was too far away for me to stop it. Without a moment's further hesitation, she bolted around the corner.

'Wait!' I cried, scrambling to follow her. 'Please!'

I hurried to the end of the corridor, rounding the corner just in time to see her disappear down the Great Staircase. She had a good lead on me already, moving swiftly as she wove around the other passengers in her path. An elderly couple fixed me with a bemused expression as I barged past them, uttering hurried words of apology.

I cursed as I reached the bottom. I had lost sight of her. From here, she could have gone into the restaurant, made for the reading room and smoking lounges or descended further still into third-class.

My mind raced. With every second I hesitated, I was painfully aware that she was extending her lead even further.

The third-class deck. That must have been where she'd gone. Robert Evans surely wouldn't let her barge into the restaurant and there was no chance of her hiding in any of the first-class communal areas. If anything, with her ragged hair and tattered cardigan, she would only make herself even more conspicuous.

I broke into a run, the iron staircase rattling beneath my feet as I descended to the third-class common area. Just as it had the day before, the stillness of second-class vanished in an instant. It was even busier than when Temple and I had first visited, a crowd of people filling the space where the shaven-headed man had been brawling.

I stopped halfway down the stairs, sweeping my gaze around, searching for the woman among the mob. A nearby group of men, each with cards in his hand and a cigarette hanging from his mouth, fixed me with a quizzical look.

There was no sign of her. I thumped the handrail. I had to find her. Had to know what she was doing outside Temple's cabin.

Then there was movement towards the back. A small group was parting to let someone pass. I craned my neck, trying to see who was forcing their way through. I glimpsed the back of a dark head, its owner jostling and shoving through the mass of people, but even from my vantage point on the staircase, I couldn't make them out with any certainty. Then she turned.

It was her. She was a good distance ahead, but there was no mistaking her. For a fleeting moment, she glanced in my direction before vanishing once more.

I sprang down the remaining stairs and plunged into the crowd. Pushing and shoving my way through, I called out for people to let me pass as I fought my way to the back of the room. I was met with irate and disgruntled faces, but there was no time for apologies. All that mattered was catching up with the woman.

She had been making for the far end of the common area, where a corridor would take her towards the labyrinth of third-class cabins. If she disappeared into one, I might as well give up my pursuit then and there. Like a diver breaking the surface, I burst free of the throng of people and vaulted around the corner.

I had barely taken two steps when a bony hand grasped me by the lapels of my coat and, with a strength that I would never have expected, thrust me roughly to the side of the corridor. Before I could react, I was pushed hard against the metal wall and the point of something sharp was pressed into my stomach.

'What do you want?' the woman hissed. She was panting, close enough that I could feel her breath on my face.

I glanced from left to right, but there was nobody in sight. Nobody to call on for help. She had me trapped.

Meeting her gaze, I could finally see just how young she was. She couldn't have been much older than eighteen, with sharp features and wide grey eyes. Those eyes ... They were feral, burning into mine with a palpable hatred.

'What do you *want?*' she repeated, her lips peeling back into a snarl.

'I just …' I was flustered, forcing the words out. 'I just want to understand.'

'Understand *this*.'

I winced, feeling the sharp point twist against my stomach.

'Whatever you think you're doing with that detective, you need to steer clear.' She leaned in closer, her voice dropping to little more than a whisper. 'Or you'll end up dead too.'

'But why—'

It was too late. Without another word, she darted back around the corner into the common area and disappeared into the crowd.

21

My shoulder throbbed as I returned to the officers' quarters with the skeleton key. It would often complain after being subjected to some kind of physical exertion, and my pursuit of the young woman at Temple's door had brought on an all-too-familiar ache.

But it wasn't just the chase that had angered the old wound. In my eagerness to catch her, I had left Temple's journal on his desk and even taken off without locking the door to his cabin. Desperate to ensure that my tracks were well and truly covered, I hurried back, conscious all the while that I mustn't be late to the restaurant. I was anxious to be present for his interview with Harry Webber, and I knew all too well that he would have no qualms about starting without me.

In that moment though, my greatest concern was neither Harry Webber nor the discomfort in my shoulder. It wasn't even Temple's journal and the connection it seemed to suggest to Winston Parker. Truthfully, I was badly shaken by my encounter with the woman.

'You need to steer clear. Or you'll end up dead too.'

Just as I had with the note under my door, I found myself wondering whether this was a genuine threat. Would she really see that Temple and I shared the same fate as Dupont if we continued to pursue the investigation? With a sense of grim resignation, I supposed I would find out soon enough. Threatened or otherwise, there was no chance of calling Temple off the hunt.

Then there was the equally troubling question of the object with which she had threatened me. I hadn't caught a glimpse of it, but it had almost certainly been a blade of some kind. I could still feel where its point had pressed against my skin. Could she have been the one to plant the knife in Arthur Blake's desk? Was that why she was so desperate to ward us off? Could she have raided Blake's cabin and pushed Dupont to his death, leaving the knife as a warning not to follow?

The questions buzzed in my mind. And yet, I still couldn't rid myself of the suspicion that it might all be a ruse. That she might actually be an accomplice of Temple's. There was no questioning that he saw me as a burden. A nuisance to be ignored or disposed of. But would he really go to the lengths of recruiting this woman to threaten me in order to achieve it?

It would certainly explain why she had been knocking on his cabin door, just as it would explain why Temple hadn't received a note of his own.

Or was I being unfair? Letting my own disdain for the detective cloud my judgement? His pursuit of her in the cargo hold had seemed impassioned and his frustration at having failed to catch her intense. It had been an impressive performance, if it was, indeed, a ruse.

As I passed through the officers' quarters, my mind swam with so many troubling possibilities that I barely noticed the commotion in the mess hall. It was only when I heard my own name being discussed that I stopped to investigate.

'Ma'am, if you'll please wait a moment longer,' Wilson was saying, 'I'm sure I can send someone to find Mr Birch.'

'Look, I'm sorry but I really have to leave,' a shrill American voice protested.

I stopped at the door and saw Wilson trying desperately to calm a stout woman of around sixty; she was dressed in a simple grey coat and hat and clutching a black handbag. It took me a moment to realise that I had seen her before.

'Wilson?'

'Tim! Thank God. This is Mrs—'

'Mrs Hewitt,' I said. 'I remember. Are you looking for me, ma'am?'

To Wilson's apparent relief, she bustled over to me, her face pinched in a worried expression.

'You knocked on our door yesterday,' she said. 'With the other gentleman.'

'That's right.'

'You wanted to know about that poor man who fell down the steps.'

'We did. You told us that you hadn't heard anything.'

Mrs Hewitt paused for a moment, breathing deeply and closing her eyes, as though to physically prepare herself for what she was about to reveal.

'My husband wasn't entirely honest with you,' she said, continuing hurriedly before I could reply. 'You have to understand, he didn't mean to cause any trouble. He's an honest man. A good man. But he has a business to look after in New York, you see. I'm sure he wanted only to avoid being involved in anything scandalous—'

'Please, Mrs Hewitt.' I laid a hand on her shoulder. 'There's no need to worry. Why don't we sit down and I'll hear whatever it is that you have to tell me?'

I pulled out a seat for her and asked Wilson to fetch a glass of water. She sat in silence, looking bleakly at the surface of the table.

'I can't stay long,' she said, fidgeting nervously with her handbag. 'Martin doesn't know I'm here.'

'That's fine,' I said, wary that I, too, had an appointment to keep. 'Why don't you start at the beginning?'

Wilson placed a glass in front of her and she took a sip.

'We did hear something,' she said. 'Martin told you the truth. The rain was coming down hard and our porthole was closed, so we couldn't hear much. But there *was* something.'

'What did you hear?'

'It sounded like two people arguing.'

I took a moment to collect myself, a lump forming in my throat.

'Arguing?'

'That's right.' She nodded eagerly. 'Just outside our porthole. I can't tell you what they were saying, but there were raised voices. It certainly sounded to me like they were arguing about something.'

I fought to keep my nerves under control. Two people arguing in the rain. Of course I had to remain critical. Had to be open to the possibility that it might not be connected. But if one of them hadn't been Dupont, who else could it have been? Who else would have had any reason to be out there?

'You couldn't make out anything at all?' I pressed, struggling to keep a slight tremor from my voice. 'Whether they were men or women?'

'No, sir, I couldn't make out as much as that. All I know for sure is that it sounded like two people fighting.'

'Was there nothing else?'

Mrs Hewitt nodded nervously. 'There was, sir. We didn't know what it was at the time, you understand. But we heard something thumping hard against the ground, like something heavy had been dropped.'

'And what then?'

She shook her head. 'The voices ... They went quiet.'

I clasped my hands together beneath the table in an effort to stop them from trembling.

'Do you know what it might have been?' I asked, keeping my voice as level as I could manage.

'We didn't at the time. But after you and the other gentleman knocked on our door and asked about that poor man falling down the steps ...' She broke off and took another sip of water.

'You believe it might have been him?'

She nodded gravely, setting her glass gently upon the table. 'Looking back on it, sir, yes. I do believe we heard him fall.'

I struggled to take it in. If Mrs Hewitt was correct, it seemed Dupont had been arguing with someone before he fell. Could she be mistaken? Might she have simply heard – as she said – something heavy being dropped?

Much as I would like to believe it, I knew that I would only be fooling myself. I thought of Temple's observation when he inspected Dupont's body, of how curious it was for him to have had his back to the companionway when he fell. If that wasn't enough, there was a sincerity in Mrs Hewitt's voice and genuine concern in her expression. She believed what she was telling me.

I glanced over her shoulder and saw Wilson, just out of earshot, casting a quizzical look in our direction.

'What time was this, ma'am?' I asked.

She looked down at the table, fidgeting with the strap of her handbag. 'I know that Martin told you we went to bed at nine o'clock,' she said. 'But it was actually closer to half-past ten. I don't know exactly what time any of this happened, but it can't have been long after that.'

'Could it have been as late as eleven o'clock?'

'No.' She shook her head determinedly. 'No, we hadn't been in bed as long as that when we heard it.'

'So, between half-past ten and eleven?'

'I'd say so. Yes.'

We were both silent as I committed the information to memory, ready to recount it to Temple.

'I have to get back,' she said. 'I told Martin I was only going for a short walk. You wouldn't believe how nervous he's been since all of this happened. Is he going to be in any kind of trouble?'

'I wouldn't have thought so.' Then, in a final attempt to reassure her, I added, 'Thank you, Mrs Hewitt. You've been a great help.'

She thanked me for the water and hurried from the mess.

'What in God's name was that?' Wilson demanded after she'd left. 'She was banging on the door for a good few minutes, demanding to speak to the officer who'd been to her cabin. I thought she'd gone mad until she mentioned your dead Frenchman.'

I didn't answer. Truthfully, I barely even heard him. Mrs Hewitt's story was missing some crucial details but, surely, it could only have been Dupont that she had heard arguing with someone outside her porthole. Was that why he had been outside? Had he wanted to take someone to a secluded place in order to have this argument? Or had he been the one taken aside? He had certainly offended both Arthur Blake and Nathaniel Morris. Perhaps they had wanted to air their grievances somewhere they were unlikely to be interrupted.

And then there was the question of his fall; the loud thumping sound that Mrs Hewitt claimed to have heard. Even if they'd been arguing, wouldn't the person who Dupont was with have tried to help? Surely, they wouldn't have just left him at the foot of the companionway. That was, of course, if he *had* fallen by accident.

I pressed the heels of my palms to my eyes. I already knew exactly which theory I believed to be the most likely. The woman from the cargo hold, having raided Blake's cabin and left a knife as a warning not to follow, must have thrown Dupont to his death, in order to claim the painting for herself.

But then, if that were truly the case, why would she visit Temple's cabin? If her involvement weren't a ruse that he, himself, was coordinating, what possible reason could she have for calling on him?

I sighed, remembering the feral look in her eyes as she'd delivered her second warning. If she was, as I feared, a genuine threat — if she was the one who had pushed Dupont to his death and stabbed a knife into Arthur Blake's desk — I was left sure of only one thing. I wouldn't be granted a third.

22

I'd heard it said that the atmosphere in the *Endeavour*'s restaurant during the evening was that of some exclusive West End club. If that were truly the case, then I liked to think that during the day, it had the feeling of a European veranda.

The glass chandeliers were lit, but it was pale daylight that glittered upon the silverware. The passengers wore blazers and cardigans, while the musicians played a relaxed suite, offering a pleasing background to the sounds of cheerful conversation and clinking crockery. It was a simple task to imagine that one might actually be in a Parisian café or a Milanese courtyard.

Temple was at a table by the window, Robert Evans nodding warily in the detective's direction as I passed him at the door. To my relief, he was alone, Harry Webber having apparently not yet arrived. Before I could approach, however, the maître d' put out an arm, blocking my path.

'Mr Birch. A word, please.'

I stepped closer and he immediately lowered his voice to a whisper.

'Is there any news? About this fellow who's died. The passengers have been even more restless than they were yesterday, demanding to know what's being done about it. I rather hoped there might be something you could tell me.'

I glanced across the restaurant at Temple, wondering how much he might permit me to say. I hadn't known quite what to expect, reuniting with him after his search for the brawler. But if the panic that I had seen during our first encounter was anything to go by, I assumed he must have been unsuccessful. He seemed deep in thought, gazing intently out of the window.

'We're making progress,' I said, hoping that I sounded more convincing than I felt.

'What kind of progress?'

'I think it's best that I don't yet say too much. Mr Temple still has a few further lines of inquiry to—'

'But what do I tell the passengers? What's the captain saying about any of this?'

'Look,' I snapped. 'I'll tell you more as soon I'm able. But for the time being, Mr Evans, you'll have to improvise.'

Evans had taken a step back, his eyes widening at my sudden frustration. Then, realising this was to be the extent of my outburst, he seemed to relax, giving a disapproving shake of his head and returning to the queue of impatient passengers. He muttered something as he turned away, though whatever it was, I suspected I should be glad not to have heard it.

Neither Temple nor I greeted each other as I seated myself at his table. Instead, we sat in silence while my mind still swirled with questions.

'*You need to steer clear. Or you'll end up dead too.*'

Of course, I had to tell him that I had come across the woman again. Perhaps I could even test him and somehow determine if the two of them were working together. The trick would be to do so without revealing where I had been. I had considered a number of different lies on my way to the restaurant, but none of them felt suitably convincing. And it would *need* to be convincing. If he were to discover that I knew about the journal in his desk – that I was confident I had all but confirmed a connection to Winston Parker – I struggled to imagine what he might do. The last thing I needed was to somehow give myself away.

After several minutes of considering my approach, I decided to begin with the visit I had been paid by Mrs Hewitt.

'I have something to tell you,' I said.

'Not right now.'

'Temple, you don't—'

'Not *now*.'

Feeling a surge of resentment, I took a deep breath, determined not to cause a scene with so many passengers on hand to witness it. Under the table, he tapped out his usual infuriating rhythm with his foot.

'Would you stop that?'

'What?' He frowned irritably.

'Your leg,' I muttered. 'Keep it still.'

'Why?'

'You seem agitated. You'll make Webber nervous.'

'I *am* agitated. We're running out of time.'

Realising it would be up to me to put Harry Webber at ease, I flagged down a waiter in a white dinner jacket and asked him to bring tea and coffee.

'Temple,' I urged when the waiter had moved along. 'Listen to me. I've just had a visit from—'

Before I could go any further, a gentleman stopped next to our table. He was squeezed into a tweed suit, his broad shoulders straining against the jacket and a waistcoat buttoned tightly against his chest. He had a square, boyish face, wide blue eyes and neatly brushed hair the colour and texture of straw.

'Mr Birch?' he asked, his eyes settling on me.

I supposed that he must have recognised my uniform. But before I could reply, Temple said, 'Harry Webber?'

Our visitor nodded.

'Please, have a seat.' Temple motioned towards the chair next to mine and Webber sat down cautiously.

'Cassie asked me to come,' he said in a thick West Country accent. 'You must be the detective?'

Temple nodded.

'And you want to know about the fellow who died?'

'That's right.'

'Funny coincidence, isn't it? A man dies in the middle of the Atlantic Ocean and there's a policeman handy to look into it.'

Temple ignored the comment. 'Mr Birch, here, has just sent for some tea and coffee,' he said. 'Shall I have Mr Evans bring you the lunch menu as well?'

'No, thank you. If it's all the same to you, I don't plan to stay.'

Temple nodded. 'Then I'd like to hear your account of the argument that took place here on Monday evening. Between Mr Blake and the deceased.'

'I thought you'd already spoken to Cassie about that?'

'It's helpful to hear the chain of events from everyone's point of view.'

Webber turned to face me. 'What about you? How do you fit into all of this?'

'I'm assisting with the investigation,' I said.

'Observing,' Temple snapped, fixing me with an icy glare that made Webber shuffle uncomfortably in his seat. I clasped my hands together under the table, feeling my knuckles tighten as I wrestled to contain a fresh wave of frustration.

'Monday evening, Mr Webber,' Temple continued. 'Could you please describe what you saw?'

'I wouldn't have thought there was all that much to tell.'

'Then we won't need to keep you long.'

Webber frowned, then shrugged his stocky shoulders. 'I can't see what good it'll do when Cassie's already described it all to you already. But suit yourself. The way I saw it, a little old fellow came over to the table while we were having dinner and asked Arthur if he could speak with him. Without so much as a word, Arthur took him by the elbow, dragged him away to the other side of the room and gave him what looked like the dressing-down of a lifetime.'

'And you couldn't hear what they were talking about?'

'Not a thing. We were sitting there and Arthur took him over there.' Webber pointed out a table against the window, just a few metres away from the musicians' podium, and then towards a wall at the far side of the restaurant.

His account certainly matched his wife's. And now that I could see the distance between the two points for myself, I realised how plausible it was that they wouldn't have been able to hear the argument. Blake and Dupont must have been the best part

222

of twenty yards away. In a full restaurant and with the musicians playing, it would likely have been difficult to hear someone speaking across the table, let alone the entire room.

'When Mr Blake returned,' said Temple, 'I understand that he explained what the argument was about.'

Webber nodded. 'He said something about the older chap being a dissatisfied customer. I didn't ask any more than that. He'd made quite the scene and people were starting to stare. Quite frankly, it was embarrassing.'

'But you hadn't seen this man before?'

'Never in my life.'

'Would you say that Mr Blake was drunk?'

Webber thought for a moment and began to fiddle with one of his cufflinks. It was a fine suit, but he wore it awkwardly. He would occasionally shrug his shoulders, as though trying to readjust the jacket to better fit over his broad frame, or tweak the cuffs, as if he wanted to roll them back over his forearms.

'I wouldn't say Arthur was drunk. He was certainly a little merry, but not drunk.'

'Your wife told us that he had downed a whole bottle of champagne,' said Temple.

Webber snorted. 'It'll take more than that to push Arthur over the edge.'

'He can hold his liquor, can he?'

'You might say that. Arthur can be a real arse when he's had too much, but it takes a lot to get him there.'

'And where might he have honed that particular skill?'

Webber shrugged again. 'He and Evelyn used to throw a lot of parties.'

'Evelyn Scott?'

'That's right.'

Temple paused. 'When we first spoke with Mr Blake yesterday,' he said carefully, 'he failed to mention Miss Scott. We hadn't actually realised he had been married until we spoke with your own wife. Would you say that their divorce is something of a delicate subject?'

Before Webber could answer, Robert Evans appeared with the pots of tea and coffee that I had sent for, along with a bowl of sugar and a little jug of milk on a silver tray. I suspected he must have insisted on serving us personally in order to eavesdrop on our conversation. But if that was the case, he was to have no such luck. We sat in silence while he poured two cups of tea and then some coffee for Temple.

'What you have to understand about Arthur,' said Webber after Evans had left, 'is that he's never been able to accept where he comes from.'

'And where exactly does Mr Blake come from?' asked Temple.

Webber poured a splash of milk into his tea and stirred it, holding the spoon with two sausage-like fingers. 'Perhaps it's not *where* he comes from, as such. It's *what* he comes from.' He sighed. 'To put it very bluntly, gentlemen, Arthur comes from nothing. Evelyn was his opportunity for a life that he's always wanted but never had. Marrying into a wealthy family like the Scotts ...' He shook his head. 'He hides it well, but it's been killing him this past year to have to give it up.'

'And how would you have described his relationship with Miss Scott?'

'I'm not sure it's my place to describe it at all.'

'With respect, Mr Webber,' said Temple. 'I am making it your place.'

Webber was silent, his teaspoon suspended in mid-air. When he eventually spoke, his eyes were fixed upon the tabletop.

'If I'm to be completely honest with you, it always seemed to me like something of a farce. Arthur was marrying into the kind of family that he thought he should naturally belong to while Evelyn got to rebel against her father for trying to pawn her off to some ponce from London. It suited them both for a little while, but I don't suppose it was ever going to last.'

'So what was it that prompted her to press for a divorce?'

'Is that important?'

'Perhaps. Either way, I'd like to know.'

Webber shuffled uncomfortably. 'Look, I'd really prefer not to say. Arthur's far from perfect, there's no denying that. But he's still a friend and ... well, they were only ever rumours.'

Temple fixed Webber with a piercing gaze. I had to admit that even I was intrigued, catching myself leaning forward in my seat. Apparently recognising that the detective wasn't going to give up without a fight, Webber sighed.

'There was talk of another woman.'

'Who?'

'I don't know. Like I said, they were only ever rumours. It all came out at Evelyn's birthday party, as I understand. Arthur was caught ... Well, I'm sure you can imagine what he was supposedly caught doing.'

'At his own wife's birthday?' I asked.

Webber nodded.

'But there's been no word since on who this woman might have been?' said Temple.

'Not that I've heard.'

Temple paused again, apparently to consider this new information.

Could I imagine Arthur Blake being unfaithful? He was certainly more than a little self-centred. But could I believe that he might try to seek out another woman? I glanced towards the bar, his description of Beatrice Walker echoing in my memory.

'To tell you the truth, I couldn't believe my luck . . . She was a pretty thing.'

Yes, I thought. Perhaps I could imagine it.

'Rumours aside,' Temple mused, 'I have to agree with you, Mr Webber. One wonders if their marriage was ever going to last. That is, if Miss Scott was only interested in rebelling against her father.'

Webber hummed into his teacup.

'Of course, she isn't the only one to have rebelled against Mr Scott.'

Webber's teacup froze halfway from the table to his lips, his whole body seeming to have tensed.

'I'm sure I don't know what you mean,' he said. He was suddenly wary, his voice low and measured.

'I understand that you left Mr Scott's employment not so long ago.'

'People take on new jobs. I don't see why that should be important.'

'But I thought that he had been training you to take over his estate.'

'Yes?'

'That's a very specific role, Mr Webber. And quite a significant one, if I correctly understand the extent of Mr Scott's property. You must have known that he thought you were in it for the long term.'

With surprising delicacy, Webber gently returned his teacup to its saucer. 'I don't see how any of this is supposed to be relevant. But if you must know, I never wanted to work for the Scotts. Not for ever, anyway. I'd looked after Frederick's horses before the war and when I came back, I needed a job. He thought it'd be more useful for me to learn how to run the estate than go back to the stables and it can be difficult to find well-paid work out in the country. So I took it.'

'So you learned how to manage Mr Scott's property and land,' said Temple. 'And then used that knowledge to leave and set up your own company?'

'That's one way of looking at it, I suppose.' The irritation in Webber's voice was becoming more palpable by the moment.

'And how's your business faring?'

'It's fine. Look, I really don't think this is what you called me here to discuss.'

Temple leaned back in his seat, a ferocious intensity in his eyes.

'You're right,' he said, sipping his coffee. 'Excuse me. It's my job to ask questions, but I do sometimes get carried away.'

'Of course.' Webber seemed amicable enough, but I suspected that we couldn't afford to push him much further.

'Could you describe your movements on Tuesday?' asked Temple. 'Just as a formality, of course. I'm cataloguing the movements of everyone who came into contact with the deceased.'

'If I must.' Webber settled back in his seat and fiddled with his cufflinks again as he gathered his thoughts. 'Every morning so far, Cassie's woken up early and swum in the pool for an hour or so. I've waited for her to come back, got dressed and then we've come here for breakfast.'

'What time does that tend to be?'

'Nine o'clock, perhaps. Is that important?'

'I'm simply trying to understand the facts.'

'Well, there's not a great deal to understand. There isn't anything much to occupy yourself with on this damned ship. On Tuesday, we went for a walk around the deck after breakfast and then we spent the rest of the morning in the reading room. I went to the gymnasium for a while in the afternoon, and in the evening, we came back here for dinner.'

'What about after dinner? Mrs Webber mentioned an incident with your car.'

'That's right. I walked her back to the cabin and then I went to check on it.'

'I understand it's been damaged.'

Webber shook his head, his brow furrowed and his jaw set, as though he was just receiving the news for the first time. 'There'll be hell to pay when I find out who's responsible. I can promise you that.'

'I can imagine. It does seem a little strange, though,' Temple continued, 'if you don't mind my saying, to have brought the car all this way. Surely it would be easier to take the train to Boston. Or perhaps Mrs Webber's parents could have met you in New York.'

Webber turned away from Temple, glancing instead in my direction. 'Cassie said that she'd told you about her parents. That they don't yet know about our marriage. I'm sure you understand why I feel it so important to make a good first impression. That car is the finest thing I own.'

Temple glared at me across the table, his foot tapping furiously against the ground.

'We have a man looking into the damage, sir,' I said, desperate to break the sudden silence. 'One of our porters. He's a decent fellow and is well acquainted with the goings-on below deck. I'm sure he'll turn up some leads soon enough.'

Webber nodded, though if he was pleased with this news, he didn't show it. 'That's good. Yes. Thank you.'

'Mrs Webber told us that you'd reported the damage to a member of the crew,' I prompted. My gaze was fixed firmly on Webber, in an effort to avoid the hateful look that Temple was still casting me. 'I don't suppose you remember his name? It would be a great help for our man to speak with him.'

'He didn't give it to me,' Webber replied. 'I'm not even sure he was on duty if I'm honest, but he seemed to think he'd seen a woman fiddling with the car shortly before I arrived. So I told him my name and cabin number, and he said he'd find me after an investigation had been carried out.'

Temple and I exchanged a glance, his frustration at my having spoken with Cassandra Webber seemingly vanishing in an instant.

'A woman?' he asked.

'Apparently.'

'Did this man get a good look at her?'

229

'No.' Webber grimaced. 'He said he'd only seen her from a distance. He called out to ask what she was doing, but she took off before he could speak to her.'

A woman in the cargo hold ... Surely it had to be the same one who seemed so intent on putting us off our investigation. We had, after all, been inspecting Webber's car when we caught her observing us. Could that be where her interest truly lay?

I thought again of my suspicion that she might actually be an accomplice of Temple's; this revelation certainly cast doubt on that particular theory. But if she wasn't with him – if she was genuinely the criminal that we were searching for – why would she knock on his cabin door?

'Mr Webber,' I said. 'It's terribly important that we speak with the man you reported this to. Could you at least describe him?'

'Well, I don't think he was an officer. At least, he wasn't dressed like you. He was wearing overalls and a cap. Sounded like he might have had an Irish accent, if that helps at all.'

'And I take it he hasn't been in touch today with any new information?' asked Temple.

'Not yet. Of course, I don't imagine he'll find anything.'

'Why's that, sir?' I asked.

'Well, how many people are on this ship?'

'Just over two thousand.'

'There you have it. How on earth is he going to determine who's responsible in just three days?'

An uncomfortable silence hung over the table, our own investigation suddenly feeling more futile than ever.

'I understand you took an exterior route to the cargo hold,' said Temple.

Webber nodded. 'That's right. You have to go onto the deck and walk a little way around the outside.'

'So you were out in the rain on Tuesday night?'

'Briefly, yes.'

'Which companionway did you use?'

'I'm sorry?'

'There are two exterior companionways between the second- and third-class decks, one on either side of the ship. Which did you use?'

Webber thought for a few seconds. 'The right-hand one.'

I forced a straight face. It was at the foot of the right-hand companionway that Dupont had been found.

'You're sure?' asked Temple, leaning forward ever so slightly.

'Quite sure, yes.'

'And what time would you say that was?'

Webber sighed. 'I couldn't tell you with any certainty. We left the restaurant around ten. I walked Cassie to the cabin and then went to check on the car. I'd say I was back soon after eleven o'clock.'

'But you didn't pass the body?'

'I expect I would remember passing a body.'

'Was there an argument?' I cut in, thinking about Mrs Hewitt. 'Did you see two people arguing? Or maybe hear it?'

A silence fell. Temple's eyebrows knotted. Even Webber looked surprised.

'No,' he said slowly, 'I didn't see any kind of an argument.'

Temple nodded, his foot tapping away beneath the table. 'Would it be safe for me to assume that you and Mr Blake are close?' he asked.

'I suppose so.'

'But I understand you haven't had dinner together since Monday evening.'

'No. Cassie seems to prefer that we dine without him.'

'Isn't that a little strange?'

Webber rubbed his jaw. 'Perhaps a little. She won't say as much, but I wonder if his outburst on Monday bothered her more than she's letting on.'

I frowned. Cassandra Webber certainly hadn't given me the impression of being particularly upset by the argument. I remembered her momentary hesitation though, just before she told us that her husband had planned to see Blake again. Perhaps he and Dupont had left more of an impact than I'd thought.

'You don't suppose she's simply uncomfortable with the idea of dining again with Miss Hall?' asked Temple.

Webber winced. 'She said that she'd told you about that.'

'Is Mr Blake not aware of your history together?'

'There aren't many who are. Vivian always insisted that we keep it quiet. That it wouldn't do for people to know she was with someone like me.' A grimace passed over his face. 'In any case, no. I don't suppose that's what's bothering Cassie. She wasn't pleased by the prospect of spending time with Vivian, but we've made no plans to see her again. It's Arthur, now, that she doesn't want to see.'

'But you *are* meeting him again before we dock?' Temple pressed.

'On Saturday night. As I say, Cassie didn't seem keen, but I insisted. We'll go our separate ways on Sunday and I don't suppose we'll see him again for a while if this commission is as important as he's making it out to be.'

Temple settled back, folding his arms. 'May I see an example of your handwriting, Mr Webber?' he asked.

Webber hesitated. I could almost feel his frustration continuing to build. 'It's not the sort of thing someone tends to just carry around with them.'

'Perhaps you could write something for us, then.'

Webber reached inside his jacket and fetched out a small notebook and a pen, prompting Temple to raise an eyebrow.

'Habit,' he said. 'I haven't been anywhere without a notebook since I opened the firm.' He placed it on the table. 'What would you like me to write?'

Temple shrugged. 'Anything. The days of the week would do.'

Webber scrawled in the book, tore out the page and thrust it roughly into Temple's waiting hand. The detective inspected it for a moment before tucking it into his jacket.

'Why do you need that?' asked Webber.

Temple ignored the question. 'When you and Mrs Webber came here for dinner on Tuesday night, did you happen to see Mr Blake at all?'

'Arthur? No. As I've said, we hadn't arranged to meet again until Saturday. Should I have?'

'He was sitting at the bar. I wondered if you might have seen him as you were leaving.'

Webber shrugged. 'I must have missed him, I suppose. It was busy in here, after all.'

'Of course.' Temple was speaking slowly, watching intently for any glimmer of a reaction. 'He may well have been distracted. He was accompanied by a woman named Beatrice Walker.'

233

'Beatrice?' Webber's voice rose a semitone. 'With Arthur?'

'You know who she is?' I blurted out before I could stop myself.

Webber recoiled slightly, apparently taken aback by my sudden enthusiasm. 'I haven't seen her since Frederick and I parted ways. But yes. She's a friend of Evelyn's. She was there on the night that Arthur and Evelyn finally fell out, if I remember correctly.'

Temple leaned forward, glaring at Webber as though preparing to deliver the killing blow. My own heart was pounding, blood thumping in my ears.

'Mr Webber,' he said. 'We believe that Miss Walker is aboard this ship. But her name isn't recorded in the passenger log. Can you think of any reason why that might be?'

Webber nodded slowly. 'She isn't called Walker any more. I heard she got married, about six months ago. The woman you're looking for is called Beatrice Green.'

23

Without a moment's hesitation, Temple sprang to his feet, snatched his fedora from the table and swept from the restaurant. I murmured a few hurried words of thanks to Harry Webber, who looked just as surprised by the detective's sudden burst of action as I was, and scrambled to follow. Brushing past a disgruntled-looking Robert Evans, we marched together in the direction of the officers' quarters.

Temple's sudden energy was infectious and for a brief, shining moment, all thoughts of Winston Parker, the shaven-headed man and the woman from the cargo hold were gone. To track down Beatrice Walker – Beatrice Green, I should say – and discover exactly what role she might have played in the theft of Arthur Blake's painting was a tantalising prospect.

We barged into the office and lifted the ship's ledger from the shelf. Spreading it open on the desk, Temple scanned the pages, running a finger down the list of names until, at last, he reached *M. and B. Green.*

I breathed a sigh of relief. 'We have her. That's a first-class cabin.'

A small, satisfied smile formed on Temple's lips. 'Good,' he said. 'Lead the way.'

We replaced the ledger and set off, my excitement building with every step.

'I have something else for you,' I said. 'Before we met Mr Webber, Mrs Hewitt came looking for us in the officers' quarters. We spoke with her husband yesterday.'

Temple nodded. 'I remember.'

'It seems that Mr Hewitt wasn't entirely honest with us.' I was speaking quickly, sure that my report would only add to his good mood. 'Mrs Hewitt says that they did hear something when they returned to their cabin from the restaurant. The porthole was closed and the rain was coming down hard, but she's convinced she heard two people arguing outside.'

Temple stopped dead in his tracks. We had reached the Great Staircase and he had already climbed the first two steps, so he was looking down on me as he spoke.

'Arguing?'

'So she says.'

'What time was this?'

'Sometime between half-past ten and eleven o'clock. At the time, Mrs Hewitt thought that she'd heard something heavy being dropped on the ground. But now, she thinks that it's possible she might actually have heard Dupont ...' I paused, my enthusiasm fading as the reality of what I was describing took hold. 'She believes she heard him falling.'

'Or being pushed ...' Temple stared into space, lost in thought as he mentally filed and cross-referenced this new detail. Then, his eyes narrowed. 'I see you've been speaking to more witnesses.'

'She came to me,' I protested. 'I could hardly send her away and you told me yourself not to follow you into third-class.'

'You could at least have shared this straight away.'

'Mr Webber arrived before I had a chance.'

'Is that right? And what, exactly, prevented you from telling me the full extent of your conversation last night with Mrs Webber? I suppose she was the one who told you that her parents were unaware of their marriage?'

'She was. But I failed to see how it could be relevant.'

Temple shook his head. 'Useless,' he muttered.

'*I'm* useless?' Before I could catch myself, my voice suddenly rose. 'I tried to share Mrs Hewitt's story with you the moment I sat down in the restaurant, but you wouldn't hear it! And if you hadn't disappeared to third-class after we spoke with Mr Morris, you would likely have been there to hear her for yourself. So, don't talk to *me* about being useless!' I climbed two steps to bring myself to his level. 'Why is it so important that you find that man? The brawler from yesterday – what crime has he committed that's so terrible you need to spend precious time seeking him out?'

'You don't need to know.'

'Of course I need to know! How am I supposed to help you with this investigation when you insist on keeping me in the dark?'

'You aren't helping,' Temple snarled. 'You are observing.'

We stood, glaring at each other. Passengers parted to walk around us, lowering their voices as they passed. Over Temple's shoulder, I saw a young family who had been about to descend the staircase cast a nervous look in our direction, then change their minds and turn back the way they had come.

I felt my cheeks flush and took a deep breath, trying to wrestle my temper under control. I swallowed back my fury. There were more important things at stake than my wounded pride.

'The note,' I said. 'The one we found in Dupont's cabin. *Saturday. Nine o'clock.* That's why you've asked Mr and Mrs Webber to show you their handwriting, isn't it? You've been comparing it.'

Temple glared at me. Then, apparently recognising the peace offering, he relented. 'Yes.'

'And?'

He shook his head. 'It's no good. Neither of them are a match.'

'You're sure?'

'Yes.' A hint of frustration returned to his voice.

'Might it be Beatrice Green's?'

Without answering, he turned and climbed the staircase, one hand on the sweeping oak banister.

For a moment, I stayed where I was. After hearing from Harry Webber that the woman in the cargo hold had also been seen on Tuesday night, I'd all but abandoned my suspicions that she might be an accomplice of Temple's. But now, after seeing yet again how much he resented our partnership, I couldn't help but wonder ... Perhaps he really would go to such lengths to get rid of me. Perhaps, somehow, they really were working together.

Even the thought of it made me bristle with rage. Surely, it couldn't be true. But if it wasn't, why would she be knocking on his cabin door?

I took another deep breath and reminded myself why I was indulging him. I forced myself to picture Dupont's body, lying on the table. To think of our culprit, roaming the *Endeavour* with a knife in hand. And to remember Raymond, waiting for me in New York. Ready to begin our search for Amelia.

I hurried to catch up with Temple. As I passed a vibrant landscape of the English countryside I thought of Arthur Blake's painting and Nathaniel Morris's words echoed in my ears. *'You'll never find anyone worth their salt who genuinely believes it exists.'*

Surely it must, for someone to have gone to the trouble of stealing it. Blake himself seemed to believe it was genuine. So did Dupont for that matter, to have boarded the *Endeavour* under a false name in order to claim it back.

But the more I thought on it, the more uneasy I felt about our conversation with Morris. If Dupont was truly a con man as he said, could all of this – the painting, the false name, maybe even the sale to Blake – be part of an elaborate scheme? The appointment that he had made on Saturday and the identity of his bankroller were both still shrouded in mystery. Perhaps there had been a plan of some kind. Something that he had intended to put into motion the evening before we docked.

My heart was in my mouth by the time we arrived at Beatrice Green's cabin. It seemed that not even a fresh confrontation with Temple could fully extinguish my anticipation at having found her. But if I had hoped for some clue that might instantly identify her as the young woman who had stalked us in the cargo hold, I was to be sorely disappointed.

Instead, there was a cold, angular quality to the woman who opened the door to cabin 103. She was dressed in a cream blouse and matching skirt, and her pitch-black hair was short, curving around the pearls that hung from her ears into sharp points on snow-white cheeks. Her blue eyes were shards of ice and a glistening string of diamonds rested on a chiselled collarbone.

She regarded us with complete uninterest as Temple explained the purpose of our visit, her lips pursed while she considered his request to come into the cabin. With a slight shrug of her slender shoulders, she stood aside to let us through.

We followed her into a large reception area, with a coffee table and two plush armchairs in its centre. There was a sofa against one wall, beneath a pair of ornate gold lamps, and an oak sideboard against another, with a wine cooler, an empty champagne bottle and a glass vase of pink roses perched on it. As if its size and furnishings weren't luxurious enough, the cabin was even brighter than those which we had visited in second-class. The windows were framed with light silk drapes, pale sunlight filling the room.

I thought of the two-bedroom cottage that Kate and I had made our home and how Beatrice Green's reception area alone might have covered the same space as our lounge and kitchen combined. There was no denying that it was comfortable, but it was far too grand for my taste.

'Nice,' Temple remarked, though the disdain in his voice was clear.

'Michael insists on having the best,' she replied, checking herself idly in a gold-framed mirror on the wall.

'Your husband?'

'That's right. I expect you'd like to speak with him. He isn't here.'

'Actually, ma'am,' said Temple. 'I'd like to speak with you.'

'Oh?' A smile spread across her face as though she was amused by the idea. Settling into one of the armchairs, she crossed one leg over the other, took a cigarette case from the coffee table and lit one. Her fingers were thin and nimble, the nails perfectly manicured and varnished in the same crimson hue as her lips. A diamond glistened on her left hand and I found myself wondering how many times my annual salary it must be worth. It was a far cry from the simple platinum band on Cassandra Webber's finger. Or, indeed, the ring which I had once placed on Kate's.

'And what would you gentlemen like to speak about?' she asked.

I cleared my throat and the detective cast a weary look in my direction. 'This is Mr Birch,' he said.

'I'm one of the ship's officers, ma'am.'

'So I gather. The uniform does somewhat give you away.'

'Ah,' I stammered. 'Of course. Well, I—'

'On Tuesday evening,' Temple interjected, 'you were at the bar with Arthur Blake.'

'Yes.' If Mrs Green was at all concerned by Temple's knowledge of her movements, she didn't show it.

'Would it surprise you to know that while you and Mr Blake were together, an item of significant value was taken from his cabin?'

'How awful,' she said coolly.

'And it would appear that the name with which you introduced yourself to Mr Blake is no longer yours.'

'Are you trying to suggest something, Mr Temple?'

The question was laced with hostility, but she didn't look at all fazed by the interrogation. If anything, she seemed to be enjoying the to and fro. She was still smiling, her hand poised in mid-air as she held the cigarette lazily between two fingers. She brought it smoothly to her lips, sending a thin trail of smoke trickling towards the ceiling.

'I understand that you and Mr Blake have met before,' said Temple.

'Once or twice. Evelyn's a good friend of mine.'

'And yet he doesn't seem to have the faintest idea who you are.'

'That *is* curious, isn't it?'

Temple bristled. 'Could you explain exactly what happened on Tuesday evening?'

'You've just told me yourself that I was at the bar with Arthur.'

'I'd like to hear the full chain of events.'

Mrs Green leaned back in the armchair and took another long drag on her cigarette, relishing the attention of her audience. She gave another little shrug.

'I was having dinner in the restaurant with Michael when I saw Arthur at the bar. We'd just finished dining and were about to return to the cabin, so I told Michael to go on without me. I said I'd seen an old friend and wanted to say hello.'

'You would describe Mr Blake as a friend, then?'

'Arthur's a pig.' The words were said without any particular malice, but I was still taken aback. 'He's an arrogant fool who

242

married my friend for her money and turned her into a joke. You wouldn't believe the things that were said behind Evelyn's back when she brought him home – the penniless artist who thought that he was high-class. I saw him drinking alone and I wanted to hear just how miserable he'd been since she sent him away. I sat down next to him and said, "It's Beatrice." He looked confused at first, staring at me with those puerile eyes of his. I supposed we hadn't seen each other since Michael and I were married, so I said, "Beatrice Walker." And do you know what he did? He put on the smug, disgusting smile that he used to charm Evelyn, said how pleased he was to see me and asked if he could *buy me a drink*.'

She dragged out the last four words, savouring the chance to show us Blake's true colours. She never raised her voice. She didn't need to. Her complete and utter disdain for him was woefully apparent.

I almost groaned aloud. There we were, chasing down the master criminal who had kept Blake occupied while his cabin was raided, when the reality was that he had simply been too foolish to realise that he actually knew the woman sitting next to him.

'I'm told that Mr Blake and Miss Scott had a happy marriage,' said Temple. 'For a while, at least.'

'No.' Beatrice Green waved the idea away. 'We all knew that Evelyn only brought him home to upset Frederick. In the end, she hated him just as much as the rest of us did.'

'Did she tell you so?'

'She didn't need to. The moment she'd married him, you could see that she regretted it. That's just what Arthur does, though. He charms and he flatters. But as soon as Evelyn let him in, he was drinking her wine, spending her money ... Everyone knew he was no good for her. When he eventually made such a fool of himself – as we all knew he would – that she cut him loose, I told her it was the best thing she'd ever done.'

I thought again about the rumours that Harry Webber had shared with us in the restaurant; that Blake had been caught with another woman. If I had struggled to believe he was capable of such behaviour, this account certainly helped to make it more plausible.

'Perhaps not everyone hated him,' said Temple. 'I understand he has a good relationship with Vivian Hall.'

'Vivian wanted someone to talk to about her art. That's all. And besides, she's an odd case. She was only ever in Evelyn's circle because her father's close to Frederick. If any of the rest of us had struck up that kind of relationship with Arthur, Evelyn would never have stood for it.'

Temple considered this for a moment. 'Would you say that Mr Blake was drunk? When he failed to recognise you, that is.'

'I'd say that he's a self-centred moron,' Mrs Green replied. 'But yes, I suppose he might have been a little drunk. He always did have a habit of drinking too much.'

'Then why stay if he had no idea who you were? He told us that you sat at the bar with him for a couple of hours.'

'To see how long it took him to remember me. I wanted to see the look on his face when the penny dropped and he realised who he was speaking to. But it never happened. He just kept smiling and buying me drinks, telling me he was an artist on his way to earn a large commission in America. When I was certain he wasn't going to recognise me, I left. It was disgusting.'

I pictured them sitting at the bar, sipping cocktails together. Arthur Blake, too self-centred to realise he had already met the woman he thought he was charming, while Beatrice Green yearned hungrily to feed on a year's worth of misery. I wasn't sure which of them appalled me more.

'What time was it when you left the restaurant?' asked Temple.

'Around eleven o'clock, I suppose.'

'And did you go straight back to your cabin?'

'Where else would I go?'

'Answer the question, Mrs Green.'

She smiled again, as though enjoying Temple's growing frustration. 'Yes. I came straight here.'

'Is there anyone who can verify that?'

'I walked back alone, if that's what you mean. Michael was still awake when I arrived, though. He'll be able to tell you what time that was.'

Temple nodded, apparently satisfied. I, meanwhile, was frantically trying to organise the chain of events in my mind. To determine whether she would have had a chance to raid Blake's cabin after leaving him at the bar. If, perhaps, she could even have slipped a steak knife into her handbag before she left.

'And where is your husband now, Mrs Green?' Temple interrupted my train of thought.

'Who knows?' She played with the diamonds around her neck. 'He mentioned something about listening to a piano recital, I think.'

'Do you often spend time apart?'

'Sometimes. We had something of a row this morning. I suppose he's decided to go and recover his composure.'

'May I ask what this row was about?'

'Nothing, really. He's been very uptight these last few days and I decided this morning that I'd had enough. I said if it was business that was agitating him so much, he could worry about it elsewhere. It seems that's exactly what he's decided to do.'

'You don't sound overly concerned.'

She shrugged. 'Michael can be hot-headed sometimes. He just needs a little time to calm down. He'll be fine when he comes back.'

Temple pondered that for a moment. 'Is there an example of your handwriting that I could see, Mrs Green?' he asked.

'What an odd request.'

'I'm afraid I can't leave until I've seen it.'

She seemed to consider, before waving her cigarette towards the neighbouring armchair. 'Pass me that jacket, will you?'

Temple showed no sign of obliging, so I lifted a pinstriped jacket from the back of the armchair and delivered it to her waiting hand. Stubbing out her cigarette, she reached into an inside pocket and withdrew a small stack of business cards, followed by an ornate fountain pen.

'What should I write?'

'Nothing of too much consequence. The days of the week, perhaps.'

She held up the little business card, pinching it between her thumb and forefinger, and cast Temple a droll look.

'Just a couple of days, then,' he said. 'Saturday and Sunday will suffice.'

246

With a quick flourish on the back of the card, she handed it over and settled back in her chair, watching Temple closely.

Peering over his shoulder, I was quietly optimistic, but one glance at her handwriting crushed my hopes. The writing on Dupont's note had been punctuated with exaggerated flourishes and sweeping calligraphy. Beatrice Green's, by comparison, was neat and refined. There was no chance of a match.

With a grimace, Temple pressed the business card into my hand. Turning it over, I saw printed in black ink above a London address:

Michael Green

Green & Carter Associates

'I don't suppose you'll tell me why you wanted to see that?' she asked.

The detective didn't answer.

'What was taken from Arthur's cabin?' she tried instead. 'This "item of significant value".'

'Mr Blake didn't mention it to you?' Temple replied.

'No.'

'Then I ought not to say.'

She shrugged and lit another cigarette.

'I can tell you that a gentleman boarded the ship in the hope of buying this item from Mr Blake,' said Temple. 'Before we reach New York. You might have heard about him. He was found dead yesterday morning, having fallen down a flight of steps while you and Mr Blake were at the bar. Quite a coincidence, wouldn't you say?'

She flashed an unpleasant smile. 'We're in it together then, are we?'

'A man has died, Mrs Green.' There was a hint of ice in Temple's voice. 'And you are speaking with an inspector from Scotland Yard. You might decide to take this a little more seriously.'

'It's rather difficult to take you seriously when you insist on asking such absurd questions. What exactly is it that you're suggesting? That I kept Arthur occupied while this mysterious gentleman raided his cabin? And what then? That I threw him down a flight of steps?'

Temple glared at her. 'What exactly *is* your reason for travelling to New York, Mrs Green?' he asked through gritted teeth.

'It's for Michael, I suppose.' She sighed, smoke flowing from her lips like silk. 'I'm insisting we go to Macy's, of course, and we have tickets for a Broadway show. But it's really his trip to the Art Fair.'

My pulse quickened. 'The New York City Art Fair?'

'That's it. Michael goes every year, hoping to pick up something rare for his collection.' She rolled her eyes, as though her husband's hobby was utterly ridiculous.

Temple didn't respond straight away, but I could tell from the way he straightened up, as though preparing for another approach, that even he saw this as a significant revelation.

'Strange,' he remarked. 'The gentleman who had hoped to retrieve Mr Blake's item was also travelling to the Art Fair.'

'I would imagine that he is one of a great many aboard this ship. They do say it's the largest art auction in the world.'

Temple's nostrils flared.

'This item,' she continued. 'The one that Arthur's lost. It's a painting, of course.'

'You said that Mr Blake didn't mention it to you.'

'He didn't.' She smirked. 'But a penniless artist is travelling to New York with a mysterious item on the same week the largest art auction in the world is in town. Please, Mr Temple. I thought *you* were supposed to be the detective.'

Temple was seething. As I watched him, I couldn't help but think nervously of the previous morning, when he had been denied permission to see Dupont's body and had stormed from Captain McCrory's cabin. I wondered how close I might be to seeing a repeat performance.

'What do you know about your husband's work, Mrs Green?' he growled. 'When he isn't collecting paintings, that is.'

'He works for the bank.'

'In London?'

'That's right.'

'And what sort of people does he deal with?'

'Michael doesn't talk business with me,' she said plainly.

'I'm sure.'

Her smile faded just enough to suggest that the detective was straying into unwelcome territory.

'What does that mean?'

He shrugged.

'Michael doesn't keep things from me, if that's what you're suggesting.' She leaned forward a fraction.

'I think your husband keeps a great many things from you.'

'You're embarrassing yourself, Mr Temple.' Her smile had now completely vanished, her voice less playful. As I watched the exchange, I began to grow nervous that Temple's frustration might truly be getting the better of him. That he was beginning to push her a step too far.

'Denis Dupont,' he said. 'He's a colleague of your husband's. But it's not a name that I imagine you will have heard before?'

Mrs Green stayed silent, glaring at Temple with pursed lips. I suspected that I, myself, was just as confused. What was he talking about? How could he know that Dupont was a colleague of Michael Green?

'Or Mr Fisher?' he continued.

'Peter Fisher,' said Mrs Green triumphantly. 'Michael's introduced me to him on several occasions.'

'They work together at the bank, do they?'

'Where else would they work?'

Temple ignored the question. He was on the offensive, pressing home his advantage. 'And how would you describe Mr Fisher? As I understand it, he's an elderly French gentleman.'

She shook her head, a perplexed expression on her face. 'Peter must only be forty, if that. I'd never seen the French gentleman before.'

'You'd never seen him before? When did you *first* see him?'

'He was here on Tuesday morning.'

Any concerns I'd had about Temple's attack quickly vanished. I saw the path that he had led Beatrice Green down and the revelation at its end. Dupont had been here. He had come to see Michael Green.

'What time?' There was a sense of urgency in Temple's voice. 'On Tuesday morning. What time was the Frenchman here?'

'I'm not sure. Eleven o'clock. Perhaps eleven-thirty.' She started to fidget nervously with her diamonds, the confidence with which she had taunted him just moments ago all but gone. She had given too much away, and she knew it.

I could almost *sense* Temple's excitement. Truthfully, it was difficult not to share it. If he had been here at eleven o'clock, Dupont must have come to see Michael Green just a few hours after visiting the restaurant and paying Robert Evans for Blake's cabin number.

'And what did he and your husband speak about?'

'I don't know. Michael took him into the corridor and closed the door.'

'You heard nothing at all?'

'No.'

'Even though they were just outside?'

Mrs Green glanced away, her nimble fingers still fiddling with the necklace. 'This is appalling,' she muttered.

'Just tell me the truth and I'll leave you be.'

'But who is he?' she demanded, a little confidence returning to her voice. 'This Frenchman? Why are you so interested in him? Why does it matter that he was here on Tuesday?'

I wasn't sure if Temple paused for dramatic effect or if he was simply deciding which details to share, but when he spoke, what little colour had been in Beatrice Green's face to begin with faded away completely.

'He's the man who was found dead yesterday morning.'

She looked away, the bravado now completely gone.

'Whatever Monsieur Dupont came to discuss with your husband on Tuesday morning,' said Temple, 'I will uncover it. If I discover not only that he was involved in Dupont's death, but that there is information which you, Mrs Green,

251

have kept from me, I can promise the repercussions will be as severe for you as they will for him.'

'You'll make sure of it, I suppose,' she spat.

'If I must.'

'Temple—' I murmured.

'They were arguing.' She snapped round to face him, her eyes cold and fierce. 'Is that what you want to hear? They were arguing.'

'About what?'

'I don't know.'

'Mrs Green—'

'I don't know! Michael had closed the door. I couldn't hear what was being said, but his voice was raised. Whatever this gentleman had said to him ...' She shook her head, and for a split second, I thought I saw something new in her expression. I'd almost have said she looked frightened. 'Whatever it was, Michael didn't like it. When he came back inside, he was furious.'

24

The reading room was one of the *Endeavour*'s more lavish spaces. It was dotted with wicker tables, all of which bore large vases of snowy white roses and were carefully laid with gleaming crockery for afternoon tea. Plush cream sofas and armchairs embroidered with floral gold patterning lined the walls, while broad windows overlooked the ocean, framed by the same velvet curtains we had just seen in Beatrice Green's cabin.

Open exclusively to first-class passengers, it was a retreat from some of the more raucous parts of the ship, perhaps for a few hours of quiet reading or to write letters and postcards to relatives at home. More often than not, the only sounds would be the rustle of paper, the clink of china teacups in saucers and the gentle ticking of a gold-faced clock.

A pianist in a charcoal suit and tie sat at a baby grand in the far corner of the room. His hands danced over the polished keys of an oak-coloured Steinway, a look of intense concentration on his face.

'That's him,' said Temple.

We had managed to procure a table at the back of the reading room, furthest from the pianist. Every other seat was occupied by a few dozen finely dressed ladies and gentlemen, all listening to the recital. That is, almost every other seat. Temple nodded towards a gentleman who was alone at a table set for four.

My first impression was that Michael Green was older than his wife. While I had guessed that she might be nearly thirty, he was almost certainly closer to fifty. His black hair was slicked back with oil and although his features were razor sharp, the slight sag of his cheeks suggested a man well acquainted with the comforts a banker's salary could afford. A thin moustache topped a small, pursed mouth and he wore an immaculate navy-blue suit, with a gold-striped tie that presumably showed his membership of some exclusive club or society. His dark eyes were fixed intently on the pianist and he was tapping his fingers on the table in time with the music.

Temple rose to his feet, steel in his eyes.

'Not yet,' I hissed, catching his arm. 'Not with all these people watching. Wait until the performance is over.'

'You must be joking,' he said loudly, earning a number of disapproving glances.

'Just wait,' I urged. 'Please ...'

Temple glanced around the room, weighing up the situation. The pianist had continued playing, but several members of his audience were now casting stern looks in our direction. 'How long?'

'Not long,' I whispered. 'Just for a few minutes.'

Temple settled back into his seat, jaw squared and hands clasped tightly on the table in front of him. His gaze was fixed unwaveringly on Michael Green.

'How did you know?' I whispered.

He frowned. 'Know what?'

'About Michael Green. Before we even spoke with Mrs Green, you seemed to know both that he was a banker and that he worked with Monsieur Dupont.'

'That's not true.'

'So I'm supposed to believe that it was all a bluff?'

'No, it wasn't—'

A woman at a nearby table turned from the pianist and fixed Temple with a glare that forced him to drop his voice to a murmur.

'It wasn't entirely a bluff. Last year, a London banker named Michael Green was investigated by Scotland Yard for fraud; an enormous tax-evasion scheme. He was never prosecuted, but we've kept an eye on him.'

'What for if he wasn't prosecuted?'

'We were sure he'd done it. Honestly, there have been several operations over the years which we think he had a hand in. But Green's a careful man and we've never managed to make them stick.'

I glanced over at Michael Green, his fingers still twitching in time with the music.

'You think this is the same man?'

Temple nodded. 'His business card.'

I thought of the card on which Beatrice Green had provided a sample of her handwriting. It still lay in my pocket, beside Amelia's yellow ribbon.

'You recognised the name of his firm,' I said.

'I did. But there was more. The Michael Green that the Yard has been investigating is a well-known collector of fine art.'

'So when Beatrice Green told you that her husband was a banker on his way to the New York City Art Fair ...'

'That confirmed it.'

I gave a satisfied nod. 'What about Monsieur Dupont? And Peter Fisher?'

'I didn't know that he'd be connected to either of them.'

'So why ask Mrs Green about them?'

'I took a chance. It paid off.'

The woman who had glared at us flashed another dark look, but I barely noticed. I couldn't deny that I was genuinely impressed.

'Where does this leave us?' I whispered. 'We know that Monsieur Dupont visited Mr Green on Tuesday morning, just a few hours after he'd been to the restaurant and paid Robert Evans for Mr Blake's cabin number. And we know that Peter Fisher is not only a real name, but that it belongs to a business partner of Mr Green's.'

'Go on,' Temple prompted.

'It seems to me the question is why Monsieur Dupont would stay in Mr Fisher's cabin. Why did he visit Mr Green on Tuesday morning? And what was it that Mrs Green heard them arguing about in the corridor?'

'I can't yet say why he would take Fisher's name. But we might already be able to explain why Dupont would visit Green.'

I stopped and thought for a moment, mulling over the details as the pianist began to play a new piece. It was a great deal livelier than the melancholy tune before, causing Michael Green to tap energetically on the tabletop.

'Could he be a client of Monsieur Dupont's?' I asked.

'Possibly.'

'You think there might be more to it?'

'Almost certainly.'

I tried to recall everything we had learned about the art dealer. Temple watched me, an expression of vague amusement on his face. Then the answer struck me like a bolt of electricity.

'You think he's Monsieur Dupont's bankroller.' I struggled to keep the excitement from my voice. 'I've got it, haven't I? You think Dupont was getting his money from Green!'

Temple nodded. 'A serious collector like Green is likely to have a private broker.'

'And it would make sense to ensure that such a broker remained in business. Even to the extent that he might provide the capital to set up a new gallery after the first was bombed during the war.'

'Perhaps.'

'And the note,' I said. 'The note in Monsieur Dupont's cabin. *Saturday. Nine o'clock*. What if that was written and given to him by Mr Green? What if Dupont was planning to steal the painting from Mr Blake and deliver it to Green before we dock?'

'It's possible. But we already agree that if the painting were to go missing, Blake would surely assume Dupont's involvement. So, if he did steal it for Green, we must still answer the question of why he would do it on Tuesday, allowing Blake four more nights to investigate the theft before we arrive in New York.'

The pride that I felt in my theory vanished as quickly as it had materialised. Temple's logic was undeniable. Just moments ago, we had felt on the cusp of a significant breakthrough. Now, we seemed as far from the truth as when we had first inspected Dupont's body.

Through the broad windows, I watched as the sun began to brush the horizon. Within just a few short hours, our second day would be over. I looked again at Michael Green, hoping dearly that his might be the interview with which we could lay this investigation to rest.

'Listen to me,' Temple murmured. 'I know you've had questions for the others. But when I speak to this man, you mustn't intervene.'

I readied myself to protest, but his earnestness caught me off guard. This wasn't about me, I realised. Michael Green genuinely made him nervous.

Before I could respond, the pianist played his final note and, to a round of polite applause, took a small bow. Without a second's hesitation, Temple sprang from his seat and wove his way through the room, leaving me to scramble clumsily behind him. In an instant, the audience still gently applauding, he was at the banker's table.

'Mr Green,' he said.

Michael Green glanced up with a cold expression that reminded me distinctly of his wife. The similarity would have been comical if there wasn't such utter disdain in his eyes.

'Do I know you?'

Temple sat down in one of the wicker chairs and placed his fedora carefully on the table. 'James Temple. I represent Scotland Yard.'

'You're a long way from home. Have we met before?'

'No.'

The banker looked at Temple, gave a shrug and then tilted his head in my direction. 'Isn't he going to sit down as well?'

I was standing awkwardly by the table, my officer's instincts restraining me from sitting beside a passenger without an invitation. Temple flashed me a scowl that barely lasted a second but gave me all the incentive I needed to pull out a chair and sit between them. I opened my mouth to introduce myself, but held back, Temple's warning not to intervene still ringing in my ears.

'I have some questions,' said Temple. 'Specifically, about your whereabouts on Tuesday evening.'

Green didn't answer. Instead, he glanced over at the pianist, who was now shaking hands with a few admiring members of his audience.

'A talented young man,' he said. 'Did you know he's Russian? It seems some of the best musicians are coming from Russia, these days. Probably not your sort of thing though, Mr Temple. I suppose a young fellow like you is more interested in jazz.'

'Tuesday evening, Mr Green,' Temple repeated. His voice was perfectly level, every syllable apparently being carefully considered. 'I'd like to know your whereabouts.'

Green looked hard at Temple, the makings of a smile just visible in the corners of his thin lips. He breathed a dramatic sigh, clasped his hands together on his lap and leaned back in his chair.

'Tuesday evening, you say? If you must know, Mr Temple, I had dinner in the restaurant with my wife, as I have done every evening this week. On Tuesday, as I recall, we had the beef. You ought to try it.'

He spoke confidently, with the air of a man who was far too aware of his own authority, and a cut-glass accent. It conjured long-forgotten memories of the officers' training academy at Sandhurst and the brash young men who had arrived fresh out of Eton and Harrow, eager to receive their military instruction.

But Green wasn't a military man. I had never truly been at home in the army, but after four years at war, you begin to recognise certain qualities in a fellow solider. It was the banker's hands that betrayed him. They were too soft. The skin was smooth and the fingernails were perfectly manicured. I caught sight of a heavy Omega glinting on his wrist. This was evidently a man who had known nothing but luxury throughout his life.

'I'm sure you will have heard that a passenger was found dead yesterday morning,' said Temple.

'Of course. Gossip spreads quickly on these ships. You'll be hard-pressed to find anyone who hasn't heard about him.'

'You knew this man personally, though.'

'I'm sure I don't know what you mean.'

Before Temple could go any further, Green snapped his fingers at a passing waiter.

'Tea,' he said.

The young man began to offer refreshments for Temple and me, but the detective waved him away irritably.

'Allow me to refresh your memory,' he said, after the waiter had moved along. 'This gentleman was an art dealer named Denis Dupont. I'd be surprised to learn that you didn't know him, because on Tuesday morning, at around eleven o'clock, he came to your cabin.'

A silence hung over the table.

'I see you've spoken with my wife,' said Green, frustration in his voice.

Temple nodded. 'Dupont was your private broker, wasn't he?'

'He was, yes. And he was rather good, if you must know. Thanks to him, I have several extraordinary pieces in my collection.'

'I'm sure. I assume that's why he visited you on Tuesday – to discuss an acquisition of some kind?'

'I suppose Beatrice couldn't tell you that part, could she?' There was suddenly a scathing tone to Green's voice. 'Yes, we were discussing business. A new acquisition.'

'What were you acquiring?'

'I hardly see how that's any of your business, Mr Temple.'

'I'd say that it's entirely my business. Twelve hours after that conversation, Dupont was killed. And just a moment ago, you tried to lie to me about even knowing him.'

Green settled back in his seat as the waiter returned with tea, milk and sugar on a gleaming silver tray. A china cup and saucer was placed delicately on the table.

I braced for Temple to insist upon an answer to his question the instant the waiter moved along, but the assault didn't come. He sat patiently, his foot tapping beneath the table as Green poured and stirred his tea. There was no sign of the ferocity with which he had grilled Nathaniel Morris and Green's wife. Of course, I had known already that he wanted to treat this particular interview with care. But only now, as he seemed to wait for the banker to be ready to continue, did I realise just how nervous this man truly seemed to make him.

Green turned to me with a pained expression. 'I suppose Mr Temple here has told you all about the various accusations that Scotland Yard has made against me?'

I shuffled, painfully aware that Temple's piercing gaze had now settled on me. 'He's ... mentioned them, sir. Yes.'

'They've been trying for years to accuse me of all manner of terrible crimes. I will admit though –' he cast Temple a wry smile – 'that this is the first time anyone has come to speak to me about a dead body. You must be a bright fellow, to have become a ship's officer. I'm sure you understand, with Mr Temple's eagerness to see me convicted of *something*, why I might feel the need to exercise a little caution.'

I found myself staring blankly at Green and then Temple, both watching me expectantly.

'The painting, Mr Green,' Temple said. 'What was Dupont acquiring for you?'

'I don't know.'

'Don't play games with me—'

'Nobody is playing games with you, my good man. Do keep your composure.' Green paused a moment and lifted his teacup delicately to his lips before continuing. 'Dupont telephoned my office in a frenzy, around this time last week, and told me that there would be a painting of immense value travelling on board this ship.'

'But he didn't tell you what it was?'

'I asked, of course. But he insisted that I wouldn't believe him even if he told me. All he would say was that I had to see it for myself. That it was rarer and more valuable than anything he had brought me before. He said that if I could help him aboard, he would be able to negotiate its acquisition.'

Seymour's words echoed in my memory. *'If that painting ever turned out to be real, it'd be worth an absolute killing.'*

'So that's what you did,' said Temple. 'You helped him aboard under the name Peter Fisher.'

'Good old Peter,' replied Green, as if speaking to himself. 'I went at once to buy Dupont a ticket. At such short notice though, virtually every cabin was already taken. Peter and I often meet at the Art Fair and, by chance, he was due to travel on this very ship. I called in a favour and convinced him to let me buy his ticket, so that Dupont could have his cabin.'

'If you don't mind, sir,' I said, 'this seems like an extraordinary amount of effort, considering Monsieur Dupont wouldn't tell you what the painting was.'

'It was a curious situation,' Green admitted. 'But if a career in finance has taught me one thing it's to find a broker you can trust. Dupont was exceptionally good and he's delivered on many occasions in the past. I trusted his judgement and I had other matters requiring my attention, so once I had arranged passage for him, I decided that we would reconvene in New York.'

'What about on Tuesday morning?' Temple pressed. 'He must have had something to say if he came to your cabin.'

Green's small shrug reminded me again of his wife. 'He came to let me know that things were progressing. He said he had a plan and that the negotiation of the painting should be complete before we arrived.'

'And even then, you didn't ask him what it was?'

'Of course I asked. But he just kept saying, "Wait and see. You won't believe me. You need to *see* it."'

'Is that why you were arguing with him?'

'I'm sorry?'

Temple gave a small smile. 'You're right, Mr Green,' he said. 'Your wife couldn't say exactly what the two of you were discussing. But she could tell us that she heard raised voices.'

'That woman.' The grimace that passed over Green's face was gone in an instant, giving way to a slick, self-assured smile. 'That's right. I told him I didn't want to wait – I just wanted to know what the damn thing was – but he refused to tell me. I'm not accustomed to being kept in the dark and I'm ashamed to say that I somewhat lost my temper.'

'And that was the last time you saw him,' Temple finished.

Green leaned back in his chair and spread his hands wide. 'I can promise you, gentlemen, nobody is more troubled by any of this than I am.'

Temple mulled this over for a moment while Green sipped his tea.

'What would you say, Mr Green,' he asked, 'if I were to tell you that I knew what painting Dupont was trying to acquire for you?'

'I would say that you must have more of an aptitude for your job than a great many of your colleagues at Scotland Yard.'

I saw Temple force back a scowl. 'Dupont approached the owner of the painting on Monday evening. But it was made very clear to him that it wasn't for sale. What plan could he possibly have made to acquire it by Tuesday morning?'

'I wish I knew. All he would tell me was that things were moving in the right direction.'

'That seems a little strange, wouldn't you say? To come to you with such a vague message?'

Green shrugged. 'He was always a little eccentric.'

'Is that so?'

'You clearly haven't met many artists, Mr Temple. If you ever come across one who isn't a few sticks short of a bundle, you'll have to let me know.'

I had to concede that Michael Green was right. I hadn't met a great many artists, but I thought of Arthur Blake and Nathaniel Morris and was forced to agree.

'Dupont could never leave well enough alone,' he continued. 'Last year, during another acquisition, he wanted to let me know that the price we discussed had been agreed by the seller. A simple message, you might think. Certainly not one that needed to be urgently delivered. In any case, I was in a meeting with a client, so I couldn't answer the telephone. Still, he called my office every fifteen minutes for nearly two hours until my secretary finally pulled me out to speak with him.'

'You would say he was obsessive, then?'

'I would say he was an old man. He would fret about things. It was just his way.'

Temple nodded, apparently satisfied. 'Let's return to Tuesday night.'

'I've told you already. On Tuesday night, I had dinner in the restaurant with my wife.'

'What about after dinner? I understand that you left the restaurant alone.'

'Indeed. Beatrice had apparently seen a friend at the bar, who she wanted to say hello to. I had some paperwork in the cabin to look over, so I left her to it.'

'And you went straight back?'

'Yes. Straight back.'

'What time did your wife return?'

Green drummed his fingers on the table. 'Around eleven, I suppose. Maybe a little later.'

'And I assume there's nobody who can verify that you spent the entirety of that time alone in your cabin?'

Green adopted a smug smile. 'You'll just have to take my word for it.'

'That presents me with something of a problem, Mr Green. You see, while you were, by your own account, alone in your cabin, not only did Dupont fall to his death, but the painting that he was hoping to acquire for you was stolen from its current owner. I'm sure you can see why that makes it somewhat difficult to believe that you knew nothing about it or, indeed, Dupont's plan to acquire it.'

'As I've said, I'm afraid you'll just have to take my word for it.'

Temple's nostrils flared, his eyes fixed on his opponent. 'But of course, Mr Green, you weren't just a client of Dupont's.'

Green tilted his head slightly, suddenly curious.

'You were a benefactor. After his London gallery was bombed, you gave him the money to set up in Bath. Isn't that right?'

Green hesitated. Just for a moment, but it was a moment too long. 'I may have provided a small contribution.'

'Out of charity?'

'I'd see it as more of an investment.'

'Of course. As you've said, Dupont was a skilled broker. I would imagine it was important to you that he remained in business. But then again, you've also just said that he was an old man. That he would fret and worry about things.'

'Your point?'

The detective shrugged. 'Only that some might think it strange for you to have supported him when, by your own account, it sounds as though he may have been nearing the end of his career. Especially so, when he planned to re-establish himself in Bath of all places. Would it not have made more sense to find a new broker in London?'

Green sat in silence for several seconds. Then he rose with a creak from the wicker chair, patting the creases from his jacket. 'Really, Mr Temple, if these are the sort of questions that you insist on asking, I think our time may be up.'

'We're not finished, Mr Green.'

'I think we are. Dupont was a valuable associate, and his death has come as a terrible blow. I will quite happily answer questions that might help clear up any mystery surrounding his unfortunate demise – and, indeed, if you truly know what it is, to find the painting he was acquiring for me – but I don't see how this can be at all relevant.'

He shook his head, a pained expression on his face. 'It's clear to me now that you really are no different to any of the others at Scotland Yard, Mr Temple. This was never about Dupont. It's simply another attempt to accuse me of some terrible crime that, one day, I dearly hope you will see I cannot have committed.'

He made to leave, striding towards the door. The sun had now completely set, and his way was lit by lanterns that glowed warmly on each table. But after a few steps, he turned back to face us, an unpleasant smile on his lips.

'Of course,' he said, 'if you should find that painting, I would very much like to see it. Perhaps I'll even give you a small reward. But I shan't hold out too much hope.'

And with that, he was gone.

25

I'll admit to being slightly relieved when Michael Green left us in the reading room. It had been like watching a sparring match more than an interview, with Temple managing a couple of times to catch him off guard, but Green ultimately parrying and sidestepping most of his advances.

Even after he'd left, the effect that he'd had on Temple was clear. The detective's foot beat furiously against the floor, his eyes fixed on the wicker chair in which his opponent had sat.

'Where to now?' I asked.

It took him several seconds to answer, and for a brief moment, I wondered if he might not have heard me. When he did finally speak, he spat out two words like a mouthful of sour wine.

'Vivian Hall.'

'Is that really necessary?' I protested. 'She's been warned of the danger and I've told you all that I learned when she visited me last night. What more do you hope to hear from her?'

'Miss Hall could have told us straight away who Beatrice Walker was, if you'd had the sense to ask. And we don't yet have a handwriting sample from her. So, yes, it's entirely necessary that I speak with her myself.'

The thought of him interviewing Vivian Hall when he was in such a foul mood was unsettling, but I knew better than to protest. Whether Temple genuinely felt a need to interview her or simply wanted to restore some of his confidence after being shrugged off by Michael Green, I couldn't say. Better to let him meet her and do my best to ensure that his frustration didn't get the better of him.

We rose from our seats and he led me from the reading room. After two days of touring the ship together, Temple was evidently beginning to find his bearings. He didn't once need me to call out directions as we returned to the Great Staircase and navigated the corridors that made up the first-class deck.

He'd certainly felt confident enough to visit third-class on his own, in his search for the shaven-headed brawler. Truthfully, with all that had taken place, from meeting Webber and the Greens to my encounter with the woman, I'd barely had a chance to consider him, nor the enlightening contents of Temple's cabin.

I was convinced, however, that one of the names in his journal must be the brawler's. Temple had told me himself that this fellow was a dangerous criminal, and the more I considered it, the more confident I became that the journal was a record of some kind, relating to the crimes committed in London by Winston Parker's cousin, Violet. The newspaper clippings had described all manner of offences. Theft, assault, even murder.

But how was Temple connected to it all? The last clipping I'd read mentioned another police officer – a man named

Pearce – being responsible for Violet Parker's arrest. So, where did Temple come into it? Why did Winston Parker's name seem to fill him with dread? And why was it so important that he tracked down the shaven-headed man?

Darkness had completely fallen by the time we arrived at Vivian Hall's cabin, a distant moon visible through the broad first-class windows. As we came to a halt, the neighbouring door opened and a gentleman in a dinner suit stepped out, bidding us a pleasant evening. Temple gave him a single nod, before knocking smartly upon Miss Hall's door. Receiving only silence in reply, he scowled, waited a few seconds and then knocked again.

'Out to dinner?' I suggested. 'Perhaps we should try later.'

Temple stared at the door as though he might somehow convince Vivian Hall to appear out of sheer force of will.

'We could wait if you'd prefer,' I said, wary of ending the day with yet another confrontation.

'No. No, you're right.'

He motioned for me to lead the way, but as I turned I heard the sound of a handle being grasped and a door thrust open. Whipping around, I expected to see Vivian Hall. Instead, I saw only Temple disappearing into the cabin.

'For God's sake, man,' I cried. 'You can't simply help your-self to—'

Before I could finish, I reached the door myself. Peering into the cabin, I was greeted with a sight that seemed to knock the very ground out from under me.

Spread on the floor of the reception room was the body of Vivian Hall.

26

'Get inside,' Temple hissed.

At first, I did nothing other than stare at Vivian Hall's body, my mouth hanging open. Surely, this couldn't be the same woman who had visited me just yesterday evening in the officers' quarters, now lying motionless upon the floor.

'Quickly, dammit!' Temple snapped.

Recovering my wits, I hurried to obey, scrambling into the cabin and closing the door behind me.

'Don't touch anything.' Temple stood completely still, a hand outstretched to hold me at bay. 'Stay exactly where you are.'

He seemed to come alive as he looked at the body, his eyes narrowed and an eager expression on his face. I might have been appalled if I weren't so completely dumbfounded. I nodded, remaining by the door as I gawped at Miss Hall.

Even when I'd had chance to prepare for it – when I'd known what awaited us – the sight of Dupont's body had troubled me. But to have the discovery of Vivian Hall sprung on us was something else entirely.

Her skin was pale, her eyes wide with surprise. She was lying on her front, a wound on the back of her head. I saw dried blood matting her dark hair.

A silver wine cooler lay by her side, gleaming, just as the one in Beatrice Green's cabin had done. Though this cooler was different to Green's in one distinct, sickening way. Its base was stained with a dark splatter of blood.

'The wine cooler,' I said, my voice a quivering husk. 'Dear God, someone's struck her across the head with it.'

Temple said nothing. He was crouching beside the body, looking intently at the wound. There was a coffee table behind him, on which a half-empty bottle of white wine stood beside two glasses. One was empty, a smudge of crimson lipstick on the rim suggesting that Miss Hall herself might have drunk from it. The other looked untouched, a generous measure of wine still inside.

'What do we do?' I asked.

Temple continued to ignore me.

'For Christ's sake, what do we do?'

'We determine how long she's been here.' He spoke sharply, his eyes never straying from the body. 'The blood is dry, so it can't have happened recently.' He reached towards the coffee table and gently touched the bottle. 'And the wine is warm.'

'You think that she poured her attacker a drink?' I asked, hearing the astonishment in my own voice.

'It would seem so. Unless she had another visitor before the attacker arrived. But whoever this glass was intended for, it would appear they didn't share Miss Hall's desire for it.'

I shook my head. 'What kind of person would let her pour them a glass of wine, only to watch her drink her own and then murder her?'

'Perhaps she had already finished her drink. And poured one for her visitor when they arrived.'

'But not pour another for herself?'

Temple seemed to consider this for a moment before looking up at me.

'What time did she call on you last night?'

'Six,' I replied. I took several deep breaths, trying not to look back at the wound on Vivian Hall's head. 'It can't have been much later than six o'clock.'

'Has she changed?'

'Changed?'

'Her clothes,' said Temple irritably. 'Has she changed her clothes?'

With another deep breath, I looked back down upon the body. 'No,' I said.

'You're sure?'

'I think so.' I pointed towards her outstretched hands. 'The lace on her cuffs. I recognise that. She was wearing a coat when we spoke, but it was poking out of her sleeves.'

Without a word, Temple strode across the reception room and let himself into the bedroom. Eager not to be alone with the body, I scrambled to follow. But as I reached the doorway I stopped, my heart sinking further when I saw what awaited us. Just like Arthur Blake's cabin, the bedroom had been turned upside down. Bed linen lay heaped on the floor, the drawers had been ripped from the desk and a suitcase of clothes had been emptied.

'Dear God,' I murmured.

'Miss Hall was carrying a painting,' said Temple.

'She was. I offered to have it in the officers' quarters — to keep it safe until we arrived — but she refused.'

'Search for it. But do so carefully. I don't suppose we'll find it. The fact that the reception room wasn't also ransacked suggests that our culprit found what they were looking for in here. Still, there's a chance they might have left something behind.'

I crouched obediently and, with a trembling hand, lifted the corner of a sheet. Over my shoulder, I heard Temple cross the room and turned to see him rummaging through the wardrobe.

'What in God's name are you doing?' I demanded.

'A wardrobe full of fine clothes. And plenty more on the floor. Easily enough for two different outfits per day, if Miss Hall was of such a mind.' He turned to face me. 'She must have been killed last night. If it had happened today ...'

I nodded. 'She would have changed.'

Temple stepped away from the wardrobe. 'What did she say when she left you?'

'Nothing.'

'Dammit, Birch,' he urged. 'Think for a moment. She didn't tell you anything at all about where she was going? Who she might be meeting?'

'I've told you, she said nothing! Only that she was in a hurry to be somewhere else.'

'But you didn't ask her where she was bound?'

'No,' I admitted. I shuffled uncomfortably, avoiding his gaze. 'I thought it rude to pry.'

Temple turned away and muttered something under his breath. I didn't have the heart even to berate him for it.

'You think she left to meet her killer,' I said. 'That it was someone she'd arranged to meet.'

'I do. If the wine isn't enough, then for the door not to have been forced and Miss Hall to have been struck from behind suggests that she let her attacker in.' He turned and looked back towards the reception room. 'She seems to have returned here to meet someone who she thought was a friend. She let them into the cabin and poured two glasses of wine. She drank her own, and then, when her back was turned, the killer struck her with the wine cooler before searching the bedroom for her painting.'

I shook my head, trying desperately to force the image of Miss Hall's lifeless body from my mind. Trying not to wonder if she had suffered, or if death had come quickly.

'But why do it at all?' Temple was speaking more to himself than to me. 'Blake told us himself – his painting could be the most valuable artistic discovery in decades. The value of Miss Hall's is surely trifling in comparison. Why has our killer seen fit to—'

'How can you speak so calmly about this? There's a woman in that room lying dead and yet you're speaking as though this matter might be something trivial.'

'What would you prefer? We can't change that she's dead, Birch. That would have been a task for last night.'

'Last night?' I repeated.

'If you'd brought her to me,' he said. 'If you had only done as I'd instructed, instead of taking it upon yourself to interview her and then simply letting her go, she might very well still be alive.'

My jaw dropped. 'You can't mean that.'

Temple didn't reply. Instead he marched past me and returned to the reception room.

'Temple,' I called, hurrying to catch up. 'You can't honestly believe that I'm responsible for this.'

'Look.' He turned on the spot and glared at me, pointing down at the body. 'Look at her.'

With a deep breath, I forced my gaze back down.

'You want to know why I objected to being accompanied in this investigation?' he demanded. 'Why I tried to insist that your captain let me pursue this alone? Here's your answer. This is what happens when amateurs become involved in things that they shouldn't. Mistakes are made. People are killed.'

I felt my hand curl into a fist. If I'd been a bolder man, I would have hit him. As it was, I let it hang uselessly by my side, clenching my fingers so tightly that my shoulder began to twinge.

He was right, of course. Looking down at the body, I knew all too well that it was my fault. First Amelia and now Vivian Hall. It was all my fault.

'You really believe this is the same thief?' I asked weakly. 'The same culprit who raided Arthur Blake's cabin?'

'Don't *you*? They both knew Dupont, they've both had paintings stolen—'

'But there's no knife,' I protested. 'Whoever raided Mr Blake's cabin took a knife with them. There's no sign of one here. They had to resort to . . .' I broke off and took a breath. 'They had to hit Miss Hall around the head with a wine cooler.'

Temple said nothing.

'We're dealing with a killer who brings a knife to steal an unprotected painting,' I continued. 'But who arrives unarmed to steal one while its owner is there? How does that make any sense? And where does Monsieur Dupont come into this? Why was *he* killed for Mr Blake's painting, and yet Miss Hall has had to pay the price for hers?'

'All fine questions,' Temple agreed. 'If we can discover who it was that Miss Hall returned here to meet, I suspect we'll have our answers. But there's another which you haven't asked.'

I didn't dare ask him what I had missed, a weight beginning to grow in my stomach.

'A painting was taken on Tuesday and another last night,' he said. 'Will there be a third tonight?'

Friday 14 November 1924

27

Captain McCrory had been suitably dismayed to hear of our discovery in Vivian Hall's cabin. Parting ways with Temple, I went straight to his office, where he had been preparing for dinner. He poured a stiff glass of brandy as I delivered the news, even going so far as to offer one to me. After replacing the cork, he sat and gazed at the surface of the desk.

'You discovered the body personally, Mr Birch?'

'I did, sir. Miss Hall had visited the officers' quarters on Wednesday to express some . . .' I hesitated, struggling for the right word. 'Some distress. I went to her cabin to check that everything was all right.'

The captain cursed under his breath. 'Do any of the other passengers know?'

'Not that I'm aware of, sir. Miss Hall was travelling alone.'

'And the officers?'

'I haven't said a word, sir. You're the first I've told.'

He had nodded, his eyes twitching towards his box of cigars. 'Can I rely on you to handle this discreetly, Mr Birch? The death on Wednesday morning has already caused enough unrest. If Miss Hall was truly travelling alone, we may stand a chance of containing this one.'

'Of course, sir. I'll see to it personally that the coroner in New York is telegrammed and prepared to receive a second body.'

The captain nodded his approval, though I'd wished there was more I could be doing.

I had suggested to Temple that we send a team of porters door to door, asking that passengers turn over any paintings they might be carrying to the Art Fair for safekeeping, but he had quickly objected. News would travel rapidly, and unless we were lucky enough to catch the killer within the first few doors that we knocked upon, they would certainly take measures to conceal the stolen paintings in the time it took to cover all of first- and second-class.

'It must be someone we've spoken with,' he'd insisted. 'Our killer was close enough to Blake to know of his painting and familiar enough with Miss Hall that she would welcome them into her cabin for a glass of wine. Someone who is travelling in either first- or second-class and would therefore have been able to steal a steak knife from the restaurant. That applies to virtually everyone we've interviewed over the past two days.'

'Except Mr Green,' I said. 'He didn't mention knowing Miss Hall.'

Temple shook his head. 'She and his wife have a mutual acquaintance – they are both close friends of Evelyn Scott. Besides which, if Miss Hall was truly the rising star that Blake claims, it's entirely plausible that, as a serious collector, Michael Green will have heard of her.'

'What about Mr Morris? He's carrying a painting. At the very least, he must be warned.'

'But what if Morris is our man? He hates Dupont, knows the story of Blake's painting and has twice been spurned by Miss Hall in his efforts to sell her work. Given his connections, he could easily sell both of the stolen paintings at the Art Fair. If he is the killer and we were to warn him, it would give him all the opportunity he needs to hide the paintings and conceal whatever proof might remain.'

'Then what do we do?' A note of panic had crept into my voice.

'We persevere,' Temple had said. 'We hold our nerve and keep to our current course. Blake, the Webbers, Morris and the Greens. They are the only names that have arisen repeatedly over the past two days. They all meet our criteria. It *must* be one of them.'

After reporting to the captain, I was in no mood to attempt conversation with the officers in the mess. Instead, I returned to my cabin, where my restless mind was filled with images of Vivian Hall's lifeless body. Try as I might, I couldn't help but wonder if Temple had been right. If, when we met on Wednesday evening, I could somehow have prevented her death.

As I settled into my bunk, the guilt truly took hold. It came swiftly, washing over me like a great wave that might swallow me whole. First Amelia and now Vivian Hall... How many more would need to suffer as a consequence of my inaction?

I thought of Miss Hall, hurrying away from the officers' quarters for her appointment with her killer. Thought of how I had simply held the door open and let her leave.

It was my fault. It would always be my fault, just as it would with Amelia. I closed my eyes, wrestling with the knowledge that, when I woke, I would have just two days left. Two days before we docked in New York and I would be reunited with Raymond. Two days in which to find the killer of Denis Dupont and Vivian Hall.

When I did wake, my mood was no lighter. Captain McCrory's briefing was once again bleak, as the officers reported even more passengers demanding to know what was being done about Dupont. He sang the same song as the previous two mornings, instructing us that any passengers who asked were to be told the death was being treated as an accident. The officers looked at him doubtfully, and I waited with bated breath to hear what might follow. But, true to his word, the captain said nothing about my report of Vivian Hall. It seemed his desire to treat her death as discreetly as possible – for Temple and I to investigate it in isolation – held fast.

As the captain dismissed us and we began to file from the mess, I heard a voice calling my name. Turning, I found Travis flagging me down.

'Birch,' he called. 'A gentleman called for you early this morning with a message. A Mr Temple.'

'Temple? He's been here already?'

Travis nodded. 'He says to let you know that he'll meet you in the reading room at midday.'

I thought of Temple roaming the *Endeavour*, finally pursuing his investigation without me, and began to panic. Could he somehow have learned that I had broken into his cabin? Had I left something out of place? Could the woman even have reported back to him that she'd seen me there?

No, I thought. He would shake me off altogether if that were the case. He wouldn't invite me to join him later on in the reading room. What, then? Why cast me off for only the morning?

I remembered his words in Vivian Hall's cabin. '*This is what happens when amateurs become involved in things that they shouldn't. Mistakes are made. People are killed.*'

'That's all he said?' I demanded. 'He didn't tell you anything more?'

'That's all. He seemed in quite a hurry.'

'To do what?'

'I'm telling you – he didn't say. He seemed excited, if you ask me. Didn't hang about to answer any questions. He had this wild look about him, like he was itching to be off.'

This gave me pause for thought. I'd hardly have described Temple as excited when we parted. Could he have found something?

The very idea of a breakthrough made my pulse quicken. Before I could pursue it, though, I noticed that Travis was glancing at the floor.

'Everything all right, Travis?'

The young man gave a short laugh. 'I'm afraid Mr Temple wasn't your only caller this morning ...'

Moments later, I burned with resentment as I made my way to first-class – to the cabin occupied by Mrs Fitch and her ratty little terrier. This was a visit that any one of the other officers could easily have paid. I ought to be with Temple, pursuing the killer of Vivian Hall and Denis Dupont, not paying homage to a sour old widow who wanted a bigger cabin.

With an effort, however, I held my tongue. I remembered Captain McCrory's instruction to keep Miss Hall's murder from the other officers. And besides, even if I were to snap back at Travis and insist that he damn well visit Mrs Fitch himself, what else would I do? Temple was in the wind, apparently chasing down some lead without me. Whatever he was up to, there was little chance of finding him before our midday appointment in the reading room. Bitterly, I accepted that the task of appeasing Mrs Fitch seemed to fall to me.

When I reached her cabin, I hovered for a moment outside. Mrs Fitch's room was only a single corridor across from Vivian Hall's, and as I stood at the door, I couldn't help but think of the moment I'd first seen her body upon the floor. I pictured the wine cooler lying next to her and the two glasses on the coffee table; thought of how the bedroom had been tipped upside down.

From the other side of the door, I heard the terrier's muffled howling, as if alerting its mistress to my arrival. With one last sigh, I raised my fist to knock. But before I had a chance to rap upon the wood, there came a familiar voice.

'Will you shut that damned creature up!'

A door was flung open to my right and I snapped around to see Arthur Blake appearing from the neighbouring cabin. As we locked eyes, he stopped, his furious expression melting away in an instant.

'Ah,' he said, rapidly adopting a cheerful smile. 'Mr Birch!'

The artist, dressed today in a pinstriped suit and striking pink tie, strode eagerly towards me, his hand outstretched. First-class suited him, I thought. To look at him now, it was difficult to imagine that just two days earlier he had been telling us how he feared for his life.

'It's very good to see you, Mr Birch. Very good indeed. What brings you to my door, then? I suppose you must have some news.'

'I'm afraid not, sir.'

'Something I can help with perhaps?'

'Actually, sir, I was visiting another passenger.'

He looked from me to Mrs Fitch's door, a confused expression spreading across his face.

'That sour old crow? Is she involved?'

'No, sir. A different matter.'

'Somebody's complained about that damn dog of hers, I suppose.'

He flashed a boyish grin, which I struggled to return. I couldn't help but think of all that Temple and I had learned about this man during the first two days of our investigation. I pictured his drunken argument with Dupont on Monday evening, his attempts to charm Beatrice Green in the bar and his rumoured infidelity to Evelyn Scott. While I wouldn't wish it upon anyone to return home and find a knife planted in their desk, it was suddenly an effort to feel the same sympathy as I had when we first visited his raided cabin.

'I had rather hoped for some news,' he said, the smile fading a little. 'Just two days until we arrive ... I'm sure you can understand, I'm becoming terribly anxious.'

'Mr Temple is pursuing the matter, sir.' I hoped desperately that there was some truth to my words.

'Of course, of course,' he nodded eagerly. 'What about Morris? Did you have any luck with him?'

'We paid him a visit, sir.'

'And?'

'He seemed not even to know that Monsieur Dupont was on board.'

'Damn. Are you sure there's nothing I can do? No way that I can help? Perhaps I could try with Morris—'

'We just need to let Mr Temple do his work. He's investigating a lead as we speak.'

'Of course. Quite right.' Blake adopted another grin, though it seemed distinctly less cheerful than the one he had fixed me with just a moment before. 'Well, I'd best go back inside. Safest place for me, I'd imagine. When you have some news ...'

I forced a half-hearted smile. Before he could vanish, though, a thought struck me.

'Mr Blake,' I called after him. 'There is actually something you can help me with.'

'Oh?'

'When did you last see Miss Hall?'

'Vivian?' He frowned. 'On Wednesday afternoon, when I went to warn her about what had happened to my painting.'

'You're sure that you haven't seen her since?'

'Quite sure.' His frown intensified. 'Is everything all right?'

'Perfectly fine, sir,' I said, the words like bile in my mouth. 'Mr Temple is simply trying to determine everyone's whereabouts these past few days. I'm sure you understand.'

'Of course, of course.' Blake nodded knowingly.

'Although,' I continued, 'I don't suppose Miss Hall mentioned an appointment to you? Someone she was planning to meet on Wednesday evening?'

'Doesn't ring any bells.'

'Might I ask where *you* were on Wednesday evening, sir?'

288

'I was in my cabin. You can imagine, I wasn't in a hurry to leave after the fright I'd had on Tuesday night. And besides, there's barely any need when one's in first-class! Although Cassie stopped by to visit me, which was jolly nice of her. Checked in on how I was doing.'

'Did she stay for long?'

'An hour or so perhaps.'

I nodded, remembering how I had bumped into Mrs Webber on the promenade.

'This lead that Mr Temple is investigating,' said Blake innocently. 'What is it, exactly?'

I only wished I knew.

28

When the gold-faced clock chimed midday, the reading room was so still that it seemed to echo from the very walls. The gleaming Steinway was silent today, sitting unused while the passengers read newspapers, wrote letters and sipped from china teacups.

Despite the tranquillity, I shuffled and fidgeted in my seat. I must have spent more time sitting among the passengers these last few days than in the entirety of my five years aboard the *Endeavour*, and it was a situation with which I was becoming increasingly uncomfortable. To do so in an exclusively first-class crowd, however, and without so much as a reason for being there, felt particularly unnatural. I found myself glancing around nervously and was grateful that Temple had at least chosen a table in the far corner, tucked away behind a large potted fern. It felt a great deal more discreet than the table in the centre of the room which we had shared with Michael Green the previous afternoon.

'Dammit, man,' I said, keeping my voice low. 'Will you please just tell me what we're waiting for?'

'We're testing a theory,' Temple replied, his gaze fixed firmly on the door at the far side of the room. 'Drink your tea.'

A pot of Earl Grey sat on the table, which he had sent for in the apparent hope of making me a little less agitated. I had poured myself a cup, but it remained otherwise untouched.

Travis had been right; Temple was certainly in a curious mood. There was a definite excitability about him; a feeling of anticipation that he seemed to be wrestling into constraint. It did nothing to calm my nerves. Nor, for that matter, did his reluctance to share whatever breakthrough he had found.

'For God's sake,' I hissed. 'You can't abandon me for hours on end and then expect to keep me in the dark like this. Tell me what we're waiting for or I'm leaving.'

'Be my guest.' Temple looked me in the eye. 'Though I'd have thought you'd like to know who you let Vivian Hall meet on Wednesday evening.'

For all intents and purposes, it might have been the most casual of remarks, tossed into the air like a comment upon the weather. But it stung like seawater on a wound.

'You've found them?' I asked, my heart in my throat.

Temple didn't reply, returning his attention to the door. I felt a sudden swell of frustration.

'That's enough,' I said, rising to my feet. 'I can't sit here any longer. Either you tell me what's happening or—'

He grasped my arm, his fingernails digging like fish hooks into my skin. Wincing, I opened my mouth to protest. But before I could speak, I realised that, still, he wasn't looking at me. Following his gaze, oblivious suddenly to the pressure on my arm, I found the object of his attention.

291

Nathaniel Morris had appeared at the door.

The art dealer seemed to scan the tables one by one, his spectacles glinting. Apparently failing to find what he was searching for, he grimaced and seated himself at an empty table.

'Mr Morris ...' I murmured. 'Is he the one we're waiting for?'

Temple nodded. 'I sent for him.'

'But he told us that he was confined to his cabin.'

Temple wrenched me back down into my seat, sending a sharp jolt of pain rushing up my arm.

'If I'm correct,' he said, 'that's not all he's been lying about.'

Despite myself, I felt my heart begin to beat just a little quicker.

'You believe that Mr Morris might be our man?' I asked cautiously. 'Is that what you think he was doing when Arthur Blake saw him on Wednesday night? He was visiting Vivian Hall?'

Temple nodded, his eyes fixed upon Morris. I took a deep breath, resisting the urge to snap at him with so many passengers on hand to see it.

'Are we not going to join him?' I asked.

'Not yet.'

'Then why send for him? For God's sake, is he our man or not?'

'We can't yet join him because he doesn't know that it was *me* who called him here.'

'How could he not know?'

'I had someone pass along a message.'

I stared at Temple, whatever excitement I might have felt at the prospect of naming a culprit vanishing in an instant.

'Who did you send?'

I watched him carefully, monitoring for the slightest change in his expression. He seemed barely to notice, his attention still fixed on Morris as he waved a dismissive hand.

'A young fellow in third-class.'

'A boy?'

'Yes, a boy,' he said irritably. 'Does it matter? I didn't trouble any of your passengers, if that's what you're concerned about. I gave him a message and a few coins, then I sent him to Morris's cabin.'

'Why the need for such secrecy?'

'It was the only way to make this happen. But it won't work twice. Believe me, we won't have another chance if this doesn't pay off.'

For several minutes, Morris sat alone at the table, checking his watch and letting loose great bellowing coughs that caused the other residents to cast unhappy glances in his direction.

I watched him closely, a sense of dread beginning to stir in my gut. Could Temple be right about this? Could Morris really be our culprit? Under the right circumstances, I decided that I could imagine him pushing Dupont down the companionway. His hatred for his old rival certainly seemed to burn brightly enough for that. But was Temple really suggesting that he had been the one to attack Vivian Hall? Or that he had broken into Arthur Blake's cabin?

It was curious to find myself thinking in such terms. If anything, I still believed that Morris seemed a more likely candidate for a third victim. Just like Blake and Miss Hall, he had known Dupont and brought a painting to be sold in New York. Since discovering Vivian Hall's body, I had barely even considered him a suspect.

And yet, it seemed he *had* lied to us about being in first-class on Wednesday evening; the very evening that we believed Miss Hall had been murdered.

He even had the look of a guilty man. The longer I peered at him, the more I realised quite how much he seemed to be fidgeting, his eyes flickering every so often to the door from behind his spectacles. A waiter approached his table, only to be gruffly waved away.

'He doesn't seem to be staying,' I said.

'I'd imagine he doesn't intend for this meeting to be long.'

'Meeting?'

'What else did you think he was here for? Morris isn't the only person I had my young assistant send for this morning.'

For a split second, Morris threatened to look in our direction, prompting me – to Temple's amusement – to duck for cover behind the potted fern.

'Who else is coming?' I whispered.

'If I'm correct, he has another acquaintance in first-class.'

'And you think this could be connected? You honestly believe that Mr Morris has had a hand in killing Miss Hall?'

'I think it could be pivotal. To Dupont as well. But we need them both if we're to know for sure. Morris *and* his accomplice.'

Temple was like a coiled spring, but I could see that there was nothing to be gained by pressing the matter. He seemed insistent that I wait and see Morris's anonymous contact for myself, his jaw set and his eyes glossed with cold intensity. There was little point in arguing.

Instead, my mind strayed to an altogether different question. One that, to me at least, might very well prove to be just as troubling. Who, exactly, was this young fellow he had recruited to deliver his messages?

I couldn't help but think again of the woman from the cargo hold and my earlier suspicions that Temple had taken her on as an accomplice to shake me loose. *Keep away or you'll be next.* That had been the warning she'd sent me. But surely, he wouldn't be so candid about using passengers to carry messages, if that was truly his game?

I glanced at the clock. Morris had been waiting for fifteen minutes, coughing into his handkerchief and glancing every few seconds towards the door. When he first arrived, I would have said that he looked impatient. But as time passed, there was an undeniable change in him. If anything, he seemed to be growing nervous.

'Come on,' Temple murmured, his foot beating furiously against the floor. 'Come on ...'

With a great sigh, Morris pushed himself away from the table, Temple's heel falling silent as the art dealer hauled himself to his feet.

'Temple,' I whispered, already hearing the panic in my voice.

'I know.' He was watching intently as Morris made his way towards the door.

'Do we follow?'

Temple shook his head, his lips moving but no sound following. Even so, I was sure I knew what he was trying to communicate; if we intervened, Morris would know that Temple had set this meeting up. What was it he had said? *'We need them both if we're to know for sure.'*

Morris stopped to ask a moustached gentleman in a three-piece suit to tuck in his chair so that he could squeeze past.

As the gentleman obliged, I thought of Vivian Hall, her body dumped on the floor of her cabin, and the notion of letting her killer walk free suddenly became too much to bear.

I rose to my feet. 'I'm stopping him.'

'No!' Temple seized my wrist.

'But he's leaving!'

'He won't admit to anything unless we have them both.'

Temple's eyes were still fixed on Morris. The art dealer was on the move again, having managed to squeeze himself between the tables and grumble a few words of thanks to the gentleman who had let him pass. I tried to tear myself free, but Temple's fingers were locked around my wrist.

'Listen to me,' I hissed. 'Whatever it is that you've learned, surely we have more to gain by speaking to Mr Morris alone than letting him go!'

Temple remained silent as Morris, now with a clear line of sight, made for the door. I tried again to pull away, my shoulder straining, but it was no use. Another few strides and Morris would be gone. Surely, we had lost him.

Then, just as he was about to disappear from view – and I had all but resigned myself to the certainty that we were letting him leave – he stopped. I felt Temple's grip on my wrist ease.

Morris filled the doorway, making it impossible to see what it was in the corridor that had halted him. But from the rhythmic heaving of his shoulders, I realised with a start that he must be talking to someone.

I felt my heart pound. Could Temple's deception have paid off? Had Morris's companion finally arrived?

I craned my neck for a better view, desperate to see just who it was that Temple had lured here. But it was no use. The art dealer still stood in the doorway, shielding the new arrival from view. Temple, meanwhile, was on his feet, eyes blazing, readying himself to pounce.

Just as I was sure that I couldn't bear to wait a moment longer, Morris turned, revealing his companion. I felt my heart sink. Of course, I thought solemnly. Who else?

I glanced over at Temple. A satisfied smile was spreading across his face as he looked upon the suited figure of Michael Green.

29

'Mr Green ...' I murmured.

The banker was scolding Morris, an indignant expression upon his face, and though they were too far away for me to hear what was being said, I could see the underlying message. He was demanding to know why he had been summoned, what was so important that they had needed to meet.

I turned to Temple. 'What do we—'

It was too late. Already, the detective was striding towards them, weaving between the tables like a man on the hunt. I scrambled to follow, and as Green caught sight of us over Morris's shoulder, his expression shifted from confusion to pure malice. Morris, following his line of sight, turned to greet us with a similarly venomous look.

'I suppose this explains it,' Green spat.

Morris began to splutter and wheeze. 'How in God's name—'

'I suggest we sit down, gentlemen,' said Temple. 'You have rather a lot to tell us.'

Morris's face turned a troubling shade of red. 'If you think we're going to tell you anything—'

'That's enough, Nathaniel.' Green took his elbow. 'Not another word. These fools have nothing to use against us. Let's not give them the satisfaction of trying.'

'I wouldn't be so sure, Mr Green,' Temple called after them. 'I know that you've both lied about your involvement in this case.'

Green ignored him, continuing instead to steer the grumbling Morris roughly away.

'And I know that you had a role in Dupont's death.'

Green stopped, this particular shot apparently finding its mark, and turned slowly to face Temple. Morris cast him a concerned glance.

'You don't know anything,' he muttered.

'Can you take that chance?'

The banker grimaced. Finally, he seemed to relent. 'Sit down, Nathaniel,' he said quietly. 'Let me deal with this.'

The four of us moved to a vacant table, Morris grumbling and coughing all the way into his seat. If I had only imagined that the reading room's other residents were watching me a few moments before, there was certainly no question of it now. In every direction, curious eyes were settling on us, probing for an explanation to the outburst.

Temple took the seat opposite Green. They weighed each other up across the table like boxers, while I, in turn, sat across from Morris. The art dealer glared at me, his beady eyes glinting behind his spectacles, and I found myself struggling to meet his gaze.

'I suppose you think you're very clever,' said Green. 'Luring us both here like this. I don't know what you think you're going to achieve.'

'As I've told Birch,' replied Temple, 'I'm testing a theory.'

'And what theory would that be? That Nathaniel and I threw Dupont down a flight of steps? It's absurd.'

'Is it?' Temple demanded. 'I suppose there's a perfectly good reason then, Mr Green, for Mr Morris to be making secret visits to your cabin in first-class.'

Morris let out a great, bellowing cough, while Green adopted the same smug smile that we had seen the previous day.

'Nathaniel and I being acquainted doesn't prove that we had anything to do with what happened to Dupont.'

'What else would you suggest it proves?'

A quick glance passed between the two men.

'If you must know,' said Green, 'I was going to let Dupont go. Nathaniel is becoming my full-time broker.'

Temple leaned across the table. 'Dupont has been dead for nearly three days, Mr Green. You'll forgive me if I find it suspicious that you've both continued to hide this arrangement from me. Unless, of course, you have another reason for keeping it a secret.'

Morris's nostrils flared. I glanced at Temple, hoping desperately that he knew what he was doing. The caution with which he had interviewed Green the previous afternoon was gone. He was on the offensive.

'I'd like to give you both an opportunity to explain what truly happened on Wednesday evening,' he declared. 'When Arthur Blake saw you, Mr Morris, roaming the corridors of first-class.'

'Evidently I was visiting Mr Green.'

'But where had you come from?'

'From my cabin.'

'Not Vivian Hall's?'

Morris frowned, his bushy eyebrows knotting together. 'I haven't seen Miss Hall in six months.'

'You didn't arrange an appointment, then, after learning that Dupont was dead, to discuss selling her latest work?'

'For pity's sake, Mr Temple,' said Green. 'I thought you had some foolish accusations to make about Dupont. What does Vivian Hall have to do with this?'

'Miss Hall is dead.' Temple fixed Green with a cold glare. 'She was murdered on Wednesday evening in her first-class cabin and the painting that she was transporting to the New York City Art Fair has been stolen.'

'That's our game, is it?' asked Green. 'We've been murdering artists and stealing their paintings? I trust you have some remarkably compelling evidence to support this.'

I glanced over at Temple. He certainly seemed at ease. He clasped his hands and settled back into his seat.

'If you'd prefer we began with Dupont,' he said, 'then that's exactly what we'll do. In fact, we'll start at the very beginning.'

'And where's that?' Green demanded.

'The true beginning of your partnership. The Liebermann.'

Green's face flickered, his expression of cool defiance fading for the briefest of moments.

'The Liebermann ...' I murmured. 'What about it?'

'Mr Green, here,' said Temple triumphantly, 'is its current owner.'

I stared at the banker. Of course, it made sense for him to be Dupont's anonymous buyer. He was, after all, a client. And if he kept the Liebermann in some private collection, that

301

would go some way towards explaining why Morris's contacts had struggled to track it down.

But how long had Temple been sitting on this information? Had he somehow deduced it from our conversation with Green the previous day, or was this what he had been investigating that morning? Whatever the answer, I burned with resentment at the thought that he had kept such a crucial detail from me, holding it close to his chest until the opportune moment.

I turned to Morris. 'So when you told us yesterday that you'd never found it, that was a lie? You knew that Monsieur Dupont had sold it to Mr Green?'

'Of course I knew. It took long enough. But yes, I found it.'

'And you approached Mr Green to try to buy it back,' said Temple. 'Is that it?'

Morris opened his mouth to speak, but it was Green who replied.

'We don't have to answer these questions.'

'I suggest that you answer whatever questions I damn well ask,' Temple snapped. 'That is, if you hope to convince me that you aren't involved in the deaths of both Denis Dupont and Vivian Hall. You don't deny that it was the Liebermann which brought the pair of you together?'

Green seemed lost in thought for a moment, his smile fading as he glanced absent-mindedly around the reading room. I wondered if he might be looking for some way to escape or distract us. Whatever he was searching for, he seemed not to find it. With the smallest of shrugs, he returned his attention to the detective.

'Have it your way, Mr Temple. As far as I can see, it has nothing to do with Dupont's death, and certainly not with whatever may tragically have befallen Miss Hall. But if it will convince you to abandon these accusations, then yes, Nathaniel first came to me six months ago. I'd say it was more to give me a piece of his mind, though, than to buy the Liebermann back.'

'I'm surprised you didn't send him away.'

'It was my first instinct, of course. But I was intrigued. Here was a man who seemed to detest Dupont just as passionately as I did.'

'Detest him?' I said. 'But he was your broker. You told us yourself only yesterday that he does good work for you. What reason could you have to detest him?'

A grim expression settled on Green's face, the remainder of his cool smile all but vanishing.

'He was blackmailing you,' said Temple. 'That's the truth, isn't it?'

Green glared at Temple.

'If you want the truth, Mr Temple,' said Green, 'here it is. I decided to part ways with Dupont a long time ago. When we first met, he was an exceptional broker. He was younger and sharper, but the simple fact is that those days were long behind him. When his gallery was bombed during the war, I thought I'd cut my losses and find another man.'

'But he wouldn't let you,' said Temple.

'Why not?' I asked.

Green pursed his lips. 'You said yesterday that you're aware of the various accusations Mr Temple and his friends at Scotland Yard are making against me?'

'That's right, sir.'

303

'Dupont claimed to have proof of these things. He told me that unless I gave him the capital to set up a new gallery, he would take it to the police, the newspapers ... anyone who would listen.'

'I thought those claims were untrue,' said Temple, a hint of malice in his voice.

Green snorted. 'It wouldn't matter if there was even a shred of truth in what he told people. It was the reputational damage that I couldn't stand for.'

'So you gave him the money for the new gallery.'

'That's right.'

'But Monsieur Dupont opened his new gallery years ago,' I protested. 'Just as the war was coming to an end.'

Green gave a bitter laugh. 'I've tried more than a few times since to let him go. But each time, he threatened again to go public with whatever it was that he thought he knew.'

'So what changed?' asked Temple.

Green seemed to think for a moment. 'Mr Temple,' he said slowly. 'You understand that I have no desire to tell you any of this. Nor do I see any reason that I should be obligated to. We're talking now about private dealings between Nathaniel and me. But if I truly have your word that it will put an end to this ridiculous notion that we are responsible for Dupont's death, I will share them.'

Temple nodded. He suddenly seemed wary, and I couldn't help but be reminded of the warning that he had given me the previous day: that Scotland Yard had been investigating Green for months with no luck. Even I could see that, if the banker was going to try to deceive us, this would surely be the time.

'You ask what changed,' Green continued. 'What ultimately compelled me to rid myself of Dupont. You're correct. It was the Liebermann.'

Morris coughed loudly into his handkerchief, causing Green to wrinkle his nose and lean away.

'As I was apparently stuck with Dupont,' he said, 'I tried to make the best of a bad situation. He may have been losing his touch, but he did still deliver on occasion. The Liebermann was one of those times.'

Across the table, I saw Morris grimace. Green was certainly speaking candidly enough, but I wondered if, for him, the Liebermann was still a sore wound.

'I was surprised, in all honesty,' Green declared. 'I hadn't heard that it was for sale and I was equally surprised that Dupont had managed to secure it. In any case, the sale was completed, and a few months later I found Nathaniel knocking on my door. At first, I couldn't believe the audacity of it. That this fellow had tracked me down just to give me a piece of his mind. But it became clear soon enough – it wasn't me that Nathaniel, here, despised. It was Dupont.'

'So, the two of you forged an alliance,' said Temple. 'Mr Morris wanted retribution for losing the Liebermann and you simply wanted to get rid of Dupont.'

'I know what you're thinking,' Green replied. 'You think we planned to achieve that by pushing him down those steps. But we're not murderers. I'm a banker and Nathaniel is an art dealer, for God's sake. We wanted to get rid of him, not kill him.'

'And how else did you plan to achieve that?'

'It was certainly a problem. But an opportunity presented itself when he told me about this voyage.'

'He telephoned you,' I said, recalling our conversation the previous day. 'Told you there would be a valuable painting on board ...'

'It was perfect. If we could find a way of taking this painting and framing Dupont as the thief, I would have the leverage required to end his extortion over me and Nathaniel could recuperate his losses incurred on the Liebermann. Our plan was to take the painting and tell him the day before we docked that the game was up. That when we left this ship, our acquaintance would be over.'

'But you couldn't take the painting, could you?' said Temple. 'Because Dupont wouldn't tell you what it was. That's what your wife heard, isn't it? When he came to your cabin on Tuesday morning and she heard you arguing. You lost your temper because he wouldn't tell you what the painting was.'

Green grimaced. 'That woman ...'

'So, how did you take it?'

'How *could* we have?' Morris grumbled. 'Mr Green has just told you, Dupont wouldn't even say what the damned thing was.'

'Regardless, Mr Morris,' Temple snapped, 'the painting has been stolen.'

'It wasn't us,' said Green plainly. 'It can't have been. Until you visited Nathaniel yesterday, we still didn't even know what it was. To think, of all things, that Dupont had somehow come across Ecclestone's lost portrait ...' The banker's eyes went wide, a sudden wistfulness briefly overcoming him. 'Of course you might refuse to believe that. But there's another perfectly good reason that counts against either of us being the thief.'

'And what is that?'

'Because when we tried, it had already gone.'

A silence settled over the table. Morris glanced at Green, a nervous expression on his face. The banker, meanwhile, settled back into his seat and fixed Temple with a small smile. He had caught the detective off guard, and he knew it.

'Mr Green ...' said Morris.

'It's all right, Nathaniel,' said Green calmly. 'It's right that they know.'

'Know what?' Temple growled.

'I devised a plan that would force Dupont to reveal the painting. I would tell him Nathaniel was on board. Not only that, but that he had learned about this painting and was planning to steal it for himself.'

'And did you put this plan into action?'

'I did. On Tuesday evening.'

I felt my eyes go wide.

'As you know already, Beatrice and I had been having dinner in the restaurant,' Green continued. 'She said that there was a friend at the bar who she wanted to have a drink with. I knew that this would allow me some time to myself, so I went to Dupont's cabin and told him the lie. It worked beautifully. The look on his face when I mentioned Nathaniel's name was a picture in itself. When I said that he was on his way to take the painting, poor Dupont sprang from his cabin without a second thought.'

'And what then?' Temple demanded. 'You followed him, I suppose?'

'Precisely. It wasn't difficult. I stayed at a distance so that he wouldn't see me, but it wasn't far and he was in such a frenzy that I don't suppose there was ever any genuine risk of being caught. I followed him straight to another cabin in second-class.'

'And did he go inside?'

Green hesitated, a sudden glimmer of uncertainty on his face. 'At first, it looked as though he might. He stepped up to the door, as if he was about to knock. But then he stopped.'

'Why?' Temple pressed.

'Naturally, I wondered the same thing. Then I realised that the door was already open. Just a crack, you understand. That's why I hadn't seen it straight away – I was looking at it from a distance, after all. But from where I was standing, it looked as though it had been forced.'

'Go on.'

'That's all there is to tell.' Green spread out his hands. 'If the painting was truly in that cabin, it seems someone beat us to it.'

'And that was the last time you saw Dupont?'

Green gave a nod. 'He was starting to panic. I suppose that, in his mind, Nathaniel had already been and taken the painting. I worried he would see me if I stayed any longer, so I left.'

Temple laid his hands upon the table. 'If this is true—'

'Of course it's true,' Morris muttered.

'*If it's true*,' Temple repeated, fixing the art dealer with a vicious look, 'and you really don't have the painting, then why, Mr Morris, did you visit Mr Green's cabin on Wednesday evening?'

The two shared an uneasy glance.

'I assume that *is* where you had been,' Temple pressed. 'When Mr Blake saw you in first-class?'

'On Wednesday morning,' Morris wheezed, 'when news began to spread that an old man had been killed ...'

'Nathaniel came to ensure that we couldn't be accused of any involvement in Dupont's death,' said Green. 'Which, of course, you'll see that we can't. We've committed no crime. Whatever happened to him after he'd led me to that cabin was nothing to do with us.'

Apparently satisfied, Green clasped his hands on his lap. The smirk returned to his face as he watched Temple, whose shoulders seemed to have slumped a fraction, prepare his next assault. The confidence with which the detective had lured them both here – the apparent belief that he might bring this investigation to a conclusion – now appeared to be all but gone.

I, however, found myself filled with sympathy. Dupont might very well have been a con man. A blackmailer, even, if Michael Green's story rang true. But in that moment, all I could think of was the old man whose body Temple and I inspected. I imagined him running from his cabin in a blind panic, not even thinking to take his coat or walking stick.

'But how did you know?' Morris demanded, waving his handkerchief like a great white flag. 'Dupont himself had no clue that we were even acquainted. How did *you* manage to bring us together?'

Temple glanced up. 'Aside from your midnight stroll through first-class?'

The art dealer growled, a deep guttural sound in the back of his throat.

'You gave quite a performance when we called on you yesterday, Mr Morris; pretending you didn't know that Dupont was even on board. But once I knew that Mr Green was a client of his, it wasn't too much of a leap to suppose he might also be the owner of the Liebermann. After all, he told us only yesterday that the old man added a number of extraordinary pieces to his collection.'

Morris scowled at Green.

'Then there was the question of the money for Dupont's new gallery.' A renewed eagerness was building in Temple's voice. 'Men like Mr Green aren't charitable. They'd much rather cut their losses and move on, especially when those losses come in the form of a frail old man. I'm well aware of Mr Green's colourful past. One can't help but wonder, if Dupont had also been aware of it, and he was truly the con man that you claimed, how he might have used that information.'

Green's smile remained in place, but something lethal began to flash in his eyes.

'You have it all worked out, don't you?' said Morris.

'Not all of it.' Temple sat a little straighter. 'I don't believe you. You stole that painting and you threw Dupont to his death.'

Green sighed. 'Really, Mr Temple—'

'And after you had done it, you saw another opportunity.' Temple leaned forward, his voice rising. I dearly hoped he knew what he was doing, my heart beginning to thump in my ears.

'Miss Hall had refused to sell her last two paintings in your gallery, Mr Morris, choosing to work with Dupont instead. With the old man dead, you made an appointment with her on Wednesday evening to discuss selling her latest work. She poured you a glass of wine, which you didn't touch because, as you told us yourself yesterday morning, your illness is preventing you from drinking. When she said that she would prefer to sell her painting at the New York City Art Fair than with you, you were enraged. And who could blame you? Even though Dupont was dead, Miss Hall still refused to work with you. Your frustration was such that you struck her across the head with the wine cooler. Then you stole her painting and were seen by Arthur Blake delivering it to Mr Green.'

Morris looked at Temple with horror. 'That is the most absurd suggestion I might ever have heard.'

'I think you ought to stop, Mr Temple,' said Green. 'We had nothing to do with Miss Hall and have told you quite plainly of our plans for Dupont. We didn't want him dead. Why tell you any of this, if not to prove that?'

Temple shot him a look of pure malice.

'Mr Temple,' I said gently, 'perhaps we ought to—'

'Prove it,' he growled, his eyes still fixed upon Green. 'Show me your handwriting.'

'I shall do no such thing.'

Temple reached into his jacket and slapped a scrap of paper on the table. 'This was in Dupont's cabin,' he said. '*Saturday. Nine o'clock*. If your story is true, this must have been the meeting you arranged to tell him that his game was up. That you had taken the Ecclestone and were going to blame him for the theft.' He glared at Green. 'Show me your handwriting. Prove to me that you wrote this note, and perhaps I'll believe that you didn't kill him.'

A frown began to take shape on Green's face, Temple watching intently for any reaction. Like spectators at a chess match, it seemed that Morris and I could only look on.

For what felt like an age, neither of them moved. Then, just as I thought I'd caught a flicker of uncertainty in Temple's eyes, Green reached for the note and lifted it up.

'How long have you had this?'

'Since Wednesday morning. When I searched Dupont's cabin.'

'And how many people have you shown it to?'

Temple didn't reply.

'Is this your writing, Mr Green?' I asked cautiously.

'No,' he said, settling back in his chair. 'No, it isn't mine.'

He shook his head in disbelief, before looking straight at Temple. 'You really don't know, do you?'

Temple was bristling, his heel tapping even more furiously than usual on the floor. A broad grin spread across Green's face, as if he was unable to hold back the hilarity of whatever he had seen in the note any longer. For a split second, I thought of the revolver in Temple's pocket.

'It's his,' Green sighed. 'This is Dupont's writing.'

Temple's face dropped, and it took me a moment to register exactly what the banker meant.

'You're suggesting he wrote this note himself?' I said.

'The man was seventy years old. He forgot things from time to time, so he'd write important details down. Whatever it was that he'd planned for tomorrow evening, he must have been worried that he'd forget the time. So he wrote himself a note.'

It was as though the breath had been knocked out of me. Three days, I thought. Three days of scouring the *Endeavour* for the author of this note, in the hope that they would reveal exactly what had happened to Dupont or lead us to Arthur Blake's painting. I looked at Temple, waiting for him to deliver some scathing response. To pull the rug from under Green's feet, like an illusionist presenting his grand finale.

But it didn't come. As Temple gritted his teeth, staring intently at Green, I realised that he had nothing.

'You say "whatever it was that he'd planned for tomorrow evening",' I said. 'Even if Monsieur Dupont had written this himself, is it not to remind him of your appointment?'

Green shook his head. 'I hadn't even made one. Nathaniel and I had failed to acquire the painting. There would have been nothing to say.'

'You're lying.' Temple growled.

'No, Mr Temple.' Green dropped the note onto the table. 'I'm afraid I am not. Now —' he stood to leave, patting the creases out of his blazer — 'Nathaniel and I have entertained you gentlemen for quite long enough and if you have no genuine evidence with which to support these accusations, it's safe to say that we're finished. But before we part ways, let's just make sure we understand a few things, shall we?'

There was suddenly a hard edge to the banker's voice. Even Morris looked nervous.

'I don't care that you represent Scotland Yard, Mr Temple. Nor do I care, sir —' he glared at me — 'about your rank as a ship's officer. We have told you the full extent of our involvement in this matter and that will be the end of it. What's going to happen now is that you will both stay away from me, you will stay away from Nathaniel and, for that matter, you will stay away from my wife. I have no clue as to who has that painting, nor how Miss Hall could have met such a tragic end. But Dupont was an old man who fell down a flight of steps. There's no murder for you to solve there. And there are certainly no answers to be found with either of us.'

Without another word, he marched briskly away, Morris in tow, leaving Temple and me to sit in stunned, miserable silence.

30

'For the love of God, Tim, what's that detective been doing to you?'

I glanced up at Wilson, tearing my eyes from the list of names that had transfixed me for the best part of an hour. My dinner sat beside it, an untouched plate of gammon and boiled vegetables that had long since gone cold.

'You look dreadful,' he said, sitting across from me.

'I'm sorry,' I replied, forcing a half-hearted smile. 'It's been rather a long day.'

It was quiet in the mess, the silky tones of a jazz record crackling from the gramophone while three men played cards at another table. In my hand I held Amelia's ribbon, hoping it might bring some comfort. But neither the stillness of the room nor the feeling of the material did anything to ease the sense of hopelessness that I had felt in the hours since leaving the reading room.

After Green and Morris had left, I'd leaned in close, lowering my voice to a murmur.

'What now?'

Temple had said nothing.

'There must be more,' I had urged him. 'Someone else to interview. Another lead to pursue.'

If he had listened to a word I'd said, he didn't show it. He didn't even fix me with his usual condescending glare. He'd simply stood, a blank expression on his face, and walked from the room.

After he'd had gone, I sat for a long while by myself, no longer caring about how out of place I might appear among the first-class passengers. There was no denying the severity of our interview with Green and Morris. Two prime suspects had seemingly been ruled out, while Dupont's note – virtually the only tangible clue that we possessed – was now rendered almost completely useless. I could understand if Temple felt somewhat deflated.

When, finally, I brought myself to leave, I returned to the officers' quarters, took a sheet of paper and listed each of the men and women we had met over the last few days. Temple had said himself in Vivian Hall's cabin that one of them must know what had happened to her and Dupont, or possess some detail that would lead us to our culprit.

But if the answer lay before me, I couldn't see it.

Wilson nodded at the list. 'Can I help?'

For several seconds, I didn't answer. I stared at the names, pleading for a solution to present itself. When it didn't, I sighed and pressed my hands to my face.

'I honestly don't know,' I said. 'Three days, Wilson. Three days we've been searching for answers and we're no closer to knowing how Monsieur Dupont died than we were when we started.'

'Perhaps you're approaching this wrong,' he suggested. 'You're looking for this chap to have been pushed down that companionway. What if it really was just an accident?'

'It can't have been,' I protested. 'On any other night, perhaps. But not for it to have happened at the same time that Mr Blake's painting was stolen.'

'You don't think someone just struck lucky? They saw that your Mr Blake was away, chanced it and came across the painting. It wouldn't be the first time a cabin was broken into – you know that as well as I do. You want this painting back? Perhaps your best bet is to start with the pawn shops in New York next week.'

I looked away, thinking how much I wanted to tell him about Vivian Hall. To speak with someone other than Temple about her murder. I held fast, though. Captain McCrory had been clear in his instruction to treat her death as discreetly as possible. For all his admirable qualities, Wilson was far from discreet. I could imagine the captain's fury if it were to get back to him that I had spoken out of turn.

A burst of laughter from the other officers shattered the silence, as one threw his cards upon the table and stormed out. The others called after him, taunting him with offers of just one more hand.

'Sharples again?' I asked.

Wilson snorted. 'Bloody fool. He's never once won a game, but he keeps coming back.'

'Perhaps one day they'll let him win.'

'Not likely. The way he plays cards, poor old Sharples is probably paying them more than McCrory.'

Wilson fetched a packet of cigarettes from his coat pocket, took one for himself and then offered one to me. I didn't often smoke – Kate hated the smell – but in that moment, I was grateful for the warmth of the tobacco. It seemed to fill me, creeping into every limb and settling my mind. The gramophone was still playing but one of the other men had changed the record, the brass section giving way to the lazy chimes of a piano.

We sat in silence, smoking and listening to the music, until Wilson finally spoke, his brow furrowed in an uncharacteristic frown. His eyes had strayed to my hand, and I realised that he was looking at the ribbon.

'I'm worried about you, Tim.'

'I don't need worrying over.'

'That's not the point. Everything that happened with Amelia ... that's still happening with Kate.' He struggled for words. 'It isn't right. The way you seem to blame yourself for it all. I know Kate gives you a hard time, but you must understand that it wasn't your fault. And now the way you're pushing yourself with this fellow's death, trying to convince yourself that he's been murdered ...'

'What are you saying, Wilson?'

He hesitated, choosing his words carefully. 'I'm saying that I don't think investigating a murder is the right way of dealing with what you're going through. Look, I'm ...' He sighed. 'I'm worried that you might not be in the right frame of mind for all this.'

I cast a venomous glare at the other officers. 'You sound as though you've been speaking to them.'

A dark expression settled on Wilson's face. 'That's not fair. I'm the only one who's tried to help since you came back.'

'And why is that?' I snapped. 'The others have been only too happy to let me cut myself off. What reason could you, alone, have for standing by me?'

Wilson looked pained. 'Five years we've served together. I've stood by you because you needed someone. And you *do* need someone. This business with Raymond—'

'What about him?'

Wilson flinched. 'That ribbon, Tim. How can you know that it's Amelia's? How can you *really* know? I don't doubt Raymond's intentions. If you trust him, that's good enough for me. But she's been gone for two years. Is Raymond's father really so influential that you believe he can bring her back?'

I felt a swell of anger, something deep and primal, begin to stir in my gut.

'Raymond is trying to help.' I held up the ribbon. 'This is proof –'

'Proof of what?'

'That he'll find her. That he'll bring her back to me.'

Wilson shook his head. 'It's a ribbon. What if, for all of Raymond's good intentions, that's all it proves to be? Have you even considered that?'

'It'd still be a damn sight more than anyone else has done.'

The pity vanished from Wilson's eyes. 'Is that so? Then I suppose everything I've said since you came back to the *Endeavour* – these past six months that I've spent trying to help you – must count for nothing. All because Raymond sends you a ribbon and the promise of his father's help?'

I stood clumsily to my feet, snatching my coat from the back of the neighbouring chair. Wilson stood too, moving quickly to block my path.

'Listen to me. I know how badly you want to find her, but this surely isn't the way. I won't watch you throw yourself into this, only to be—'

'Leave me, then!' My voice rose, my shoulders heaving. 'You talk about standing by me? I don't need you, Wilson. And I certainly don't need your approval.' I brandished the ribbon. 'This is all I have. Do you understand? This is everything. And if you can't let Raymond try to bring Amelia home, then you can just get out of my way.'

The two other officers stared at us from across the mess, cards still in hand. The only sound was the crackling of the jazz piano.

Wilson took a step back, his shoulders slumping. 'You don't hear half the things the others say about you, Tim. They say that you're not right in the head – the way that you've cut yourself off, the way you just can't seem to move on. I never wanted to believe it. I *knew* that my friend was still in there somewhere. But d'you know what?' He shook his head, his disappointment palpable. 'Maybe I can see it now. Maybe they're right about you.'

I barged past him, my heart pounding in my ears. This time, he made no attempt to stop me.

I stumbled into the corridor, and the moment I was certain that I was out of earshot, collapsed against the cold iron wall. I screwed my eyes shut, as tightly as I could, and pressed the heels of my hands to my brow. My breath came in ragged gasps, my mouth dry.

I could feel them all in the corridor with me, pressing in. The feral woman. Dupont, pale in death and soaked to the bone. Even Vivian Hall, her dark hair askew. They were all there. Surrounding me, boxing me in.

I clenched my hands into fists and heard Raymond's voice, beckoning me to New York, promising that he could help. That he could bring her home. And finally, there was Wilson.

'D'you know what? Maybe I can see it now. Maybe they're right about you.'

I had no idea how long I stood there in the corridor. It might have been a minute or could just as easily have been an hour. I eased my eyes open and dropped my hands to my sides. I was alone.

Glancing back towards the mess, I thought about returning. I had to apologise to Wilson, see what I could salvage. But deep down, I knew that it was too late. Already, I supposed he would have joined the other officers, asked them to deal him into their game and conceded, at last, that they had been right about me.

It was a painful image, and one that filled me with resentment. No, I thought. This wasn't the time for apologies. Instead, I found myself overcome with a sudden determination. A silent fury that, just a few days earlier, I would scarcely have recognised in myself. To hell with Temple and his injured pride. We had an entire day left. We could still pin our culprit down. And we would start tonight.

Tucking Amelia's ribbon into my pocket, I set off eagerly in the direction of second-class. The sound of a string quartet and the tantalising smell of roasted meat drifted from the restaurant, but I paid them no notice, taking the Great Staircase two steps at a time.

As I walked, my feet thumping against the carpet, I began to formulate a plan. Temple had been certain that one of the men or women we had questioned must be our culprit. Someone close enough to Blake that they somehow knew the existence of his painting, he had said. And familiar enough to Vivian Hall that she would invite them in for a glass of wine. Surely, if we could determine where each had been on Wednesday evening, we could deduce whether any of them might at least have had the chance to kill Vivian Hall.

My mind strayed to the list of names that I had compiled in the mess. I could feel the paper tucked inside my coat pocket as I mulled over what I knew of their movements. It was, admittedly, a pitiful amount. Arthur Blake had spent the night in his cabin, where he was visited for an hour by Cassandra Webber. Nathaniel Morris had been to see Michael Green, while Harry Webber had checked on his car. We knew nothing of Beatrice Green.

And yet, as I marched through the corridors of second-class, there was one whose name we still didn't know. She sat at the bottom of my list, the only alias by which I knew her roughly underlined three times in pencil. The woman from Temple's cabin. The woman who had reportedly scratched Harry Webber's car, stalked us through the cargo hold, threatened me — twice now — with the same gruesome fate as Dupont, and knocked upon Temple's door. If she was our culprit — if she had been the one to push Dupont to his death and strike Vivian Hall with the wine cooler — then all the interviews we had conducted so far might very well count for nothing. She had to be found. That, I decided, needed to be the focus of our final day. Finding her, naming her and determining how, exactly, she was involved.

I rounded the corner and stopped dead, hardly believing the sight before me. Directly ahead, no more than ten paces away, was the woman. She was standing at Temple's cabin door, as she had been the previous afternoon, wearing the same grey cardigan, her sandy hair clinging to her cheekbones in the same ragged strands.

I stood and stared – then, recovering my wits, I darted back around the corner. Slowly, with my back pressed against the wall and my heart pounding in my ears, I peered into the corridor.

There was no mistaking it. I had seen her closely enough when she cornered me in third-class to recognise her anywhere. But that wasn't all that caused my pulse to quicken. What really troubled me was that the cabin was open. Temple was standing in the doorway and they were speaking.

Still peeping around the corner, I strained to hear what was being said, but it was no use. Whatever they were discussing, they were speaking too quietly. There was a yearning expression on her face, though, as if she was pleading with him. Temple, meanwhile, appeared to be listening intently, his arms folded and his eyes narrowed. Then, with a nod, he stepped into the corridor, locked his cabin door and motioned for her to lead the way.

I clenched my fists, my resentment building to such a height that it was all I could do not to round the corner and bellow at them. They really were in it together. After all my speculation, it seemed I had my answer. The chase in the cargo hold, the threat sent to my cabin ... It must all have been carefully orchestrated. But what for? Had Temple really gone to such lengths in order to get rid of me? Was it so important that he take on the investigation alone?

There was nothing else for it. I had to follow and confront them. I waited until they had reached the end of the corridor, then hurried to pursue.

They walked together through second-class, engaging in brief snatches of conversation. I wanted desperately to hear what was being said but hung back, making sure that I could take cover behind a corner if it looked as though they might turn and catch sight of me. Perhaps they were laughing at me. Swapping thoughts on how they could shake me loose once and for all. With every step my anger grew, until, at last, the woman stopped at a cabin and ushered Temple inside.

Squaring my shoulders, my fists trembling, I marched to the door. I thought briefly of the dressing-down that I would receive from Captain McCrory if word reached him of one of his men demanding entry to a passenger's cabin in a fit of rage. And yet I ushered the thought away. In that moment, it occurred to me that I simply didn't care.

I took a deep breath and raised my fist to knock. No more lies. No more secrets from this damned detective. For the first time since we had set out on this investigation, he was going to tell me the truth.

But before I had a chance to rap on the door, there came an almighty crash from the other side. Something large had either been knocked or thrown to the floor.

In an instant, my resolve to enter the cabin and confront Temple disappeared. I stood, perplexed, my hand suspended uselessly in mid-air.

Gently, I placed my palm on the door. Then I brought my ear to it. I heard a muffled grunting and the shuffling of feet, before feeling the heavy thud of something large being hurled against the wall. I flinched away from the impact. What in God's name were they doing?

I glanced up and down the corridor, looking for help. Hearing the muffled sound of shuffling feet again, I realised that no one was coming. Whatever madness was going on behind this door, it would be up to me alone to put a stop to it.

With one last deep breath, I grasped the handle and threw it open.

The desk and chair had been knocked to the ground, scattering paper and clothes across the little cabin. The woman was standing in the far corner and, to my left, I saw with a start that Temple was wrestling with the shaven-headed brawler from third-class. He stood behind Temple, his face contorted with effort as he attempted to wrap a belt around the detective's throat. Temple had raised his hands, teeth gritted and eyes bulging as he strained to keep the thin strip of leather at bay.

For a split second, nobody moved. All three fixed me with the same vacant look of surprise, as though suddenly unsure of how to proceed. Then two things happened at once. Temple, taking advantage of the distraction, released one hand from the belt, closed it into a fist and plunged his elbow into his assailant's stomach. At the same time, the woman lunged for me, flinging herself the short distance across the cabin. Utterly unprepared, I raised my arms to shield myself, but she barrelled into me and her momentum sent us both crashing into the wall.

From the corner of my eye, I saw that Temple, having wrenched himself free, was reaching for something inside his jacket. But the shaven-headed man was only distracted for the briefest of moments, and in an instant had tackled him heavily to the floor. I caught a glimpse of black metal as his revolver flew from his hand and scuttled across the floor.

The woman was on me, snarling as she rained down blows with her fists and elbows. I flung my arms up to shield myself, but while I was able to deflect the worst, they were coming down too readily for me to mount any counter-attack.

Turning my head to escape a particularly savage lunge intended for my face, I saw that Temple was grappling once again with his attacker, the man's fingers reaching for his throat. Then I glimpsed the revolver. It was lying on the floor, just a few feet away.

With a flash of pain coursing through my shoulder, I seized the woman by the wrists, hauled her away and lunged for the gun. My hand found the leather grip and, flailing wildly, I swung the weapon up to face Temple's attacker. With a loud crack, I squeezed the trigger and saw the shaven-headed man go rigid with the impact of the shot. He slumped unceremoniously to the ground.

The woman, seeing that her companion had fallen, wasted no time in springing to her feet and running for the door. But Temple was after her. Heaving his attacker's body away, he snatched the revolver from my hand and lurched into the corridor after her.

'Stop!' I heard him cry through the open door. 'Stop where you are, or I'll shoot!'

Trembling with adrenaline, I lay panting on the floor. My shoulder was throbbing with the effort of heaving the woman away, each breath sending a fresh ripple of pain through the old wound.

Temple's assailant was heaped just a few feet away from me, motionless, his lifeless eyes staring up at the ceiling. His face was hideously contorted, as though capturing the very second the bullet had found its mark. Unable to hold his terrible gaze, I turned away. After bringing my breathing under control, I dragged myself to my feet and, panicking, searched my pocket for Amelia's ribbon. Finding that it was still there, I blew a sigh of relief and stumbled into the corridor, clutching my shoulder as I went.

If the woman had turned right when she'd fled the cabin, she would have rounded the corner almost straight away and disappeared before Temple had a chance to pursue her. She'd gone left, though, requiring her to run the entire length of the corridor and giving her no chance of reaching the end before he had a line of sight on her with his revolver. Now she was walking slowly towards us, her hands raised in surrender.

As I appeared at his side Temple clapped me on the back, causing a fresh wave of pain to erupt.

'What the hell is going on?' I hissed at him.

He didn't reply. I glanced at the revolver and saw that, like mine, his hand was trembling.

'Temple,' I pressed, 'who are they?'

'Later. For now, let's just get her inside.'

31

Before anything could be done about the woman, Temple and I agreed that our priority must be to contain the fallout from the attack.

My first concern was the noise; that the sound of the gunshot and of his apprehending the woman would draw a crowd of curious onlookers into the corridor. Mercifully, the revolver was small, firing with a short, sharp crack, instead of the deep boom that might be expected of a larger weapon.

Still, I spotted a few inquisitive faces. I tried to speak to those who did peer around their doors for a glimpse of the commotion, to assure them that there was nothing to worry about. But at the sight of my officer's uniform, they all retreated hurriedly into their cabins.

My secondary concern was the body. I had fired wildly, with the simple goal of hitting Temple's attacker as quickly as I could, and I had caught him squarely between the shoulders. The shot hadn't been powerful enough to pass cleanly through him, so I rolled him onto his front, hoping to prevent too much blood from oozing onto the carpet, and covered him with a sheet from the bed. Then I accosted a passing porter and sent him running to fetch another man and a stretcher. They returned within just a few minutes, and before long, the body was ready to be carried away.

'Take him quietly,' I instructed. 'I want as few passengers to catch wind of this as possible. And not a word to the other men. Do you understand? I will be reporting this to Captain McCrory myself and if I hear any talk among your colleagues, I'll know where it came from.'

'Yes, sir,' the first porter replied. Then with a grimace, 'Where would you like us to take him, sir?'

I considered for a moment, and in the absence of a morgue, thought miserably of the glorified cupboards which were now being used to house both Dupont and Vivian Hall.

'Put him below decks.'

I knew I was in a bad state as we watched them hurry away with the stretcher. My hands had just about stopped trembling, the adrenaline apparently wearing off. But with the impact of crashing into the cabin wall and the subsequent effort of heaving the woman away, my shoulder was throbbing with an intensity I hadn't felt in years.

I couldn't say whether Temple had noticed. If he had, he made no comment.

'I haven't killed a man since the war,' I said.

'His name was Doyle,' the detective replied grimly. 'And you needn't feel guilty. There isn't a man or woman alive who'll grieve for him.'

I waited for him to expand, remembering his insistence that Doyle was a dangerous criminal. If I was hoping for more, though, it seemed I was to be disappointed.

Unsure of quite how to respond, I motioned towards the cabin. 'What about her? We don't have anything even remotely resembling a cell to hold her in.'

'There isn't a brig?'

'We're a passenger vessel.'

'Can we lock her in the room?'

I shook my head. 'Not unless you can find the key. I searched Doyle before the porters took him away. He wasn't carrying it.'

'She'll need watching, then.'

I thought for a moment. 'There's a man called Wilson. He's a friend of mine, another officer. We'll send for him and work out a plan.'

Temple nodded, while I wondered if Wilson would have any interest whatsoever in coming to help me. If our roles were to be reversed, I suspected I'd think twice after the way I had lashed out at him in the mess. The truth, however, which I arrived at with a sorrowful realisation, was that there was nobody else I could turn to.

All the while, the woman sat silently on the lower bunk, her eyes darting around the cabin. I saw a bruise just beginning to show on her wrist where I had pushed her away. I forced myself to remember that this was the woman who had twice threatened to see I shared the same fate as Dupont. The woman who had stalked us in the cargo hold and, just moments ago, had lunged at me across the cabin with the apparent intention of ending my life. Still, I felt a sharp twinge of shame.

'What happened in there?' I demanded.

'He was hiding behind the door,' said Temple. 'Got the jump on me as I stepped into the cabin.'

'That's not what I meant. I thought ... I thought she was with you. When I saw her outside your cabin—'

'You were following me?'

'Do you really wish that I hadn't been?'

Temple scowled. He straightened up as though he might protest, but seemed to think better of it, his shoulders slumping again. 'She said she had something to show me,' he relented. 'Something to do with Dupont.'

'And you just went with her?'

'She said it couldn't leave her cabin. Told me I had to come and see it.'

'You reckless—' I stopped myself and took a deep breath. 'Did it not occur to you who she was? That she was clearly the woman watching us in the cargo hold?'

'Of course it did.'

'Then why did you go?'

He shook his head, his eyes to the floor. 'After this afternoon, with Morris and Green ...'

'You were desperate,' I said. 'Is that it? Your theory turned out to be wrong and you just wanted a breakthrough.'

'I had this, didn't I?' He waved the revolver at me, suddenly defensive again.

'And look how much use it was.'

'I could deal with it.'

'No, you couldn't!' I heard my voice rising, unable to hold back my frustration any longer. 'If I hadn't followed, where would you be?'

He didn't answer.

'And now I've—' I stopped and took a deep breath to steady myself. 'Now I've killed a man.'

'I told you—'

'I know what you told me,' I snapped. 'That no one will grieve for him. But it doesn't matter. I've killed a man and it's your fault. This wouldn't have happened if you'd trusted me. If you'd just let me help.'

For once, Temple seemed to have no retort. Instead, a heavy silence hung in the air.

I nodded towards the cabin door. 'Who is she?'

'I've no idea. Doyle and I have crossed paths but I've never seen her before. She told me her name was Elsie. Not that we can believe her.'

'Well, what do they want? Do they have Mr Blake's painting? Or Miss Hall's?'

'No.'

'But what if they were the ones who had already been to Mr Blake's cabin? When Mr Green followed Monsieur Dupont—'

'This isn't about Dupont.' Temple shook his head, refusing to meet my eye. 'Listen, Birch ... I don't want you to be involved with this. It's a bad business—'

'Winston Parker,' I muttered. 'This is about Winston Parker, isn't it?'

At the sound of his name, Temple flinched. I thought of the discovery that I'd made in his cabin; of the reports of Parker's crimes in London and my certainty that Doyle's name was one of those listed in the journal.

'You can argue all you like,' I said sternly. 'But I won't be shut out any longer. I don't care if you want to keep whatever it is that you're doing in New York secret. I've had enough of it all. Whoever she is, that woman intended to kill me and I won't leave your side until I understand why.'

Temple glared at me, the revolver still in his hand. With an effort, I held his gaze. Finally, he shook his head, stuffed the gun inside his jacket and returned to the cabin.

There was a long silence as he assessed the woman, picking the chair up from the floor and seating himself in the middle of the little room. If he meant to intimidate her, it didn't seem to work. She was like a coiled spring, glaring at him with palpable resentment.

I, meanwhile, hovered a foot or two behind. Eager as I was to observe, I was unable to forget that the last time this woman and I had come face to face, my life had been threatened at the point of some sharp, unidentified weapon. Even if Temple was right, and she wasn't the one who had left a knife in Arthur Blake's desk, it was a difficult memory to shake loose.

'You're a young one,' said Temple. 'You can't have been doing this for long.'

The woman said nothing.

'Is Elsie really your name?'

Again, she didn't reply.

'This will go much better for you if you answer my questions.'

For several seconds, she simply continued to glare at him. Then she gave a single nod.

'You're with Doyle, then?' he asked. 'He didn't force you to do any of this?'

'Does it matter?' she snapped.

'Yes, it matters.'

'I'm with him, then.'

Temple was about to respond, but Elsie blurted out, 'It don't matter that you locked up Violet. The Parkers have still got people in London. We didn't get you, but someone else will.'

'Except Violet's gone, hasn't she?' Temple's voice suddenly rose. 'And now Doyle has, too – put down like the rabid animal that he was. You're all alone out here, Elsie, and you've just tried to kill a police officer. So, if you want to leave this room with anything besides a noose, you're damn well going to answer my questions.'

Elsie said nothing, glaring at Temple as though she might launch herself across the cabin again. I, meanwhile, found myself thinking once more about the newspaper clipping I had found in Temple's cabin. The story had been about Violet Parker, Winston Parker's cousin, who was being tried in New York for crimes in London. Was that how Temple was involved? From what Elsie said, *he* had been the one to lock Violet up.

'Why are you interested in Mr Webber's car?' I asked, taking advantage of the silence.

'Who?'

'Mr Webber,' I repeated. 'You scratched his car on Tuesday night and you were there when we came to inspect it on Wednesday. What does it have to do with any of this?'

'I don't know anything about a car.'

'Don't lie to us. You were *seen* scratching the car.'

'I don't know about any car!' Elsie hissed. 'I'd never been down there until I followed you two.'

'Then why did you follow us?'

334

'I was watching you, wasn't I?' She nodded at Temple. 'Trying to get this one alone, so I could bring him to Doyle.'

I shook my head, trying desperately to order the events in my mind. 'You're lying. On Tuesday night, you were seen—'

'Enough,' Temple growled. 'This isn't helping.'

I frowned to myself, recalling our conversation with Webber in the restaurant. If Elsie wasn't the woman who had scratched the car, who had his witness seen?

'I suppose it was the Parkers who provided you with this cabin,' said Temple. 'A place to lure me.'

'Or to hide your body.' She cast him a venomous look before turning her gaze on me. 'We'd have had him if it weren't for you.'

'Leave him be,' Temple snapped.

Suddenly, a new-found eagerness flashed across Elsie's face, a smile forming in the corners of her mouth. 'He doesn't know, does he?'

'I said leave him.'

'What's he told you?' she demanded, oblivious to Temple's protests. 'That he's the golden boy of Scotland Yard?'

'Shut up.' Temple spoke through gritted teeth, his fingers flexing; threatening, it seemed, to reach again for his revolver.

'That he brought down the meanest crook in London?' Elsie continued. 'Single-handed, was it?'

'I said shut up.'

'He's not even a detective!' she cried, her voice rising. 'They sacked him! They gave him a job to do and he mucked it all up. You want to watch yourself, mate. Last time this one had a friend, he went and got 'em killed!'

335

'Quiet!' Temple sprang to his feet, sending the chair flying backwards. His face was contorted with rage, and for a split second, I thought he might be about to strike her. Elsie, apparently having had the same thought, flinched away, her bony arms flying up to cover her face.

But Temple just stood there, his shoulders heaving. Seeing that he had managed to restrain himself, Elsie lowered her arms and began to giggle quietly.

Before Temple could muster enough composure to speak again, the door opened and I turned to see Wilson peering inside.

'Tim ...' His eyes were wide as he surveyed the overturned desk and chair, the clothes and paper strewn across the floor and Temple looming over the grinning Elsie. 'What the hell's happened?'

32

The restaurant was quiet, most of the diners having either returned to their cabins or retired to the reading room for brandy and cigars. The musicians on the podium were putting away their instruments, while the bartender polished glasses with a white cloth and arranged them neatly on the shelves behind him. Velvet drapes had been drawn across the windows and the glass chandeliers had been extinguished, the only light now coming from the candles that flickered gently on the tables.

Despite having the room almost entirely to ourselves, Temple and I had still chosen a table in the corner. I don't believe that he cared, but I was uncomfortably aware, as we passed the remaining passengers dressed in their dinner suits and evening gowns, of how dishevelled we must have looked. We received a number of confused glances and Robert Evans treated us to his usual disapproving frown as we wove between the tables, though nobody tried to stop us.

The combination of the ambush and his failure that afternoon in the reading room seemed to have affected Temple even more than I had first realised. He slumped into a chair, propped his elbows upon the table and ran a hand through his thick hair. Perhaps it was a trick of the light, but the dark bags beneath his eyes looked more pronounced and his skin seemed even more pale. The self-assurance with which he had first marched into Captain McCrory's office and insisted upon seeing Dupont's body had disappeared. He looked defeated.

'What will you have?' I asked.

'Scotch.'

I almost laughed. At last, I thought. Something that we can agree on.

Moments later, I returned from the bar with two double measures of Glenfiddich. My shoulder was still throbbing with the effort of fending off Elsie's attack, and as I took a seat opposite Temple, I thought of Kate. I heard her asking, *'What have you got yourself into, Tim? Why couldn't you leave it alone?'*

We sat in silence, nursing our drinks. Over Temple's shoulder, I could see a young couple a few tables away, chatting quietly and gazing into each other's eyes. At the opposite end of the restaurant, laughter erupted from a group of men with thick moustaches and bellies that strained against their patterned waistcoats.

I'd given a great deal of thought to telling Temple that I had visited his cabin. To admitting that I had seen the notes in his journal and read the reports of Winston Parker's crimes in London. In the end, I'd decided against it. I wanted to know the truth. To understand exactly why Elsie and Doyle had stalked and attacked us. But I was also desperate to conclude our investigation, and the risk of him being so infuriated that he cast me off altogether seemed too great.

No. If I was to have answers, I would need to take a more subtle approach.

'Who are they?' I asked, setting my whisky down upon the table. 'Truthfully. Elsie and ...'

'Doyle.'

'Elsie and Doyle,' I repeated. 'What did they want? The cargo hold, the threat sent to my cabin ... What was it all for?'

Temple simply sipped his whisky, a blank expression on his face.

'What did Elsie mean?' I pressed. 'When she said that you aren't a detective.'

'Nothing.'

'She said that they sacked you. That someone had died. That doesn't sound like nothing to me.'

Again, he made no reply.

'When we first met,' I said. 'On Wednesday morning. You said that you were travelling to New York on police business. How can that be true, if you're not with the police?'

This time, I stood my ground and let the question hang in the air.

'It's complicated,' he said quietly.

'So start at the beginning. What does this have to do with Winston Parker?'

Finally, Temple sighed and leaned back in his chair. 'All right,' he muttered. 'If you want to start at the beginning, Mr Birch, that's what we'll do.'

He took a deep breath and then sipped his whisky as if to steady himself. His reluctance made me uneasy, though I tried not to let it show. These might very well be the answers that I had been craving for days. I couldn't shy away.

'Elsie and Doyle belong to a vast criminal organisation,' he said. 'Founded twenty years ago in New York – as you seem so astutely to have observed, by Winston Parker.'

'You think Mr Parker is a criminal?'

'We know he is. On the face of it, he might very well appear to be a perfectly legitimate businessman. But beneath the surface, he's up to his neck in bribery, violence and extortion. If you could trace it, you'd probably find that he's somehow connected to most of the crime in New York. But he's clever. He operates through agents and trusts, doing everything he can to ensure that none of it can ever be associated with him.'

'Is this not something for the American police to deal with?' I asked.

'It was. In all honesty, Scotland Yard couldn't have been less concerned about what Parker was up to in New York. What brought him to our attention was that, during the war, he set his sights on London.'

Temple sipped his whisky again before continuing. I peered at him closely, breathing in every word.

'Winston's agent in London is his cousin. A woman called Violet Parker.'

'That's who Elsie was talking about back in the cabin. She said that you'd locked up someone called Violet.'

Temple nodded. 'It's difficult to be sure, but we believe that Winston first sent her to England in 1917, while everyone's attention was on the war, and that she's been building up their operations ever since. Slowly, at first, to the point that we didn't even realise it was happening. But they've been gathering momentum during the last few years, and now they're running a fully fledged criminal network. It's reached the point that what they're doing is now too large to be tackled like an ordinary crime, so a number of officers were assigned to infiltrate the organisation.'

'And you were chosen?'

'I volunteered.' Temple shook his head at the thought. 'Foolish, really. But I suppose pride does strange things to people.'

'But why was any of this necessary? If you knew that this Violet Parker was the ringleader, why couldn't you simply arrest her?'

Temple paused before replying, apparently taking a moment to gather his thoughts.

'You have to understand how intelligent these people are,' he said slowly. 'How patient. At first, we didn't know Violet Parker existed. Christ, we didn't even *think* to look for a woman. All we knew was that some kind of American organisation was racketeering in London. It wasn't until we had officers within their operation that we realised the full extent of what was happening. Once we knew just how influential they were – how many people they had in their pockets – it became clear that it wouldn't be enough to simply catch Violet. They might be family, but if Winston couldn't see her released, he would surely just have her replaced. We needed something that could topple the entire organisation. Something that couldn't be dismissed or paid to disappear in court.'

'But she *has* been caught?'

Temple gave a sombre nod. 'Yes, she's been caught.'

I had expected him to sound pleased, but there was something in the way he continued to avoid my eye that told me his story was far from over.

'What happened?' I asked quietly.

He took a deep breath. 'Once I was accepted into the organisation, I was partnered with Doyle.'

I thought of the shaven-headed man. Tried not to picture the way his body had gone rigid in Temple's cabin with the impact of the gunshot.

'You told me that nobody would grieve for him,' I said.

Temple shook his head, looking wistfully into the distance. 'I've never come across a more violent, sadistic human being. To take pleasure in killing is bad enough. But Doyle ...'

He stopped to compose himself.

'I was partnered with him for months. I helped him with robberies and collecting extortion money, but all the while, I was meeting with the Yard to report my progress. For a long time, we had nothing. We were none the wiser as to who was in charge, where the money was going or how extensive the operation even was. Then, we discovered Violet Parker. She was careful. So careful that, for a long while, it seemed impossible to pin her to any of it. We finally struck lucky, though. I was given instructions to witness an execution – one of the shopkeepers who hadn't paid his share of the Parkers' extortion money and was being killed as an example to the others. She wanted to show them just what would happen if they decided to take a stand too.'

Temple shook his head, his eyes wide and distant. 'I'd heard of a few executions happening while I was with Doyle. But this was different. There was a rumour that Violet would be overseeing this one personally. I knew it was the opportunity we'd been waiting for. The chance we needed to catch her in the act. But my next report wasn't due until after it had taken place. I thought about going straight to Scotland Yard, but we all knew that it was being watched. I wouldn't be surprised if it turned out Violet even had people inside.'

He paused to sip his whisky.

'But there was another officer who'd managed to work his way into the organisation,' he continued. 'He was due to report back within the next few days. So I told him what I knew. I convinced him to meet me, gave him the details of the execution and said that he had to convince the Yard to carry out a raid.'

'What was his name?'

Temple looked for a long while at the surface of the table. 'It was Pearce,' he said at last. 'Edward Pearce.'

I felt my hands begin to quiver. Pearce had been mentioned in the newspaper clipping; the officer who had supposedly been tortured and murdered by Violet Parker.

'Did he succeed?'

Temple nodded. 'He did. And Violet Parker was arrested at the scene.'

'So what was Elsie talking about?' My voice was trembling. 'She said that you were sacked. That someone had been killed.'

Temple shook his head grimly.

'Pearce,' he said, what little colour was left draining from his cheeks. 'I knew it would be suspicious if we were seen together. We weren't partnered with each other so, as far as Parker's people were concerned, we had no reason to be in contact. I thought we'd be safe if we met somewhere crowded. I had him come to Covent Garden, one of the busiest places I could think of, but I suppose it did no good. I don't know who saw us, but ...'

343

He stopped to clear his throat.

'Whoever it was that picked him up, they were too late. He passed the message on, the raid went ahead and Violet Parker was caught.'

'So what happened?'

Temple shrugged. 'Pearce wasn't there. Of course, we knew straight away that they must have got him, but there was nothing to be done. The next day, they started sending—'

He stopped and took a deep breath, as though physically struggling to finish the sentence.

'What?' I pressed, dreading the answer. 'What did they send?'

Temple drained his glass and brought it down heavily on the table. Over his shoulder, I saw the young couple jump in surprise.

'Fingers,' he said. 'The day after Violet Parker was taken into custody, a note arrived at Scotland Yard, demanding her release in exchange for Pearce. We didn't respond, so for ten days, each morning, we received an envelope containing a finger.'

I felt sick, my mind filled with images of brown paper stained black with blood. We sat in silence, and I thought of the way that Raymond described Winston Parker in his letters. The American Dream personified, he had once said. Surely, he couldn't know that this was the kind of activity with which Parker was involved. Looking at Temple, I began to wonder if *I* really wanted to know. If these were truly details that I wanted to hear. But I knew that I had to. I was too far in to turn back now.

'You couldn't have known,' I said weakly. 'You were doing your job. You caught Violet Parker.'

Temple said nothing, leaning back in his seat and fiddling with the empty glass.

'Did they really sack you?' I asked.

He nodded. 'But not for that. Don't misunderstand, everyone knew that what happened to Pearce was my fault. They couldn't wave me off, though. Not when I'd given them the tip-off that brought in Violet Parker. No, I made another mistake.'

He cleared his throat again. He was starting to slur his words ever so slightly, the whisky apparently taking effect.

'It was the seventh day after we'd taken Violet into custody and another envelope had just arrived. The guilt ... You can't imagine it. The thought of another man going through this because of you. Because *your* mistake got him caught.'

I saw where his story was leading.

'You were going to let Violet go,' I said quietly. 'You were going to make the exchange.'

Temple didn't reply at first. A heavy silence hung over the table as I waited for him to finish his story.

'They stopped me, of course.' His voice was beginning to tremble. 'I had no plan and, in all honesty, I think I knew that it wouldn't work. I knew they would catch me. But I had to do *something*. When that seventh envelope arrived, still wet with Pearce's blood, I just needed to know that I'd tried. That I hadn't sat back and let it happen.'

I nodded, suddenly filled with sympathy for him.

'I was dismissed immediately,' he continued. 'The Yard had been looking for a reason to send me on my way ever since they found out about Pearce. When they caught me trying to let Violet go, they had their excuse. But they had a problem, too. I needed to appear as a witness at her trial – to give an account of everything that I had seen during my time with Doyle – and the Yard couldn't have me step up to the dock after dismissing me for jeopardising the investigation. As unreliable witnesses go, I don't see how it could be much worse. So it's been done quietly. My attempt to free Violet Parker has been covered up and I've been put on non-active duty, with my dismissal planned for after the trial.'

'That's why you're going to New York,' I said. 'That's your "police business", isn't it? If Violet Parker's an American citizen, that's where she'll be tried.'

Temple spread his hands wide, meeting my gaze for the first time since we had sat down. 'There you have it. That's my story. I'll appear in court next week and then my career will be over.'

We sat in silence for a long while, as the weight of Temple's story settled in.

'I suppose Elsie's note makes sense now,' I said. '*Keep away or you'll be next*. I assumed it meant Dupont, but that was never true. She was talking about you. She was trying to frighten me away. To catch you by yourself so she could take you to Doyle.'

Temple didn't answer.

'But this business with Dupont and Miss Hall,' I continued. 'Where does that come into it all? If you're no longer working for Scotland Yard, why are you so set on pursuing it?'

Temple might not even have been listening any more. He stared vacantly at the surface of the table.

'You're trying to prove yourself,' I realised. 'Is that it? You're hoping that if you can solve their murders and recover the paintings, it might compel Scotland Yard to take you back.'

Again, Temple said nothing.

'Do you really think it will work?'

His eyes flicked up, filled with venom.

'What about you, Birch?' he spat. 'What's your story?'

'*My* story?' My tone was a good deal more defensive than I had intended. His sudden hostility had taken me by surprise and the whisky was going to my head, a week's worth of sleepless nights starting to take their toll.

'That's right. You've heard my sad little tale. Surely you won't keep yours from me?'

'I'm sure I don't know what you mean.'

'Then I'll elaborate for you.' He leaned forward in his seat, glaring at me intently. 'The wound in your shoulder is fairly self-explanatory. You've been wincing and trying to avoid putting any strain on your right arm since we were jumped by Doyle and Elsie, but there doesn't seem to be any blood and you're clearly doing your best not to let it show. Perhaps you're trying not to let me see it. Whatever your reason, you know how to move without straining it too much, suggesting that you've lived with it for some time, so I suppose you must have earned it during the war. That's not what interests me, though. I want to know about the ribbon in your pocket.'

I gawped at him, completely unsure of what I could say.

'I saw you on the promenade,' he continued. 'On Wednesday morning, just before we called on Cassandra Webber. You were watching those children playing with a skipping rope, and you were fidgeting with a yellow ribbon. You have it even now. For God's sake, you were attacked by a pair of criminals belonging to the most vicious gang in London tonight and the first thing you did was make sure it was still in your pocket.'

I opened my mouth to speak, but he continued before I had a chance.

'Now, I would imagine it isn't a requirement for a ship's officer to carry a yellow ribbon in his pocket, so I can only assume it must have some personal value to you. There's a story behind it. Some quality that means you can't bear to be away from it. *That's* what I want to know about.'

He let the assessment hang in the air, the intensity that had come over him when he first inspected Dupont's body returning. He leaned over the table, his eyes filled once again with the same piercing energy that had burned within them over the last three days.

I took a deep breath to steady myself and looked him squarely in the eyes. 'We're not talking about the ribbon.'

'Did your wife wear it?'

I didn't reply.

'Your ex-wife, perhaps?'

'That's enough,' I said through gritted teeth.

'What happened? Did she leave you?'

'I said *enough*.'

'Or maybe it wasn't your wife at all,' he continued, his voice rising. 'You seem like a family man – perhaps it belonged to one of your children. But why value it so highly? Why take such care to always have it with you? I suppose it might be a reminder of someone, either a wife or a daughter who's no longer here to wear it, though I can't imagine which. Fine, your wife might leave you. But your children wouldn't—'

'That's enough!'

The young couple seated at the table behind Temple stood up to leave, throwing disapproving glances at us as they went.

For a long while, we sat quietly, not making eye contact. The remaining passengers began to file from the restaurant and I was aware of the bartender peering at us curiously from across the room. Finally, feeling my cheeks flush, I broke the silence.

'What do we do now?' I asked bitterly.

'About what?'

'What do you think? Dupont! Miss Hall! Where do we look next? Who do we speak to?'

Temple thought for a moment, tapping a fingernail rhythmically against the whisky glass. 'We don't do anything.'

'What do you mean?' I snapped but Temple was standing to leave. 'How can we do *nothing*?'

'Go back to your duties, Mr Birch,' he said solemnly. 'Report to your captain that we've tried and failed. This investigation should be resumed by the police in New York. It's clear to me now that we need more men and more resources than you and I can muster between us.'

'You can't be serious. You've said yourself that the police won't stand a chance – not once the passengers have all disembarked. This has to be resolved before we reach New York. It has to be us!'

'Let it go,' he said. 'We're done.'

Saturday 15 November 1924

33

After Temple had left me in the restaurant, I returned to Elsie's cabin, where Wilson had mercifully agreed to stand guard in the absence of a key.

Having searched both Elsie and Doyle and found no sign of one, and with no cells of any kind in which to keep her prisoner, he had decided while I had been away that we would return to the officers' quarters for the skeleton key. I pointed out the fact that Captain McCrory would only allow it to be used in the most severe emergencies, as well as the ethical quandary of imprisoning a passenger in their cabin. But as Wilson quite rightly – and more than a little bluntly – argued, Elsie had attacked both a passenger and a ship's officer, and in just over a day we would dock in New York, where she would be handed to the police. For the time being, the most important consideration was that she be secured.

Elsie, of course, hadn't said a word as we explained how she would be spending the remainder of the voyage. She had sat silently on the lower bunk, her bony knees brought up beneath her chin and her wild eyes flitting frantically between Wilson and me.

After we were satisfied that she was securely held, I had declared I should be the one to report the incident to Captain McCrory in the morning. There was no need for Wilson to be implicated any further. He had merely grunted in reply and then retired to his cabin, leaving me to ponder miserably that, with my outburst in the mess, it seemed I really had pushed my friend too far.

Settling into my bunk, I had struggled even more than usual to slip into a restless sleep. I had killed a man. Acted in blind panic and ended his life. I had locked a passenger – a frightened, angry young woman – in her cabin and I had somehow dragged Wilson into the middle of it all.

And then there was Temple. I thought that I would be relieved to finally understand the full truth of his connection to Winston Parker. Instead, I couldn't help but feel betrayed by his decision to abandon our investigation; by his apparent revelation that we no longer stood a chance of unmasking the culprit ourselves.

I found myself stinging with resentment. But, if I was honest with myself, that resentment was only partly fuelled by Temple's surrender. The truth was that he had wounded me in an altogether more painful way before leaving the restaurant. Despite it all, he had noticed the ribbon and even the injury to my shoulder. And he had asked about Kate and Amelia.

Lying in my bunk, I held the ribbon close and thought of all the months I had spent searching. Of the way Kate had glared at me, hatred in her eyes, when I first announced that I would be returning to the *Endeavour*. The numerous letters in which I had recounted my grief to Raymond.

With a sigh, I recalled the conversation that I'd had with Wilson.

'I'm worried that you might not be in the right frame of mind for all of this.'

He was right. It hadn't been clear to me while Temple and I had roamed the *Endeavour*, but it was evident now. Dupont. Vivian Hall. Even Temple ... It was all too much. I had to prioritise. To focus wholeheartedly on Amelia.

And so, as I wove the ribbon between my fingers, I resolved that I had no choice but to banish all thoughts of the investigation from my mind. The question of whether Dupont had fallen or been thrown down that companionway would fall to the police in New York. As would that of who had struck Vivian Hall with the wine cooler, and taken both her and Arthur Blake's paintings.

I was all too aware that these questions might very well remain unanswered. In fact, I was sure that they would. How the police would resume this investigation when the culprit had disappeared into the streets of Manhattan, I couldn't fathom. But, however uncomfortable that prospect made me, it seemed I had no other choice. Temple had given up, wallowing in the shame of his looming dismissal from Scotland Yard. And if there was one thing he had made abundantly clear to me, it was that I wouldn't solve this mystery alone.

When morning came, I felt groggy. My little cabin had only a small porthole, but even if it had been larger, there was barely any daylight to be enjoyed. I lay in my bunk for a long while, reluctant to step into the cold air any sooner than I had to, and listened unhappily to the rumbling of the *Endeavour*, the howling of the wind and the endless churning of the ocean.

One small mercy, I supposed, was that the aching in my shoulder had subsided since my brawl with Elsie. As I massaged it my mind drifted to Raymond. I thought of the moment I had opened his last letter. Remembered his insistence that I visit, the offer of his father's resources, and then, finally, discovering Amelia's ribbon, tucked inside the envelope.

We were going to do it, I told myself. The ribbon was just the start. Together, we were going to find her.

I dragged myself from my bunk, the chill morning air seizing me the instant I threw back the covers. I washed in cold water and donned my uniform, ready to attend the last of Captain McCrory's daily briefings before we docked on Sunday morning.

As I brushed down my coat I was surprised to feel the outline of a sharp corner resting in my pocket. Fetching it out, I found myself holding a small rectangle of crisp white card, on which the words *Saturday* and *Sunday* had been written in a neat hand. I turned it over and realised that it was Michael Green's business card, the address of his office inscribed in fine black print. With everything that had happened since Temple and I met the banker's wife, I had all but forgotten that I kept this sample of Beatrice Green's handwriting.

I gazed at the card, as though it might yield some hidden secret if I could just concentrate hard enough. All I could think of, however, was our last conversation with Michael Green and the smug assurance with which he had threatened Temple and me in the reading room. With a scowl, I tossed it onto my bed.

As I arrived in the mess hall, I was glad to see that Wilson was already there, wolfing down a large bowl of porridge. I was anxious to apologise for the previous evening; both for having involved him with Elsie and for lashing out at him over dinner. But at the sound of my approach, he glanced up, a new-found thunder in his expression. His eyes burned into mine. Then he shook his head and returned to his breakfast.

For several seconds, I stood where I was. With a great swell of frustration, I considered marching over, sitting down and demanding that we talk this out. That he hear my apology and we put the previous night's events behind us. But with an effort, I restrained myself.

Wilson had tried time and again to reach out to me – to speak to me about Kate and Amelia – and I had thrown every effort back in his face. Rejected each show of kindness and hint of concern. He was entitled to his anger.

At precisely nine o'clock, Captain McCrory arrived, and as we did every morning, the officers stood to attention. I listened closely as the man on duty spoke about the various preparations being made for our arrival. Dupont was briefly mentioned, but only so far as to announce that a coroner had been telegrammed and would be waiting in the harbour to receive his body. Then, finally, came the report that I had been dreading.

'There's also been talk, sir,' the officer said, 'of a gunshot in second-class.'

With bated breath, I watched for several seconds as the captain seemed to consider this new information.

'Has anyone been shot?' he asked.

'No, sir.'

'Do you not think that if there truly had been a gunshot, then someone would likely also have *been* shot?'

'Sir,' the officer bravely protested. 'This has been reported by three different passengers, each of whom say that they distinctly heard what sounded like a gunshot. They're extremely concerned—'

The captain raised a hand, silencing the officer in an instant.

'I understand that tensions are high,' he said. 'Many of our passengers are, no doubt, still worried about the gentleman who was found on Wednesday morning. But as I have now explained several times, his death was the result of an *accident*. Nothing more.' There was suddenly a hard edge to his voice. 'We are just a single day away from New York. Keep your eyes and ears open, and if there is genuine evidence that a shot was fired last night, I will examine it. Until such an occasion, you will treat this as what it almost surely is. Gossip, gentlemen. Tomorrow, the passengers will disembark and this unpleasantness will be forgotten. The best thing we can do today is contain it, not encourage it.'

Many of the officers looked unenthused by the captain's instructions, but it seemed nobody had the courage to question them. I suspected they all saw just as clearly as I did that there would have been no point. There was an absent look in the captain's eyes, as though he were picturing the moment, barely twenty-four hours from now, when he would fetch the cigar box from his desk, step from the *Endeavour* and, at long last, begin his retirement.

It was a strangely uncomfortable moment. That being said, I was relieved to see that the two porters who had stretchered

Doyle's body away had followed my instruction and kept their silence. Or at the very least, that any idle chatter they might be spreading about yet another body being housed below deck seemed not to have made its way to the officers' mess.

The report now concluded, the captain dismissed us and we filed from the room. I tried to call after Wilson, but he was the first to leave, barging his way to the door before I could catch him.

34

It was with a sense of dread that I slipped the skeleton key from my pocket, unlocked the cabin door and eased it gently open. After our last meeting, I half-expected Elsie to launch herself across the cabin at me the moment I entered, and with the key in one hand and a plate of food in the other, I was painfully aware of how unequipped I would be to defend myself.

To all intents and purposes, however, she might not even have moved from the spot in which Wilson and I had left her the previous evening – sitting on the lower bunk, her back to the wall and her knees to her chin. Her eyes snapped up to meet me, and she seemed to tense as I pushed the door closed.

I set the plate down on the bedside table and retreated to the other side of the cabin. Elsie watched me for a moment. Then, apparently satisfied that I wasn't a threat, she snatched a chunk of bread from the plate and tore at it, like a dog pouncing upon a piece of meat.

'Did I hurt you?' I asked, nodding towards the bruise on her wrist.

She glared at me, her eyes filling with hatred at the very suggestion.

'Well, if I did, I'm sorry.'

Still she said nothing. I glanced around the cabin, feeling curiously as though I was intruding. The little room was in disarray from the ambush, both the desk and chair lying on their side, while clothes were strewn across the floor. On the lower bunk, it looked as though she might have drawn the covers around her during the night, but the top bunk was bare, the sheets having been taken to cover Doyle's body.

'I need to ask you something,' I said, with as much authority as I could manage.

She stopped mid-chew, her eyes narrowing.

'Last night, Mr Temple told me about Winston Parker. About what he's doing in London. He spoke about blackmail, murder, even torture.' I looked her in the eye, almost too afraid to ask my question. 'Is it all true?'

Elsie swallowed and carefully returned what remained of the bread to the plate. Looking down at the floor, she gave a single nod.

I picked up the chair and sank into it. It was curious to feel so disappointed – so betrayed – by the apparent unmasking of someone I had never met. By all accounts, Winston Parker was a man who countless people looked up to; who many saw as a beacon of the success that they, themselves, might one day hope to achieve. Even Raymond, on the occasions that he had mentioned Parker in his letters, had always done so with adoration.

I supposed the truth was that I didn't want to believe it. I wanted to deny that Parker had sent assassins aboard the

Endeavour, just as I wanted to deny Temple's story about his comrade from Scotland Yard. But to deny it from Elsie, a woman who openly claimed to be following Parker's own instructions, was an impossible task.

'They're going to kill me,' she said bluntly.

I glanced up at her. Troubling as this sudden prediction was, there was something strange in her voice. I'd have expected to hear fear, maybe even anger. Instead, there was only a vague sense of resignation.

'You'll be in police custody.'

She snorted at me. 'I thought you said that your friend had told you about them?'

I frowned.

'You really don't get it, do you? The Parkers own half the police in New York. I won't even see the inside of a cell, like as not. They'll hand me straight over.' She looked me directly in the eye. 'Then they'll come for you.'

'Why me?' I asked.

'We would have had that copper if it weren't for you. Do you think Mr Parker's going to take kindly to that?'

'But how would he know?'

She looked away, a guilty expression flashing across her face. With a sudden realisation, my heart sank.

'You're going to tell them, aren't you? You'll tell them that I'm the one who stopped you from killing Temple.'

'If it buys me a quick death, then yes.' She flexed her fingers, and I found myself thinking about Temple's story. About the officer called Pearce and the bloodstained envelopes that had been sent to Scotland Yard.

'I don't believe you,' I said. 'The only reason you sent that note to my cabin was so that I'd be away from Temple when you jumped him. You wanted to spare me, to ensure that one less person was killed.'

'I sent it so I could get him alone,' she snapped. 'I followed him for two days. Working out where he slept, where he spent his time, if he was travelling with anyone. Just as I was starting to work him out, Wednesday morning, he meets you.' Malice glinted in her eyes. 'Don't think I've got any interest in helping you. I sent that note because he'd be easier to pick off if you weren't around. If handing you over to the Parkers means I get a clean death, believe me, I'll do it.'

'But Winston Parker doesn't even know who I am.'

'It doesn't matter,' she said. 'He'll find you. He can find anyone.'

I paused a moment, watching her carefully. 'Anyone?'

She nodded. 'Doesn't matter where you try to hide, they'll find you sooner or later. The Parkers have people everywhere.'

For a long while we sat in silence. There had been pure certainty in Elsie's voice. She believed what she was saying.

'What would it take,' I said quietly, 'for you not to tell them that I saved Temple?'

She gave a sad smile. 'Nothing. There's no sense in lying to them and I haven't got the means to outrun them. I wouldn't last a week before they found me, and when they did, it'd be worse than if I'd gone willingly.'

Realising I was getting nowhere, I stood to leave, motioning towards the plate.

'I'll need to take that.'

She snatched up the remaining bread and handed the plate over.

At the door, I stopped, turning back one last time to face her. 'I'll speak to Mr Temple. Tell him what you've told me. There *must* be some kind of protection that the police can offer you.'

'It's no use,' Elsie replied, her mouth full. 'Kindest thing you could do would be to take that revolver of his and put a bullet in my head. But leave one for yourself.' Her eyes were wide and distant. 'It'll be cleaner than whatever's waiting for the pair of us in New York.'

35

Having locked Elsie's cabin, I climbed to the bridge, hoping that the open ocean would help to clear my head. Sharples, the officer Wilson and I had seen being thrashed at cards the previous night, was on duty, and he fixed me with a suspicious look as I approached. But upon learning that I was there to relieve him, he became a good deal more agreeable.

I took up my position by the window; the sky was clearing and the waves were calm as the helmsman guided the *Endeavour* at a steady thirty knots through the Atlantic. After a short while, a porter came with a rag and polished the clock, the navigation instruments and the great brass handle of the engine order telegraph. I even sent for a pot of Earl Grey. But the stillness of the bridge wasn't having its usual soothing effect.

Of course, I was still shaken by my conversation with Elsie. It was clear now that Winston Parker was, indeed, a man to be feared. If Elsie were to deliver on her threat and tell him that I had helped Temple to escape his death, I doubted that even Raymond could offer me sanctuary.

But it wasn't just the thought of crossing Winston Parker that plagued me. Try as I might to put Dupont and Vivian Hall from my mind, it somehow felt wrong not to be on my way to meet Temple or chase down another lead in our investigation.

Someone aboard the *Endeavour* had struck Vivian Hall with a wine cooler. They had thrown Denis Dupont down that flight of stairs and they now possessed both of the stolen paintings. But instead of chasing them down, I was standing and watching as we inched closer to New York. To the moment the culprit would step from the *Endeavour*, free, should they see fit, to strike again.

An hour passed, each minute more uncomfortable than the last. Then, just as I could stand it no longer, the telephone rang on the wall behind me. Grateful for the distraction, I lifted the brass receiver from its cradle.

'Bridge.'

'Is Birch up there?'

'Speaking.'

'It's the officers' mess,' the voice crackled over the line. 'There's someone here asking for you. A porter.'

'A porter?'

'That's right. He seems eager to speak with you. Says his name's Seymour.'

Seymour ... With everything that had since happened with Temple and Elsie, I had all but forgotten the mission I had assigned the young fellow.

'Are you still there?' the voice demanded.

'Yes,' I said. 'Yes, put him on.'

There was a fumbling noise as the receiver was passed over. Then a familiar voice came eagerly down the line.

'Hello? Mr Birch?'

'Seymour. What is it?'

'I have some news for you, sir. About that car in the cargo hold. I've been asking around the other men, trying to find out who was nearby on Tuesday, and I have something that I think you'll be keen to hear.'

Despite myself, I couldn't help but feel a flutter of excitement. 'What do you have?'

'A witness, sir! My friend, O'Shea. He was *in* the cargo hold on Tuesday evening and he saw a woman interfering with the car. He chased her off and the gentleman who owned the car arrived to inspect it shortly after. O'Shea says he seemed terribly unhappy about the damage that she'd done.'

My excitement vanished as quickly as it had begun. Harry Webber had shared this news with us already. Although there was a small detail in Seymour's account which Webber hadn't been able to divulge.

'O'Shea,' I murmured. 'I know that name ...'

The line went quiet, and I could almost sense the guilt passing over Seymour's face.

'Hold on a moment,' I said. 'He's the fellow you sold your whisky to, isn't he? The one you said had come into some money.'

Out of the corner of my eye, I saw the helmsman, suddenly interested, cast a curious glance in my direction.

'That's right, sir.'

'How can we trust this man? What was he even doing in the cargo hold?'

'I wondered the same thing, sir. When I raised it with him, he said that he was just stowing something for another passenger. He's a decent sort, sir. You can trust him. He likes a drop of whisky, but then don't we—'

'Is that everything, Seymour?' I could hear the frustration in my own voice. 'There's nothing else?'

'That's all, sir.' Even over the phone line, I could hear the enthusiasm drain from the young porter's voice. 'This is quite important though, isn't it, sir? It seems to me that you need to find this woman.'

I paused. Though he couldn't have realised it, Seymour's question had prompted a sudden realisation, flickering in my mind like a spark.

'Mr Birch,' Seymour crackled over the phone. 'Are you still there, sir?'

Before he could say another word, I returned the receiver to its cradle.

Again, with all that had since happened, I had allowed myself to neglect the revelation that on Tuesday night, the woman who Seymour's friend, O'Shea, had seen scratching Webber's car hadn't been Elsie. That is, at least, if she had been telling the truth; that when she followed us to the cargo hold on Wednesday afternoon, it had been her first visit.

Could that be the detail that Temple and I had missed these past few days? Could the woman who had *truly* damaged Harry Webber's car be the key to all of this?

For the life of me, I still couldn't fathom what scratching the car might have to do with either the murders or the thefts of the paintings, but it was surely too much of a coincidence for it to have taken place on the same night – virtually at the same time – as Dupont's death. If we could determine who this woman was, might everything else fall into place?

My mind raced. Of course, I thought to myself eagerly, the woman's identity wasn't the only unsolved mystery. Dupont might well have written the note from his cabin himself, but the question remained: what, exactly, had he planned for tonight at nine o'clock?

I glanced up at the window and surveyed the endless ocean. How many miles were between us and our destination? Just how long did I have until we docked and two thousand people – the culprit among them – disembarked? Might there already be another body somewhere on board the *Endeavour*, which Temple and I hadn't found? A third painting stolen? Would there be a fourth by the time the engines fell silent in the morning?

To hell with Temple. He might have given up, but I couldn't do the same.

Setting my untouched teacup to one side, I moved to the table at the back of the room, cleared a pile of naval charts and took out the list of suspects that I had compiled in the mess the previous evening. Gripping a pencil, I flipped the paper over and began to write out the details that we knew of Dupont and Vivian Hall's movements.

Monday Denis Dupont boarded the Endeavour and approached Arthur Blake in the restaurant, where he was dining with Vivian Hall, and Harry and Cassandra Webber. He attempted to buy the painting back from Mr Blake, a conversation which led to a heated argument and Dupont being sent away, unsuccessful.

Tuesday Dupont visited the restaurant early in the morning and paid Robert Evans for Mr Blake's cabin number. He then visited his client, Michael Green, to report that the acquisition of the painting was proceeding well, but wouldn't

*reveal its identity or location. That evening, Mr Green tricked
Dupont into leading him to Mr Blake's cabin, only to find that
the painting had already been stolen.*

*<u>Wednesday</u> Dupont's body was discovered at dawn on the
starboard promenade. Vivian Hall's whereabouts are unknown throughout the day. However, she visited the officers'
mess at six o'clock in the evening, before leaving for an appointment in her cabin with an unknown individual. During
this appointment, she was struck about the head with a wine
cooler and killed.*

I set down my pencil, admitting to myself that this was a
disappointing account. From the moment he arrived at Blake's
cabin and discovered the painting had been stolen, we knew
nothing more of Dupont's final movements. All we had to go
on was Mrs Hewitt's claim that she had heard him arguing
outside her window, between half-past ten and eleven o'clock,
before falling down the companionway. Likewise, we seemed
no closer to knowing who Vivian Hall had hurried to meet on
Wednesday evening. Nor why the culprit brought a knife to
Arthur Blake's cabin, but arrived apparently unarmed to their
meeting with Miss Hall.

Eager to try a different approach, I turned the paper over
and began, once again, to examine the list of names. My eyes
drifted first to Beatrice Green and Cassandra Webber. As the
only women, if O'Shea had seen any of the suspects on my
list scratching Harry Webber's car, it must surely have been
one of them. But both presented problems.

At the same time that the first painting was stolen, Dupont
was killed and the car was damaged, Beatrice Green had been

in the bar with Arthur Blake. Cassandra Webber, meanwhile, had been alone in her cabin. While it seemed nobody could confirm this alibi, I could think of no reason for her to damage her own husband's car, nor how she would even know about the painting in order to steal it. Blake told us himself that he had gone to considerable lengths to ensure that both she and Harry Webber had no idea it even existed.

I supposed that Green and Morris could have recruited a woman to scratch the car while they put their plan into action. Temple certainly seemed to have found it easy enough to recruit an accomplice to deliver the messages that lured them yesterday to the reading room. The question remained, though: neither of them knew Harry Webber, so why scratch the car?

Perhaps it was Vivian Hall who O'Shea had seen. She'd admitted herself to having no alibi for Tuesday evening. Perhaps she'd damaged it out of spite, having seen Harry and Cassandra Webber together. It seemed unlikely. When we'd spoken in the mess, Miss Hall had seemed completely indifferent to her relationship with Mr Webber. I struggled to imagine her being overcome with jealousy.

I thumped the table. How could we have come so far, spoken to so many people and gathered so much information, only to be no closer to the truth than when we had first inspected Dupont's sodden, lifeless body?

There *was* a solution. Someone on my list had the missing paintings. They knew what had truly become of Vivian Hall and Dupont. I was sure of it.

Abandoning the list, I returned to my position by the window and watched as the *Endeavour*'s great iron prow carved through the waves. Perhaps I was approaching this in the wrong way: searching for the answer in the information that we already had when, in fact, we were still missing some crucial detail.

But loath as I was to admit it, Temple had been thorough in his investigation, painting as vivid a picture as possible of Dupont's movements and dealings. We even knew the story of Arthur Blake and his failed marriage to Evelyn Scott.

In that moment, something came into focus. A question that we hadn't answered but which suddenly felt of the utmost importance. And I knew exactly where to find the answer.

'Is everything all right, sir?' the helmsman asked.

Despite us being the only two men on the bridge, I took a short while to realise that he was speaking to me. Following his gaze, I looked down and saw that I was gripping the brass handrail so tightly my knuckles were turning white.

'Quite all right,' I said. 'As you were.'

I strode to the back of the room and snatched the telephone receiver from its cradle.

'Hello?' I said. 'Sharples? It's Birch here. Would you mind coming back up to the bridge? I need to step away.'

36

I was becoming increasingly apprehensive as I returned, once again, to the restaurant. There had been no answer at her cabin door, nor had I found her in the reading room. Even to those who knew it well, a ship the size of the *Endeavour* could often feel like a labyrinth, and if she wasn't here, I would have no clue where to look for her next.

As was always the way during the lunchtime service, the room was heaving, with every table occupied and a growing queue of impatient passengers trailing into the corridor. Standing at the door, I looked out at a sea of men dressed in blazers and ladies in fine dresses. Waiters weaved between the tables, serving plates of fish and slices of pie.

I scanned the room, feeling the first twinge of disappointment as my gaze flitted from one crowded table to the next. Then, at last, I spotted her. Breathing a sigh of relief, I made my way through the teeming restaurant towards the window, where she sat with two other finely dressed ladies, each nursing a glass of white wine.

'Excuse me,' I said, as I reached the table. 'Mrs Green?'

Beatrice Green glanced up, her cool eyes filled with the same disinterest with which she had greeted Temple and me on Thursday. I recognised the diamonds glistening at her throat, but today she wore a matching snow-white skirt and blouse, as if to make her shadowed eyes, ruby lips and ink-black hair appear even more sharply defined against her porcelain skin.

'I'm sorry to bother you, ma'am,' I said, my voice trembling. 'Timothy Birch. I visited your cabin—'

'I remember. Is it just you today, Mr Birch?'

'It is, ma'am, yes. Mr Temple is . . .' I hesitated. 'I'm afraid he's unavailable.'

'I see.' Her eyes flitted back down to her wine glass. 'I suppose you have some more questions for me.'

'Only one, actually.'

'Oh?' She sounded intrigued, but I was aware of the curious gaze of her two companions. While I was relieved to see that Michael Green hadn't joined his wife for lunch, his parting warning to us not to speak with her again still rang in my ears.

'I wonder, Mrs Green, if it would be possible for us to speak privately?'

A smile spread across her face. She drained the rest of her glass and, once again, I had the distinct feeling that she enjoyed the to and fro of this process.

'You should know that Michael told me you'd met with him yesterday,' she said. 'I haven't the faintest idea what you and your detective said to him, but he was terribly unhappy when he came back to the cabin. I can't imagine he'd be pleased to know that I'd spoken with you again.'

I felt my heart begin to sink, realising that she must surely be about to send me away.

'But as it happens, Mr Birch, I am without a drink.' She stood and lifted a small white handbag from the table. 'You can buy me another.'

I was acutely aware of Mrs Green's companions whispering to each other as I followed her to the bar, and for a brief moment, I started to wonder if I was making a mistake. Perhaps it wasn't too late to apologise and wish her a pleasant day. There was no need for this to go any further.

Only it *was* too late. Already, she had arrived at the bar and the bartender was pouring a generous glass of white wine.

'And for you, sir?'

'Nothing for me.'

Mrs Green's features morphed into a pained expression, her mouth pursed. 'Are you going to make me drink alone, Mr Birch?'

'I'm on duty, ma'am.'

She didn't reply, an uncomfortable silence descending as she turned away and brought the glass to her lips. Recognising an impasse, I turned reluctantly to the bartender.

'A small white wine, please.'

Mrs Green's face lit up. As the bartender poured another glass, I noticed that he had been holding the bottle ready throughout the whole exchange. It was a routine that he must have seen countless times.

'I don't mean to delay you for long, Mrs Green,' I said, trying to sound more confident than I felt. 'I have just one question that I hoped you could help me with.'

'What is it today, Mr Birch?' She rolled her eyes playfully. 'You aren't going to ask me about this gunshot that the idlers in second-class have been wittering on about, are you?'

I winced, causing her eyes to go wide.

'It isn't *true*, is it?'

'It's being investigated, ma'am.'

'Has anyone been hurt?'

'No,' I said hurriedly. 'I promise you, Mrs Green, there's no reason to be alarmed.'

'You might want to try telling that to some of your other passengers.' She set her glass down on the bar and nodded towards the two ladies at her table. 'Cecilia over there is desperate to get off this ship. She was only just starting to get over this poor man of yours who fell down the steps. Hearing this morning that shots are being fired just a single deck below has sent her into a terrible frenzy. The poor thing says that she'll never travel on the Aurora Line again.' There was a wry smile on Beatrice Green's lips. 'Of course, she *is* a terrible bore. It doesn't take much to upset her, but I gather from what I've heard on the other tables she isn't the only one.'

I looked out across the restaurant. 'Will you assure her for me that everything is in hand?'

'I suppose so. But I must admit, I'm even more curious now than before. So tell me. What *did* you come to ask me about?'

I took a deep breath, aware that once I had asked my question, there would be no turning back. I could almost feel Temple next to me, shaking his head in disapproval.

'When we spoke on Thursday,' I said, 'you told us that Mr Blake was married to Evelyn Scott for a year before she sent him away.'

Mrs Green's eyes narrowed a fraction at the sound of Blake's name.

'By all accounts,' I continued, 'he spent that year drinking, taking advantage of her family's wealth and doing all that he could to make a fool of her. I would imagine that Frederick Scott would have happily seen the back of him much sooner.'

She gave a sharp laugh. 'I'll say.'

'But as I understand it, it wasn't until there were rumours of another woman that Miss Scott finally pressed for a divorce.'

Mrs Green took a long, slow sip. 'I thought you were looking for Arthur's painting,' she said.

'We are. Mr Temple believes the painting has been stolen and—'

'And that Evelyn is involved?'

I fiddled nervously with the stem of my own glass, forcing as much authority into my voice as I could muster. 'We're trying to build a clearer picture of Mr Blake's movements before he boarded the *Endeavour*. Who he was close to, how his work was faring, how he spent his time. His divorce from Evelyn Scott appears to have been a significant event and I believe it would be helpful to know all that we can about it.'

She looked at me, drumming her slender fingers on the bar as she considered my question. All around us, I was aware of the clinking of glasses and cutlery, the chatter of passengers at their tables and the laughter of the other patrons at the bar. A bottle of champagne opened with a loud pop, and just a few yards away, I could hear Robert Evans taking dinner reservations at the door.

'What exactly is it that you want to know, Mr Birch?' she asked, any sign of playfulness now long gone.

I took a deep breath. 'If Mr Blake was unfaithful to his wife, do you know who the other woman was?'

Mrs Green took a cautious sip as she considered her reply. 'I shouldn't tell you any of this,' she said. 'Evelyn's my friend and, frankly, I don't see what their divorce could possibly have to do with Arthur's painting.'

I nodded, readying myself to concede defeat.

'But I will tell you. Because I want you to truly understand what a despicable creature Arthur is.' She took a deep breath. 'You've heard, I suppose, about Evelyn's parties?'

I nodded. Harry and Cassandra Webber had both spoken about Evelyn Scott's garden parties. I could easily picture the long gravel drive, the gleaming manor and the perfectly mown lawns, bustling with guests.

'Arthur always drank too much at those parties.' Mrs Green swirled her wine around in its glass. 'He has a fondness for champagne and, as you seem to know already, he likes to ensure that his appetite is satisfied.'

I remembered the accounts of Blake's outburst when Dupont approached him on Monday evening, just a few yards from where we were now. Cassandra Webber had said that he was drinking champagne then as well.

'I'd been with Evelyn. We were smoking cigarettes on the veranda when it dawned on me that I hadn't seen Michael in some time. I knew he hadn't been looking forward to the party – he hates being away from town for very long – but it was his first time meeting my friends and it looked awful for him to have disappeared. So I went to find him.

'I searched everywhere. On the front lawn, in the gardens, inside the house … I was running out of places to look, but I hadn't yet tried the rose garden. Michael's never had any interest in gardens, but it would have been a good place to hide, if that was what he was trying to do.

'So I walked down there to have a look. As I got closer, I heard a woman behind the hedges. I couldn't see her, you understand, but she was protesting – almost pleading with someone. She was saying, "Please, you mustn't. Your wife will see."

'I didn't recognise her voice and I had clearly heard something that I wasn't supposed to. But before I could walk away, a man began to speak, in a voice that I most certainly knew. He said, "It's all right. She's up at the house. She'll never know."'

I felt a weight in the pit of my stomach.

'It wasn't Mr Green,' I said cautiously.

'No.' She shook her head slowly, savouring the moment. 'It wasn't Michael. It was Arthur.'

Before I could stop myself, a grimace danced across my face. Mrs Green gave a small laugh, apparently pleased by my reaction.

'Of course, as soon as I heard his voice, I went into the garden,' she continued eagerly. 'And there he was, holding this girl's wrist. She had been trying to pull away, and when he saw me, Arthur was so surprised that she managed to wrench herself free. She barged past me and ran straight back up to the house.'

'What did you say to Mr Blake?'

'Not a word. I left him there, went back to the house myself and told Evelyn exactly what I'd seen. Once the party was over and the guests had all left, Frederick had Arthur thrown off the grounds that very night.'

379

I took my first sip of wine, despairing at the thought that, during our first meeting, I had considered Blake to be the victim in this investigation. That I had been adamant Temple and I would return the painting to him and unmask whoever had left that knife in his desk. Now, with the image of him drunkenly grasping at a young woman's wrist, I didn't just feel foolish. I was repulsed.

'Mr Blake didn't tell us about any of this.'

'I'm not sure how much of it he would even remember. Arthur always made a fool of himself at Evelyn's parties, but I had never seen him as drunk as he was that day. He stumbled into a waiter on his way back up to the house, knocked a tray of champagne glasses out of the poor boy's hands and then screamed blue murder about how he was going to have him fired. Not that Frederick would ever have allowed him the authority.'

I winced at the image. 'You did say that he didn't recognise you in the bar on Tuesday night.'

'He hadn't the faintest idea who I was. If he remembers what he did in that rose garden, I'll be amazed. He probably didn't even know the girl.'

'Did *you* know her?'

'No.' Mrs Green was glancing towards her companions, apparently losing interest now that she had shown me Blake's true colours. 'She was a guest, but I hadn't seen her before, so she can't have been one of Evelyn's friends. I suppose she must have been someone's date.'

'You have no idea at all?'

She frowned at me, apparently growing irritated by my persistence. Then she sighed. 'She was American. I can tell you that much.'

'You didn't hear anything to suggest her name?'

'Perhaps. But you have to understand that I can't be sure.'

I nodded eagerly. 'I understand.'

'All right,' she sniffed. 'I don't see what good it will do you, but it was Cassie. I think he called her Cassie.'

My stomach dropped.

Cassie. Cassandra Webber. It had to be.

'Mr Birch?' Beatrice Green was frowning, her head tilted slightly as she watched my reaction. 'Is something the matter?'

I cleared my throat, trying quickly to compose myself.

'Tell me, Mrs Green,' I said quietly. 'Did you meet a man called Harry Webber at this party?'

'The name isn't familiar. Why? Should I have?'

'He was employed by Mr Scott at the time, training as an apprentice to run his estate. I wondered if you might have seen him there.'

Green gave a little shrug. 'Evelyn might have introduced us, I suppose. But then, I don't see why she would have wanted me to meet one of Frederick's staff.'

It had to be Cassandra Webber. What was it that Mrs Green had just said? *'She can't have been one of Evelyn's friends. I suppose she must have been someone's date.'*

'You're being very cryptic, Mr Birch,' she snapped. 'And I don't care for it. For heaven's sake, who are these people?'

Still trying to order my thoughts, I mumbled a few words about confidentiality.

'Mr Birch, if you won't tell me anything more, I'm going to return to my table.'

I straightened and cleared my throat again. 'I think that would be best.'

With a look of exasperation, Beatrice Green drained the rest of her glass, plucked her handbag from the bar and turned to leave. But after a few steps, she stopped and faced me again.

'Good luck,' she called, her lips twitching into a smug smile. 'I do hope you find Arthur's painting.'

After she had gone, I pushed my glass away. Taking off my officer's cap, I propped my elbows upon the bar and ran my hands through my hair.

Blake had tried to force himself on Cassandra Webber. It certainly made sense. Harry Webber had told Temple and me that she hadn't wanted to go for a farewell dinner with Blake tonight, though she wouldn't say why. He had speculated that she had been bothered by Blake's argument with Dupont, but if she had actually been the woman who Beatrice Green saw in the rose garden, I could understand her reluctance to share a dinner table with her attacker.

Did Harry Webber really not know? Had nobody told him what his friend had done? I supposed not – he surely wouldn't have kept in such close contact with Blake if he did.

And what about Blake himself? This wouldn't be the first report of him drinking so much that he couldn't remember his actions. Vain as he might be, I couldn't imagine him sharing a table with Cassandra Webber if he remembered what he had done – or, at least, attempted to do – at his own wife's birthday party.

Surely someone would have told him? But if the only person who witnessed it was Beatrice Green and she hadn't even known who Cassandra Webber was, Blake might never have been reminded who the object of his unwelcome affections had been.

I couldn't think. I needed quiet. The bartender uncorked another bottle of champagne with a loud pop. To my right, two passengers clinked their glasses and to my left, I heard Robert Evans speaking to a passenger.

'A table for six? Certainly, gentlemen. Would you like to reserve it under just one cabin number or two?'

If I had still been holding my wine glass, I was quite sure I would have dropped it.

It's a curious moment, when a problem that has troubled you so much suddenly starts to make sense. I practically ran to Temple's cabin, barging past the maître d' and taking the Great Staircase three steps at a time. Passengers parted to let me through, casting strange glances in my direction as they pressed their backs against the corridor walls, but I paid them no notice.

I rapped on Temple's door, panting heavily. My shoulder groaned from the effort of my sudden sprint across the *Endeavour*, but I didn't care. I knocked again, more sharply than the first time.

When it finally opened, my heart sank. He hadn't changed since he'd left me in the restaurant. His shirt sleeves were rolled up to his elbows, his collar was wide open and his waistcoat unbuttoned, hanging loosely from his shoulders. His thick hair was a mess and his eyes were bloodshot; I hoped from nothing more than lack of sleep.

'Birch—'

'Listen,' I cut across him. 'Just listen. There's something you need to know. Something new.'

Quickly, I repeated everything I had just learned. At first, he looked uninterested, but as I told my story, I could see him becoming more attentive. He stood up straighter, his eyes narrowing in concentration.

'What do you think?' I asked breathlessly, as I reached the end of my story. 'I'm on to something, aren't I? Surely, this is important.'

Temple took a slow, deep breath and I realised that my hands were trembling in anticipation.

'Come inside,' he said. 'We should talk.'

37

'What do you mean, no?'

Resolute, Temple shook his head. 'It's not strong enough. It doesn't add up.'

I took a breath. I had been proud – embarrassingly so – of my breakthrough. As I'd run to his cabin, I had pictured him clapping me on the back and his eyes lighting up when I shared my triumph. Instead, he had sat in complete silence as he made me recount Beatrice Green's story, gazing at the floor as I described every detail until, at last, I reached the crucial point. The one that I was so sure would finally bring this investigation to an end.

'It all adds up,' I said. 'We've been wrong all along. Dupont must have seen Harry and Cassandra Webber in the restaurant with Mr Blake on Monday evening and realised that they could help him get to the painting. When he returned to the restaurant on Tuesday morning, he wasn't going back for Mr Blake's cabin number. He was after theirs!'

'Why not ask Vivian Hall for help?' replied Temple. 'Dupont knew her already. Surely, she would have been easier to recruit as an accomplice.'

'Would *you* involve a client with something like this? Asking Miss Hall to help him steal a painting would hardly have convinced her to sell another in his gallery. And in any case, Dupont didn't even see her on Monday evening because she was at the bar! She didn't return to the table until after Robert Evans had sent him away. I suppose Evans would have given him her cabin number too. But he must already have decided that it was Mr and Mrs Webber he was going to turn to.'

Temple was still reluctant. 'You genuinely think that Cassandra Webber is our culprit?'

'Listen to me,' I said, forcing calm into my voice. 'I don't want to believe it either. Truly, I don't. Mrs Webber is … She's kind and she's decent. But you can't deny that she has a clear motive for stealing Mr Blake's painting.'

Temple nodded. 'If she really was the woman who Blake cornered in that rose garden, then there may be motive. But the same could be said of virtually everyone we've met these last few days. Take Beatrice Green, for one.'

'What about her?'

'Dammit, Birch,' he hissed. 'You saw just as clearly as I did that she despises Blake. Who's to say that *she* doesn't have his painting and this story about Cassandra Webber isn't something she's fed you to cover her own tracks? What if she's trying to mislead you just long enough to reach New York and make her escape?'

I shook my head. 'It has to be Mrs Webber. The cabin numbers prove it—'

'The cabin numbers *help*. Yes, they give us a potential connection between Mrs Webber and Dupont. But they don't prove that she killed anyone, nor that she has taken the damned paintings.' He raised his voice, seeing that I was preparing to argue. 'Your theory is that Mrs Webber has taken Blake's painting as some kind of retribution for whatever Beatrice Green witnessed at Evelyn Scott's birthday party, correct?'

'That's right.'

'If it was truly Mrs Webber that Green saw and she wanted to get back at Blake in some way, why would she wait more than a year to do it?'

I thought for a moment. 'Perhaps she's never had the chance. Perhaps when Dupont found her and told her about the painting, she realised that this was how she could punish him. If anything, it's a ... a crime of opportunity.'

Temple shook his head. 'A crime of opportunity,' he muttered.

'What?' I demanded, struggling to hold back my growing frustration.

'Listen to yourself! Do you have any idea just how absurd you sound?'

'At least I'm trying!'

'It would be better for everyone if you didn't.'

I felt my cheeks flush, caught off guard by just how much this last remark stung.

'What about Miss Hall?' he continued. 'Are you suggesting that Mrs Webber killed her too?'

I nodded. 'She'd have had the opportunity. I saw her on Wednesday evening, on her way back from first-class. She'd been to check on Mr Blake, but he's told me himself that she was only there for an hour. Surely, that would have left plenty of time for her to murder Miss Hall before returning to her own cabin. Perhaps the visit to him was even to give herself an alibi, should she happen to be seen. She knew by that point that we were investigating. It's entirely possible that she—'

'But why, Birch?' Temple urged. 'Why would Cassandra Webber murder Miss Hall? Would she really be so furious to learn that her husband had been with another woman before her? And then why take her painting? It simply isn't strong enough. And what about Harry Webber? Where does he fit into this theory of yours?'

'Mr Webber doesn't know.' I had considered this already and struggled now to withhold a hint of triumph from my voice. 'Both murders took place while he was checking on his car – something Mrs Webber *knew* he would do every evening. Don't you see? The woman who was seen damaging the car on Tuesday night – we thought that it was Elsie, but it was Mrs Webber! She must have damaged it herself as a distraction. To keep her husband away from the cabin and buy herself time to take Blake's painting.'

Temple frowned. It was a small movement, but enough to make me wonder if I was winning him over.

'Say I agreed there was something in this,' he said. 'Why would Dupont approach Cassandra Webber but not her husband? Fine, it might have been their cabin number that he wanted from Robert Evans. But why not involve both of them?'

'I don't know for sure—'

'And Dupont's death.' He closed his eyes and pressed a hand to his forehead. 'Are you saying that Mrs Webber killed him after she'd taken the painting? Why? To cover her tracks? Those are sizeable holes in your theory, Birch.'

'And that's why we need to question her.'

Temple shook his head.

'It adds up,' I urged. 'We might need more to pin her to Miss Hall. But it seems entirely possible that she damaged Mr Webber's car to buy herself time and then took Mr Blake's painting while he was away.'

Temple kept his eyes fixed firmly on the floor.

'Please. We have to question her.'

'We're not going,' he said quietly.

'Why not?'

'Because you're wrong,' he snapped. 'Twisting the evidence to support your own theory. For God's sake, you're talking about accusing Cassandra Webber of murdering Vivian Hall over a simple case of petty jealousy!'

He sprang from the bunk and turned his back to me. I burned with resentment, as though feeling every jibe and insult that he had cast in my direction these past few days all at once.

'This is it then,' I said. 'You really have given up?'

He sighed. 'You might be on to something with the cabin numbers.'

'So why won't you interview Mrs Webber?'

'Because we're not there yet. There are too many questions still unanswered. I just need a second to—'

'No,' I said. 'I see what's really happening and it's a new low. You have ignored me, shunned me and insulted me at every possible turn. Every time I've tried to help, you have pushed me away, and now I have the answer, you won't hear it because you're too proud to consider that I might have pieced this together when you couldn't. I *shot* a man last night to save your life and yet you still won't even entertain the idea that I might be of use. Well, no more.' I stood to leave. 'If you won't finish this, I'll do it myself.'

Temple frowned. 'Where are you going?'

I didn't answer.

'Birch,' he said. 'Where are you going?'

Still, I ignored him.

'Birch, stop!'

It was too late. I had thrown the cabin door open and was marching down the corridor with renewed purpose. I no longer needed Temple. I was going to question Cassandra Webber myself and bring this damned investigation to an end.

38

I must have stood outside Cassandra Webber's door for several minutes as I tried to regain the composure I had lost in Temple's cabin. I had to be calm for this conversation. I needed to think clearly.

But when the door opened it was Harry Webber who appeared, a bemused expression on his face. He seemed to fill the doorway, the same tweed suit still straining against his broad shoulders.

'Good afternoon, sir,' I said as boldly as I could manage. 'Pardon the intrusion, but is Mrs Webber here?'

'Cassie? Not right now. She's gone to the pool.'

An uncomfortable silence hung in the air. I suddenly felt foolish, my cheeks flushing.

'Is this about Arthur?' he asked.

'Yes, sir. It is.'

'You have some more questions to ask, do you?'

'I . . .' I could feel myself faltering, my new-found confidence rapidly disappearing. 'Perhaps I ought to come back later.'

Webber frowned at me. 'Where's your colleague? The police officer.'

'It's just me today, sir.'

He nodded. 'I didn't like that fellow much. Cassie seemed to think you were all right, though. She said you were kind.'

I struggled to hold a straight face, the first seeds of doubt taking hold. Could Temple be right? Could I honestly see this woman striking Vivian Hall with a wine cooler? Or planting that knife in Arthur Blake's desk?

'If you need to speak with her so urgently, why don't you wait inside?' said Webber. 'She's been away a little while now. I can't imagine she'll be much longer.'

I took a step back. 'I really think I ought to come back when she's here.'

'Don't be daft.' He stepped aside, holding the door open. 'There's no sense in you leaving only to come back again.'

I peered into the cabin, the confidence that had spurred me here having all but evaporated. Still, I knew that I couldn't go back. I couldn't face Temple again without having at least put my theory to rest.

'If you really think she won't be long ...'

I stepped inside and Webber closed the door.

'Have a seat if you like.' He waved me into the chair at the desk. 'I'd offer you something to drink while you wait, but ... Well, there isn't exactly much to offer.'

'That's quite all right.' I forced a smile. 'I thought Mrs Webber tended to swim first thing in the morning?'

'She wasn't feeling quite right this morning. Decided to go this afternoon instead.' He seated himself on the lower bunk and with a crack that seemed to fill the little cabin, clasped his hands together. 'You had some questions?'

'Yes, sir. For Mrs Webber.'

'Won't they be for me as well?'

'I really ought to wait for her to come back.'

He bristled, his eyes narrowing a fraction. 'What's this about, Mr Birch? You're acting rather strangely, if you don't mind me saying so.'

'Please, sir.' I shuffled uncomfortably under his gaze. 'Mrs Webber has to be here.'

Webber's mouth dropped open, his lips parting in a perfect circle. 'Oh, God,' he whispered. 'You think she's involved with what happened to that gentleman.'

'I just need to speak with her.'

'You do, don't you? That's why you're here!'

I swallowed back the lump in my throat, my hands clasped tightly together to stop them from trembling. 'Yes, sir.' I forced the words out. 'I think she may be involved.'

Webber pressed a hand to his forehead. 'I trust you have some fairly convincing evidence to support this.'

'I do, sir. We have learned about a possible motive for her to have stolen the item that was taken from Mr Blake's cabin. I hope it isn't true, sir. Honestly, I do. But I need to—'

'What motive?'

I took a deep breath. 'When we asked you on Thursday about Mr Blake's divorce from Miss Scott,' I said cautiously, 'you told us there had been rumours of another woman.'

Webber's eyes went wide with astonishment.

'Please, sir,' I urged. 'It wasn't—'

'You think ... Arthur and Cassie?'

'No, sir. Please listen. The night that Miss Scott sent Mr Blake away, I understand they were hosting a party.'

'It was Evelyn's birthday. I took Cassie with me ...'

I nodded. 'Mr Blake was caught making advances on Mrs Webber at the party. That's what prompted Miss Scott on send him away.'

Harry Webber ran a hand through his hair, a pained expression on his face. 'Where have you heard this?'

'Beatrice Green. She was at the party as well and saw it happening in the rose garden. But you must understand, sir, Mrs Webber didn't return Mr Blake's advances. I'm told that Mrs Green's intrusion gave her the opportunity she needed to break away and she ran straight back to the house.'

Webber's hands curled into fists. 'Arthur, you filthy ...' He took a deep breath, apparently trying to calm himself. 'So now you think Cassie's stolen Arthur's painting. For what, to punish him? To teach him a lesson?'

'Yes, sir. I believe the gentleman who approached your table on Monday evening found her on Tuesday morning and convinced her to help him take it.'

'That's the man who died, isn't it? You think she's involved with that as well, do you?'

'That's why I'm here. I need to ask some more questions.'

He pressed his hands to his face. 'Cassie ...' he murmured. After several seconds, he lifted his hands away, his eyes red with the pressure. 'How sure are you about this? Even if Beatrice is right – if it really was Cassie that she saw with Arthur – there must be some mistake. Cassie's a good woman. She wouldn't do something like this.'

'I'm sorry, sir,' I said, wishing for Temple's cold delivery. 'This must come as a terrible shock—'

He waved my concern away. For a moment, he simply sat, his head once more in his hands.

'What happens now?' he asked. 'Will your detective arrest her?'

'I just need to ask her some questions.'

'He will, won't he? If you think she's responsible – that she's killed this gentleman and taken Arthur's painting – there'll be the police to answer to.'

'I ...' The lump had returned to my throat. 'Yes. I suppose there will be consequences.'

A silence hung over the cabin. I was woefully out of my depth. Despite my resolve, I wished desperately that Temple was there with me.

'Is there anything I can do?' I asked.

When Webber finally looked up, the resignation in his face was painfully clear. 'There are some cigarettes,' he said, his voice completely flat, 'on the desk behind you. Pass them over, would you?'

'Of course.' I scrambled to my feet, eager to be of some use. To look away from the suffering that I had caused. Aching with guilt, I yearned for Temple's ability to detach himself. For the harsh indifference which he seemed to instinctively feel for his interviewees.

I rifled through the papers on the desk, turning over Cassandra Webber's notes and papers in search of the cigarettes.

It was only when I moved the last document, frowning to myself at having found no trace of them, that I froze. That I realised – far too late – what I had missed. Something I should have noticed several minutes ago but, in my foolishness, had overlooked.

My heart was pounding in my ears, my mouth dry.

'Mr Webber,' I said, hearing the tremor in my own voice, 'we never mentioned Mr Blake having a paint—'

I barely felt the blow. I was aware only of a sudden pressure at the back of my head, the sound of breaking glass and the floor reaching up to strike me.

39

I wasn't sure if I had been knocked briefly unconscious or if the blow to my head had come with such ferocity that I simply hadn't had a chance to register my fall to the floor. Either way, as I lay face down upon the carpet, my skull throbbed, my ears rang and the room span.

I felt something warm on my forehead. Raising a hand to investigate, I brought it away to find blood on my fingers. I must have struck the desk as I fell. From the corner of my eye, I saw the remains of a glass ashtray scattered around me like glittering pieces of confetti.

'So now you think Cassie's stolen Arthur's painting.'

I cursed my foolishness. Temple would have noticed straight away; we had never mentioned Blake's painting to Harry Webber when we met him in the restaurant. How could he have known what we were accusing his wife of stealing?

I winced and a drop of blood trickled around the corner of my eye.

'It was you,' I said. 'Dupont never met with Mrs Webber, did he? It was all you.'

He had been pacing restlessly around the cabin, but at the sound of my voice he stood over me, his face contorted with rage. 'Why couldn't you stay away?' he hissed, his voice trembling. 'Why did you have to involve *her*?'

I closed my eyes, my skull throbbing. 'Listen to me.' I planted my hands on the floor and heaved myself onto my knees. 'Whatever this is about, we can—'

Before I could go any further, Webber seized my coat with both hands and dumped me roughly on my back. This time, I made no attempt to pick myself up. My limbs had turned to stone, my shoulder searing. I shut my eyes, holding the carpet as though I might somehow fall off it. When I finally opened them again, I saw that he was removing his cufflinks.

'I didn't want this,' he murmured. 'I didn't want any of it.'

'We can talk about this,' I rasped.

'No.' He tossed the cufflinks onto the bed and wrenched back his sleeves, his forearms thick as branches. 'You can't leave. Not now. I can't let you tell anyone what I've done.' He dropped to his knees, looming over me. 'And I can't let you involve Cassie.'

With that, I felt his hands close around my throat, the calloused skin rough against mine as he began to squeeze.

'It was for her,' he hissed through gritted teeth. 'It was only ever for her.'

I clawed at his hands, trying frantically to tear them away. Suddenly, I no longer noticed the throbbing in my skull, the burning in my shoulder or the spinning of the room. I couldn't breathe. I had to get free. I pounded my fists against Webber's arms and head, but he seemed barely to notice, his eyes wild and his face twisted in sheer, murderous determination.

'That's enough.'

Webber's grip loosened just a little, and over his shoulder, I saw Temple. He was standing in the open doorway, a furious expression on his face and his revolver raised.

'Step away,' he commanded. 'Step away from him or I'll shoot.'

Webber's face contorted in pure fury, but his hands remained locked tightly around my throat. Temple cocked the revolver with his thumb.

'Last chance,' he snarled.

Slowly, Webber's hands slackened. I gasped, clutching my neck as I gulped down air.

'You were right, Birch,' Temple called, his eyes blazing. 'Or at least, you were right about the cabin numbers. It seems you've taken Mrs Green's story a little too much to heart, though. If you'd only given me a moment to think, we could have worked this out together.'

'Worked *what* out?' Webber spat.

'That Dupont never met your wife, because on Tuesday morning, she swam before breakfast.' The detective's grip seemed to tighten on his revolver. 'Instead, when he'd paid Robert Evans for your cabin number and came here, he met *you*.'

With surprising speed, Webber snatched up a fragment of the shattered ashtray and held the point to my throat. 'That's enough,' he said, his voice suddenly hoarse. 'Put that gun down.'

'Or what? You'll kill him? Another death on your hands. Is that how you plan to get out of this?'

For what felt like an eternity, they stared at each other. I lay still, the broken glass at my neck. I could feel myself beginning to panic again, my relief at Temple's arrival burning out as I realised just how hopeless our situation was. Whether Temple shot him, or Webber finished me off with his own makeshift weapon, there was surely no way all three of us could walk away from this stalemate alive.

Then a new voice entered the room.

'Harry ...'

Over Temple's shoulder, Cassandra Webber stepped into view. Her blonde curls were damp from the pool, her face creased as though she was in physical pain. She shook her head, her eyes flitting between her husband's astonished expression, Temple's revolver and the glass shard at my throat.

'Harry, what have you done?'

'Cassie...' His voice began to tremble. 'I didn't ... It wasn't supposed to—'

'He's been lying to you,' said Temple. 'I suspect he's been lying for quite some time. Are you going to tell her now, Webber? Or shall I?'

I felt the glass brush my skin. Another drop of blood ran down the side of my face, but I didn't dare wipe it away.

'Tell me what?' Cassandra Webber pleaded.

'That he's broke,' said Temple. 'It was quite clear after our meeting on Thursday that your husband's firm is failing. I suspect it did start off well when he first left Frederick Scott. He won his first few clients, bought his car, proposed to you ...' The detective kept the revolver pointed squarely at

Webber's head. 'But you told us yourself that he no longer discusses the details of his business with you. When I asked him how his company is faring, he was similarly reluctant to discuss it. It seems to me that Mr Scott's influence over your husband's clients has finally started to take its toll.'

'Stop,' Webber murmured.

'Does it not strike you as odd,' Temple continued, ignoring the protest, 'that he insisted on bringing his car on this voyage? His pride and joy, you told us. You said he wants to drive it on Broadway, but I suspect he's brought it for an altogether different reason. He spoke to Birch and me about the importance of a good first impression. Said that his car is the finest thing he owns. I'd imagine the truth is that when you share the news of your marriage with your parents, he hopes the sight of the car will convince them he's a successful businessman, instead of a complete failure.'

'Stop ...' Webber moaned again.

'How bad is it, Webber?' Temple growled. 'Just how broke are you? Enough that you would decide to help an old art dealer steal a priceless painting from your friend? Enough that you would keep it secret from your wife?' His voice was suddenly laced with menace. 'Enough that you would betray the old man and try to take the painting for yourself?'

'I said stop!' he cried.

'Harry ...' said Cassandra Webber quietly, her gaze fixed on the glass shard in his hand. 'Put that down.'

He looked down at me, his eyes wide with panic. But the weapon remained firmly in his grip.

'That's what happened, isn't it?' said Temple. 'Dupont saw you in the restaurant with Blake, and on Tuesday morning he came to find you. As luck would have it, he arrived while Mrs Webber was swimming in the pool, and he told you all about the painting.'

Cassandra Webber shook her head. 'I don't understand. Why would he need Harry to help steal a painting?'

'Because after Blake made it clear on Monday evening that he wouldn't sell, Dupont knew he would surely be blamed if anything happened to it. That was why he needed your husband. You told us that Mr Webber had insisted on going for dinner with Blake this evening. One last hurrah before you go your separate ways in New York tomorrow.'

'That's right ...'

'We found a note in Dupont's cabin – a reminder that he had written for himself of an appointment today at nine o'clock. I suspect he planned to approach your table again while Mr Webber found some excuse to slip away and raid Blake's cabin. Blake couldn't blame Dupont, because the old man would have been in his sights the whole time.

'I'm sure it might even have worked. But on Tuesday evening, your husband saw Blake at the bar with Beatrice Green and realised he had an opportunity. He knew that he could take the painting for himself and leave Blake to assume Dupont was responsible. After all, Blake had gone to great lengths on Monday to make sure neither of you knew anything about the painting. He lied about his reason for travelling, took Dupont away from the table to discuss it and even made up a story about him being a disgruntled client. Mr Webber could claim total ignorance and Blake – the very man he was hoping to fool – would have been his greatest supporter.

'So that's what he did. He told you he was going to check on his car, broke into Blake's cabin and took the painting. But it all went wrong, didn't it, Webber?'

Nobody spoke. Harry Webber stared at Temple, apparently frozen, and I thought briefly about taking advantage of his distraction to wrench myself clear or snatch the glass from his hand. But if I misjudged my approach and brought on the rage with which he had attacked me just a few moments earlier, I would never be able to overpower him. Temple would have no choice but to shoot.

'Dupont saw me,' he murmured. 'I have no idea why, but when I stepped out of Arthur's cabin, he was there. Waiting for me.' His voice trembled. 'He saw that I had the painting and he knew straight away what had happened. I tried to leave but he followed, insisting that I had to give it back.

'I told him to leave me alone. Said that I was sorry but I needed it. But he wouldn't go away. He was desperate – you could hear it in his voice. I went outside, into the rain, and that's when he grabbed the painting. It was coming down so hard. There was so much water in my eyes. I couldn't see anything. I didn't even know how close we were to the steps ...'

'And you left him there,' Temple spat. 'A frail old man, dying alone in the rain.'

A silence briefly descended, before being interrupted by Cassandra Webber.

'But why were you outside, Harry? What were you even doing out there?'

'He had to hide the painting,' Temple answered. 'And around the outer deck was the only route from second-class to the

403

cargo hold. You see, he wasn't lying entirely when he told you that he was checking on his car. He went to the cargo hold, hid the painting in his car and – the crowning detail – scratched it himself so that he could tell a convincing story about why he'd been away for so long. That's right, isn't it, Webber? If we went down there this very moment, we would find Mr Blake's painting.'

Harry Webber said nothing.

'Where is it?' Temple demanded. 'In the boot? Under a seat?'

'The boot,' he said quietly.

'No.' Cassandra Webber shook her head, confusion in her eyes. 'No, a woman was seen scratching the car.'

'All a ruse,' said Temple. 'I suspect your husband was seen scratching the car by a member of the crew and convinced the witness – most likely with a bribe of some kind – to tell a story about having actually seen a woman. It's quite clever really. He could have just had the witness claim not to have seen anything. Instead, he sent us in completely the wrong direction by making us believe we were looking for a woman. That particular gamble backfired fairly spectacularly, however, when Mr Birch here believed that *you*, Mrs Webber, were the woman who had been seen.'

Without a word, she stepped forward, knelt beside her husband and took the shard of glass from my throat.

'Harry ...' she whispered. 'Why have you done this? Why couldn't you just tell me?'

'I didn't ...' Webber's voice was breaking, tears forming in his eyes. 'I just wanted to make you proud. To be what you needed. What you deserve.'

She cupped his cheek in one hand. 'We'll fix this,' she said. 'I promise. We'll stay together. I'll speak to the police. Defend you if it goes to court—'

'It most certainly will,' said Temple. 'I'm afraid we haven't reached the end. We haven't yet come to Miss Hall.'

'Vivian?' Even now, in the face of her husband's crime, Vivian Hall's name brought venom into Cassandra Webber's voice. 'What does she have to do with this?'

'Miss Hall is dead,' said Temple. 'Murdered on Wednesday evening by Mr Webber.'

Suddenly, Webber was hostile again. 'You don't know that,' he spat. 'You don't have proof.'

'I have one clear piece of evidence. Whoever Miss Hall met in her cabin – whoever it was that ended her life – it was someone to whom she was close enough that she would invite them in for a glass of white wine. But when we found her body, that glass was completely untouched. As your own wife told us herself, when describing how much champagne Blake had drunk on Monday evening—'

'Harry doesn't drink wine.' Cassandra Webber turned back to face her husband. She pulled her hand away, a look of horror spreading across her face.

'I presume you showed Miss Hall the painting,' Temple continued. 'Or did she somehow work out for herself what you'd done?'

For a moment, Webber looked as though he might resist. He glared at Temple, some of the fury returning to his eyes. But the fight seemed to leave him, his shoulders slumping.

'I suppose there's no hiding from it,' he said quietly. 'I went to her. On Wednesday morning. I took her to see the painting and asked if she would help me sell it when we reached New York. I told her that she could have a share; that I knew it was valuable but I needed her knowledge of the art world to make a decent sale.'

Any pity left in Cassandra Webber's expression melted away. Suddenly, she was glaring at her husband.

'Did she recognise it?' asked Temple.

'I can't say. But when she asked me who the artist was, I couldn't tell her. And when I tried to convince her that I'd come by it in England, it was clear she didn't believe me.'

He breathed a heavy sigh, struggling to meet his wife's piercing gaze.

'She asked for some time with it. She wanted to inspect it. To consider how much it might be worth. So I did as she asked. I let her have it for the day and told her I would collect it from her cabin that evening. But it was too late. Arthur had visited her that same afternoon. He'd told her it was Dupont whose body had been found and that a painting had been stolen from his cabin.'

Webber shook his head, his voice quivering.

'She knew it then. Knew perfectly well where the painting had come from. She told me that if I didn't let her keep it, she would tell everyone what I'd done. She'd tell Arthur.' He turned to face Cassandra Webber. 'She'd have told you ...'

'And you couldn't allow that,' said Temple. 'You waited until her back was turned, then you struck her with the wine cooler. You turned her cabin upside down to find Blake's painting and you even stole hers, to make it appear as though that was the intention all along.'

Nobody said a word. Harry Webber looked at his wife, fear in his eyes, and despite myself, I felt a sharp stab of pity for the pair of them. When she spoke, though, her voice was low and hostile.

'Mr Temple, would you put that gun down, please?'

Temple didn't move.

'Mr Temple,' she snapped. 'Put it down.'

Reluctantly, he lowered his revolver. Dragging myself to my feet, I went to stand by his side. My throat was raw and my head still throbbed, but the room had at least stopped spinning. Temple handed me a handkerchief from his jacket, which I pressed to the cut on my forehead.

'The knife,' I said hoarsely. 'In Mr Blake's cabin.'

Temple nodded. 'Taken from the restaurant, presumably at the same time that he saw Blake with Beatrice Green, and stabbed into the desk as a warning not to come looking for the painting.'

Harry Webber frowned. 'What knife?'

'There's no sense in denying it,' Temple snapped. 'You might not have intended to use it, but lying won't help you now.'

'There was no knife,' he protested. 'I searched Arthur's cabin, found the painting and left.'

'But we saw it,' I said.

'There *was* no knife!'

I cast a glance at Temple. Could there somehow be a second man? Webber had admitted to everything else; why would he hold back about leaving the knife?

'It was me.'

In unison, the three of us turned to face Cassandra Webber.

'I left the knife in Arthur's cabin.'

'Cassie …' Webber's eyes went wide.

'I'd never have used it,' she said defiantly. 'I only ever wanted to frighten him. To punish him.' She placed a hand on Webber's chest. 'Harry, there's something you need to know. Something that Arthur did.'

Webber nodded, his lip curling with fury. 'Evelyn's birthday. In the rose garden.'

She frowned at him. 'How do you …?'

'Beatrice Green told us,' I explained. 'She's the woman who saw you both, who gave you the opportunity to break away.'

Cassandra Webber seemed to consider this for a moment, before giving a single nod. 'I was glad to hear that Evelyn had kicked Arthur out, after what he'd tried to do. I was even more glad to hear from Harry just how much he'd struggled with it.' A look of contempt flashed across her face. 'But when he bragged to us on Monday evening about this commission that he'd received in New York – about all the money he stood to make from it – it just seemed so wrong. So unfair. When we left the restaurant on Tuesday, Harry said he would be checking on his car again. I knew from when he'd gone on Monday that I would have time to visit Arthur's cabin and—' She broke off. 'And stick the knife in his door.'

'But the knife wasn't in Mr Blake's door,' I said. 'It was in his desk.'

She nodded again. 'When I arrived, the cabin door was already open, and the place had been raided. I'd snuck the knife from the restaurant in my purse and knew that I still needed to get rid of it somehow, so I slipped into the cabin and stuck it in the desk.' She looked at her husband. 'If nothing else, I thought I could add a finishing touch to whoever had been there before me.'

There was no pride in her voice, and yet I still couldn't help but feel disappointed. To learn that Mrs Webber – seemingly the only decent person we had met during our investigation – was innocent of Dupont and Vivian Hall's deaths had come almost as a relief. For a brief moment, I caught myself wishing that I hadn't raised the question of the knife.

'That's where you'd been on Wednesday evening,' I said. 'When you found me on the promenade. You told me that you'd been to check how Mr Blake was holding up. I suppose that was only half-true, wasn't it? You wanted to see what sort of effect you'd had.'

She nodded, causing my disappointment to burn a little brighter.

'What happens now?' she asked.

'The paintings will be retrieved from Mr Webber's car,' replied Temple. 'Mr Blake's will be returned and Miss Hall's will be taken as evidence. After that, Mr Birch will make a full report of our findings to the captain and telegram ahead to New York. Regardless of his intentions, your husband has killed two people. When we dock tomorrow morning, the police will be waiting.'

'And me? I took that knife to Arthur's cabin. What consequences will there be for that?'

'None.' Harry Webber seemed to straighten a little. 'I'm in enough trouble already with Vivian and Dupont. It can't do me any further harm to say that I left a knife in Arthur's cabin.'

Her eyes went wide. 'I won't let you do that for me.'

'My mind's made up. And with everything I've done already, I'd imagine the police will have no interest in taking your word over mine.'

She seemed to consider this, a sombre expression on her face. 'I suppose you'll face trial—'

'In England,' Temple cut in. 'The Americans won't want to deal with this. A crime committed by a British citizen in international waters ... He'll be on the first ship back to Southampton.'

'And until then?'

'He'll be confined to this cabin.'

'You're not going to take him away? To arrest him or ... or anything?'

'There's nowhere for us to take him. As I understand it, there's no brig or cell that we can lock him in. We'll return in the morning to escort him from the ship but, for now, there's nothing but ocean in every direction.' Then, as something of an apparent afterthought, he added, 'I'm sure Mr Birch can arrange some alternative accommodation for you this evening.'

'No.' She took her husband's hand. 'I'm staying with him.'

'Mrs Webber—' Temple began.

'I'm staying,' she snapped. 'If being his wife isn't enough for you, I'm staying as his legal counsel.'

Webber looked at her, pure disbelief painted across his face. Temple, meanwhile, seemed to consider for a moment. Then he gave a little frown and turned to me.

'Can you walk?'

'I think so.'

'Then it's high time we claimed our prize.'

Without another word, he opened the cabin door and beck-oned me through. Before he closed it, I glanced back through the crack for one last look at them. They were kneeling upon the floor, holding each other among the glittering fragments of broken glass.

40

The hours that followed our final visit to Harry and Cassandra Webber passed in something of a blur.

Having locked the couple in their cabin, I sent for a porter, asking specifically for Seymour, and gave the young fellow instructions to stand guard outside until I told him otherwise. He had nodded vigorously, still indebted to me, it seemed, for my leniency over the whisky he had been keeping under his bed.

'Yes, Mr Birch. Of course, sir.'

Once satisfied that the Webbers were suitably contained, our first port of call was, of course, the cargo hold.

Leaving the comfort and luxury of the passengers' accommodation behind, my heart pounded as we descended a final time to the lower decks. Heaving the metal door open, we stepped into the gloom, the hold stretching endlessly ahead of us. But unlike the last time we visited, I barely noticed the cold or the lack of light. All that mattered as we stalked through the warren of wooden crates and leather cases were the paintings.

The headlights of the Ford Model T soon leered at us through the shadows like two great eyes. For a split second, in what little electric light was available, the long scratch on its side flashed.

With Temple hovering at my shoulder, I eased open the boot. Seeing only a woollen blanket, I felt a flicker of panic, until he lifted it away to reveal a pair of square-shaped bundles nestled underneath.

Gently, as though it was made of glass, I lifted the first. It was smaller than I had expected, wrapped in brown paper and tied with a thin piece of white string. Loosening the string and peeling back one corner, I glimpsed a wooden frame. Then the grey of a stormy Devonshire sky, pillars of pale sunlight breaking through the clouds and settling in patches upon a tumultuous sea. Stripping the rest of the paper away, I saw bracken on the crest of a moor, and standing among a vivid bed of pink and purple wildflowers, a woman, her back turned, the wind tugging at her hair and the hem of her dress as she surveyed the raging storm.

This was it, I thought. Arthur Blake's painting.

I remembered the way that Blake had described it when we first met in his cabin. *'The Devon coast in the background. His use of colour and light. The brushwork ... To someone truly familiar with his work, it could only be Ecclestone's.'*

It was a curious feeling to at last hold this painting in my hands. Though I knew nothing in particular of Ecclestone, I could almost sense the value of this piece. Perhaps it was the reputation that it had garnered these past few days. The measures that Blake had taken in order to conceal it, or the lengths that Denis Dupont, Harry Webber, Nathaniel Morris and Michael Green – even, apparently, Vivian Hall – had gone to in order to claim it as their own. I almost felt guilty as I

413

remembered Miss Hall's own portrait, still wrapped up in the boot of the car. Having now set eyes on it, I could see why this painting was so widely desired.

I couldn't help but wince as Temple clapped me on the shoulder. Not a word was said between us, and yet, it felt like the greatest compliment. Even so, I struggled to look him in the eye.

He had been in something of a sedate mood since leaving Harry and Cassandra Webber, as though suddenly exhausted by reaching the end of our investigation. As he surveyed the lost Ecclestone, however, he allowed himself a grin. I supposed that, in his mind, he had achieved exactly what he had set out to do. He had recovered the paintings and exposed the killer. With a bit of luck, it might just be enough of an achievement to salvage his career when he returned to London.

I felt similarly mellow. While I was glad to have reached the end of our search, in a strange way it didn't feel like a victory to hold the fabled Ecclestone in my hands. Two people had lost their lives for the sake of this painting, and I, myself, had acquired a new scar.

Despite knowing in my mind that Harry Webber, alone, was guilty of her murder, I couldn't dismiss the feeling that I should have saved Vivian Hall. That I had held the door of the officers' quarters for her and let her walk, without protest, to her death. I had hoped that if I could unmask her killer, that feeling might ease a little. There was no sign of it doing so yet.

Temple and I said very little as we climbed from the cargo hold to Arthur Blake's cabin, the painting once again bundled up and tucked under my arm with Vivian Hall's.

As we walked, I pictured Blake's happiness at being reunited with it. He would, no doubt, be overjoyed. But I couldn't help feeling that this, too, was a hollow victory. I thought of him grasping Cassandra Webber's wrist in the garden of his wife's ancestral home, too drunk to even remember his actions the following day, and the idea of handing him an item of such value felt like a bittersweet end to all of our work.

It seemed, however, that this reunion was to be delayed. When we returned to first-class and knocked on Blake's cabin door, all we received in reply was silence. We waited a moment and Temple knocked a second time. Again, silence.

'Typical,' the detective muttered.

'We'll try again later,' I assured him. 'If it comes to it, we can find him in the morning. He'll surely return for his things when we dock.'

'You're suggesting we leave?'

'I don't see what else we can do.'

'What about that?' He nodded at the painting.

'I'll hold on to it.' I tightened my grip on the paper bundle. 'Miss Hall's, too.'

'I'd feel better if I kept them.'

'They'll stay in the officers' quarters. We'll deliver the Ecclestone together to Mr Blake when we dock, and you can do whatever you need to with Miss Hall's. Until then, there's no safer place for them.'

Temple thought for a moment, then gave a curt nod, apparently satisfied. At long last, it seemed he might be starting to trust me. Turning away from Blake's cabin door, we began to walk back the way we had come. Light poured through the broad windows into the first-class corridor, and glancing out at the ocean, I glimpsed clear blue sky. It was the fairest weather that we had seen all week.

'Tell me something,' I said. 'Truthfully.'

Temple raised an eyebrow.

'How long had you been outside Webber's cabin?'

'Does it matter?'

'Of course it does.'

'Why?'

'Because ...' I took a deep breath. It was a question I had been itching to ask since we'd left the Webbers, but I'd held myself back, almost too afraid to hear the answer. 'When I went to find Mrs Webber – when I was so sure she was our culprit – did you already know it was actually her husband we needed?'

Temple frowned. 'You're asking if I used you as bait.'

'You can hardly blame me for wondering.'

'I suppose that's fair.' For several seconds, he was silent. 'I suspected,' he said at last. 'But I wasn't sure.'

'So you did use me.'

'Briefly. You had him talking, and he'd told you himself that he didn't care for me. Until he turned violent, it made sense for me just to listen.'

'But what changed? If you didn't know that it was Mr Webber and you didn't believe it was his wife, why did you come after me at all?'

'The cabin numbers.'

'You told me they weren't proof.'

'I told you that they weren't enough by themselves. But you were right that they established a possible connection between Dupont and Mr Webber.'

'And you seemed to have already known that he was lying about his company.'

'Of course. The stories about Frederick Scott's influence over the other landowners, Webber's reluctance to speak about his business, the speech that he gave us about first impressions and then the fact that he brought his car with him ... You put all of those things together and it wasn't much of a leap to assume his company might be in trouble. Even his suit gave him away.'

'His suit?'

'You must have seen the way he shuffled and fidgeted in the restaurant. It didn't fit him. And yet he's still wearing it today. Does that suggest a successful businessman to you?'

I shook my head, growing increasingly frustrated by all that I had failed to notice.

'I suppose his coming meeting with Mrs Webber's parents must have been the tipping point,' I said. 'The thought of them somehow discovering that his business was in such a state when he had married their daughter in secret must have been a terrible one.'

'I suppose it must.'

'But if you knew that the cabin numbers established a connection between Mr Webber and Monsieur Dupont,' I protested, 'why did you let me go? Why didn't you believe me?'

'I hadn't had a chance to fully consider it. After you'd left to find Mrs Webber and I had a minute's peace in which to think, it started to fall into place. Once I'd realised it might actually be her husband that we were chasing, then of course I had to follow you. As I said back in the cabin, if you'd just waited, we might have worked it out together.'

417

I was about to launch a rebuttal, but held my tongue. I wouldn't admit it out loud, of course, but he was right. He had even asked, before I'd stormed from his cabin, for a moment to think, and I hadn't listened.

'How did you know about the car?' I asked. 'How could you tell that Mr Webber had scratched it himself?'

'When it occurred to me that he might have needed somewhere to hide the paintings, it made sense. You remember when we inspected it on Wednesday? I said that the scratch was too straight to be accidental but too shallow to be genuinely malicious. It's like Mrs Webber said – that car is his pride and joy. He couldn't bring himself to damage it properly.'

'But the witness account of a woman causing the damage ... What made you question that?'

'It didn't make sense for a woman to have done it – at least, none of the women who were close to Dupont or the painting. Mrs Webber had no reason to and Beatrice Green didn't seem to even know who he was. I suppose Miss Hall might have done it, if she'd been jealous of his marriage. But you've told me from your conversation with her on Wednesday that there doesn't seem to be any love lost on that front.'

'None whatsoever. At least, not that I could see.'

'But if you consider the possibility of Webber raiding Blake's cabin, leaving Dupont at the bottom of those stairs and then damaging his own car, the idea of him covering his tracks by bribing a witness to say that they'd actually seen a woman didn't seem too outlandish.'

We walked in silence as I took in Temple's deduction. A pair of gentlemen in three-piece suits gave us a curt nod as we passed them.

'I think you're right about him bribing the witness,' I said.

'Oh?'

'The porter that I'd tasked with looking for leads on the car learned that Mr Webber spoke with a man from the engines called O'Shea. He'd apparently come into some money over the last few days, which he used to buy a bottle of whisky. My man even speculated that he might have earned it by doing a job for a passenger.'

'There you have it, then.'

'But you still haven't answered my question.'

'Oh?'

'How long did you wait outside the cabin door?'

Temple hesitated. 'I was only a couple of minutes behind you.'

'And Mrs Webber?'

'She arrived shortly after I did, but I meant for her not to come in at all. I had no idea what kind of effect she might have. As it happened, she seemed quite useful.'

This felt like a severe understatement, but I decided against pointing it out.

'And what will you do now?'

'I suppose I'll begin preparing a report.'

'Will you present it when you return to London?'

He nodded. 'The moment I return. And hope that it's enough to win my superiors over.'

'I'll need to do something similar. Captain McCrory will be expecting to hear about our findings.'

Temple snorted. I thought back to our first meeting, when the captain had so adamantly insisted that Dupont's death was nothing more than a tragic accident. He wouldn't enjoy hearing just how wrong he had been.

As we reached the top of the Great Staircase, an American gentleman in a pinstriped suit passed us, barking instructions to a porter regarding the manner in which his luggage was to be unloaded the following morning.

As they disappeared around the corner and his voice faded away, I thought of the *Endeavour*'s engines falling silent. Of the passengers disembarking and the coroner waiting to receive the bodies of Doyle, Dupont and Vivian Hall. And, of course, of Raymond, waiting for me in the harbour. Ready to greet me with open arms so that I could resume my search for Amelia.

'Listen,' I said, bringing us to a halt. Above our heads, a pale sun shone through the glass dome. 'Meet me for a drink later this evening. I expect we'll go our separate ways tomorrow, but we've done a great thing together. We ought to toast our success.'

Temple hesitated, a glimmer of uncertainty on his face.

'One drink,' I said. 'What harm could it do?'

After a moment more he nodded. 'Where do you suggest?'

'It will need to be somewhere out of the way. I'm obliged not to drink on duty and certainly not in sight of passengers. I have duties to tend to as well, so it will have to be late. Why don't you meet me up on deck, at the prow of the ship? Eleven o'clock?'

'The prow of the ship?'

I nodded. 'There's no chance of being seen up there. Not at that time of night. Meet me there and I'll bring some whisky.'

'Until tonight, then.'

He turned to leave, but seemed at the last second to stop himself, meeting my gaze with a quizzical expression. Then he jabbed out a hand. I was so taken aback that for a short while I wasn't certain quite how to respond. Recovering my wits, I grasped his hand and for a fleeting moment he squeezed, before releasing me and stalking away.

I wasn't sure how long I stood there afterwards, the paintings tucked under my arm as crowds of passengers parted to walk around me. I had been entirely unprepared for the gesture and I suspect it must have taken a good minute to recover my composure enough to descend the Great Staircase.

With Temple gone, whatever pride I had felt in bringing the investigation to a close quickly began to fade. The last few hours had certainly provided a compelling distraction, but with the paintings recovered, Elsie's warning of the fate that awaited us in New York loomed over me.

I certainly couldn't bring myself to kill her, even if she was the one who suggested it. And yet, I also knew all too well that I couldn't allow her to let Winston Parker know of the role I'd played in preventing Temple's assassination. Even now, her warning still rang in my ears; that wherever I fled to, Parker would find me.

Something had to be done.

Arriving at the officers' quarters, I hovered at Wilson's door, deliberating over whether to knock and try to make things right with my friend. But I remembered the glare I had received that morning in the mess hall and decided against it, continuing instead along the corridor to my own cabin. I had work to do.

41

Temple was already waiting on the deck when I arrived. He stood with his back to me, leaning on the railing with his hands tucked into the pockets of his coat. He'd apparently left his fedora behind, a breeze tousling his thick hair in the soft glow of a dozen electric lamps. Ahead of him, out to sea, there was nothing but impenetrable darkness. Glancing up at the sky, I saw that the clouds were too thick even for stars.

I didn't join him straight away. Instead, I hung back, wondering if I had made a mistake. If I ought to have let us part ways on the Great Staircase. It wasn't too late to simply turn and leave.

But I chased the thought from my mind. One last drink. And then I would have no need to see James Temple ever again. I took a deep breath and forced a smile.

'Sorry to keep you,' I called.

He turned to greet me, one eyebrow raised. 'I wondered if you were going to stand me up.'

I chuckled, my breath steaming in the winter air as I held out Seymour's confiscated bottle of whisky in one hand and two glasses in the other. Temple took one and I poured us each a generous measure. I glanced around instinctively as I poured, but I needn't have worried. At this time of night and with the temperature as low as it was, I had been correct in my assumption that there would be no passengers in sight.

We clinked glasses and I took a sip, the warmth of the liquor comforting against the chill.

With his free hand, Temple pulled his coat closer around him. 'We really couldn't have met somewhere inside?'

'I've told you. I can't be seen drinking on duty.'

He growled and sipped at the whisky. 'How's our prisoner?'

I sighed. I had visited Elsie's cabin again since parting ways with Temple, bringing her more rations of food and water. It had been a considerably shorter visit than the one I had paid her that morning, with not a word spoken between us. It seemed we both knew where we stood.

'I'll be glad to see her handed over to the police when we dock,' I said.

'That makes two of us.'

'Although she does seem concerned.'

'Oh?'

'She seems to think that there are police officers in New York who will give her to Winston Parker.'

Temple winced.

'Is she right?'

The detective thought before answering, carefully weighing each word. 'There are certainly officers in New York who'll be on Parker's payroll. Whether they really would hand Elsie over to him ...' He shook his head, his breath steaming in front of him. 'I couldn't say.'

'Doesn't that bother you?'

'It wouldn't matter if it did. It might be a different story in London, but I've never been to New York. I have no contacts there. Nobody to confide in. I could offer to have a quiet word with the officer we surrender her to, but with the influence that Parker supposedly has over this city, I'd have no way of knowing whether that man might actually be one of his.'

'And you don't have any sort of problem with that?'

He paused again, something cold in his eyes. 'She meant to kill me, Birch. You, too. I'll follow procedure to the letter when we hand her over. But frankly, if Parker gets hold of her then she's made her bed.'

I thought about the raggedy young woman who had attacked us. Remembered the bruise on her wrist and the way she seemed to be perpetually tensed, her wild eyes flicking frantic-ally around the room, searching for even the slightest hint of danger. I suppose I understood Temple's indifference. But I didn't have the stomach to share it.

'What about you?' I asked. 'Are you worried? About the trial, I mean.'

'The trial will be fine. We have our evidence. We know everything that Violet's done. There's no chance of her leav-ing that courtroom without a prison sentence. It's returning to London that has me worried.' He hesitated, looking out to sea, then said quietly, 'But I suppose whatever happens, happens.'

We sipped our drinks, the whisper of the breeze and the churning of the black ocean the only sounds to be heard. I kept my eyes fixed firmly on the horizon, trying to think of anything but the dark water below. Of the short distance between us and the surface, and the cold, crushing weight of the waves.

'There's something else I've been thinking about,' I said hurriedly, suddenly desperate to break the silence. 'Mr Webber told us that Monsieur Dupont was waiting for him outside the cabin when he emerged with the painting. I hadn't thought all that much about it at the time. What with …' I mimed holding a weapon to my own throat. 'But I suppose that Dupont was only ever there because of Mr Green. You don't think …'

'Yes. Webber must still have been in the cabin when Green and Dupont arrived.'

'So, if Mr Green had stayed a moment longer …'

'He would likely have seen Webber emerging from Blake's cabin and saved us a great deal of trouble.'

I felt a sudden fury stir in my gut. Green might not have meant to kill Dupont, but there was no denying that the old art dealer would never have tumbled down those stairs if he hadn't been lured to Blake's cabin. Green might as well have cut out the middleman and done the deed himself, I thought bitterly.

'We might even have saved Miss Hall,' I murmured, speaking as much to myself as to Temple. 'If Mr Green had waited a moment and caught Mr Webber, he'd never have had a chance to involve her.'

'You mustn't think like that. What happened to Miss Hall was Webber's fault and his alone. We all must take responsibility for our wrongs and he's no different.'

A pained expression passed over his face. I supposed he was thinking of the officer who Violet Parker had killed, though I knew better than to press the matter. Instead, I raised my glass to my lips.

'I overstepped last night,' he said sharply. 'In the restaurant.'

I froze, my glass suspended in mid-air.

'I was frustrated,' he continued. 'Desperate. But that's no excuse for the things I said. To lose a child is ...' He cleared his throat. 'I want you to know that I'm sorry.'

A fresh silence descended, infinitely more uncomfortable than the last. For a split second, it was as though there was nothing else at all to be heard. Even the ocean seemed to quiet itself.

I slipped my free hand into my pocket and drew out the yellow ribbon. I thought of Amelia, and the night I had returned home to find her gone. I thought of Kate, and the loathing that she bore for me. And I thought of Raymond, waiting for me in New York, ready to begin our search.

'Her name was Amelia,' I said quietly. 'She didn't die. At least, not that we know of. She ...' I took a deep breath to steady myself, my head beginning to spin. 'I had been away – nearly three weeks, on a crossing very much like this one. When I returned home, she had vanished.'

I was aware of Temple watching me closely, though I couldn't bring myself to meet his gaze. I was quite certain that if I did, I would lose what little nerve I had mustered.

'There was a search. People from all the neighbouring villages came to help. The police were involved. But there was no sign of her. Days passed. And then weeks. But there was nothing. She had just disappeared.

426

'After the first month, the other villagers went home. After the second, the newspapers stopped writing about us. By the end of the third, even the police had all but given up. They think she's dead. You can see it in their faces – those people who came to help us. They don't think we'll ever find her. I don't believe it, though. I can't. Because it's ...'

I stopped a moment, my voice breaking. 'Because it's my fault. My wife begged me not to join the *Endeavour*. She asked me a hundred times what she would do if she needed me. If something happened while I was at sea. But I paid her no notice. Told her that nothing could possibly happen. Look how wrong I was.'

I tipped back the remaining contents of my glass, the liquor burning my throat. I could see for myself in the gentle light how violently my hands were shaking.

'It's been nearly two years now. My wife won't see me. The officers here think that I'm some kind of recluse. But do you know what the worst part is? It's that we still don't know what happened. We don't know if she was taken, if there was an accident of some kind or if she ran away. Only that she's gone.'

'Christ.' Temple shook his head and gazed out to sea. 'The things you'd give – that you would do – just to ...'

I watched him struggle for the words. I knew, of course, what it was that he was trying to say.

'Anything,' I said, slipping the ribbon back into my pocket. 'You'd do anything.'

In the absence of a table to rest it on, I turned around and placed my empty glass carefully on the deck. My hands were trembling so violently now that I was surprised I could even move them, my heart racing and my breath coming in ragged gasps. Tears stung at the corners of my eyes, but I gritted my teeth, forcing them back.

Temple, meanwhile, was still staring out to sea, lost in thought and oblivious to the fact that I had moved to stand directly behind him.

'Listen,' he said. 'Timothy—'

But he didn't get any further. In a single, swift movement, I hurled myself at him, throwing all my weight into a shove that caught him squarely between the shoulder blades and sent him toppling over the railing. It was over in seconds; too quickly for him even to cry out. He simply fell, his arms flailing helplessly as he plunged towards the dark water below.

42

It started with a letter.

The stairs creaked and echoed around my lifeless home as, just a week before, I descended to find an envelope waiting for me on the doormat. There was no other post – it was still far too early for the postman to have called – and my first thought was that it might be a message from Kate or a new piece of information regarding Amelia. My pulse quickened at both possibilities.

But as I looked at the handwriting, the fantasy of being re-united with my family vanished as quickly as it had materialised. There was no mistaking who the letter was from. Since the end of the war, I had received at least two of them every year. And yet this one was different. While every other letter had borne my full address and an American postage stamp, this particular one was marked with only the word *Timothy*.

I picked it up and took it to the kitchen table. It must have been delivered by hand. Did that mean that he was in England, or had he tasked someone else with carrying it all the way from New York? If he was here, why put a letter through my door, instead of visiting me personally? Or if he had sent it, what could possibly be so special about this message that he would have it hand-delivered from America?

I took a deep breath and peeled open the envelope. Reaching inside, I drew out a letter, neatly written, as always, upon a crisp sheet of fine paper:

My dear Timothy,

I'm sorry it's been some months since I last wrote, and I hope that you are keeping well. That is, as well as can be expected during this terrible time.

I hope you know that, as ever, the offer still stands to visit me in New York. While I understand, of course, that you have urgent matters requiring your attention at home, I remain certain that you would feel the benefit of some time away. I'm all too aware of the pain that you are feeling. Taking time to rest and recuperate with friends would surely do you the world of good.

We are all well. My father is still hard at work, as always, and my son continues to give me a great deal more lip than I would care for. But enough about my own concerns, as I know that they are trivial in comparison to yours.

Timothy, I've written before that I wish there was some way I could be of help to you and your family. That I could somehow bring you all together once more, and play some part in putting this terrible tragedy behind you. My friend, I believe I may have found that opportunity.

As you know, my father is a well-respected businessman here in New York. But in recent years, he has embarked on a series of new ventures, one of which is in London. It saddens me to report that my father has not been well received in

England. Your country and mine might have fought together in Europe just a few short years ago, but it seems that the world of business is a different battleground, and many of our British competitors have not taken well to an American setting up shop in their city. There have been workers' strikes, awful things said in the newspapers and even accusations — all unfounded, of course — of criminal activity.

Herein lies my problem, Timothy. Absurd as it might seem, a small number of these people have spun such an incredible story of criminal intent that they have caught the ear of Scotland Yard. As I write this letter, I understand that a police officer will soon travel to New York to testify in a trial against my father, all on the grounds of claims and evidence that have been entirely fabricated. Indeed, my father believes there is a chance that this man is not even a true police officer, and that he might actually be in the employ of these corrupt, deceitful people.

We are fearful, as I'm sure you can imagine, of the damage it would do to my family if such a man was allowed to stand before a judge and voice these false accusations. This, my old friend, is where I hope that we can help each other.

I enclose a photograph of the man who is due to speak against my father. As luck would have it, he will be travelling aboard your ship, the Endeavour. Timothy, in light of our friendship, and the bond that we forged on the battlefield in France, I beg that you help me to protect my family, by taking action to stop this man from reaching New York.

I know that you are not a violent man, and that by making this request I am asking a terrible thing of you. But I swear to you that if you would help me to protect my family in this

431

way, my father and I will devote every possible resource at our disposal towards reuniting you with yours.

I know that your wife still refuses to see you and that the police have all but given up on their search for your poor daughter. You cannot rely on them to make this right. My father, however, has wealth and influence in equal measure, and is prepared to make these available to you.

As a token of my commitment, and, I hope, a demonstration that I can keep this promise, I have taken the liberty of assigning a man to this investigation already. He is one of my father's finest and has been in England now for some weeks. While there are currently precious few leads for him to pursue, he reported to me just a few days ago that his search has led him to a certain trinket, which I understand belonged to your dear Amelia. I have enclosed the item with this letter, so that you may see it for yourself and understand just what it is that I am offering in return for your help.

I am offering hope, Timothy. I am promising you what the police cannot. If you can find it within yourself to help me protect my family, I swear to you that this trinket will be just the beginning. There will be no resource that my father and I refuse you. No stone that we will leave unturned in our search for Amelia. Together, we will bring your family together again.

Whatever you decide, I will trust your judgement and wait for you in the harbour when you dock in New York.

Your friend,

Raymond Parker

Upon finishing the letter, my first response was to scramble for the envelope, searching frantically for the trinket that

Raymond claimed to have found. This item of Amelia's. Reaching inside, my fingers brushed something soft. A piece of fabric, was my first thought. With trembling hands, I drew it out. Then, as I looked upon what Raymond had sent, my stomach turned. Had I not been sitting down, I was quite certain that my legs would have given way.

In my hands was a yellow ribbon. Amelia's ribbon. The one that she had worn virtually every day. Even, by all accounts, on the day she disappeared.

My heart thumped in my ears, a hundred questions swirling in my mind. Where could Raymond possibly have found this? Why would it not be with Amelia? Did its discovery suggest that she was still alive?

I turned it over, feeling the material between my fingers. I had begun to lose hope that I would ever set eyes on it again. Started to believe that I would never see it flutter in Amelia's hair or watch Kate tie it in a perfect bow. Finally, when the shock of being so abruptly reunited with it had begun to ease, I returned my attention to the letter.

Raymond had mentioned his father fleetingly in previous correspondence, but even in England, I had heard of the American businessman, Winston Parker. If the snatches of gossip that I had read in the newspapers were to be believed, he was certainly a wealthy man. Perhaps he might even have the means to follow through on Raymond's promise.

It was a tantalising prospect: to have Amelia returned and Kate forgive me. To have our old life restored. But to ask for something like *this* ... Even if Raymond could deliver — if it was truly possible that he could reunite me with Amelia — could I do what he asked of me in return?

A photograph had fallen from the envelope and lay face down on the table. With the ribbon still in my hand, I picked it up and turned it over, to examine the person who apparently intended my friend such harm. I saw the head and shoulders of a man in his late twenties, with a lean, angular face, a brow furrowed in an expression of ferocious intensity and a head of thick brown hair. He was dressed in a police uniform, and on the reverse *James Temple* was written neatly in pencil.

I dropped the photograph with a start. Did Raymond honestly expect me to kill a police officer? He had said himself in his letter, I wasn't a violent sort. Was this really the condition on which he offered his support? After all these years, were these his true colours?

I could scarcely believe it. Raymond wouldn't ask me for something like this. The man I knew wouldn't even be *involved* with something like this. And yet, the handwriting was undeniable. As were the details of our previous conversations. It was, unquestionably, my friend asking me to commit murder in exchange for his help.

Then, inevitably, came the most uncomfortable question of all. The question that frightened me most. If Raymond was right – if this James Temple really was travelling aboard the *Endeavour*, and the two of us were to meet – would I do it?

I barely slept that night, and as I caught the train to Southampton the following morning, to assist with the preparations before the *Endeavour* set out for New York, my mind swam.

After an uneventful start to the voyage, it was on Tuesday that my curiosity got the better of me and I checked the ship's ledger for the cabin number assigned to *J. Temple*. Then on Wednesday morning, we received the news that Denis Dupont's body had been discovered.

It had occurred to me that if I found myself lacking the nerve to follow through on Raymond's request, it would be a simple enough task to claim that Temple and I had never crossed paths. There were over two thousand people on board. Perhaps I could even say he had travelled in third-class or under a false name, so that I couldn't find him in the ship's ledger. It was comforting to know, if I ultimately decided that what Raymond asked was too great – too terrible – just how believable it would be that we simply hadn't met over the course of the crossing.

And yet there he was. Standing before me, plain as day, demanding that the captain allow him to see Dupont's body.

I wasn't a believer in fate, as such. It's difficult to imagine that life has a path carved out for you when you've been dealt a hand like mine. But I'll admit to being astounded when I first opened the door to the officers' quarters and found him standing in the corridor, demanding to speak to the captain. I suppose it was fortunate that, even then, he didn't seem to pay me much attention, as I was quite sure that the expression on my face must have been one of either complete amazement or sheer terror.

Moments later, when the other officers bandied the idea of sending him away, I knew that I had to seize this chance. At the very least, I had to get the measure of him. To hear what he said and decide, for myself, if I believed the story that Raymond was telling. So I volunteered to be the one who introduced him to the captain, and agreed willingly when it was decided that I should accompany him in an inspection of Dupont's body.

After bracing myself to entertain Raymond's request, I'll admit to being at something of a loss when Temple stormed from the captain's office, having refused to accept me as an escort. Should I pursue him or dismiss the meeting and tell Raymond that we had never met? I hadn't forgotten that Raymond had known Temple would be aboard the *Endeavour*. With a growing sense of unease, I began to wonder: would he know if I had encountered him but failed to follow him, too?

Of course, the decision had been made for me when, just a few hours later, Temple sought me out and relented to being chaperoned on his investigation. Even in that moment, as we sat together in the officers' mess, I hadn't yet decided what I was going to do. If the war had taught me anything about myself, it's that I am not a man who is predisposed to violence.

But still, Raymond's promise echoed in my ears, and the prospect of having Amelia returned was more tantalising than ever. So I decided I would set out with Temple on a fact-finding mission. Before I could take any course of action, I had to study this man and find out exactly what truth there was to Raymond's story.

What I hadn't counted on, however, was the full extent of the mystery surrounding Dupont. And so began four of the strangest days that I had spent on board the *Endeavour*: trying to learn all I could about James Temple, while simultaneously relying on his skills as a detective to uncover the truth of Dupont and Vivian Hall's murders.

My visit to his cabin on Thursday morning proved an enlightening diversion. The newspaper clipping that I'd found certainly seemed to confirm a connection to the Parkers – even if it was to Violet, as opposed to Winston – and I later supposed that the journal full of names and addresses must have been part of the testimony that Raymond had mentioned Temple delivering in his letter.

To know that Raymond was telling the truth didn't come as a relief, though. As desperately as I wanted his offer to find Amelia to be genuine, I still paled at the thought of what he was asking in return. Temple was insufferable, but I didn't want to kill him. Just as I didn't want my friend to be involved with the charges that I was becoming increasingly certain the Parkers were guilty of.

Our encounter with Elsie and Doyle on Friday evening complicated matters even further. At no point had I entertained the idea that I might be just one of several agents deployed by Raymond and his father to pursue Temple, and now, having killed one and been witnessed doing so by the other, I knew I was inextricably involved.

As Elsie herself warned me, unless I could find some way of removing her from the equation, there was no longer any option to convince Raymond that Temple and I had never crossed paths. She was going to talk, and I imagined my friend would be significantly less willing to search for Amelia when he learned that I had not only failed to kill Temple, but had actually saved his life.

Even so, as I thought about young Elsie, with her bony limbs and wild, restless eyes, I knew that killing her wasn't a solution I could consider.

The most curious thing, I suppose, about this particular predicament, was that after nearly a week of deliberating, it was Elsie who convinced me to go through with Raymond's request. Her final warning when I visited her on that Saturday morning cemented in my mind that Raymond could deliver on his promise. Winston Parker had people everywhere, she had said. He could find anyone. I saw the fear in her eyes as she said this. Heard the certainty in her voice. If Raymond could truly make his father's resources available, however blood-soaked they might be, then I finally believed that he would find Amelia.

When the moment of action came and I found myself staring blankly at the spot where, just seconds before, Temple had stood, my knees went weak and I thought I would be sick. My shoulder burned with the effort of sending him over the rail and my breath plumed in front of my face in short, ragged bursts.

As I threw myself into him, he had dropped his whisky glass onto the deck and I was overcome with a sudden panic that at any moment, someone would come running towards the sound and I would be discovered.

But I soon realised that nobody was coming. I was completely alone. Forcing myself to take deep, slow breaths, I picked up the glass with trembling hands and tossed it over the railing, along with my own and the bottle of whisky.

Moving quickly, I turned away from the prow and made my way back inside. The ship was quiet as I barged past the porters polishing the Great Staircase and sweeping the floors in second-class. They tipped their caps and gave friendly calls of 'sir' as I passed, but I barely noticed. I was on a mission, and now that my plan was in motion, I couldn't stop.

When I reached my destination and the cabin door opened, Cassandra Webber looked exhausted. Her eyes were bloodshot, her face drained of all colour and her arms folded across her chest.

'What do you want?'

'I have news,' I said, fighting to keep the tremor from my voice. 'I think you'll want to hear it.'

For several seconds, she simply glared at me. Then she stood aside. Harry Webber sat on the edge of the bed, head bowed and hands clasped in front of him. He scowled at me as I stepped into the room, his hands balling into fists.

'Well?' Mrs Webber sighed.

I cleared my throat, noticing that the shattered fragments of the ashtray still lay upon the floor. 'I'm sorry to report that there's been a terrible mistake.'

Ever so slightly, her expression softened.

'Miss Hall and Denis Dupont are no longer thought to have been the victims of any crime,' I continued, unable to meet either of their gazes as I forced the words out. 'It's now quite clear that their deaths are the result of a tragic accident.'

'But—'

'A tragic accident,' I pressed, meeting Cassandra Webber's eye. 'When we dock tomorrow morning, I suggest that you both continue on your way and try to put these events behind you.'

'What about Mr Temple?'

I winced, trying not to picture the detective thrashing and clawing at the dark water. Nor the crippling terror that he must have felt as the *Endeavour*'s lights drifted into the distance.

'Mr Temple has found new reason to believe that the theory he presented this afternoon was incorrect,' I replied.

'I don't understand. So Harry's free to go?'

'Yes. Although I must insist that from this moment, neither of you speak a word about either Mr Blake or Miss Hall's paintings.'

Her face darkened again and I saw Harry Webber's incredulous expression. Their astonishment was palpable, but it was clear that neither of them would challenge the lifeline they had just been thrown.

'You can leave now, Mr Birch,' she said quietly.

I swept from the cabin without a moment's hesitation, too ashamed to look back.

'Is everything all right, sir?' asked Seymour, still standing dutifully on guard outside.

'Perfectly,' I replied, the words like salt in my mouth. 'Return to your quarters, Seymour. There's no need for you to stay here any longer.'

He frowned, a confused expression on his boyish face. 'But, sir—'

'Leave, Seymour! Just ... leave.'

He jumped at my sudden outburst. Then, with an almost mournful nod of his head, he turned away.

In that moment, the guilt almost overcame me, but I forced it back down. There was no time for such sentiment, nor to stop and contemplate what I had just done. There was still one task that needed seeing to. I continued along the corridor and, pausing at another cabin door, drew the skeleton key from my pocket.

I held out the palms of my hands as I entered the cabin, Elsie's eyes snapping up to meet me. As I closed the door gently behind me she tensed even further. I heard a low growl through her gritted teeth and wondered if she thought I was heeding her advice; if she was waiting for me to draw a revolver.

'We need to talk,' I said quietly, keeping my distance. 'That's all. We just need to talk.'

'What do you want?'

'I know it's not your fault. I understand. The Parkers sent you after Temple – they *made* you do it.'

Her face twisted into a scowl.

'But they can't know about Doyle,' I continued. 'They can't know that I killed him.'

'They'll ask what happened to him,' she spat.

'I know. And if you go back to them, you'll need to tell them. But what if you didn't have to go back? What if I could help you disappear? Set you up so that you didn't have to do anything more for them?'

She hesitated. Just for a moment, but it was all I needed. She was listening.

Moving slowly, I reached into my coat pocket. Elsie tensed.

'It's all right,' I said.

She watched me warily as I slowly produced a slip of card and held it out. 'What's this?' she snapped, snatching it from my outstretched hand.

'Please ... let me explain.'

As I spoke, her eyes softened, glimmering for perhaps the first time with something other than pure disdain. It was something I had desperately wished I would see and that I knew I was going to need in order to make a successful bargain. It was faint. But where seconds before, there had been nothing but fear and resentment, there was now a flicker of hope.

Sunday 16 November 1924

43

After we had docked in New York and the engines had finally fallen silent, the officers formed a line in the mess and Captain McCrory shook each of our hands in turn. While many were disheartened to see him leave, the captain himself was in as jovial a mood as I had ever seen. His eyes gleamed as he worked his way down the line, the box of cigars tucked under his arm.

'Mr Birch,' he said, seizing my hand in a firm grip.

'The very best of luck in your retirement, sir.'

He nodded gruffly and was about to move on to the next man, when he turned back. 'Birch,' he said. 'Did you ever hear from that detective again?'

'Not a peep, sir.'

He clapped me on the arm and continued on his way. There was nothing more to be said.

When Temple had first stormed from the captain's office, having refused to accept me as an escort, I had been too pre-occupied with the question of whether to pursue him to give it a great deal of thought. But in time, I had come to think of it as an incredible stroke of good fortune. Even before I had made my decision about Raymond's letter, I knew that my course of action would be considerably easier if, as far as the captain was concerned, Temple had never bothered to rear his impudent head again. By calling me later that morning to meet him in the officers' mess, and beginning our investigation without the captain present, Temple had inadvertently made it a much simpler task to keep his return a secret.

To ensure that it remained so, I had made just one report of our progress to the captain since we had embarked on our investigation. That report came on Thursday evening, after we had discovered the body of Vivian Hall.

I hadn't been sure, at first, if I was going to share even this. Temple hadn't shown the slightest interest in meeting McCrory again. For a short while, it seemed the easiest thing in the world to say nothing and simply let Temple believe I had made a report.

But I knew it was too fine a line to walk. If the captain were to speak with the coroner when we docked and learn that a second passenger was due to be taken away with Dupont, questions would be asked. Likewise, Wilson had seen me with Vivian Hall in the mess. It would have been all too easy for him to make some passing, innocent comment that aroused the captain's suspicions. And so on Thursday evening I had made my one report.

Of course, I hadn't told him the whole truth. I had said that Vivian Hall had visited the officers' quarters on Wednesday evening in some distress. The captain didn't need to know, however, that this had been caused by the threat to her painting. I had chosen instead to say that she was suffering with a heart condition and had been feeling particularly unwell since leaving Southampton. She was travelling alone and had visited the officers' quarters in the hope of meeting a medical officer, before ultimately succumbing to her condition on Thursday.

In the end, it seemed I needn't have worried. The captain had been so eager for a quiet crossing that he swallowed my story without question, even going so far as to ask me not to mention Vivian Hall to the other men. That had suited my purposes beautifully. Having assured him that I would be the one to deal with the coroner – that there was no reason whatsoever for him to involve himself – I was quite confident of keeping the details of her death to myself.

I was so confident, in fact, that I didn't even report Doyle's death. Looking back, that had been something of a calculated risk. I had succeeded in passing a second death under the captain's nose without suspicion. A third might be a step too far. It wasn't a situation that I was entirely comfortable with, but after he had been so eager to wave away Vivian Hall's death, I reached the conclusion that Doyle's could go unreported.

Shortly after the captain had disembarked, the coroners boarded and I escorted them below deck, to claim the bodies of Doyle, Dupont and Miss Hall.

Before returning to my cabin the previous evening, the telegram office had been my final stop. The man operating the equipment had looked unnerved as I dictated to him that two more bodies were to be recovered in the morning, but he dutifully tapped out the message. Whether it was something in my voice or in my expression that held him back, he seemed quickly to realise that I was in no mood to be argued with. Once they had been taken away, I made my own way down the gangplank. Halfway down, I stopped, took a breath and tucked my hand into my coat pocket, brushing my fingers against the ribbon. It was a curious feeling. My hands might very well be dirty – filthy, even – but I still felt as though a weight had been lifted. I wasn't proud of what I had done. I suspected that I never would be. But it was over now.

A pale sun shimmered overhead and I pulled my coat tighter around me with my free hand, clutching a battered leather suitcase in the other. People were jostling and calling out to each other on all sides; porters carrying luggage, mothers ushering children towards the immigration office and a young boy calling out the *New York Times* headlines. Barrels and crates of cargo were being loaded onto carts and wagons, and the Stars and Stripes fluttered at the top of a towering flagpole. Despite the flurry of noise and movement, though, I couldn't possibly miss my friend.

The last time I had seen Raymond, six years ago, he had worn a soldier's uniform. Now he was dressed in a fine Italian suit, his cheeks were fuller and perfectly shaven, and his hair was slicked back with oil.

He grinned as I approached and when I held out my hand in greeting, he waved it aside, pulling me instead into a tight embrace.

'Timothy!' he beamed. 'It's been too long, my friend. Far too long!'

Before I could reply, he took a step back, grasping me by the shoulders and holding me at arm's length. He smiled broadly, but there was suddenly cold in his eyes too; something I had never seen in all the months we spent together in France.

'How was your journey?'

'It was ...' I caught sight of two broad-shouldered men in black suits watching us with blank expressions from a few yards away. With a deep breath, I looked Raymond straight in the eye. 'It's done,' I said quietly.

'Excellent.' His expression softened again and he moved to stand beside me, one arm wrapped around my shoulders as he guided me away. 'I know I asked a lot of you, Timothy. But I can't tell you just how much you've helped my family. Come this way – there's a car waiting for us. We have a lot to talk about.'

As we left and the enormity of what I had done truly took hold, I began to ache with guilt. But as Raymond spoke about the London magistrates that his father could call upon and the private investigators that he would send from New York to search for Amelia, I knew, deep inside, that it had been the right thing.

Holding the ribbon in my hand, I let my friend guide me through the thronging crowd. While we walked, I thought for a moment of Elsie, who would soon be embarking on a life-changing journey of her own. I knew that I had nothing to worry about, though. Not after the agreement that we had reached last night.

She would disappear into Manhattan, another face in the crowd, and take herself far from the reach of the Parkers. With her, she took three items that, to anybody who happened to spare a glance as she passed them on Broadway, would seem completely inconsequential. But to Elsie, they were the promise of her silence and a new, prosperous life.

In her pocket, she carried Michael Green's business card, and tucked under her arm, a pair of paper bundles tied with string.

Acknowledgements

When I first sat down at my kitchen table to write *A Fatal Crossing*, I'd probably have struggled to believe that I would even finish it, let alone that it might one day be published.

The truth is that it was a bit of fun. An idea for a story, which I just wanted to get out of my head and down onto paper. Fast-forward four years and it's been quite a journey. One for which I have several people who I need whole-heartedly to thank.

First, thank you to my agent, Harry Illingworth, for taking a chance on a twenty-six-year-old with a first draft and a daft idea about one day being an author. I couldn't have found a better chap to help me realise that dream, and that's only in part because you're a fellow Yorkshireman.

Next, a big thank you to my editor, Emily Griffin. Thank you for all of your insight and invaluable suggestions, and for the many (*many*) questions that you've indulged from me over the past nine months. You and the team at Century have brought *A Fatal Crossing* to life, and it's been such a privilege to work with you throughout this process.

Thank you to everyone who first read the book back in November 2019 and gave me the confidence that it might actually be something people would want to read. My mum and dad, Neil, Gillian, Sarah and Soph – I'll be eternally grateful to you all for giving me that very first push. And, of course, for not guessing the ending.

Finally, the biggest thank you of all to my girlfriend, Hayley. Thank you for always believing I could do it, especially on the many days that I didn't. Now that we're here, I hope I've done you proud.